Immortal Lover

By Carlos Martinez

"In the pursuit of glory, beware the allure of lust, for true joy resides in your relationship with others."

Table Of Content

Dedicated to my mother Miranda Martinez, my father Junior Martinez, but most importantly my mentor, best-friend, and co-worker, Anthony Northup

Chapter 1
Masquerade

"Immortality isn't as bad as they all say." Masquerade smirked at his sworn enemy, who lay sprawled on the floor. Masquerade pushed him down aggressively, Jace's eyes lowering, staring back fiercely.

"Come on, there's no need for this!" Jace pleaded awkwardly, stumbling over his often mixed up words. His anxious demeanor often slurred up his language skills. Jace had sweat covering his lower back, highlighting his shiny tan body. Masquerade already had him pinned to the floor, he knew that the janitor's closet wasn't the best place to do this.

"Oh my god, stop talking so loud. If someone so much as walks by this locked door, my foot will be up your ass." Masquerade mocked, ironically his own vocals staying rather loud. He started to laugh hysterically in grief filled anger. Jace shook at the thought of his previous dialogue, and looked utterly terrified.

"I will hurt you, so please do worry. You don't even know the beginning of what you have done. You make me seem like a bad person, after all we both know what love can do to a person. How much longer can you put up with this act, Jace? After all, you are the one who tricked all of us and used me to get closer to her." He sighed between sentences. "That's why we aren't friends anymore. Crazy how you can ruin a great friendship, right Jace?" Masquerade said. "You're probably wondering how I'm still alive, huh?" Masquerade stared into Jace's soul, muttering.

"You're immortal. There's no way you can be alive after that! You're a liar, and I should've known!" His voice croaked with force, although he had no energy to scream.

"You think I believe you? Oh no, I know you, Jace; I know who you really are. You're just a psycho." Masquerade snapped back in a rather sassy tone.

"You think that, but the truth will show itself soon." Jace attempted to get comfortable under his terrifying grip.

"You're very funny; you can't gaslight or manipulate me this time. Not anymore!" Masquerade teased in a baby voice. "I absolutely hate your guts." Masquerade continued to bash him with heavy clenched fists. His voice and throat hurt from trying to hold back tears and trying to keep up this act. Jace stared at him. No sight of tears, no signs of emotion, no sign of guilt. His mind was completely empty, void of any signs of remorse.

Masquerade fought the urge to unleash his anger and beat him. He still loved Jace partially; he couldn't hurt him. Masquerade locked his eyes back on Jace. He put his emotions in check and bottled it up like normal. Jace's thoughts were filled with trying to protect Jynx from her damned cursed family, but that was Masquerade's job, not his.

Wiping away his tears, he stared Jace in the eyes. "What really happened then?"

Jace swallowed. His body was still covered in sweat, "Jake lied to you!" He bellowed. "There's no way you can actually believe that liar! We have to stop him together; you already know Jynx wouldn't want this..."

His eyes lowered, and he tried making sense of it all. "How can something like that be a lie!" He screamed. "You can't hide behind that stupid mask forever!" Masquerade grabbed Jace by the head. His face seemed to melt. Tears rolled down both Jace's and Masquerade's faces, a last resort to show emotional distress.

"It didn't have to be like this Masquerade."

Masquerade, a normal fifteen year old boy, was known for his loud mouth. He calls himself normal, but most would say otherwise. Masquerade was born as the last 'batch' of his fifteen siblings. Yes, fifteen of them. The abundance of people in their family made it a large struggle to provide for the family. He always thanks 'God' for their fortunate lives, and his father gets mad at him for it, considering he's a god himself. His father, Zeus, a deity with a reputation for having numerous offspring, was a notable figure in their world. His father had always been distant and always kept secrets from Masquerade and his entire family. He always disappeared for work vacations spanning a few weeks to several long months. Masquerade wanted to crack the code on what secrets his dad really held, but was always disrupted by problems of his own; family drama. It usually starts in the morning, when everyone in his room has to wake up.

If you couldn't tell already, Masquerade was born as quintuplets. Which means he has four basically identical brothers. For some reason his mother thought it was a good idea to force them to sleep in the same room. Masquerade, blinded by the huge rays of sunlight emitting from the window, stood up on his bunk bed, smacking his forehead against the ceiling of the room. Already, two of his brothers were arguing about who had to do their laundry today.

He was tired of the back and forth, considering there was a calendar that marked their own specific dates for the days that they had to clean. His four brothers stood up, all gathering in a circle. Dark, Hyper, Lazer, Infinity, and Masquerade. To cover the rest of his family, they had to buy almost two grand on groceries alone. Tazer and Bow were his youngest brothers. They are 6 years old. The middle batch included Crystal, Nature, Feisty, Moon, and Split. All were female and 16 years of age. Masquerade didn't have much time to bond with them.

The eldest batch consisted of Gray, Love, Fate, and Power. They were seventeen, and he loved Gray the most. The other three, for whatever reason, were mean to him. Masquerade couldn't find out why, yet.

They lived in the countryside away from town, growing crops, holding livestock, and whatnot. "What's the plan?" Masquerade consulted, the other four still rubbing their eyes in tiredness. In the midst of the early morning, was the smell of bacon.

The smell attracted them all as soon as they left the room. "It's cleaning day. . ." Dark said through a hoarse voice. The sun's rays beamed through the curtains, making Dark's dark hair glow a golden brown. They all sat down at the table, staring at each other weirdly, awaiting breakfast. Plates weren't served, so he doesn't get why they were even in the dining room. Hyper was bouncing his leg as usual. The sounds of sizzling meats and buzzing ovens arose from the kitchen.

"COME EAT!" She screamed, the usual alarm for the family, they all had great ears for an odd reason. His entire family had come down from their rooms, except his dad. According to himself, his father can travel at light speeds or, at least, used to. They believed he was an old war god, but there was never enough evidence to prove so. No one believed his speed because, half of the time, he wasn't even at the table when Mom called. Masquerade looked at his dad's spot. Empty. *His ass probably can't even travel faster than the mailman, and she's old.* Masquerade thought. His dad appeared. Short and stubby footsteps. Foot by foot, he slowly made it to his spot. His steps made loud creaks from the old wood. *He needs to shave.* He observed his obvious ingrown hairs on his wrinkled chin.

"And you need to shut the hell up," His dad looked at Masquerade. Masquerade jumped in shock.

"I forgot that you can mind read. . ." Masquerade said while frowning, trying not to smirk.

"And I almost forgot that you set yourself on fire last week." His dad said as he served himself, which, for Masquerade's sake, was clearly taken out of context.

"Haha, He got scared of the fireworks," Hyper said. Everyone else chuckled: New Year's Day didn't go well for him. Everyone took the story out of context 24/7. To start off, it was a dark night during the firework show. In an attempt to cool himself off, he tried to bath himself in water. The tank he picked up however, wasn't water, instead a thick oozing fluid of pure gasoline. Which he poured on his entire backside, and got on his hands. He plays with his hair and face a lot, so it wasn't a mistake when he went to light the next firework, that his entire body went up in flames. Masquerade shoved a biscuit in his mouth to shut himself up before he said anything else stupid.

Everyone looked unphased and zoned out, as they weren't awake yet, which Masquerade could definitely change. He wanted to start the day in an excited manner. He looked at his Mom, who had dad in a stare-down. The scrappy sound of forks irritated his father, who looked ready to shoot the place down with large blasts of lightning.

"Seriously, you gotta stop making fun of Masquerade. I get he says rather hurtful things-"

"Actually, I'd like to keep it to myself; he just invades my personal privacy," Masquerade smirked like a smart-ass; he liked starting unnecessary drama. "Maybe you should stop reading our minds!" He barked, thinking of a sweaty man's bare buttcheeks, his father's eyes retaliated. He smirked upon seeing the image in Masquerade's head.

He started chuckling at his dad, who couldn't do anything in an argument with two. His dad looked at him angrily, which indicated that he put the 'god pulse' on him. Unable to articulate the sensation, Masquerade found himself grappling with the unexplained power coursing through him.

"You better not use that power on him, Zeus. I swear I will seriously hurt you," Masquerade's mother threatened.

His dad didn't listen and used the 'pulse' on him anyway. He knew he did because he felt it. A short and quick beat that scared him every time. When his dad activated that ability, he could know your exact location at all times, so you couldn't hide from him. The ability also sometimes summoned harsh storms overnight, which rarely happened. It also didn't matter because he could just summon storms anyway. He also knew the ability gave the person nightmares, which haunted him. Masquerade's dad didn't play around when it came to punishment.

"I knew what you FIVE did the other night..." Zeus exclaimed, glancing at Dark, Hyper, Lazer, and Infinity. He knew he had to run, and so did his siblings. His father wasn't great at a foot race, so if he ran, he doubted Zeus would actually chase him. After a while, Zeus would forget about the punishment, or he would simply just not care.

Masquerade sped out the creaky front door quicker than lightning. Four more flashes followed after. Masquerade assumed it was the other four following him. Destroying the breakfast table, they sped through the front yard and out onto the still gravel paved roads in harsh seconds. The leaves and grass blew with the gusts of wind created by their increasing speeds. He glanced behind him to see Dark, Infinity, Hyper and Lazer following in a line. They had to escape far and long enough so their father would eventually drop the grudge. He knew he could beat Dark and Infinity in a race. But not so much Hyper or Lazer. If it came down to it, he would have to sacrifice his siblings for his own survival. His dad was definitely making them clean the gutters whenever they returned, which is better than cleaning the stables though. He sped past trees and branches. A dust trail followed their paths. Hyper caught up like nothing. Gravel stones flew everywhere with his deep steps.

"Looks like someone is finally faster than the four-wheeler, huh? Where are we hiding any-way?" Hyper mocked. Masquerade gave him a cold leveling stare.

"Who's we? Fend for yourself, loser!" He swerved into Hyper's body, making him unbal-anced. Hyper quickly moved out of the way and intruded into Masquerade's left side. He made his path towards the forest. They had made a tree house together a few years back, and he guessed Hyper was headed there, too. He maneuvered through the trees. He tried losing Hyper, but he was too fast. Masquerade led him to the tree house. Hyper looked confused, yet challenged at the same time. Hyper quickly followed up the same tree, attempting to join him. Masquerade felt a second heart pulse in his body, like there were two beating lumps of muscle inside him. His ear twitched. Hyper looked scared as Masquerade lifted his foot, and gusts of wind lifted the two into the air, greatly higher than the tree house, and other tree in the area.

Masquerade looked down to see they were forty feet into the air. Hyper looked cocky and scared at the same time. Masquerade smiled at the moment, even though he might die from the impact. He flipped his body in the air so his feet were facing Hyper. Gusts of wind blew Hyper away and blew Masquerade further forward. Infinity and Dark looked nervous from above, their eyes scanning for a place to land. Masquerade fell to the ground. He fell through a tree and broke his arm, branches cracking and snapping off. He landed with a quick thud. He worried for Hyper for a moment, completely forgetting about his own injury. He touched his arm slowly but felt no pain, or blood. He looked at his arm. It was healing, a thick steam emitting from his hand. He looked confused.

Zeus had mentioned something about his children having godly healing abilities. Mas-querade thought it might be his inner god power kicking in. He sped to where Hyper fell; he was fine somehow. Masquerade helped Hyper up. He had guessed he also had that weird god-healing power.

"Is the race over yet??" Masquerade mocked him back, still making sure he was okay.

"That's not fair; you unlocked your signature power before me!" Hyper replied. Masquerade discarded the fact it sounded like they were in some video game.

"This can't be my signature power! If Mardo's future sight is real, my name wouldn't be *Masquerade*." He continued. He recalled that Mardo was another god that his father had relations with for a while. Mardo was known for his great future sight. He helped name Zeus' sons based on their future powers and events, which was weird because he absolutely sucked at naming kids.

"It has to be something flashy, like something you would find at a masquerade dance maybe?? Duh." Masquerade blurted.

"Why wind then?" Hyper replied.

"I don't know, you're asking like I decided what my powers would be. I'm confident there's more to it, I bet this is Zeus's genetics kicking in. Y'know he's the god of the skies itself." Masquerade said. Lazer was the first to unlock his signature, which was lasers. You could probably figure that out by looking at his name, hence why Mardo named him that.

"It'll be fair since you both have your signature powers now." Hyper said. Masquerade let the gusts of wind carry him up again, leaves following the gusts. Hyper looked up like Masquerade was stupid and annoying. He looked at the beautiful view. The trees, the river, the farm, and the barn animals all looked nurturing from above. His mom was staring at them from the gray faded red porch, clearly telling them to get home. Masquerade flew towards the house steadily, his wind prowess failing to respond to him. He had no idea how to fly.

His mother looked proud and disappointed for Masquerade, she had that look very often. He jittered his way to the house with quick thrusts of blowing wind. He was taking too long, but all that mattered was that he tried. (What his mom would say). Hyper was already inside, and Masquerade was still trying to decipher his name. Mardo clearly had no clue how to give real names, for example who names their kid "Hyper"? He threw himself into the ground, trying to look cool while landing, but breaking his big toe instead. Masquerade flew through the lawn and almost fell again. Quickly, he tried making it up the porch. The rest of the family gathered at the porch. Usually when a family member gained their signature, their granted a ceremony. Masquerade was finally next to take the challenge.

"You got your signature power already??" Nature asked while Masquerade was faintly levitating; he still found it weird it sounded like he was in a video game.

"No fair. . ." Dark mumbled under his breath.

"I don't think it's my signature, though; wind isn't usually found as a masquerade, don't you think?" He replied and repeated.

"Uh-huh, sure, your name always reminds me of the book Romeo and Juliet; you think you'll find a lover when we go to school?" Nature replied.

"No, he won't. You're going to school to learn, not to find lovers." His mom said, trying to fix the destroyed table.

"Speaking of, Mom, did you meet Dad in high school?" Crystal piped in, staring at the two.

"We had met in high school but didn't date until college."

"Don't you think they should be punished since they, you know, ruined breakfast?" Zeus complained.

"Oh, for sure, make me clean the gutters. Such an original punishment," Masquerade exclaimed. Everyone chuckled as Zeus looked ready to banish Masquerade to Tarturus. His Mom sent everyone back to their room while she fixed breakfast once more, and a large cake for Masquerade's ceremony. The two-story house was falling apart, trying to hold together a family of 18. Five-bedroom house and two bathrooms didn't stand well under constant chaos.

His basement led to the sewers, which were fun to race in. However, it is very creepy any other time. The dining room had a long, royal wooden table. The kitchen was attached to the dining room. They had a kitchen that was naturally seen in a restaurant, because whoever cooked had to cook for 18. Their mom had arranged a schedule for people to help her cook. Masquerade barely had ten hours a week though, because he always made a mess instead of cleaning.

Every time he was reminded of his abnormal kitchen, he remembered the first time his mother had ever brought him to the grocery store. It was a scary experience for Masquerade. He didn't like public interaction in his pre-teen years, which was only years prior. It started off in haste, as usual. Nature usually goes with mother, but she was sick that afternoon. Mother would roam the house looking for the first person to ask.

Masquerade seemed to be caught, eating cereal at 1 PM in the afternoon. His mother's soft tone asked nicely, "Masquerade honey, Nature's sick, and I was wondering if you could come to the store with me?" Although Masquerade hated going, it didn't bother him at the time. Usually, when Nature went, she always came back with some crazy peculiar junk food. Masquerade knew what he wanted to pick out once he got there. He jumped in the car with his mom in the front seat. Reminder: this was the first time Masquerade had been out of the house, away from the fields.

Not too long into the trip to the town, it seemed normal: rows of trees and the occasional recurring river. Which was really the same river, but Masquerade was too dumb to know that at the time. The car rolled into town, and he was already excited to see the suburbs. He could see other houses and multiple lawns in the front views of the road. A car was parked in each driveway, which surprised him a lot, as well as the occasional two or three vehicles. The car turned, and there the grocery store lay. It was a big building. Bigger than anything he has witnessed until now.

The car parked, and Masquerade got out excitedly, waiting for his mother. There were cars parked everywhere. As soon as he walked in, the smell made him never want to leave. There were these stands where people would scan items and ask people, 'If they found everything right.' It made him excited. He looked to his left, and he saw a booth that looked like it was selling coffee. If anything, that's what he wanted to buy.

Following his mother around, he saw many food items he wanted to try. Although he guessed he would only allow for one. Masquerade slowly pushed the cart while his mother picked items from the neverending shelves. Although he had never worked an hour of his life, he knew the cashiers wouldn't be happy to ring up a full cart of packing groceries. He looked around in the aisle he was in. Name brands of many treats lie on the shelves: Cheetos, Cheez-Its, and Doritos.

They all grabbed his attention. His mother grabbed multiple bags of chips and other treats for the house. Aisle by aisle, they made their way. For a house of 18, they already had 2 and a half carts filled with groceries. Masquerade was getting tired, pushing two around with every bearing step forwards. When the time for checkout came, they approached a young man with black hair. His hair, however, shimmered dark blue in the light.

He had a friendly smile, ignoring the fact they had almost 3 entire carts full. His nametag read the name, 'Stitch.' It was an odd name for sure, but it wasn't any weirder than Masquerade's. He hesitated before starting to lay the items on the belt, as he needed to use the restroom.

"Hey, Mom, I'm going to use the bathroom quickly. I'll be back out to help put the groceries away..." Masquerade said; his Mom nodded in return. As he walked down the check lane, there was another person. Bagging the groceries for Stitch. His nametag read 'Jake'. Masquerade ignored him and continued walking to the bathrooms.

Masquerade had never used a public restroom before, so as he walked in, he had no clue what a urinal was. He had to pee, so he tried using the urinal. The bathroom contained only one stall, which was being occupied. Only later would Masquerade care if someone was in the stall or not.

It took a while for him to do his business, sparing getting into the details. As he was washing his hands, the person in the stall had finished and flushed. Masquerade didn't know why, but he felt fear rising in his chest. The person made slow steps to the stall door, and Masquerade could see he was wearing black dress shoes. The person slowly fiddled with the stall lock before saying something that would haunt Masquerade.

"I absolutely love the smell of fear, young one. . ." The person bellowed. Masquerade did not know how to respond.

"Who are you!?" Was the only sentence he could spit out of his mouth. The stall door flung open with great speed. The noise startled him more than it should have. In the doorframe stood a normal-looking man, but he radiated fear. Something about his eyes startled Masquerade, something about the irises that were a glowing fiery lava color.

"I will show you, boy," The person said in a distorted voice, becoming severely low-pitched and deep. The person's hand and fingers were distorted into longer and deformed black claws. All the way from his forearm had turned a black charred substance. His legs grew in length as well with the same superior sleek black, and his eyes were overwhelmed with fire. His mouth had fire and thick lava spurting from it. Masquerade wasn't the smartest of people, but even he could tell this was a demon straight from Hell itself.

The demon stared at Masquerade demonically, ironically. Its claws were long enough to slice his head off in one swipe, so he didn't do anything stupid yet. He watched observantly, thinking about what he was going to do. He had two obvious choicesFight this demon head-on or bolt for the door.

Both resulted in death in Masquerade's head. Its finger scythes would slice him to bits if he tried even touching the door. Fighting it would be even worse. Now, to start, Masquerade didn't believe in any gods up until now, besides his father. He prayed to god that he would get out of this situation alive. And you wouldn't believe it, but God had answered his prayers.

Although whoever helped him hadn't helped very much, it was still helpful. Made directly from the gods themselves, a sword had been summoned into Masquerade's hands. The blade was made with metal that could kill demons directly. The demon's face said it all.

"That blade, that metal. Where did you acquire such power?" The demon asked as if he wasn't paying attention at all. He recoiled a bit at the sight of the blade.

"This?" Masquerade raised the blade high. "Why, are you scared of it?" He mocked the demon, which wasn't a good idea. A straight-up monster versus an arrogant teenage boy, an uneven match. Masquerade didn't care. He never cared for others' well-being, not even his own. He charged the fire-spitting demon.

Masquerade hadn't had any combat training in his life at all until now. Although, he felt a warrior's spirit deep inside him that had come out just now. The demon lifted his finger, trying to attack. He responded by parrying the finger, snapping it off effortlessly. The demon looked surprised. His fingers were thin, and so was the black material hoisting his legs. In a quick swipe, Masquerade sliced one of the monster's feet off.

The demon tried turning around to counterattack, but Masquerade already plunged the sword into the demon's chest. Successfully, he used the rest of his strength to pin the monster to the wall.

The sword kept him stuck to the wall. The demon responded by using his finger to stab Masquerade's ankle. In response, he recalled the sword and sliced his entire arm off. No blood had been spilled. The demon didn't seem to have any. With the momentum of the last swing, he swung the blade once more, beheading the demon in one go. The monster started disintegrating from its feet. Before it had reached his head, he spit out his last sentence.

"Well played, godling; however, this will not be our last encounter..." The monster said before parishing into dust particles. This wasn't his last encounter with such forces. What should've been a quick little grocery shop started a hunt and war between Masquerade and a mini army of demons.

The next encounter was much more violent, as he almost died twice in the same night. It started in flux, with everyone trying to get out of the house on Halloween night. Masquerade was wearing a clown costume and was trying to get out the door faster than everyone else. He wanted to get started already. Masquerade slid his body out the window, and Hyper followed.

"Where do you think you're going by yourself?" Hyper whispered as they snuck out to the garage. Masquerade winced and forced a fake smile.

"I wanted to get to the rich side of town before anyone else. That way, we get the good candy first." He said, climbing aboard his own dedicated four-wheeler and starting it. Hyper nodded, and his face said it all; he wanted to trail behind. Masquerade put a thumbs up before the two revved their engines and flew past the volleys and fields of trees. They don't get out often, so the trip to town was a stressful drive. After minutes of cruising, the two made their way to the 'rich' side of town, through an old country gravel road. Heavy trails of dust were left dispersed through the air.

The huge houses stood three or two stories high and had beautiful balconies and front porches, everything gleaming a warm gold. Hyper's eyes were filled with a sense of excitement. Masquerade smiled and tugged him forward. Hyper had an old vampire costume on, with the fangs being chipped, it still looked good on him however. The first house they decided to go to was a heavily decorated mansion. Purple, black, gold and red lights lit up the entire yard.

The skeleton and other monster decorations stood high and looked more realistic than Masquerade had hoped for. He could swear they were alive, which was the first red flag of that fateful night. The mansion had a glowing red carpet that led to the huge cascading golden doors. The windows were tinted black. Hyper hesitated before knocking on the door, but little did he know he didn't need to. The golden rings on the door flung themselves upwards, and the doors thrusted open with great velocity.

They both reluctantly walked in, like they were openly invited, which for their sake, seemed like the case. Hyper was shivering, but Masquerade reluctantly kept him close. Upon entering, massive golden pillars held up a pristine white marble ceiling, and the floor, adorned with purple etchings, was made of sleek black marble. In the middle of the circular room was a huge crystal purple and quartz white chandelier. It gleamed in the moonlight through the large open skylights in the room ceiling. Hyper whimpered and turned to leave. Masquerade followed suit.

Then the doors slammed shut. They both turned around, and directly under the chandelier was a fairly short man. His hair was chopped shortly and faded black to white. His outfit was interesting. He wore a black compression shirt that had anatomically correct bone placement, from the rib cage, the pelvis, and even the leg bones. He was muscular, and his sweatpants were pure black that had stripes that were arranged from any color of the rainbow. The man was weirdly attractive, in an odd sense.

"Oh, I know you two! Masquerade and Hyper, no?" He smiled weirdly and looked Masquerade up and down weirdly. His eyes were weirdly mesmerizing, they compelled the two boys forward. "Well, my name's Bone, and it's a pleasure to meet you." He said, his voice making Masquerade feel oddly weak. "Mardo told me a *lot* about you two!" His body was lingering as he walked towards him weirdly. Hyper was staring him down attentively, awaiting something violent to occur.

"Yeahhh, wait a minute, how-" Masquerade stammered as he maintained eye contact with him. His voice lowered, and he was getting mad that he didn't even have control over his own body. Bone's fingers fiddled around his own waist for a moment, then he raised them and grabbed Masquerade by the chin, making him look up into his spiraling eyes.

"Ohh? You have very nice eyes, young man." He said, almost like he wanted to pluck them out for himself. Then he smiled, which made Masquerade's stomach feel uneasy. "You're very handsome, you know that?" He looked him up and down again, checking him out. "I can't forgive you though." His tone changed and the white bone layout on his shirt changed to a glowing red, and his eyes started sparkling red sparks of light energy. Masquerade felt intense anger rise inside himself, but for no reason at all.

"Your father is disgusting, and no one likes him!" Then Bone trickled his hand to touch Masquerade's, and he quickly snapped three of his fingers in half. He looked up and saw that Bone had broken his fingers. Masquerade could feel the anger built up in Bone's brain for some odd reason.

He got to his feet and prepared to attack him, but then his shirt changed colors again. They quickly went to a depressing blue. Almost immediately, the mood changed, and a heavy cloud of sadness settled over Masquerade, his shoulders slumping as his gaze dropped to the floor and he could feel the pressure of the emotion. "Sorry! I didn't mean to; it's just-" He said in a moody tone. "I can't control my emotions right now; I think you can though-" He said with his finger on his lip weirdly.

Then Hyper blitzed across the room quickly, trying to attack the man. His shirt color changed grayish in an instant, and they both froze in place. They couldn't move. "Nice try." He said as his shirt changed orange. "I liked you, but your father is too atrocious for me to keep you alive." Then gold, orange, red and yellow flames burst from his wide spread hands. The flames licked across their bodies and quickly set ablaze their costumes. That didn't kill them, however.

Bone's shirt turned purple, and arcs of lightning dragons started swarming the circular arena room. Masquerade climbed to his feet as the Chinese modeled dragons tried biting him. He dodged and tried to punch Bone. He just smiled and caught Masquerade's fist with a fast agile movement.

Bone taunted, "Mardo said you'd be powerful! Where's all the strength then?" Then Masquerade flung straight across the room and broke through one of the walls with a quick force of wind. He got to his feet and saw trails of ice and whispering water started filling the floor quickly. Masquerade tried remembering who this guy could be and why he had so many powers. He tried swimming towards Hyper to protect him, the water's cold breeze quickly paralyzed him. Then, everything was gone in an instant, like the entire event from before was only an illusion.. Another man stood in the middle of the room, right next to Bone, who's shirt had completely turned back to normal.

"Cut these boys some slack, would you?" His soft voice said, and Masquerade quickly ran to cover Hyper, who was on the floor, hurt. He turned around. His eyes pierced the soul; they had golden rings in them with an overlay of black and red. His hair was extremely fluffy and black but with purple and pink highlights. His presence tied Masquerade to the floor. "They're just trying to trick or treat!" He said and grinned as he bowed down to the two. "Sorry about my son here, but I can get you guys going really soon." Masquerade wanted to ask for his name. NBefore feeling his pockets become heavy, upon checking, he found a Kit-Kat candy bar. "Oh, don't worry about that, I'm Sura!" His heart dropped, and then the next thing he knew, he was four hundred feet in the air, about to land on his own house. He was only saved by his father, Zeus, who was able to control the winds to stop their fall.

The next encounter was the last, and it was the scariest, especially since it happened the night prior. This is what made their father angry at them because they were playing around in the sewers when they were forbidden to do so. It started in the cellar, where his batch were going to attempt to map the sewer tunnels that intruded under their house.

"Are you just gonna stare at us like a serial killer, or are you gonna get down here?" Dark teased him. Masquerade tried walking down the stairs, but he fell forward instead and fell down them like an idiot. The four looked down at him once he reached the bottom. Hyper and Dark were laughing while Infinity and Laser held a peachy smirk. Masquerade got to his feet, his eyes were still adjusting to the foggy darkness. The background contained the dark silhouettes of huge pallets that held many different animal livestock. They walked down the large stone floored basement, their shoes making echoes in the dark. Then, a beam of light flashed Masquerade's eyes. Lazer stared into his eyes.

"Flashhhlight eyessss." Lazer mocked. Masquerade pushed him lightly, and Laser chuckled. Clearly, Lazer has laser powers, as it's literally his name. His eyes could turn into large beams of light, which was useful, but not in this case.

"Lead the way, Mr. 'Flashlight eyes'," Masquerade insulted.

"Will do," Lazer replied. The four followed Lazer towards the sewer well, the brick wall being illuminated by the deep white consulting from his eyes. Masquerade looked down on the wishing well, his conscious impulsive thinking about jumping down the hole for a good moment. He looked at his brothers, glaring across their eyes one by one. They knew immediately what he was up to. Infinity tried grabbing him, but he was faster. Masquerade jumped over the wall and straight through the well. He looked upwards while falling. The other four stared at him, disappointed in their brother.

The rocky ragged walls lightly scraped his arms, making faint scratches in his skin. Then Hyper fell in, either accidentally, or he was copying Masquerade. The fall was long, following the sound of air disrupting. Masquerade hit the floor with a thud. He landed on a wet and soggy hay bale that smelt like a corpse. He put it there just to pull this stupid prank. Hyper fell right next to him, smiling deviously.

"YOU GUYS ARE GOOD TO COME DOWN!!!" Hyper screamed as his voice echoed up the long stone pipe. Masquerade smiled at him. Dark landed, then Infinity, and after a while, so did Lazer.

"It smells down here." Lazer pouted as his flashlight eyes slowly flickered and turned off. Masquerade shot him an incredulous look.

"No shit, it's a sewer." In unison, Masquerade and Hyper remarked. Lazer frowned.

"I swear if anyone teases me down here, I will leave." Lazer said in a serious tone while trying to maintain a serious look. Masquerade started slowly running, so his feet kicked up to his butt, purposefully splashing the sewer water in Lazer's face.

"Haha, eat gray water." Masquerade teased. Lazer looked at him. "If you leave, we will all jump you, I hope you know." Masquerade stared back. Lazer scowled, seemingly limited to this expression.

"Fine, whatever. I also don't want to lead anymore, what if I get jumped by a bunch of rats." Lazer worried.

"You can move faster than a whole four-wheeler, and you're worried about some rats?" Dark questioned. Lazer looked Masquerade up and down and made a disgusted face.

"Yeah, especially when they look like Masquerade." Lazer blurted. Everyone started laughing immediately, their echoes being heard throughout the stone walls. Masquerade booked it and started chasing Lazer, ignoring the low layer of sewer water covering the floor. Lazer ran through the maze of smelling tunnels, making sure to check behind him occasionally. He turned and maneuvered the sewers, trying to lose him. The others didn't even bother following, they just stood and watched from afar. Masquerade tried remembering the layout from years ago, when their parents actually let them in there. Even then he tried remembering why it was such a forbidden act for them to explore. After getting lost in his thoughts, he realized that he had lost Lazer.

His body pulsed unexpectedly, his brain sending shivers throughout his nerves and spine, He felt off, as if his senses were deactivated. A new emotion filled his body, an underlying emotion of scarcity. He felt scared, yet he didn't know why. Focusing ahead, he noticed the walls were brighter than usual. He felt as if someone was observing him from afar. Upon glancing behind him, he noticed the sewers seemed darker to him. The shadows were extended and made a horror-esque scenery. A cold wind brushed past him. From the corner of his eye, he saw a figure wash past quickly. Masquerade gazed into the emptiness of the tunnel.

Where did Lazer go? Masquerade had decided to chase the figure. Frost covered the already damaged concrete walls, making a sheet of white fog. Once he passed the corner, the figure was gone. His eyes wandered, and his brain hurt.

"Show yourself!" Masquerade screamed. His voice echoed through the stone-paved walls. Masquerade slowly levitated in place, as it would definitely give him an edge in a fight against a total stranger.

"If you say so." A voice whispered before a frigid gust of air swept in. The air blew Masquerade right into the wall behind him. His head rang. Masquerade tried focusing, but there was a mist in the air. The chill made him feel weird, disrupting his thoughts. A figure approached him, a figure in the mist, a human silhouette.

"So, who are you?" The figure's voice pierced Masquerade. It said it in a concerned tone, almost like he actually wanted to meet Masquerade. He felt consulted to answer the man's question.

"I, I don't know." Masquerade tried to think, his brain was blank. He couldn't explain it. His mind was filled with fog, frost, and shadows. His mind glitched, making his arms twitch upwards.

"You don't know who you are?" The voice asked. Masquerade fell on his knees and tried to think. His brain had frozen, like a brain freeze, making him not able to function. Masquerade tilted his head to look up at him. He stared back chillingly, with white glowing eyes.

"Is this brain stuff you?" Masquerade managed to spurt out of his now frozen-dry lips. His brain remained filled with fog.

"What do you say? You can't think for yourself? Little one?" He said disrespectfully, his footsteps inching ever so closely. Then, a red light approached from behind. A laser beam pinged the back of its head, sending him falling forwards. The figure staggered a little. Another green beam followed the red, but the creature in the fog dodged easily.

"MASQUERADE, RUN!'" Lazer screamed, "THERE ARE TWO OTHERS, HYPER HAS ALREADY ESCAPED." Lazer said before he faded off in the other direction, the thick fog masking his shadow. Masquerade got up immediately and ran the way he came from. *Two other things?* His mind was still filled with frost, rendering him unable to control his thoughts effectively.

Masquerade sprinted down the tunnel. The figure wasn't following, but trials of ice slithered like snakes against the walls and floor. The ice traveled almost as fast as him, spreading across the walls and ceiling. Masquerade levitated. *I have to teach myself to fly.* Masquerade flew upwards, almost hitting his head on the ceiling. He smirked to himself.

He blew gusts of wind from his feet and blitzed the ice trailing him, flying almost as fast as an electric scooter. He flew down the tunnel with ease, the ice still following.

"You think you're so clever, huh?" A voice alarmed in his head. It made no sense considering there was no one to speak to in the area. It was as if the voice could speak from the walls. Masquerade's brain froze again. He glanced, and the figure was standing before him. He couldn't stop the momentum from his blast of wind earlier, falling directly into the clutches of the man. The figure gut-punched the wind out of Masquerade. Caught between cold air and an even more chilling fist, Masquerade threw up blood. He was thrown the other way, and the figure chuckled. He hit the floor roughly, scraping up his knees and elbows.

Masquerade stood up once more and tried running the other way before Hyper showed up from the end of the tunnel. Hyper grabbed Masquerade and sped off heroically. Hyper was significantly faster than before he remembered. Masquerade saw two other figures at the end of the tunnel, guarding the exit. They had large claws that highlighted their blackened appearance. He sent gusts of wind downward, so the two's feet were taken off balance and fell to the floor. Then he sent gusts flying up so they hit the cement upwards, breaking off bits of rock. Then he sent them down with one final gust, crushing them between the stones. A three-hit combo.

Hyper blitzed by them and went upwards. He went fast enough to run up the wall. It all happened so fast, that it was over before he knew it. Hyper left through the wishing well. He dropped Masquerade next to Dark. Dark, Infinity, and Lazer were already there. Hyper looked exhausted. "So much for fun." Masquerade chuckled.

"Yeah, totally; at least it wasn't rats." Lazer exclaimed jokingly. Hyper collapsed to the ground and breathed heavily in exhaustion.

"I'm alright, just got to catch my breath." Hyper trailed off. Masquerade looked at Dark, who looked pissed. Infinity looked disappointed. Hyper was exhausted, and Laser looked normal or unphased.

"Who were those people?" Masquerade questioned; the group ignored him completely and collectively. His brain pulsed all of a sudden, the third time the entire day. A chill rang through his body, his eyes felt lazy, like he couldn't keep them up any longer. Everyone looked at him weirdly, almost the same expression painted across their faces. Either because they felt the same or because something was eerily off. Dark's eyes closed, and he fell to the floor. Masquerade blacked out, falling to the floor with a thud and a shockwave through his body.

That brings them to the present; it was nighttime, and a breeze filled the room. Masquerade used heavy guts of winds to blow his blanket away from him. He jolted up in his bed, full of electrical energy. He was pissed, but he didn't know why. It was chilly, and he felt his heart beating louder than usual. He felt like he just woke up from a nightmare. He was wide awake. He had no idea how long he had slept for, his eyes wandering around the darkened aesthetic. He glanced around and saw a tiny blanket of frost covering the walls and floor, making the overall temperature greatly chilling.

Dark and Infinity were gone from their beds, and Hyper and Laser were sound asleep. His ears adjusted to the scenario, and his eyes widened, hearing his Mom scream. It was dark; night had fallen since he passed out. He felt lightning pulse through his veins and arteries. He sped straight through the window, remembering the events before he blacked out.

The sound of broken glass attracted attention. Shards of glass stabbed into his arms, he reluctantly ignored the sharpening pain. The second he got outside, he was hit by a wave of cold air. A blizzard raged through the yard with lightning strikes raining down in the midst of the blizzard. He saw multiple silhouettes in the midst of the storm. Then, the memories flooded back all at once. Masquerade glanced at the figure. *It's all our fault,* Masquerade thought.

He sprinted towards the man in the fog; he knew it was a bad idea. The blizzard obscured his view greatly, making him unable to observe anything around him. *Where is everyone???* Upon reaching the intruder, his fists reached outwards, attempting to attack. The figure dodged and looked at him accordingly, his eyes just as piercing as before.

"You again?" He said. his voice grated on his nerves, tempting him to claw at his own ears. It was chilling, and he didn't want to be near it. Every time he spoke, a chill ran down his spine, serrating through his veins. His brain was freezing once more, and he tried searching for anyone else for assistance. He saw his dad lying on the ground. His dad's body showed no signs of fluid movement, a tear shed in his eye. Masquerade looked at the figure, then to his father, and back to the man. The blizzard, an icy curtain, blurred his vision, preventing him from acknowledging his father's demise.

"Right on cue. I was about to silence this liar for good!" His voice reverberated through the blizzard.

"Masquerade! Don't listen to him!!" His dad's voice screamed, proving he was alive. However, he was severely injured since he couldn't stand.

"Oh, trust me, it's better to listen to me than this piece of shit." He said while he kicked the body on the ground. The blizzard died down a little in a quick flash, almost like his anger was the factor for its stopping. The halt in the storm was long enough for Masquerade to see his face. His hair gleamed an unsettling white, complemented by round spectacles framing cold, light-blue eyes. There were dark spots blotches on his face, which he guessed were blood. *Whose blood?* He observed.

"So, are you gonna do anything? If not, I guess I could introduce myself." He paused. "I'm Echo. An old ally turned foe, thanks to your father's betrayal. Now, I've arrived to reclaim something and, perhaps, settle an old score." Echo said.

"Your dad was the only one willing to fight," he mocked. "Your siblings were too scared of me. I don't know why since they don't know me." Echo said. Masquerade just stood and watched. He couldn't move.

"I'd be scared if I saw your ugly ass appear in my front yard, too" Masquerade snapped at him while he tried attacking Echo once more. He pushed his body through the ultimate cold of the blazing winds. Echo dodged every single one of his attempts to attack.

"Oh, really? Cockiness suits winners, not sore losers like you," Echo echoed, dripping with irony. He raised his fist, and ice chains bound Masquerade to the floor.

He glanced around quickly while he could. He saw a group gathered around someone on the floor. The blizzard made it hard to see, but Masquerade glanced down to see what Echo was wearing. Some overalls and a neon green shirt, all blood-stained. His entire arm had blood over it like he impaled someone with his arm alone. He was clearly some sort of construction worker, or, in Masquerade's eyes, just some clown. Echo saw Zeus was trying to crawl away, so he stomped on his chest and pinned him to the ground.

"No moving until my servant has what I came for." Echo said. He suddenly remembered his mother, who was screaming earlier. He attempted to tend to his mother, but the ice chains kept him stuck. He stared into Echo's eyes, his dark gaze glaring through the heavy wisps of snow and ice. Echo looked scared all of a sudden, as if his eye contact had some kind of danger, or if staring at him activated a flight or fight response. He didn't know why since he didn't do anything, then another figure approached from the deep depths of shadows.

Masquerade couldn't make out who it was, but he knew Echo was scared of him for a quick and odd reason. Then, like a swarm of flies, pink and red fire erupted from the spots where blood was covering Echo's body. The figure approaching had the same pink fire blasting from his deep injuries. It was Dark. He grinned at the moment of luckiness, able to stand against the evil that swallowed their family. Echo was screaming in horrid pain as the fire burnt his arm and left one side of his face broken and burnt crisp. Dark was bleeding badly, but his injuries seemed to be healing from the pink-blazing fire.

"Where's Mom??" Masquerade asked, his ice chains still holding his weight. The group of figures behind watched.

"You know our god's blood can't get into other's hands, Dark!" Nature's voice screamed from behind.

"It wasn't my fault! He's powerful; my blood doesn't matter. He probably doesn't even know about *that* stupid blood myth anyway." *His blood's hot pink, hot pink meant his blood could be used as a weapon instead of a cure.* Masquerade recalled what his father told him long ago. Echo stood up on his feet, ready to face Dark, ignoring the searing pain of flames.

"Mom's still inside. If you go find her, I'll deal with him." Dark said coldly, his smile hid behind a bright pink light that was wavering due to heavy wind gusts. Masquerade's hearts dropped. *She was screaming. Why was she screaming? And there's a servant?* He broke free of the weak frozen chains, and bolted towards the house. His body bursted into Tazer's room quickly, breaking down the door. His Mom was sitting on the floor, sobbing, Tazer was crying, and there was a figure holding what seemed like Bow.

The humanoid was holding him like a baby, like it was **his** baby. The crib toys were still on, singing their glitching lullaby. Masquerade felt a new rage hidden deep within his soul, one he's never felt before. He looked at the intruder. His mother raised her eyes and looked at him directly. He felt his eyes change shape, like a slit pierced through the iris, his already heart-shaped iris.

The intruder looked behind him to see Masquerade, who didn't seem to care that he was there. The humanoid appeared to have a werewolf-esque appearance, and upon turning to face the light, Masquerade inquired that he did have Bow in his hands, still acting like Bow belonged to him. His mother looked at Masquerade's hands, observing them attentively. He was too emotional to even glance at himself, nor towards anywhere besides the stranger. Every emotion filled his veins at once, his heart pumped with twice as much power, charging his fists with absolute power.

The lightning in his veins started pulsing like it told him to just attack already. His senses were overloaded, and he let go of all his energy.

In a flash, he was across the other side of the room, with Bow in his hands. The dust came off the old planks and followed the rush of wind that just occurred. A large cut intruded on the shoulder of the figure. Its open blood scattered through the air, and there was a quick flash of lightning that emulsified from Masquerade's arms. Following the lightning was a large blast of thunder. He quickly realized that the sensation of energy in his veins, was his fathers great lightning power awakening.

Masquerade put Bow on the floor safely. His hands ached and pulsed. With one pulse, he pushed the wind upwards to get on top of the intruder. His hand radiated a bright yellow glow, which he thought was a sheath of great electrical energy. Upon unleashing its power, an explosion erupted, propelling the intruder through the wall in a fiery burst. Coming from Masquerade's hand, the wall exploded and creaked. Splinters of wood exploded through the room. Smoke exerted from his arms, as his hands still sparkled with explosive energy.

His mom looked scared and proud at the same time, smiling indefinitely. His other hand remained glowing, ready to unleash a powerful destructive blast. He concentrated the power to make the glow brighter, shining the light on his mother. Her arm was gone, cut clean. She was healing since she had the god factor too, but it wasn't healing well. *That must be that guy's power.* He retreated and glanced back at the hole in the wall.

The figure stood up again at the hole in the wall. He looked at him, and the figure stared back. Masquerade's body suddenly had cuts everywhere, like invisible swords had come out of nowhere and barraged his body. His forearms were cut with extremely sharp cuts. His new power allowed them to heal perfectly, however. The villain could cut things using his mind, he made a mental note about this piece of information. Masquerade charged his foot with his new explosive power, the yellow light shining through the material of his brown shoes. His foot ached, and then he released the power, another explosion boosted him towards the figure, leaving damage in the floor. He charged his hand next, the yellow light further illuminating the room. The villain snapped his long fingers. Deep sword cuts wounded Masquerade, but that didn't stop him from pushing forwards.

With a forceful release, the explosion tore through the house, reducing it to rubble in an instant. The shockwave redirected the blizzard for a split moment. Splinters flew everywhere, smoke covered the sky, and a mushroom cloud formed. His cuts weren't healing suddenly, and he observed that his blood wasn't hot pink like Darks, just red.

There were splinters stabbed everywhere in Masquerade's skin. His mother looked horrified. Masquerade's body ached. *Explosions are theatrical, much like a masquerade,* he mused as he lunged back into the fray against the villain. The figure kicked his calf to try and make him fall, which worked, and he fell to the floor. Another wave of cuts shaved through his body. This time, they did not heal. They left searing slashes on his face and hands. He was blacking out again, losing his vision inducingly. *One. Last. Time.* Masquerade felt another jolt of energy shock his body, as if he were getting revived. His scars and cuts healed, and he got up once more.

"I gotta give you credit for trying, but that won't be enough. Sorry kid." The demon had spoken for the first time. Masquerade felt a wave of guilt upon looking at his mother, who was crying. He glanced at Tazer, who was now with Dark and the others. "You only caught me off guard. I assure you it won't happen again." He looked at Bow, and he was laughing. He had no clue what was going on.

Masquerade tried attacking again, but the villain threw him to the side, using a power resembling telekinesis. He didn't even grab Masquerade or touch him, for that matter. He walked towards Bow menacingly, who was still laughing. Then, a bright laser pinged the villain's head out of nowhere. Hyper and Laser approached, trying to reach Bow, but the intruder did first. He reached over and swooped Bow into his arms. He threw Hyper at Laser with his telekinesis and started walking towards Tazer and the others. Bow wasn't laughing anymore. His mom moaned in pain, and Masquerade charged his entire arm again, the same aching occurring from before. His entire forearm glinted a bright yellow.

The explosion that came was massive, he aimed his entire arm upwards. Destroying the rest of the house and blasting the blizzard out of the way. He made sure not to hit anyone directly. The night sky was clear as day, and the winds spread throughout the open yard. He speed-blitzed the villain immediately after, not letting him take a breath, but an attack did not land. Masquerade felt a sharp pain in his chest, he was eye-to-eye with the intruder however. Following his mothers scream, a tsunami wave of sword cuts wavered through every single part of Masquerade's already damaged body.

He now realized there was a large sharp scythe through his chest. The scythe hoisted him up, like he was staked. *I should be dead by now.* The villain lifted the scythe to show everyone the body, just to mock them for whatever stupid reason. Then he waved the weapon, so Masquerade flew out towards the ground while the scythe retreated through his guts and chest. He couldn't move, as his spleen was entirely ripped out. The villain had Bow, and Masquerade couldn't move anymore.

I should be dead. I should be dead. I SHOULD be dead. His mother was screaming. The villain stepped on Masquerade's chest. *Were they retreating? Why do they need Bow?* He doesn't blame his siblings for not doing anything. After all, what could they do? He saw his dad still on the floor. Dark was on the floor. The pink flames were gone. He couldn't do anything. Masquerade tried getting back to his feet. The other siblings were actually attempting to fight the other guy, and he couldn't move. Even to help his siblings, his Mom, and his dad, he couldn't. He was useless.

Echo approached and pointed at him, "Kill that one, please." Masquerade's heart pulsed. A sudden cold feeling pierced through his body. Then, an entire ice spike stabbed through his back. Everyone looked in shock. Too shocked to scream and too shocked to react. *What could they even do? My dad's supposed to be a super soldier, but he lost to a newbie with ice powers?? I should be dead dead dead.* He felt his body thump, his eyes falter, and his muscles relax. He blacked out, without knowing what just happened. When he opened his eyes, he saw a figure staring at him. He was in a completely different area than just a few seconds ago. A golden light flashed in the stone room he was contained inside. The room was beautiful, the black and gray stones enlightened by a fresh light of royal gold. He observed it carefully, and he had no clue where he was.

"How did you die?" The 'person' said in front of him

"I died? This is the afterlife!?" Masquerade screamed. He bled out, he assumed. While he was there, he noticed that his entire body was healed, the pain was gone, and his soul felt replenished. The place felt so beautiful that he never wanted to leave. He observed the god that he was in the presence of.

"You're...you're, Anubis, servant to Osiris, weighing souls and helping the afterlife. God of the Dead..." Masquerade said while confused. The jackal nodded in approval. "Speaking of, where is Osiris?" Anubis gave Masquerade a puzzled look.

"Osiris, my old partner and leader, is dead. As his dying wish, I had taken his spot and left to watch over the afterlife. Although you got it all wrong, Osiris isn't some god you should automatically start worshiping just because I exist." Anubis said. "You know Zeus exists? Poseidon? After all, none of those are the gods you should be amazed by, as the real godfather is Misa and his sons Peace and Mardo," He continued.

"Mardo!? That's my uncle, and Zeus is my dad!" Masquerade exclaimed and most likely lied. Anubis looked surprised to hear this. He grabbed his chin in astonishment.

"Oh really? Sad to see that you died then, huh." His voice was calming, alleviating the overall vibe this place of harmonization gave.

"Well. . . I don't think Mardo is actually my uncle, maybe just a close friend?" He stared for a long moment. Anubis nodded and gestured his fingers towards him.

"It's time I weigh your soul now." He said, "And atone for your sins." Masquerade staggered backwards.

"II don't want to die." Masquerade announced, his voice scattering against the stone. Anubis stared back coldly.

"No one wants to die, young one." His voice was soothing and calming. "Now come, please, you're running out of time."

Out of nowhere, his blood felt like it was pumping backward, like his heart was absorbing his blood instead of pushing it. Everything reversed around him, giving that effect you get when you travel at a great speed, the blurs of lines appear around him. It felt like he was falling from Heaven itself. Then he jolted awake, his eyes adjusting to the dark lights. Bow was gone. The intruders were gone. He looked around. Everyone was gathered around him. All of them were gasping for air and all tired. Terrified and tired, he bets all of them are still processing what just happened.

"How are you still alive??" Nature's hoarse voice croaked through the gasps of his entire family.

"I don't know-" He answered. He believes he shouldn't tell anyone what just happened. *Did I fake death? I need an excuse. There is no way they think I just survived that based on pure luck. How am I still alive? How, how, HOW? There's only one real answer. . . Surviving this, was it just luck? Or am I something more? Immortal, perhaps?*

Chapter 2
Jake (Past)

Jake fixated on his impending act, idly staring at the wall in Stitch's basement, a sharpened knife dancing between his fingers. The anticipation fueled his restless mind. He couldn't wait for the moment to eliminate the one who always thwarted his triumphs.

The anticipated cue played in his mind—footsteps echoed upstairs, a pattern only he recognized. Swiftly, Jake gripped the doorknob, maneuvering out from the basement, his movements purposeful. Regretting not studying the house layout, he silently advanced toward the stairs, a planned murder demanding finesse.

Two voices murmured upstairs, their words indistinguishable. Jake, now at the end of the stairs, gripped the railing, positioning himself near a closet. Moonlight streamed through the front door, casting beams. He played with the knife again, nerves and anticipation palpable. A silhouette appeared at the top of the stairs, and Jake's heart sank—he wasn't ready for this. Glancing up, he saw the shadow facing away, engaged in conversation with someone else.

"Why are you still up, following me? Are you hungry too?" Questioned the female voice—the intended victim.

"No, just making sure you're alright. There might be an intruder. I'm sure of it," innocently replied the other voice, Mark, Stitch's father.

"Only slightly creepy, especially since it's the middle of the night. But whatever, treat yourself if you must," retorted the female voice. seizing the opportunity, Jake stealthily retreated from the stairs. The two figures descended into the kitchen, where the basement door awaited. The male figure arrived first, progressing into the kitchen before abruptly halting. Gripping his face, he feigned forgetfulness, adding suspense to the impending encounter.

"My glasses, dear, can you grab them for me." The female's footsteps stopped. She slowly retreated back upstairs while murmuring some swear words to herself. The male turned towards the basement door. He walked up to it and started playing the knob. Jake swiftly ran up the stairs quietly. The man was still distracted. Jake faintly touched his knife, enchanting it with growing capacity. The knife glowed a faint purple. He hid it behind his back mysteriously.

"Can't find them honey?" He whispered in the same exact voice as her husband, showing off his vocalized prowess. The woman turned around quickly, alarmed.

"No, I can't, but since you're here, you grab them." The woman slowly walked towards him from the dark void of the room. Walking towards the door, unaware of her unwilling demise. The woman reached towards Jake before stopping and looking at him suspiciously. From the faint light, you could tell Jake didn't look like her husband.

"Mark? You look different." She leaned in closer, looking into his eyes softly. Jake smiled softly in return. She grinned for some reason, leaning in for a kiss. Jake grabbed her chest, purposefully grabbing her bra and tugging it off a little. His powers put perfectly into play, exactly how he planned it. He pulled her close and kissed her. The woman looked closely at him from a closer view than before. Jake slowly changed his appearance over time, more and more looking like Mark, her husband.

She smiled seductively. Jake grabbed her chest again. Slowly pulling her bra off even more. She took her shirt off in response.

"You know, Mark, you're being more dangerous than usual, especially considering you rejected me earlier," She exclaimed while giving him 'that' stare. Jake didn't respond; he just stared back with a manipulative gaze.

Jake smiled. The woman was too aroused to notice. Jake kissed her again. She breathed heavily. Jake pinned her against the wall as she moved softly. Jake slowly trailed his fingers toward her stomach, tickling her gently. From there, he trailed his finger back up towards the back, removing the bra strap. The woman looked Jake in the eyes while having a fearful expression on her face.

"You aren't Mark." She said slowly. Her bra remained slightly off, revealing cleavage. The knife had already reached its destination. The woman didn't even notice by now. Jake could feel her emotions with the knife stabbed into her thoracic cavity. She was seduced, scared, and sad all at the same time, the knife proved useful. The pain hit her all at once, and through the manipulation; she screamed.

Jake pulled the knife out quickly and jabbed it again, straight into her waist. Looking straight into her eyes, he retaliated with the knife, and stabbed her eye. He then pushed her away with enough force to make her fall over. She grasped her eye in wrenching pain. Jake looked at her in a disappointed manner, whispering defeat in his eyes. He then heard footsteps blasting upwards towards him.

Jake simply nodded his head and disappeared into thin air. He was gone, nowhere to be seen, nowhere to be heard. The door right next to Mark's room busted open in an instant, Stitch, his former friend. Stitch observed the area, his eyes scanning the scene. Mark stood over the impending body, looking like he did the deed, as Jake purposefully dropped the knife next to her body. Stitch looked terrified, looking at his own father, whose feet were planted right next to the lifeless body of his mother. Mark turned around, realizing what had just happened, realizing that he was perceived as the one who committed murder.

"It's not what it looks like, trust me." The door right next to Stitch's room lay open. A little girl stood, watching the scene as well. Jake didn't know her, but he knew it was possibly Stitch's little sister.

"Why, why would you do something like this? WHAT COULD POSSIBLY GO THROUGH YOUR MIND TO MURDER YOUR OWN WIFE!" Stitch screamed at his father.

"I am telling you, it wasn't me. You have to trust me." Mark echoed, trying to remain composed.

"How am I supposed to believe that? Nothing but lies! Am I supposed to believe some ghost killed my Mom? HUH!?" Stitch asked. Jake smiled at the thought of being called a 'ghost'.

"Now I want you to grab the knife and slit your wrist, not too hard, not too light, just perfect. Please." Jake bellowed to Mark. The other two couldn't hear him, his whispers of evil were only audible to the framed innocent dubbed Mark. Jake was already controlling Mark with his powers.

"What, wait, who said that?" Mark said, looking around for a ghost that he couldn't see. He looked miserable in the heat of the moment.

"Oh, so now you're hearing things?!" Stitch said. Mark bent over wistfully, grabbing the knife chillingly and slowly as his body was trembling, attempting to fight against Jake's word magic.

"Huh, wait, no. I'm not doing this! This isn't me! I'm not moving!" Mark mumbled to himself. Jake couldn't do anything but keep a sinister smile. Mark grabbed the knife swiftly. He held it across his wrist, the knife quivering against his tough skin. He sweated the moment. The knife cut through elegantly and quickly into his wrist. The girl and Stitch watched in horror, their father's and mother's blood staining the carpet below. Jake quickly changed the point of view towards Stitch only, so no one else could hear him.

"Now, Stitch, I want you to mindlessly beat your father until you physically cannot continue," Jake bellowed to him, the little girl's ear twitched for an odd reason. Stitch had a gaze of familiarity in his eyes, slightly recognizing the voice, as an old friend's. Jake, once again, changed his point of view towards Mark again.

Stitch sprinted at Mark, punching him reluctantly with heavy fists. Stitch kept going, his fists gathering blood that shone brighter than any moon. Jake watched happily, being the ultimate catalyst for the event of chaos that insured in front of his view. Mark took all the blows for one reason. The reason being that he fully believed it was his fault that his wife was dead. In this case however, it was. Stitch continued until his body physically couldn't throw any more punches. Mark pushed him down the stairs.

"Now, as your last cry for help, I want you to grab a match and set your house ablaze. With the intention of either killing yourself in the process, or turning yourself in to the police." Jake grinned at him, his smile almost never disappearing. Mark stared in fear as his eyes went blank, showing no signs of grief whatsoever. Mark did as told. He stood up slowly, trying to break out of control of the mind games that Jake placed upon his body.

He walked towards his nightstand, grabbing a box of matches. He grabbed one match as Stitch and her sister watched, and didn't, or couldn't move a muscle. Mark lit it, dropping it right onto his wife's body, who was still alive by a few deep breaths of pain. Two stabs didn't do the job, but the fire would.

The fire raged with an insatiable hunger, devouring the house in seconds. Stitch, adrenaline pumping, seized Jynx and burst into the next room, determined to rescue as many as possible. He grabbed Jynx's twin, an almost identical male version of her. Chaos reigned, the flames casting eerie shadows on their desperate faces.

Mark, panic gripping him, fumbled for his phone, fingers trembling as he dialed the emergency number. The dispatcher answered, and Mark relayed the address with urgency. A tense wait ensued, each passing second intensifying the perilous situation.

Stitch desperately tried to be a hero in the inferno but was thwarted by rising flames. Meanwhile Jake, a silent spectator to the destruction, observed as he effortlessly orchestrated the collapse of an entire family's world, for seemingly no reason at all.

Mark stood by the window, paralyzed by terror as he could feel his entire world crumble. He turned towards his children, desperate to console his son. He tried to offer comfort, but Stitch's emotional detachment was evident. Pushing his father aside, Stitch approached the girl, a potent mix of determination and sorrow in his eyes. The room hung heavy with the weight of their shattered lives, and the intensity of the moment surged as Stitch prepared to confront the aftermath of the devastating fire.

"You'll eventually realize when you need this." Jake spoke to only the girl, Stitch and her other brother, Mason, unable to hear the voice. He said to the girl, but nothing occurred.

Mark couldn't turn this around no matter what he tried, he still didn't even know who really killed his wife. He stared as blue and red flashes illuminated the streets below, their lights unable to light up the world that he was ripped apart from. He stared at the remains of the family. Twins, and an older brother. The mother is dead, and the father is locked up for good, whom, despite his actions to keep them all happy, will never see them ever again, or will never have the same relationship with them ever again. Mark turned around as the cops invaded the burning house. The squad investigated the body before noticing Mark, seeing the knife, a dead body, and a box of matches. They looked at him, completely disgusted. The four rushed to the room.

Mark threw his arms into the air and knelt on the floor, the officers rushing towards his helpless body with steel cuffs. They arrested him as the house elegantly collapsed. Stitch watched from outside on the lawn, tearing up as the family shattered just like that. Moments passed, the three siblings watching their house reluctantly burn, plank by plank, memory by memory, they told their favorite stories that occurred in that beloved house.

"Remember when we had that cockroach infestation and we had to fog the entire house? This reminds me of that time. . ." Mason said, holding a teddy bear that resembled an old relative that passed years ago. Stitch grabbed his hand, rubbing it slightly, letting the little boy cry.

"Yeah but remember when mom bought that bearded dragon for us, that ate the cockroaches for us!" The little girl, Jynx, exclaimed, looking for the good in the situation.

"I remember Heisenberg! He really loved those bananas, huh?" Stitch responded. Mason smiled through tear filled eyes.

"Me too!" He said, holding his teddy bear upwards. Despite the roaring fateful night, Stitch grabbed his siblings by their hands and began their walk towards the 24/7 open gas station.

"Let's go grab some banana shakes in his name then." He spoke with a whisper to his younger siblings.

As the scene died down. Jake reappeared. He retrieved his knife, by then everyone was long gone. The body was reduced to ash, Jake smiled. Her eyes remained glowing, a hot pink color, this made Jake feel fearful, but he knew his play in this all was finally done. All through, the body was all black ash, he stabbed her once more. Jake kicked the body one last time and walked away slowly. He has done his job. Finally.

Chapter 2
Jynx (Present)

Jynx looked the teacher up and down, disgusted. She hated this class. She glanced around, catching the eyes of three different guys and the new girl, she frowned in response. She looked down at her notebook, noticing the scribbles covering the entire page, where she drew something horrid. She hates to remember that day, she hates every aspect of it. Her veins were pacing again, and her back was sweating again, a cold sweat that covered her in a thick blanket of underlying anxiety. She still has PTSD from that day. The classroom's noise level lowered in Jynx's mind, like someone turned a knob down on an old TV. She couldn't stop it from happening, she didn't know why it kept replaying in her head. Despite wanting to be a psychologist, she had no clue how mental illnesses work.

Her brain pulsed and stopped, feeling every lobe highlight themselves, looking for an answer to cure her chaos. Her eyes blacked out, her head falling down on the desk. She opened them, she was there, once more. She opened her eyes to her mother's screams, and a clank of metal that ringed against the carpet. Jynx hopped out of bed, scared and thoughtful. She kept her blanket over her shoulders. The hallway light was on, blazing through the under crack of the bedroom door. She walked slowly towards the door. Her mother was still screaming. Jynx slowly approached the door and put her hand on the knob. Her brother was screaming her father's name.

"Why, why would you do something like this? WHAT COULD POSSIBLY GO THROUGH YOUR MIND TO MURDER YOUR OWN WIFE!" Stitch screamed at his father.

"I am telling you, it wasn't me. You have to trust me." Mark echoed, his voice sounded unconvincing than ever before.

Her brother's voice boomed from down the hall very loudly. Jynx opened the door swiftly. She glanced down the hallway at her parents' room. The door was wide open. There were three figures. Her mom, who was either passed out on the floor, or dead, her dad, and her older brother. Her twin was nowhere to be found, most likely passed out.

The white walls near the room were smeared with an absurd amount of blood. Mom was on the floor. Dad was face to face with her mother's body. A knife lay right next to his hand. Jynx could feel her fear coursing through her body as her hands trembled with her accelerating heartbeat and drops of cold sweat dripping down her back. *Did my father kill her?* Jynx stopped in her tracks and watched. Her dad locked eyes with her brother. "It isn't what it looks like, believe me." Her father testified, his voice sounding more and more deceitful.

"How am I supposed to believe that? Nothing but lies! Am I supposed to believe some ghost killed my Mom? HUH!?" Stitch asked.

"Wait, what? Who said that?" Her father said chillingly. Jynx looked around for another speaker, although her ear twitched, slightly feeling a disturbance or air.

"Oh, so now you're hearing things!" Stitch screamed. Her father hesitated for a moment. He leaned down and grabbed the knife. He slowly pulled it upwards. Jynx watched in horror as her father slit his own wrist in a split second. Her father hesitated again before walking into his room. Her brother frowned, watching the murderer attentively.

In the aftermath, Stitch, consumed by a mixture of grief and anger, approached their father. He swung with all his might, but her father showed no reaction. A twisted smile played on his lips, absorbing the blows. Stitch relentlessly attacked, the room echoing with the sound of violence. Jynx, frozen in horror, watched the relentless assault unfold, the seconds stretching into agonizing hours.

As Stitch exhausted himself, her father, still waiting, seized the opportunity. With one swift, calculated swing, Stitch tumbled down the stairs, the thuds signaling his unconsciousness. Amidst the chaos, Jynx remained unnoticed, a silent witness to the tragic drama.

A mysterious voice, oddly familiar, pierced the heavy air. "No one speaks of this moment. You know it had to be done." Her father met the gaze of the unseen speaker and nodded solemnly. Jynx felt her heart shatter, the pieces scattering in the wake of an unthinkable truth. Mark, a shadowy figure in the background, grabbed a match and ignited it, casting an eerie glow on the scene.

In the aftermath, her father called the authorities, surrendering himself to the consequences of his actions. Stitch, still dazed at the foot of the stairs, wept. Their father tried to offer comfort, but Stitch, rising with newfound strength, approached Jynx. Kneeling down, his eyes locked with hers, and in that moment, she felt a strange pulse coursing through her body. The world seemed to blur as Stitch's eyes changed color, leaving Jynx in bewildered awe.

"You'll eventually realize when you need this." A very unfamiliar and consulting voice told her, she felt something reverberate through her empty grief filled soul. Stitch had then grabbed her and her twin brother from their rooms, escaping out the front door. Her father was fined, and everyone knew he was the murderer of Jynx's mother. Her father got arrested for a life sentence. She still had questions, but she never got them. Moments passed, the three siblings watching their house reluctantly burn, plank by plank, memory by memory, they told their favorite stories that occurred in that beloved house.

"Remember when we had that cockroach infestation and we had to fog the entire house? This reminds me of that time. . ." Mason, Jynx's twin said, holding a teddy bear that resembled an old relative that passed years ago. Stitch grabbed his hand, rubbing it slightly, letting the little boy cry.

"Yeah but remember when mom bought that bearded dragon for us, that ate the cockroaches for us!" Jynx exclaimed, looking for the good in the situation.

"I remember Heisenberg! He really loved those bananas, huh?" Stitch responded. Mason smiled through tear filled eyes.

"Me too!" He said, holding his teddy bear upwards. Despite the roaring fateful night, Stitch grabbed his siblings by their hands and began their walk towards the 24/7 open gas station.

"Let's go grab some banana shakes in his name then." He spoke with a whisper to his younger siblings. With that turn of events, her mind flailed, levitating in a blank state.

She still had to find out why her father would curse her like this. Her mind flailed around in this dream state for a bit. This was usually when she would wake up from the memories, but she didn't. She was in a cold black nothingness. She opened her eyes finally.

Her brain unlocked a memory, unforeseen to anything she has experienced before. She was in a car, very late at night, the lampposts illuminated the night street. It was raining, drops of water highlighting the metal sheet of the automobile. She looked around the car to see who it was. In the driver's seat was Jake. The passengers consisted of her brother, Stitch. Jynx's eyes gleamed in fear. She looked out the window. The street lights faded away solemnly, indicating they were taking her out of town. She was now just realizing she was tied up. The highway faded as the car turned. The concrete pavement changed into a gravel mess of rocks. They were taking the back roads to a sketchy place deep in the country. Jynx kept glancing at the two. They didn't say a word, so Jynx didn't dare speak back.

The car rolled across the gravel slowly. Jynx breathed softly, it was hard to breathe all of a sudden. She found herself breathing harder. Jake looked back at her, a chill running through her body when their eyes met. Jake smiled softly and focused back on the road, his hands reluctantly cruising on the wheel. Jynx felt a sharp emotional stab in her chest.

Something pissed her off about Jake, but yet she was too scared to feel actual anger. Her eyes wandered around the car, trying to notice the minor little details of this void memory.

Nothing but a dark road ahead, for miles upon miles. Stitch and Jake were quiet, not even music played, just pure dark silence, besides the constant beating of rain. The car rumbled to a stop in front of a dilapidated, eerie house, its windows shattered and the wind howling through its creaking boards. They both got out of the car. They talked for a moment, nothing but mumbles to Jynx's ears. Then, the car door right next to her swung open. Jake grabbed her with no hesitation.

Jynx's eyes widened. She was terrified, too terrified to do anything. Raindrops rolled down her face. She tightened her eyes shut, feeling the warmth of the house steadily creep on her skin as they carried her in forcefully. She still kept her eyes shut, despite the warm and helpful entrance. There was another pair of footsteps following, who she guessed was Stitch. Another door opened, and Jake put her down on a chair. Jynx opened her eyes, and she was in a lab room. Stitch walked in and tied her down to the chair even more, chains and straps consulted her thin wrists. Jake looked at her disappointed, and Stitch looked sad and inept.

"It has to be done, Jynx." Jake said. Jynx stared in fear, remembering the quote from her previous memory. Stitch had a tear roll down his face. "First off," Jake said as he grabbed a syringe. "We'll start by running a blood test." Jynx tightened in her seat. While Jake got the syringe ready, she examined the room. A few tables around with random equipment on them scattered the room.

She squinted towards the back. A few bags hung, a few body bags. One with hot pink hair drooping from the bottom of the bag, signature pink hair. Pink hair only her mother had. Jynx felt her heart drop. Jake approached her slowly with the light equipment ready. Stitch remained by the door, watching.

"Hopefully, you aren't scared of needles." Jake mocked. The syringe entered her arm. Jake slowly pushed the syringe, and the needle entered. Jynx stared carefully. She didn't know what he was looking for. The blood retracted.

The blood came out normal. Normal red. Nothing out of the usual. Jake stepped back with the syringe and placed it on a scale. He dropped the blood on his finger. Then he licked it, licked HER blood. He made a weird face, his eyes wandered around, and he locked them with Stitch.

"It's normal," he said chillingly. Jynx's body shivered. She looked at the syringe. The blood was normal, but she was confused about what 'normal' meant. "For stage two, I'm going to need you to stay quiet, understood??" Jake started. Stitch came from behind her and unstrapped her. She fell to the floor on purpose. She didn't want to get up. She didn't want to imagine what 'Stage Two' was. She didn't want to know. Jake stood her up with his aggressive hands.

She opened her eyes. She was eye-to-eye with Jake. "Her eyes seem normal, too, Stitch." Jake grinned. "She's already failing your stupid test, idiot." Jake said. "I didn't waste gas money just for nothing interesting to happen." Jake put his hands on Jynx's shoulders. He pushed with full force, and she fell to the ground. "I guess I should test durability, huh." Jake looked her up and down. Stitch stayed in the corner, just watching.

"Stand up," Jake said with a commanding voice. Something about it made her get up straight away. She looked at her feet, her knees unfolding and her hands shifting to make her posture perfect. *Why did I stand up? That wasn't me.* She looked at Jake in fear. "Just now realizing my ability?" Jake mocked, he smiled a stupid little grin. "Punch yourself now." His pupils jittered a bright red for a second in the moment he said the sentence.

Jynx clenched her fist as hard as she could. Her arm moved unwillingly. She tried to stop it. Her arm lifted up and socked her jaw in, she fell to the floor, barely catching herself. Jake looked at her, laughing. Stitch watched and did nothing. *What a great brother you sure are.* Jynx shed a tear, afraid of what Jake would do next.

"Get up again." Jynx stood up, unwilling once more. Jake looked around for a moment. He touched a handle at the side of the table. He rolled out the drawer and pulled out a sharp knife. Jynx's eyes widened, quivered, and secreted tears. She started crying. Tears rolled down her face that eventually fell to the floor. Drops started appearing on the gray cement floor. Stitch looked down now, too cowardly to do anything. Jake held the knife up and slid it right next to the syringe.

"Grab the knife." His voice demanded. Jynx used all her strength to stop herself from moving. Her body gave in, and she inched towards the table. She lay her fingers on the table, using every bit of muscle she had. "Hurry." Jynx swiftly touched the knife. She gripped it and held it on her chest. A sinister smile curled up on Jake's face, sending shivers down Jynx's spine.

"Stab yourself in the thigh." Jynx's eyes said it all, fear and everything building up in her chest. More tears rolled down her face. She looked at Jake in absolute terror.

"Please, no," Jynx's voice pleaded, cracking with desperation. Jake smiled in return. The blade thrust mercilessly into her left thigh, a searing agony engulfing her. She screamed in pain. She tried turning around to look at Stitch. The knife quivered in her thigh. She couldn't let go. "Now stab it out and hold the knife in your mouth" Jake instructed. Jynx followed as tears ran off her face. The knife lay between her teeth. Blood stained her leggings. It dripped down, adding more to the damp floor, dyeing it red. Suppressing her anguish, Jynx clenched her teeth, awaiting the next command in dreadful silence.

"Slit your tongue." Jynx tightened the knife in her hand and followed. Blood dripped from her mouth. Blood and tears streamed down her face. "Now, slit your wrists, one final goodbye to your brother as well." Jynx turned around. Her brother stared at her. No guilt, no signs of remorse. Not a single tear or thought behind his eyes. Disappointment etched across her face, Jynx wept, a tumultuous storm of emotions within her. Waterfalls of tears streamed down. She grabbed the knife and held it to her wrist.

"Wait!" Jake said, remembering something deceitful. "There's one more test to run." Jynx stopped the knife, falling to her knees. Jake quickly stepped up to her, rubbing her shoulders aggressively. They locked eyes for a great moment of silence, before she felt the interrupting feeling of something tugging at her insides. A feeling of swirling in her stomach, a spiritual presence eventually gathering beneath her muscle and skin. Her soul. Then just as quickly as she stabbed herself earlier, Jake jumped up in shock, his body flailing backwards in fear.

"A soul test. She passed." He said, locking eyes with Stitch. "She must die. Her soul had a glint of pink!" He recalled. "The same as her mothers!" Jynx couldn't understand what they meant, the meaning behind their words were shrouded with mystery to the young woman.

"Slit your wrists, both of them, and stare at your brother the whole time." Jynx grabbed the knife, and held it at her wrist for a long moment. Staring at Stitch. Jynx couldn't mutter a word to him. Jynx locked eyes with him. "The only thing we share is one last name." Jynx quoted before the knife slid straight through her wrist to the bone. Blood was pressured to the floor. Squirting. She held the knife weakly and did the same to the other side. "Now, before you bleed out, slice cuts all over your body. Arms, thighs, face. Everything." Jynx's eyes already started feeling low.

Jittering the knife over her body, she complied with Jake's demands, marking scars in a painful dance of obedience. She felt decentralized to the pain. Her eyes felt weird. She looked out the window. She saw a figure running towards the house. The figure blasted through the window, and Jake looked surprised. Stitch looked unphased, like he was the one that alerted them to save her.

Four more people filed through the broken window. Glass shattered through the room. Jake was already out the other door. Stitch stood as officers consulted him. "Are you the one that called?" He said, and Stitch nodded, she now understood why he remained useless in her rescue, because he had been the one to alert the authorities. Jynx had started to black out by then. All she knew before she hit the floor was that she was safe. She woke up again, this time in a rush.

Jynx finally woke up in the classroom. Her best friend, Jace, was waiting for her. Giving her that "Not this again." look. Jace tapped his fingers on the desk as Jynx adjusted to the school ambience. She walked towards Jace awkwardly.

"Sorry, I was tired." She lied. The two walked outside the classroom. Jace looked worried for Jynx. She already told Jace about her crazy family, but he still suspected there was something more. Jace kept staring at her, worried. Jynx walked to her jammed locker and threw her stuff aside. Her thoughts raced with danger. "Do you want to go out for lunch or not?" Jace asked lightly, his fingers racing.

"No, not today. I have a feeling something interesting is going to occur today. I wanted to eavesdrop on people's conversations. I heard there might be a few new students." Jynx explained. The two walked towards the lunch room. A crowd covered the doors as usual, everyone was trying to get in there first and whatnot. Jynx went to the back of the line.

"Jynx!! Come up here; we saved you a spot in line!" The voice alarmed her. She looked over, and the sporty popular boys wanted to talk to her. They were all jerks, always teasing her of her family history. Approaching them, she found herself at the front of the line. She showed up and budged in front of all of them. They looked confused.

"Oh, was this not the spot you saved?" She blurted in a condescending tone. Daemon looked at her.

"No, it wasn't. I wanted to talk to you. Not an invitation to budge in front." He said jokingly.

"Well, why would I want to do that? I'm kind of hungry, so thanks for the spot, Daemon." She replied and smiled. The other boys stared at her. She stared back, and as she did, all their eyes wandered away. She turned around and called Jace over. The boys looked around at Jace. Jace budgeted and squirmed through the lines, trying to reach Jynx. The other boys teased him and blocked his way, saying lines like 'why would you be friends with that freak'. Jynx walked through them and pulled Jace towards her.

Jace stared at her like she was weird. Jynx grabbed her tray and served herself lunch. She scanned her ID and went to sit down. She was disappointed she heard nothing about any new kids at all. She sat down at her table. Jace sat down next to her, still concerned.

"So, are you going to tell me what was going on in the classroom?" Jace asked, concerned. They both stood at the table, boredom racing.

"It was nothing, Jace. I was just tired, okay?" She replied in a sassy tone. She ate slowly, making a face at him. Jace stared back.

"Okay, okay, yeah I get it." He said. Jynx looked around curiously. She sat right next to the popular kids' table on purpose, wanting to hear of any drama.

"Have you heard that there are gonna be some new kids coming this week?" One of them piped up. "Yeah, I heard somewhere that there were five of them!" Another continued. "Maybe they will be at the dance tomorrow night." Jynx forgot about the dance, her eyes widening. She continued to eat as she was eavesdropping the entire conversation.

After lunch, she continued to class. She hunched down in her seat and zoned out all period. Before she knew it, the day went by. Jynx talked to Jace one last time before hopping on the bus. She sat down in the middle of the dirty bus. She looked around. The bus revved up as she got comfortable. The bus started moving slowly, rolling out of the school.

Lost in thought, she gazed out of the window, the world a blur. Suddenly, something seized her attention. A peculiar house emerged, surrounded by a diverse crowd, each member boasting vibrant, rainbow-colored hair. She watched as the bus came to a stop. Against her better judgment, she chose to disembark, the suspense of the unknown drawing her closer.

Her house was still a while away, but she wanted to see the new crowd. She got off awkwardly. While she was watching the house, the bus left quickly. She counted eighteen people. Twenty, including what seemed like a landlord and a furniture mover. She fixated on that house. A fairly large house, Jynx looked around, attempting to find something interesting.

The family was separated in groups, almost like it was on purpose. Lined up first were two young toddlers, and second were a batch of five teenage boys her age. The third line also consisted of five, all girls slightly older than her. The fourth had four, that looked like adults. Then, another two, who she assumed were the parents. It was cool to her, how they arranged themselves like that. A chaotic yet organized family. She watched, as one of them turned. His hair was hot pink, and faded into black undertones.

His gaze held firm, nodding with eyes shaped like hearts. An unsettling connection pierced through her. His eyes stabbed into her soul. He smiled and turned back, saying something. Jynx looked away, embarrassed. She turned away and started walking. Autumn leaves fell from the trees. She crushed the leaves as she walked.

The crunching noise continued all the way back home. She slowly opened the door, not trying to get caught coming in. It was a bit late, later than when she's usually home. Stitch stood in the kitchen, cooking something. She walked in fully and shut the door, smelling the garlic scented air. Jynx walked in slowly, watching her brother from the kitchen. Stitch looked into her soul from the oven.

"I got a call earlier. . ." Stitch trailed off, looking at her. Stitch retaliated, "It was our dad. He wants to talk." Stitch stared at her.

"What?! What does he want, what did he say!?" He paused. "Are you waiting for my answer?" Jynx asked. She reached for her pocket, grabbing her phone from her pocket. She turned it on, glancing at the missed notifications. *1 missed call from an unknown number.* The phone read.

"He wants a conversation, I feel it isn't the best choice, but I do want to talk to him." Stitch said. "I didn't give him a clear answer yet, because I wanted your opinion. Mason already said yes," Stitch exclaimed. Jynx thought about it for a long moment.

Agreeing reluctantly, she added, 'Yes, but not right now. Let a few weeks unfold before deciding. I assume he's out by now." Jynx replied. "I want him to get on his feet first," she smirked.

"Good answer. Anyway, I cooked for you. So enjoy it." Stitch said as he walked back to his room with a bowl of soup in his hands. Jynx stared at her phone for a long Moment. *It has not been 25 years.* She thought to herself. *They served him a life sentence, and he hasn't even spent half of that. Something's definitely up.*

Chapter 3
Masquerade

Masquerade looked at himself from the smudged mirror. He sported a sleek tuxedo paired with stylish black jeans. He looked at the counter. Picking up some cologne, he sprayed himself. Dark circles still clung to his eyes, remnants of three sleepless nights. There wasn't much to pack, since he had destroyed the entire house in previous events. It was exhausting, considering the fact that he basically died. A gloomy atmosphere had enveloped everyone lately, a sentiment Masquerade couldn't fault them for. He put some deodorant on and made sure he looked good before walking out of the bathroom.

Once he opened the door, Dark, Lazer, and Infinity were waiting in a single-file line. Hyper was enjoying his new bed, jumping up and down. Their new residence boasted an air of splendor. It was the same old sharing-a-room thing, but this time, the rooms were bigger, and each room had its very own bathroom. There was one extra room that was being used as a secondary living room for the family.

Lazer teased, strolling into the bathroom, "Took you quite a while, pretty boy." A mischievous smirk played on Masquerade's lips as he observed, while Dark and Infinity engaged in a playful scuffle for bathroom supremacy.

"Ladies, ladies, chill out. We all have time." Masquerade mocked the two. Dark and Infinity looked at each other and then looked at Masquerade in unison. "If you jump me, I will seriously kill you," Masquerade bellowed down to them. The two looked Masquerade up and down.

Dark smiled, "You know Lazer wasn't lying. You look great for the party." Lazer smiled at himself from the mirror. Infinity shuffled around in the bathroom, trying to look busy.

"Thanks, you know I'm kinda excited to be going to school for the first time, you know?" Masquerade said as he cracked his knuckles. "But I'm still nervous," he said.

"Consider this, Masquerade. We'll be in the same grade, so it won't be as nerve-racking," Infinity reassured.

"I mean, I guess???" Masquerade babbled. As they prepared, the anticipation for the school's homecoming party hung in the air. Mother and father were stressed at the fact that Bow was kidnapped. They reached out to multiple friends to try and rescue him. His dad refused to confront Echo. Masquerade didn't know his dad's past well. A shadow of doubt lingered in Masquerade's mind; he fervently hoped that Echo's ominous words held no truth.

He slowly laid down on his bed, waiting for everyone else, his dark floating anxiety overwhelmed him. His parents had to split them in half and take them in separate cars. Contemplating the upcoming events, Masquerade resolved to snatch a quick nap before heading out.

He got jerked awake by Hyper. "We're leaving!!!" He screamed excitedly in Masquerade's ear. Masquerade got up. He scrutinized his reflection in the mirror, ensuring every detail was impeccable before stepping out. He followed everyone out the door as they filed into their new mini van.

Everyone pretty much had their permits or licenses by now, but the family couldn't afford to give them their own cars. Masquerade zoned out as his dad mindlessly tried navigating the city to find the school. You'd think a god would be filthy rich, but Zeus wanted to keep his heritage 'on the low'. After multiple turns and swerves, they pulled into a filled driveway. Neon hues illuminated the school's facade, casting a vibrant glow.

Mesmerized by the captivating lights, Masquerade allowed himself a brief moment of admiration. The others were already getting out. Masquerade stepped out of the old rusty van. Staring at the school, he slowly made his way towards the doors. His siblings sped past him with uncertainty. Masquerade let them in front of him as he kept the door open for them to file out.

The others looked eager to get in, but Masquerade was nervous. He followed the others in the building, trailing behind them slowly. The older siblings looked like they knew what they were doing, it was almost like they had been to school parties before or just normal parties in general. Masquerade's underlying anxiety quickly dissipated as he realized that he was a descendant of a god that can blow up stuff.

Masquerade's gaze wandered across the room, a mix of excitement and apprehension clouding his eyes. Inside, there was a huge dance floor with neon lights and a huge stage playing loud drumming music. The stage had no singers or bands but a DJ for a change. There were smoke machines and multiple strobes. The party was one entire open room, with the bathrooms being the only direction with a door. Around the dance floor were multiple tables set with food and drinks, in a large semi circle.

There were people everywhere, but no one noticed the group of fourteen that just walked in. It seemed they threw the homecoming party in the schools commons area. Although unfamiliar with the intricacies of such gatherings, Masquerade understood that students from grades 9 to 12 were welcome. Masquerade would be in his sophomore year starting now. He walked towards admission, where his siblings already beat him too. The staff, brimming with enthusiasm, wore radiant smiles as they managed the reception. They were eager to see them.

"SO! You guys are the new students. We already got a note about you from the principal. New sophomores, juniors, and seniors, you know the freshman will be disappointed they didn't get a batch of quadruplets or quintuplets in their grade. Also, let's not forget the twins in first grade! Exciting stuff. I don't even get how your parents managed to have three batches of that many!" One of the admission staff piped up in a very exciting tone.

Masquerade put on a fake smile, assuming that's what his siblings were doing. "Yeah! We figured we could make some friends before actually starting school," Nature said in a fake, overly nice tone. "So, just so we all know, how big is the school, and how many people in each grade?" Nature questioned. Hyper ceased fidgeting with his bow tie and turned his attention to the staff, expressing his interest.

"Well, the town is pretty average. The school is the county's state school, and we usually have around 150 students in each grade graduating year. I hope this helps emphasize your school size." the staff said. The other staff looked as if she was doing a roll call and counted each of Masquerade's siblings.

"Ten for admission, since there are fourteen of you, A hundred and forty dollars, please," she said assertively. The other staff appeared disappointed; it seemed like they were genuinely interested in having a conversation. Masquerade fumbled his pockets and pulled 150 dollars out clean. One hundred dollar bill, and a fifty dollar bill.

"Here, and the change back, please," Masquerade said while maintaining eye contact with the clerk. The clerk's expression dazed off. Her eyes locked with Masquerade's. Her expression changed from assertive to calm in mere seconds. Almost like she was high and even amused at such a gaze. Even Masquerade was confused about what was happening. The clerk stared into Masquerade's eyes like they were mesmerizing. Masquerade looked back; he didn't understand, but he played along. His eyes pierced her soul.

His mind was flooded with a scene he clearly hadn't experienced. It was a foggy and unclear memory, where he was on the couch, and his "husband" was sitting next to him. Clearly, it wasn't his memory but rather hers. His so-called husband got up from the couch and walked into the kitchen. Seeing the undid dishes pinched a nerve in his brain. His expression changed, and he slowly made his way to her. The husband hesitated and staggered a bit. He was clearly drunk. For no reason at all, he struck his wife. Full force slap, followed by another. He screamed something, but the memory faded before Masquerade could hear it.

"Your husband beats you?" Masquerade's revelation hung in the air. The others around him wore expressions of surprise, yet they remained silent for a moment.

"Y-Yeswait, how did you-" she stuttered. Masquerade focused THAT gaze back onto her. Almost like a little spell, she stopped again and continued admiring Masquerade. *Weirdo. I thought she knew I was a minor?* Masquerade sensed the exact emotion she was experiencing. He looked away for a second before continuing the gaze.

"Change, please?" Masquerade's demand cut through the air. The clerk stared into his eyes for a good twenty seconds before fumbling her hands under the register. She quickly fumbled out the wrong amount and gave it to Masquerade awkwardly. "Thanks, I'll see you around." Masquerade smiled. He motioned for the others to continue into the party. He counted the money in his hands. He was supposed to get 10 back in change but instead got a full 50 back. He smiled and walked into the midst of the pulsating neon lights.

Now, people began to take notice of their presence. The crowd looked at the group weirdly. A lot of the people looked excited, while a number of them looked weirded out. Firstly, Masquerade walked towards a counter with an array of different colored drinks. The rest of his siblings dispersed and went to do their own things, leaving him alone

Behind the counter was someone his age, probably a high school student putting volunteer hours in for graduation. She looked surprised and excited to see him, although Masquerade had never seen this person before. Another person approached from under the counter. Her partner, another girl his age. The neon lights bathed the two, reflecting back since they both wore neon pants and neon shirts. They were both clearly blonde, but the heavy neon spectrum made it hard for Masquerade to tell.

"Hi! How can we help you today?" They both chimed in at the same time, almost like they were following a script. Masquerade observed the menu closely. Arranging of Coke products to Pepsi products and many traditional drinks.

"Yes, just one, uh, large lemonade, please," Masquerade stammered awkwardly. He looked around, making the situation more awkward than it already was.

"Of course! We'll get that ready for you. Three dollars, please," one of them chimed. Masquerade focused his eyes back on one of them, making eye contact. He wanted to test the eye charm he used on the cashier earlier. He looked deeply into the drink tender's eyes, hoping to get the same reaction as earlier.

The lady initially regarded him with a strange expression before succumbing to the charm. Masquerade didn't know how to explain it, but it was almost like he was entering her brain.

Seeing her memories and reading any thoughts she thinks of. Although it's an invasion of privacy, Masquerade can charm them, making them want to do whatever he wants them to do. Earlier, he persuaded the clerk to give him extra cash back, which worked. Masquerade didn't want anything from these other two, except to test the new power.

The girl stared back, with disgust at first, that quickly changed to a face full of interest. Her name was Makenzie. He knew from eye contact, and their brains connecting. He stared deeper, focusing the gaze. She looked more interested with every second that passed. While the other girl made the lemonade, the two made intense eye contact. Masquerade invaded her brain even more, learning about her birthday, which was today. Makenzie had just gotten her new car.

"So. . . Makenzie? How do you like your new pickup?" Masquerade raised his voice in confidence while still maintaining direct eye contact. Makenzie looked at him with a confused face that slowly turned back after looking back into Masquerade's spiraling eyes. Makenzie managed a soft smile.

"It's great, really; I didn't expect my dad to actually get me one. Although it's my 16th birthday." Makenzie replied. She still looked confused, but she played along for an odd reason.

"Oh, Happy Birthday, Makenzie; I hope you have a great one." Masquerade smiled as he grabbed his drink and slowly retreated away.

"Wai-" Makenzie said as Masquerade walked away. He smiled to himself as he realized that he didn't pay for the drink. He walked into the crowd, seeing who would be his next victim. He felt bad for playing people into doing stuff they probably didn't mean to do, but it was cool and mesmerizing to him.

After all, with a power like that, who wouldn't use it? Masquerade approached a duo dancing further in the corner of the dancefloor. A male with light brownish messy hair was dancing with a shorter female with blond hair and a black undercut. She had a hairstyle meant for boys, but still looked pretty with it. The two didn't notice Masquerade yet.

They danced with great chemistry. Masquerade watched for a bit before interrupting them. "I'm new here, and I thought I wanted to make some new friends, and well, uh, you looked cool," Masquerade announced. He looked nervous; he didn't want to use them.

"Huh? New? Well, I guess, I would know you otherwise, Mr. Flashy hair!" The male said. "I like it, though, so don't take offense." he put his hand out, indicating for Masquerade to shake it. "The name is Jacob..." Jacob introduced himself.

"Hi, Jacob, thanks for the compliment. The name's Masquerade," He said while shaking Jacob's hand. A nice firm handshake that complimented his already nice manners. Jacob knew how to greet people, and he had a nice smile.

"Oh? *Masquerade.* I like it, almost as flashy as the hair..." He said while looking at Masquerade with a weird look. Masquerade almost recognized the stare. The two stared at each other for a while before Jacob broke the silence.

"Huh, it doesn't work on you, either." Jacob narrowed his stare and his eyes became broadened. "That's why I'm so hooked on her, you know." He continued. "My charm doesn't work on either of you." He smiled at him, Masquerade further relating to the boy.

"What! Do you have it too? You know! Like an eye charm, I can make people like me, and do stuff for me, and read their minds by staring at them." Masquerade explained.

"Oh yeah, me too, just not the whole mind-reading thing, although I can make people say things for me, which is pretty much the same thing; you just skip the extra step." Jacob analyzed. "Anyways, this is Kai, my girlfriend." Jacob said. Kai nodded at Masquerade.

"Oh, so we're already pretty similar, almost like a lost brother, haha" Masquerade conducted. "Although I already have too many of those, fifteen siblings in total."

"FIFTEEN? That's nonsense. I only had 2; one of them's dead, though." He said in an oddly happy tone.

"Oh, well, one of mine was kidnapped in an attack held against my father a while ago. . ." Masquerade glanced around the dance floor, realizing he revealed too much information to a total stranger.

"No reply. I'll talk to you later. I have a dance to finish" He said as he gestured towards Kai. Masquerade nodded and walked away, acknowledging that he made that entire conversation awkward. Sipping away at his lemonade, he strolled toward a collection of secluded chairs.

No one else sat there, so he decided it would be a great resting place for know. He wanted to test the power some more, but he didn't want to do that to innocent people. He observed the lively crowd, searching for intriguing individuals who might make for engaging conversations. He scanned the crowd to see if he could find any of his family dancing as well.

As Masquerade lost himself in the sea of anonymity, a mysterious figure emerged from the shadows, her presence shrouded in an air of intrigue. A voice, sultry and amused, cut through the ambient sounds. "Hey, you look interesting!" A woman's voice secluded.

His attention was drawn to his right, where the silhouette of a woman materialized. The play of light and shadow concealed her features, leaving only the allure of her masked visage. Masquerade couldn't help but feel the magnetic pull of this enigma.

"Yes, come sit down," Masquerade pulled a chair out for her. As she got closer, he could make out more details. Dark brown hair that had a very unnoticeable faded pink color at the end. Masquerade made eye contact with her immediately. "My name's Masquerade."

"Huh, cool hair and cool name. I think I'll really get to like you. My name is Jynx." Jynx said as she examined Masquerade. "I like the way you dress. Your style is really cool" she said as she looked him up and down. Masquerade was already very confused. Was she flirting with him?

"Oh, thanks, everyone I spoke to so far liked both my hair and my name." He said, finally maintaining eye contact with her.

"Oh, I also really like your eyes, HEART SHAPED PUPILS? Are those natural???" Jynx exclaimed with excitement.

"Huh? Oh yeah! 100% natural." Upon making eye contact, he realized there were no thoughts coming from her brain, no memories, nothing at all. It was empty. Masquerade couldn't read her, the same as Jacob, except he kind of liked it better that way.

"I'm certain I met your brother already. He didn't want to talk to me." She said in a giddy tone, her smile glistened with the red glitter lipstick she wore.

"Oh, that must be Dark. Just so you find out sooner rather than later, I have fifteen siblings; fourteen currently go here." The two maintained eye contact.

"FIfteen! That's crazy. What are the ages? I heard there were five new sophomores alone. How does it work?"

"Well, the sophomores are my grade. There was a batch of five: me, Hyper, Lazer, Dark, and Infinity. We're all 15 years old." Masquerade explained. "Juniors, Crystal, Nature, Feisty, Moon, and Split. They are 16." "And the Seniors, Gray, Love, Fate, and Power. They are 17."

"Oh, that's a wild family, two batches of quintuplets." Jynx said, her expression showing extreme signs of interest. "Wait, you said fifteen siblings, you only named thirteen."

"Yes, the other two were twins, Tazer and Bow." Masquerade went further in detail. "Although Bow was, uhh, yeah. . ."

A pang of guilt crossed Jynx's gaze as she stared at him. "Yeah, I understand. Well, it looks like you're in my grade!" She exclaimed. Masquerade smiled lightly. He stood up firmly and let out his hand to Jynx. Jynx stared at him with a blank expression. "What? Are you expecting me to dance? Haha, I barely just met you" Jynx said, slapping his hand away in a playful way. "You gotta earn it first," she said, staring at him with a flirtatious smile.

"Oh really now, and how am I supposed to do that?" Masquerade snapped back to her. Jynx stood up quickly, shorter than Masquerade, but still puffed her chest up to him and looked up at his face.

"I don't know, come find out. . ." She said as she started walking away quickly. Masquerade looked hurt but challenged at the same time. He was going to play her little game.

"Oh, okay, I see," Masquerade said as he followed, catching up quickly, "So, what exactly am I finding out?" Masquerade asked.

"Oh my god, you're such a dork," Jynx said. "I was just messing around! That's all, however I want some of that lemonade you have."

"Come on, obviously I was just messing around as well," Masquerade chuckled. "I'll show you where I got this. Lemonade?" Masquerade said as he looked at the half gone drink in his hand. He led her to the stand that Makenzie held, however she was walking twice as fast as him, so really she was the one leading him. Makenzie and her friend were still certainly there.

"You came for more, I see," Makenzie said, smiling slightly at Masquerade. However, she didn't have the same expression towards Jynx. "Oh hey, Jynx, looks like you've found the new kid." Makenzie said in a greeting tone.

"Yes, he's pretty cool, and he's not the only one. There are thirteen more scattered around here. Maybe you could try counting them and score." Jynx said. Makenzie was avoiding eye contact with Masquerade. He stared at her again, seeing if it could maybe work again.

"Two pink lemonades, please," He said, gazing into her soul just so casually. Makenzie stared back, immediately falling for the trap. Masquerade could feel her emotions. Jealousy, jealousy for someone she just met. Makenzie was thinking about some boy, some boy named Felix. An average popular high school junior. Although clearly in love with Felix, she couldn't resist Masquerade's stare. Masquerade side stared at Jynx, who was staring at him. Jynx quickly looked away. Through Makenzie's thoughts, he found out Jynx was also fairly popular, sort of.

"So, how's Felix treating you?" Masquerade said with full confidence. Mackenzie looked confused again, and so was Jynx.

"What, howhow do you know about him? You're new here aren't you?" Makenzie said, disregarding the heavy eye contact. She brushed off the weirdness, "I guess not so great, thanks for asking." she smiled.

"Huh, that's weird that you knew they were talking. How exactly did you know that, Masquerade?" Jynx faced his direction.

"Ooh, what a cool name. Is it supposed to be a nickname? " Makenzie and her friend Zoey exclaimed.

"I have my ways, Jynx," Masquerade said with emphasis on her name. "Let's just say I have some special powers, alright?" Masquerade said.

"Oh, for sure, I do too. You're not special," Jynx lied, gradually closing the distance to Masquerade, as if playfully interrogating him. Makenzie slid their cups of lemonade to the two, breaking the tension. Masquerade grabbed the drinks and handed one to Jynx.

"Yeah. . . you're acting a bit weird. Just take your drink and stop acting like a cop," He said as he playfully nudged Jynx away from him. Jynx looked at him vengefully as she aggressively sipped her lemonade at him. "Where to next, captain?" He teased.

"Oh, hush up, we're going to look for my friend Jace. He'll surely know what to do with you." She smiled at him as she led Masquerade towards the dance floor.

"Oh yeah? Jace, he better be cool" Masquerade tried making conversation as he followed Jynx. She ignored him. It was hard for him to follow, because Jynx was swerving in many directions, her shortness didn't make it easier. The huge crowd was not making it any better. After a while of maneuvering the labyrinth of people, Jynx stopped on the other side of the dance floor.

She approached a tall white boy with brown hair. He had an innocent type of face. He assumed this was Jace, who was sitting with a group of more boys. They were all snickering as Jace muttered something.

"Jace! I know you're with some friends, but I'd like you to meet Masquerade." Jace stared at him weirdly before standing up. The other boys shut up quickly and all stared at him as if he were some celebrity. Jynx pulled the two aside, away from the large crowd.

"So, an emo? Weird, why would you dye your hair like that?" That was the first thing Jace said. Masquerade didn't know if he should be mad or confused.

"Sorry, my hair isn't dyed, though, it's fully natural." Masquerade said. Both Jynx and Jace looked surprised at this comment.

"What, even your hair is natural??" Jynx said, all surprised.

"Yes, I know. It's amazing, isn't it? Masquerade smiled at her, playing with his hair.

"Huh, that's cool, but I don't really like those eyes," Jace said while staring directly at them. Masquerade hesitated for a Moment. *Could I deactivate it somehow?* He thought to himself. Jace still focused his entire face on his swelling eyes, their minds interconnecting. Masquerade could read him, but it was different this time around, there was a thick layer of purple fog covering his brain. This made it hard to read anything that was going on in that complicated brain of his. Then, Masquerade felt a large blow dealt to his abdomen, and his eyes stung like dissolving acid. He jumped upwards in reaction, catching Jynx and Jace looking at him oddly.

"Yeah, a bit bright, I know," Masquerade quickly blurted, regarding his eyes. Jace smiled at him.

"Yeah, I like him," He said while walking away. "Thanks for the introduction, but I have a very important conversation to attend to."

"You'll like him once you get to know him, trust me," she said with a promising smile.

"I trust you," Masquerade said, his expression radiating confidence. "So, have I earned that dance yet?" Masquerade inquired, seamlessly transitioning as they strolled around the dance floor. Jynx smiled at him while glancing sideways.

"I don't know. I don't feel like you've proven yourself worthy just yet." Masquerade stepped behind her and smoothly circled to her opposite side. Jynx looked at him weirdly as they walked. Masquerade purposefully walked with a tilt, so they slowly made their way to the floor. Jynx stared at him like he was a psychopath.

"Do you not know how to walk straight, or what?" She said in a playful, aggressive tone. Masquerade smiled at her. Jynx smiled back, not having a single clue to what Masquerade was doing. Masquerade then pushed Jynx onto the dance floor, grabbing her hands elegantly.

"No way you just did that," Jynx said, awkwardly staring and smiling at him. Jynx grabbed his hands slowly and paced a slow dance, tapping her foot to the beat of the song.

"You have to teach me because I have no clue what I'm doing," Masquerade grinned at her. He copied the pace she was at.

"You really, really suck for this, but if you want a dance, then I'll give you a dance." Jynx said in another playful tone. Masquerade flashed her a charming smile, punctuated by a confident wink. Jynx winked back. She stepped one foot back and took his hands in hers. She gave Masquerade a "just copy what I do." look. Masquerade did the same sequence. Jynx signaled her fingers towards him and did the famous swirl.

"You know, you're pretty good at dancing for someone who doesn't know how," Jynx teased him in a rather flirty voice.

"Thanks for the compliment, but seriously, I have no clue what I'm doing." Jynx was a master at this, but she was still giving Masquerade that "I'm still so killing you after this" look. The two performed the sequences again and again before the song ended. Jynx pulled Masquerade to the side and looked straight into his eyes.

"Now that's over with," Jynx smiled. Masquerade looked at her before Jynx slapped him with medium force. A kind of slap that didn't mean that much but at the same time, meant that much. She had a huge, cute grin spread across her face as she stared at Masquerade.

"I probably deserved that-" Masquerade trailed off.

"Not probably, you did."

"Yeah, you're probably right."

"NOT PROBABLY, I am." She asserted dominance. "Anyways, I should probably get going. Sorry for the slap, and thanks for the fun night," She said as she stared at Masquerade, who wasn't that taller than her. He stared at her for a moment, trying to think of what to say.

"Yeah, of course, I'll see you tomorrow, I guess; you gotta show me the way. I've never been to school before, you know,"

"Oh really, I'd be more than happy to show you around," Jynx said excitedly. "You've never been to school, so have you just been homeschooled?"

"Yeah, pretty much. I'm excited to see how real school is going to work out." Masquerade held his hand out, shaking Jynx's hand. "I guess this is goodbye until tomorrow?"

"Omg, you really are a huge dork, but yes, I'll see you tomorrow, Masquerade..." She said as she walked towards the nearest exit. Masquerade stared at her down and smiled as she left.

"Who was that now?" A familiar voice said from behind. Masquerade turned around, and Dark approached from the depth of the dark, ironically.

"A new friend, why have you been talking to people at all or no, you fucking loser?" Masquerade teased him, his personality changing immediately.

"Oh shut up, Masquerade, of course I talked to people," Dark said, fidgeting with his hands. "I just came looking for you to see if YOU were talking to people."

"Clearly I was!" Masquerade said, gesturing his hands towards the exit Jynx had just exited from. "I gotta tell you something anyways, come sit over here. . ." Masquerade said as he walked towards an array of tables. The two settled into the cushioned chairs at a corner table, surrounded by the lively hum of the dance floor.

"Go on, tell me what you need" Dark exclaimed while rocking the chair backward.

"I don't NEED anything from YOU. I just want, umm, advice, maybe?" Masquerade trailed off. "So, uhh, I have this weird power. I can kind of charm up people I stare at, only if we make eye contact, though," Masquerade explained, with weird hand gestures. "And I just need help. I can control it, like right now, the charm isn't activating on you, but surely it works on men. It applies to both genders."

"Oh wow, you came to me for this advice?" Dark questioned him while staring at his eyes.

"Yes, you had an uncontrollable power with that exploding pink fire blood thingy, and plus, you always give the best advice." Masquerade stared at Dark. "You know, like Hyper wouldn't be able to keep focus and probably start talking about random things like burritos or something..." Masquerade said as they both chuckled. "Infinity is too mature and has no experience with unexplainable powers, and Lazer is just, how do I put this, plain stupid." Masquerade explained.

"Well, thanks for the compliment, but surely the older siblings have more experience, so still, why ask me?" Dark underestimated himself.

"Well, I feel uncomfortable talking about it to them, plus I wanna keep the power secret, you know? We can get out of sticky situations with it. I trust you to keep it hidden, so just let me use it on you!" Masquerade looked at him with a convincing expression. Dark stared back like Masquerade was mentally ill.

"What kind of question is that? Of course!" Dark announced. "And yes, I'll keep it our little secret," Dark teased. Masquerade gave him a light convincing smile.

"Okay, so anyways, I'll use it, but I need help controlling it. I have to hold back constantly to stop it from affecting people, so do you have any advice so it's not such a burden on me?" Masquerade asked.

"I'll give you the advice afterward, but for now, just let it upon me. . ." Dark fixed his posture, acting like he was about to get shot by a cannon. Masquerade softened his gaze and looked into Dark's eyes. The effect went into play immediately. Masquerade was able to enter his brain right away. Dark's mind was blank for a moment, then he started thinking about unicorns and rainbows, like Dark was playing with him, but at the same time, Dark's gaze hardened on him. Masquerade chuckled, and Dark grinned at him.

Hey, do you think we can make this a new way to communicate silently? Dark's voice echoed in Masquerade's head. He was trying to think of how he could answer back without saying it aloud.

Yes, I think this works pretty well. Masquerade thought back at him. Dark looked scared, excited, and confused all in one expression. Masquerade smiled at him. *Now, for advice?*

Yes, of course, I had a power similar to yours, with the corrosive exploding hell blood. After it awakened against Echo, my blood never came out normal. So, after every wound, it would explode on my arm. It didn't hurt. It was just very annoying. I overcame this by reversing the feeling. At first, you have to subconsciously deactivate it; after a while, your brain will automatically do it manually.

Like breathing and blinking, so then when you want to activate it, you do the opposite. Pretty much, you act like you want to 'deactivate' it. Even though it's already deactivated, your brain will swip swap it, so instead of you trying to deactivate it, it will instead activate it. You're essentially manipulating your brain into swapping deactivation with activation. So it will take time, but you will get it eventually, trust me. Dark explained so well that Masquerade was amazed.

Oh, wow, that was, like, the best explanation I could get out of almost anyone. See! This is why I came to you. Anyway, yes, I'll start deactivating it on my own until I get to do it subconsciously. Masquerade unfocused his gaze, and eyes, for that matter. He forced himself to deactivate the power. Doing so didn't hurt, it was just very annoying, like when you have to blink manually or breathe manually, exactly what you're doing now.

He had to focus so it didn't activate on someone like his mom. He didn't want the charm to mess up some random lady. Masquerade stood up and roamed the dance floor. He decided he was going to try and get popular before he even started school. After all, his little charm might help him reach this goal. Masquerade released his focus, and his eyes sparkled with a mix of determination and charm.

Chapter 4
Jynx

Jynx begrudgingly woke up to the blaring alarm, driven by the looming school day and her unresolved trust issues with her father. School started at 8:30, so she set her alarm for 7. She stood upright in her bed, looking at the curtains, and early sunlight beamed through them. She picked up her phone, checking her notifications since she fell asleep early. Many missed calls and texts from Jace and a few other unimportant messages from boys at her high school. Jynx quickly showered and did the other things in her routine. Brush teeth, brush hair, dress, etc, etc.

She headed out the door today without saying anything to Stitch. She wanted to wait for her dad. After all, she still couldn't bring herself to fully trust him – her father. The doubt lingered like a haunting whisper in her mind. He's probably out to kill her next, which was only a distant probability in the back of her mind. Jynx still didn't understand why he killed his own wife.

Jake said something about the females of her family always having a dangerous power, a threat to Jake, but Jynx didn't manifest any special powers whatsoever, and from what she had known, neither did her mother. The morning air was chilly, the car window adorned with a delicate frost, mirroring the cold uncertainty that enveloped Jynx. She opened the door, started the car quickly, and sat down.

She glanced at her cup holder, seeing the leftover pink lemonade. Thoughts of Masquerade lingered, and Jynx found herself intrigued. What untold stories hid behind his enigmatic facade? He was certainly interesting. Jynx started the car and slowly drove down the road. She had to pick up Jace. An unsettling feeling gnawed at Jynx, casting a shadow over her morning, though she couldn't pinpoint why.; her brain felt oddly clear, but she couldn't name why. After making a few more turns, she arrived at Jace's house. He was already outside and ready as usual. Jace walked up to the door quickly.

"Hey, what happened last night? You didn't answer me when you got home." Jace said as he opened the door. Jynx shot him a playful yet exasperated look, her way of expressing affectionate annoyance.

"Well, jeez, Jace, you do know I have my own life too." Jynx said, knowing damn well she wasn't busy last night. Jace stared at her with a priceless expression on his face.

"Yeah, I guess, but you could have returned a text? I was worried." Jace said in a concerned tone.

"Please stop acting like my boyfriend. If I don't feel like returning a text, then I don't have to. I know I get it; you're worried my dad is going to try killing me, PROBABLY, but still. I can protect myself. Or maybe he changed, WHO KNOWS! We'll see what fate God has for me." Jynx explained. Jace's expression remained blank as he stared at her.

"Whatever, but what if your dad is released due to the government sending him to spy?" Jace pointed out, his concern knitting a web between them.

"Are you a conspiracy theorist?! You sound stupid right now Jace, I just need to focus on the present and deal with this later." Her words came out rushed, mirroring her speeding car.

"Sorry, I see you're stressed, mainly because you're also speeding. . ." Jace chuckled. She slowed down and finally realized what felt off today. She noticed an unusual quietness in her mind—the memories, usually on constant replay, were strangely silent. They weren't constantly bothering her. She smiled, wondering what caused her brain to be free from the constant fog of darkness. She saw the school approaching in the horizon, reluctantly matching the speed limit.

Next week, a two-week school trip awaited her and Jace, an adventure that promised more than just exciting sights and experiences. She'd figured she'd probably talk to her dad when she gets back, hopefully coming to a truce with him. She pulled into the school's parking lot. Arriving early was her habit, a blend of efficiency and the desire to share a few words with friends as the day started.

She got out of the car with Jace trailing her. She walked towards the entrance. Entering with Jace, the first thing she saw was a large group of people grouped together at a table.

She walked in and instinctively went to get breakfast. Walking past the table, she saw the center of attention. Masquerade and his siblings. Only four of his siblings were there. She assumed they were the ones a part of Masquerade's quintuplet batch.

Hyper, the bundle of energy, stood out with his bright yellow eyes and white hair adorned with playful purple highlights.Masquerade, with his bright pink hair. Another one with eye bags and red eyes had dark purple hair that faded into a rough brownish color (Dark).

The second to last had a middle part. He also had purple hair and white streaks (Infinity). The last had red and blue overly fluffy hair, with alarming bright sectoral heterochromia eyes. One blue and one red (Lazer). She felt a spark of jealousy as she saw the group were mostly girls.

Jace saw that jealousy immediately, instantly reading her. She brushed it off and started walking towards the breakfast stand, trying to ignore the lack of attention from Masquerade. Jace opened his mouth, but Jynx just nudged him.

"Hey!! Jynx, come here!" A voice alarmed from behind her. She quickly looked back and saw Masquerade moving himself through the little group of people. There was only a group of nine or maybe ten, but still a big grouping for their school.

She smiled to herself without realizing it. She hoped Masquerade wasn't going to drop her friendship because of others. The other siblings followed Masquerade like he was their leader. Jynx had a mini panic attack, mainly because these guys were exactly out of some superhero movie. It was so cool being friends with even one of them.

Masquerade approached her with his other siblings. "So, are you still going to show me around the school like you said? The bell rings in about an hour and ten minutes" Masquerade said. The group of people behind him looked disappointed. Jynx smiled at him before responding.

"Hey, while you're at it, you can tour the rest of us!" The energetic chimed in. He walked up to her quickly and held out his hand. "Hi, I'm Hyper," Hyper exclaimed in a high-pitched tone. Which she assumed was just his voice.

"Sure, why not? I'm Jynx by the way," she said, masking her excitement about guiding these intriguing newcomers. "Uhh, we'll start with the cafeteria and the high school commons area, which you guys seem to be familiar with." Jynx exclaimed, trying to hide she was excited to tour them.

The five boys just stood behind her. Hyper was moving uncontrollably, which was ironic because he always seemed to always be hyper. She guided them into the serving room. Two of them were discussing their school schedules, showing obvious signs of aggression.

"Hey, no, no, I have first-period algebra, that's clearly better than your geometry," Infinity said.

"Infinity, no, geometry is harder than algebra. Are you stupid? I swear you're more dumber than Masquerade sometimes." Lazer exclaimed.

"'More dumber' is a double positive. You're both stupid. You could've just said 'dumber'." Dark said in a low tone. They both looked at him like they were going to jump him.

"Oh really, I guess I'm the stupidest here then. I ended up in pre-algebra," Hyper said while squinting at his schedule. Everyone started laughing, Hyper frowned slightly.

"Just to make it easier on you, the red and blue-haired is Lazer, the middle part is Infinity, and the dark-haired is Dark" Masquerade leaned in. "Also, we're always like this, so this is normal." He whispered while grinning at Jynx.

"Thanks, I like all of them!" Jynx giggled.

"I feel like you guys always like ganging up on me. It's not fair bro." Lazer said in a serious voice.

"We do. Now shut up and let's get breakfast" Dark said. Now that Jynx thinks about it more, Dark is the leader of these five, the one who keeps them all managed and together. They all got their food, and Jynx led them where to sit down. The five sat down, Masquerade sat next to her, and the others picked random spots.

"Guys, I'm kind of nervous, you know, like what if I get bullied since you guys always say I have a big nose," Hyper said while everyone else shoved their faces with scrambled eggs. The five chuckled aggressively while Jynx found that hurtful.

"Hey, don't worry about it. You don't have a big nose. No one's gonna bully you" Jynx reassured him. Hyper's eyes lightened up after she said that.

"Thanks! I like you; don't listen to what Masquerade tells you. He's the real idiot." Hyper smiled with his bright face. Masquerade's expression dropped, and he smiled a little. Jynx giggled at him while Hyper was staring.

"You want to talk about the ball then, huh?" Masquerade said while finishing his food. The other three laughed under their breaths.

"Yeah, he broke our window because he chucked a ball at Masquerade. It was funny," Lazer said to Jynx while taking his last bite. Jynx laughed.

"Well, you know he surely has the energy to do something like that," Jynx replied.

"Oh yeah, we know that part very well," Infinity said sarcastically. "You know he broke four out of the twenty or so four-wheelers we have? In one day?" Lazer continued. Jynx was more surprised at the fact that they had twenty four-wheelers than how Hyper managed to break four of them.

"You have twenty??" Jynx said, surprised. "Really!? How did he manage to break FOUR of them?"

Hyper (Flashback)

Hyper knew that whatever he was about to do was probably a bad idea, but someone needed to have a little fun in their life. He stared down at the mudded ATV. The wheels were currently stuck in the mud, and at this point mud stuck to every part of his body. He knew Split would find him eventually, who was riding behind him somewhere.

She was the only one willing to go out with him today. He didn't get why anyone else was excited since it had rained the previous night, because they would all get the chance to go mudding. He revved the engine again, knowing really well it wasn't going to get unstuck at all.

Hyper stared down at his hands, contemplating if he should really do this. He stood up and opened the engine hood of the quad. He motioned his hand, and lightning scattered around it quickly. Sparks of purple jittered into the metal parts of the vehicle. Then, with full force, he jolted lightning into the engine. Immediately, the engine started on fire. This didn't phase or stop Hyper, however.

Next, he closed the hood to the quad and sat back down quickly. He zipped lightning on both of his arms, conducting the volts into the gas. The four-wheeler quickly contracted before shooting past the mud. Hyper smiled as the wind soared across his face. The four-wheeler shot upwards, and mud exploded upwards from the heat and propulsion of the steam.

Hyper lost control and shifted the wheel leftwards. Hyper felt a pulse of fear shiver through his body as the ATV shifted in the direction of a thick tree. The fire on the engine grew quickly. Hyper jumped off the vehicle as it crashed straight through the tree. Moments after, Hyper watched, in midair, as the quad straight up exploded into many pieces. He landed on the floor with a loud thud, the thick mud cushioning the long fall.

The explosion caused all the parts of the ATV to scatter everywhere. A sharp piece of metal quickly shot into Hyper's leg as he was already sprawled on the soft, muddy forest ground. Hyper winced in pain, watching the smoke trail into the sky. He hoped that indicated Split where he was. He quickly jutted the sharp piece from his thigh. He watched as his body quickly healed itself, he loved that part of his family. He found it satisfying how he could heal ANY injury with great ease.

The blood clotted quickly, and soon after, the muscle tissues reconnected. The blood stopped, and the skin quickly covered the wound. He smiled as he stood up, wet mud dripping down from his face and his soaked clothes. He looked off in the distance and noticed Split. He smiled and waved obnoxiously at her. He waited for her quad to catch up to them. Split smoothly swerved the wheeler to a stop right next to Hyper, almost hitting him but still missing him by a few inches. She analyzed the scenery, noticing the disassembled quad.

"Way to go, dumbass. How the hell did you even manage to blow the entire thing up?" Split said in the meanest and most playful tone. She glanced at his attire, giggling offensively. "Damnnnn, I can't tell if that shirt was originally brown or if it was white. You might as well live with the pigs since you look so alike," Split chuckled.

"Oh my god, shut up bro. I was simply testing something, and clearly, my hypothesis was wrong. Here's what I discovered: Lightning doesn't help get four-wheelers unstuck." Hyper said in a low tone. "Well, actually, it did get it out of the mud. It just detonated seconds after." Hyper chuckled.

"Oh wow great job, Mr. Scientist, looks like I won't be jumpstarting anything with lightning now," She giggled. "Anyways, hop on. We'll go get you a spare one if you still want to race," Split suggested. Hyper smiled as he walked towards the vehicle. Split looked at his arms, terrified for no apparent reason.

"HYPER, CAREFUL, YOU'RE STILL OVERCHARGED WITH LIGHTNING!" Split screamed at the top of her lungs. Hyper didn't notice until now; his veins were glowering with electricity. He felt overcharged; holding an incredibly unhealthy amount of lightning inside of him. Hyper couldn't stop himself in time before making contact with the vehicle.

Anything he touched was automatically charged with lightning, even the ground he was standing on was static. One finger tap was enough. Earlier, Hyper had to directly touch the engine to barely jumpstart it, but now the overcharged lighting overhyped it. The quad exploded immediately. Split jumped off in time, surprisingly.

Hyper flinched, getting ready for the sharp metals to penetrate him, but when he opened his eyes, the scraps of the vehicle were floating in the air. They had a low layer of blue lightning surrounding the metals. A coat of lightning that was able to create a forcefield of magnetism.The lightning he let out was so much that it made the metal magnetic. Hyper walked around it, acting like he had stopped time.

"OUCH, HYPER, YOU'RE ELECTROCUTING THE GROUND!" She whined as she quickly climbed a tree. "Damn it, Hyper, your lightning power is way too powerful, even for yourself. YOU HAVE TO DISCHARGE YOURSELF!" She screamed at him again.

"SPLIT, STOP SCREAMING AT ME. I DON'T KNOW HOW TO!!" He screamed back. "Don't even think about coming close to me. I might fry you and your beautifully styled split light blue and purple hair." Hyper chuckled, pointing his fingers towards her.

"Your hair looks frizzy from up here. I think I might know what's wrong with you." She said while she cowardly hid in the tree. "Just don't come close to me, and I might tell you."

"Okay, I'll sit still," Hyper sat down in the mud again, cearly still bouncing his leg.

"You're sick. It happens every once in a while to all of us. It's just that you're different from the rest of us. You have way more raw lightning power than us. SOOO, pretty much, we have to find a way to make you sneeze." Split said as she looked up at the clouds. "I think. You have WAY too much raw power." Spiral dark storm clouds started forming above them, charged lightning wavered all over the clouds.

"Yeah, this doesn't look good for either of us." Split said stupidly. "If you conduct too many volts, you'll fall into a deep sleep." Split said while climbing further into the tree.

"Hey, you know it's not the best idea to climb higher. You have a higher chance of getting struck," Hyper said.

"No, I won't. You'll conduct any lighting in the area" Split pointed out.

"Not if I direct it towards you," Hyper grinned at her, pointing his fingers told her once more.

"Is that a threat? Plus, can your dumbass even manage to pull a stunt like that?" Split insulted him. Hyper laughed.

"I don't know. I guess you'll be the first and the last to figure that out," Hyper replied.

"Knock it off! That doesn't even make sense, stupid," Split said as thunder rumbled the skies.

"Shush, I feel something," Hyper said, all the lightning conducted itself into one huge bolt in the clouds. Particles charged and exploded. Making the sound of disrupted air, and sending shockwaves of dense air outwards. The bolt charged itself as it shot straight down, striking Hyper, coming directly from above him. Split screamed as Hyper was unaffected by the blast of energy. Then, the thunder masked her screams, seconds soon after, it started pouring into the area.

"Just as I thought things couldn't get worse," Split stared down at Hyper. "Hey, know any ways you could, you know, SNEEZE ALREADY!?" Split emphasized.

"No, maybe there's another way to 'discharge' myself," Hyper said, trying to think of a way where he could release all the lightning in his body. The rain hardened, and the lightning in the air was gone. The clouds still remained, and Hyper's white hair shone with the deep droplets from the rain. Split was still staring at him from the tree.

"HEY, since it's raining, maybe you could catch a cold! Then the sneeze would come faster." She was shivering up in the tree. "So, that means take off all your clothes!!!"

"You sound very weird screaming that in the middle of the forest, but sure, I'll take my clothes off," Hyper said as he took his shirt off. Cold raindrops pricked his skin, and an uncertain thought crossed his mind—could rain make him sick? "Hey, don't you have ice powers??? Why can't you just use those to make me sick,"

"Well, obviously, Hyper, I don't have a brain. I decided I would go mudding with you, so there's not much up here than you think. . ." She said while tapping her skull.

"DO SOMETHING THEN AND STOP COMPLAINING, hit me with a blizzard or something," Hyper said. He observed the floating metal pieces around him, tapping them with ease. He slowly walked towards the magnetized metal. He touched one of the pieces, messing with the fabric forcefield. In an instant, all the metals quickly retracted to the one he touched, making a ball of crushed ATV parts. Then, out of nowhere, a wave of cold air and snow rushed over the landscape. Hyper jumped in shock, his already wet hair freezing with a thick layer of frost.

Hyper shot her a look, a mix of disbelief and amusement, as if questioning her sanity. "Seriously? You could have warned me beforehand," Split stared at him with a stupid grin on her face. The blizzard continued as Hyper stood there and couldn't do anything about it.

"Hey, be ready. I'm going to lower the temperature of the blizzard, then I'll flash you with a wave of heat, for sure that'll make you sick," Split explained. "Constantly entering or experiencing hot and then cold temperatures after a while, your body will get sick, causing a flash cold." Split explained further, "So that means be prepared." her powers allowed her to control temperatures, and multiple different elements. Hyper rolled his shoulders and squinted his eyes while the blizzard raged on.

"Okay, I think I'm ready. Also, please don't give me frostbite, those are the hardest to heal from because it's not even damage, It's just straight-up frozen," Hyper said while he did some jumping jacks.

"Yeah, whatever, I'm gonna start now. . ." Split said as she waved her hand out towards Hyper, turning the blizzard off and increasing the heat. The rain instantly vaporized and boiled on point, making the general temperature even higher. Hyper stared up at Split, trying to endure the temperature, making a weird face. She looked uncomfortable, but she clearly wasn't hurt. Then, in an instant, the heat dropped again, forcing his body into confusing itself. In seconds, the heat wasn't a problem, and he was already shivering.

"This is just as annoying to me as it is to you. Don't worry Hyper." She said from her stupid tree. "I hate producing heat, it's uncomfortable and sweaty,"

"EASY FOR YOU TO SAY, YOUR BODY'S BUILT TO ENDURE THE TEMPERA-TURES, MINES NOT!" Hyper snapped. "AND HURRY UP AND MAKE IT HOT AGAIN,"

"Okay, okay, jeez, stop yelling at me," Split said while casually making the air dryer and hotter than the Sahara desert. Then, Split continued making the air frigid and cold, repeating this process over and over. Split went until she felt Hyper would be sick.

"There, we're all done, now, SNEEZE!" Split verbally harassed him. She stared down at him when he hadn't responded. "Hello?"

"Yeah, I definitely feel sick," Hyper responded. Hyper rubbed his nose, a telltale sign that the flash cold had taken hold. His once vibrant energy now replaced by a subdued vulnerability. "Oh yeah, it definitely worked," He said in a concerned, sick voice. He looked at Split with a bright red nose and rose-red cheeks. Hyper snuffled his nose at her.

"Oh yeah, just get ready for a shitshow now," Split said sarcastically. "And by the way, don't take that too literally and actually shit yourself," She giggled at her own terrible joke.

"Shut up, I can feel a sneeze coming," Hyper said. "If I blow up, please tell Mom I never loved her," Hyper overreacted.

"I think you got the phrase wrong there a bit, bud," Split chuckled at him.

"No, seriously, she's like, always on my ass for no reason at all," Hyper said.

"Yeah, she has to, or else you'll single-handedly redefine our family tree, one explosion at a time. You expect her not to watch over you 24/7 when you do shit like blowing up TWO of her four-wheelers," Split explained to him precisely.

"Hyper chuckled, thinking, 'Well, when you put it like that, I sound like an irresponsible little brat who can't control himself."

"You couldn't have explained yourself any better, Hyper."

"You're so mean to me. Sometimes, I wonder if you even like having me around," Hyper complained with a hint of vulnerability. Split stared at him like he was stupid. Then Hyper sensed it building—a sneeze, a release of pent-up energy, a storm waiting to break free. Hyper could see the fear in Split's eyes. She tried climbing the tree further but couldn't.

"Hyper, I swear, this better not kill me. If it does, I swear, I'll, like, actually kill you," Split said.

"Since when did we change the roles? Now you sound like the one who doesn't know what she's saying. You can't kill me when you're dead already." Hyper said before sneezing. The lightning built inside his body released at once. Exiting at light speed, a shockwave occurred, breaking the nearest trees in an instant. The lighting traveled with the shockwave. Dispersing the leftover parts to the quads. Split managed to get lucky and not get caught in the traveling shockwave of lightning. She dodged the initial blast by jumping off the tree.

Hyper looked amazed at the damage he had done. All the trees in the area were rooted from the ground. Leaving holes in the soil. The shockwave also made an indent in the sky. The clouds disappeared with the blast. Hyper looked at Split weirdly, who was finally able to get closer to him.

"Whatever, Hyper, why the hell are you backing up from me?" She said, inching towards him.

"I don't know. Why are you trying to touch me?" Hyper said while laughing nervously.

"I don't really know, but let's get home now." Split said while facing the direction of home. The two ran home quickly, stopping in the front yard.

"I'm going to go get another one, and then I'll meet you inside so we can plan a prank against Masquerade, okay?" Hyper concluded.

"Oh yeah, for sure, and what exactly are you planning on doing?" Split interrogated him.

"None of your business," Hyper said while walking toward the warehouse slowly.

"Whatever, weirdo, but count me in for the Masquerade prank." Split said with a mischievous grin before disappearing inside.

With cautious steps, Hyper pushed open the creaking warehouse door, his eyes scanning for the familiar form of his signature four-wheeler. They all had their own designated quads. The ones he and Split took were the extras they had. They only had one left now. Hyper found his quad quickly. The one he had wasn't cool at all; it was the older model, and it wasn't as good as everyone else's. He got on it and tried starting it as quietly as possible, which was pretty much impossible.

Quickly, he drove it outside and towards the path that took him to the river. It took him around ten minutes to reach the heart of the river, but with a shortcut, it took only half that time. He took a deep breath.

"I'll miss you, old bud, but if I destroy you, I'll get the older model, and that's just for the greater good." Hyper said before driving the whole thing into the river. Hyper gazed at the scene he'd created, a frozen tableau of emotions etched into the canvas of the river's surface. He stood there, swaying his arms slowly. He watched the quad sink slowly. A tear traced its path down his cheek, and Hyper, wiping his eyes, found himself caught in a silent sob. He sniffled, grappling with the raw emotions surging within. Hyper stood there, silently acknowledging the gravity of the moment. Time seemed to stretch as he grappled with the weight of his actions.

"That's only three? What happened to the fourth one?" Jynx asked while she was still cracking up from the story.

"He later went and dissected the last extra when we had. He claimed he wanted to 'learn more about mechanics' when we all knew he just broke the last one, so we were forced to get him a new one." Dark explained. Hyper put his head down awkwardly.

"It's okay, Hyper. We all make mistakes," Jynx reassured him. "And where's this Split? I would like to meet her,"

"Yes, of course, but seriously, we should start the tour. We took a while telling that story," Masquerade said.

"Wait, they said they were going to prank you? What did they do?" Jynx asked.

"They smuggled me into a bean bag chair and threw me down the basement stairs. . ." Masquerade chuckled. The face Jynx made was priceless.

"That's not even funny. That's just hurtful," Jynx said in an honest tone. "But yes, we shall start the tour. Stand up please" Jynx continued. "I assume you guys know where your lockers are? We'll start there, so show me the way..." Dark, Infinity, and Masquerade stood up in perfect unison, which really confused and amazed Jynx. Lazer and Hyper stood up off sync from the rest of the trio. She smiled at them and gestured to them to guide her. "Oh, and by the way, I want to meet Split. She seems fun and veryyyy sarcastic,"

"You'll have many opportunities to meet every single one of them," Masquerade said.

"Yeah, we're all crazy, but it's easy to catch and play along," Hyper said while fidgeting with his hands. The five walked in a certain formation. Dark led, while Infinity and Masquerade trailed not far from him. Then Hyper and Lazer were behind those two.

Jynx followed behind all of them. She found it fascinating how organized and ready they were as a big family. She observed closely as they walked. Dark led the group through the halls. He looked like he knew where he was going. Jynx recognized this side of the halls.

Then, the five opened their lockers all in front of her. All five of them lined up right next to each other. In order went Masquerade, Lazer, Dark, Infinity, and Hyper last. Jynx's locker was right next to Masquerade's. She walked up to her locker with her backpack in hand.

"Oh, well, isn't that nice? My locker is just right here," She said as she opened her locker. The five stared at her weirdly as Jace walked down the hallway.

"May I help with the tour?" Jace asked politely while awkwardly staring at Jynx and the quintuplets at the same time. Jynx cast him a quizzical glance, pausing before uttering a word.

"Uhh, no, I got this under control. You can wait until the first period." Jynx exclaimed. She looked Jace in the eyes, clearly telling him to leave. Jynx would be nicer to Jace if he wasn't in her business 24/7. 'Oh, your dad's out? When are you going to talk to him?' or, 'I'm just trying to keep you safe.' and the most popular, 'What if Jake comes back?' Jynx regretted telling him things. It almost felt like he was sent to interrogate her sometimes. Jynx had told him everything ever since they became close friends.

She told him information she wouldn't give out to anyone else, even if she was paid. She told him about Jake, how he tortured her, how her dad murdered her Mom, and definitely how Stitch acted extremely weird during these said conflicts. Family drama, she told Jace everything.

It was almost like he was a third brother since Mason didn't say a word to Jynx, and Stitch was pretty much a father figure at this point. Jynx wanted to pinpoint the lab Jake brought her to, but she could never find it. Jace was never any help in the first place. He's constantly on Jynx's ass about staying safe, so she didn't feel bad when she ghosted him sometimes.

"But, I can be of good service, you know. I know this school better than you do" Jace challenged.

"Is that a challenge? Because I definitely know more than you. . ." Jynx replied hastily.

"If you want it to be, it can because I don't think it'll make a difference. Since these idiots probably won't even listen" Jace said while gesturing towards them.

"Hey! That's rude, don't say that about them, they're extremely smart. You're just saying that because you know I like them better than you," Jynx said.

"That's just hurtful. I didn't mean it, you know. Plus, I thought they didn't go to school until now, so how smart can they be?" Jace said, raising an eyebrow in playful skepticism.

"Just shut up already before I block you again. I'm still mad at you for sticking your nose in my business. So you better make up for it on the trip." Jynx said, leaning in with a mix of irritation and amusement.

"Wait, what trip? Would it still be possible for me to go?" Masquerade chimed in, a hint of excitement in his voice. "I have money readily available if it's needed."

"I just insulted you, and now you want to go on a trip with us?" Jace raised his voice.

"I mean, sure, I don't see a problem. Don't friends insult each other often?" Masquerade smiled at him. Jace smiled back while he fidgeted with his phone in hands. Masquerade gestured his body towards his siblings.

"Which one of you wants to tag along on the trip??" Masquerade asked. "I mean, if you all want to tag along, that's fine too. It just depends on the bill." Unsurprisingly, all of them started chiming in, saying they wanted to attend. Masquerade smiled lightly.

"Well, I guess we got our first destination. All five of you on the first out-of-country school trip? That's wild. Especially when we board the plane." Jace exclaimed. "Sounds like a lot of fun since you guys have supernatural powers, right?"

"Uhh, yes, I guess? If you put it like that, you make it sound like we're mutants," Lazer said. "Don't you?"

"Well, yes, everyone probably has some sort of powers, but from what I've heard, you have multiple and very good control over them," Jace said while he looked at them like they were some group of Greek gods. "Do something cool,"

Jace raised his voice in a childish yet eager way, his curiosity getting the better of him. The five all glowered at Jace as lightning quickly sparked from their bodies. The lightning scattered across their bodies, not leaving a few feet from them. Jynx even found it cool. Masquerade held his hand up, and smoke emitted from the palm of it. He observed his hand as he moved his other in a weird motion.

"I've been trying to work on it for a while now, but this is the best I can do," Masquerade exclaimed. He pointed his arm upwards like he was raising his hand. Except his palm gestured upwards. He then pulsed his body upwards, slightly levitating with thin and noticeable gusts of wind. Then, from the top of his hand, it started glowing a bright yellow, almost like it was about to explode. Then, a pretty green firework explosion erupted from his hand. It was beautiful. The fireworks then sparkled and crackled into mini sparks. It even surprised his brothers, who were watching in awe. Jace had his mouth wide open.

"Is that all for show? Or does it hurt? Can you control the color? Can you make different types of fireworks and explosions? Can you recreate a nuke?! Can you change the size and the shape?" Jace started mumbling question over question.

"I knew you could create explosions, but not fireworks?" Dark said, a surprised yet proud smile playing on his lips.

"ANSWER MY QUESTIONS!" Jace screamed excitedly. "Also, I want a full showcase and presentation on each of your powers too," his eyes glinting with anticipation.

"Uhh, to start, yes, they hurt. They're real explosions, so you don't want to be on the other side of the hand. I can change the color and size of them, but only the fireworks. I can't change the color of a normal explosion. Also, it's hard, so don't test me. I can do sparklers as of right now and, of course, the normal artillery." Masquerade explained deeply. "Also, I can only erupt and ignite them from my hands and, oddly, my feet." He smiled.

"That's so cool," Jynx said while admiring him.

"The explosions are cool enough, and you have lightning control?" Jace said while walking towards him. His eyes examined Masquerade all over.

"Oh yes," He said as lightning erupted from his hand, creating a sword made of straight lightning.

"Is that even real?" Jace said as his fingers strayed closer to the bolt in his hands. Jace smudged it with his hand, shocking his body. He quickly recoiled and still had a huge smile on his face.

"Also, I have an affinity for wind as well," Masquerade said as he started lightly levitating. He closed his eyes as he was trying to focus. Then, everyone there started flying in the air. Jynx felt a light breeze tickle her as if she were standing on top of a fan. Then, everyone slowly fell back to place as Masquerade gestured. Jace looked as if he were jealous and amazed at the same time.

"Oh yeah, we could definitely use you on the trip," Jace exclaimed while having an excited expression on his face.

"I think Mr. Zander and Mrs. Glicher said powers weren't allowed to be used on the entire trip," Jynx piped up. Masquerade loomed around his locker while impatiently waiting.

"Maybe we should just go check in with her," Jace said, a note of impatience creeping into his voice. "After I get a showcase of these guy's powers,"

"That's pretty much all I can do," Masquerade said while looking at Dark. "You're next," He said, pointing at Dark. Dark stared at him weirdly.

"Well, I guess. I mean, it's a bit disturbing, so prepare yourself?" He said while rolling up his long-sleeved shirt. He put his thumb in his mouth slowly, putting it cleanly in between his teeth. Biting down, the pink blood from his thumb oozed out slowly. Jace had an excited expression printed on his face. The blood trickled down his arm as he looked at it. Then, the blood quickly exploded into a burst of pink flames. Dark raised his arm up as the fire spread across it.

"Oh, pink blood turns into pink fire," Jace observed, "So how long does it stay?" Jynx was staring at it with her lit-up, excited eyes.

"It stays until I deactivate it," He said as the flames quickly dispersed out of thin air. "Also, I can do this." Dark exclaimed as he put his entire hand in his mouth. He smirked as he looked at Masquerade. Biting down with full force, blood expulsed from his mouth, but the blood didn't come out like it normally should. The blood floated in midair for a few moments before it started forming a little insect. The blood formed into a little pink butterfly. The blood from his hand still oozed out, falling on the floor.

The butterfly flew around the group. Flying around majestically, it stopped in front of Jynx's face. It flew in place, staring at Jynx. Then, the butterfly deformed as the blood dispersed but still flew in place. The pink blood quickly reformed into a pretty-looking flower. The flower had no stem, and it lay on Jynx's hair for a moment. She tried touching it, but the blood deformed again into a butterfly. The blood that was coming from Dark's hand traveled to the beautiful insect. Adding to its wings, they became abnormally big for the butterfly.

The insect gracefully flew towards Jace. Landing on his hand, the butterfly deformed once again. It slowly but surely turned itself into a long pole that Jace was able to hold. The pole quickly formed into a sharp edge, revealing a mighty and shiny pink sword. Jace held the sword with respect, swinging it around like he was some sort of samurai.

Then, the sword's blade ejected into an array of beautiful pink flames again. The pommel, grip, and cross guard remained inflammable by the fire so Jace could actually hold it. The fire was hard to control, even for Jace. It quickly ran up his arm. However, Jace did not scream in pain. He had a relieved expression on his face as the fire unharmed him.

"The fire will heal or hurt whoever I 'command' it to hurt or heal," Dark explained. Then, Jace jerked away from the fire for a quick moment before standing still again.

"Ouch, the fire hurts worse than a normal burn, but the healing portion really feels refreshing almost," Jace described while rubbing his arm where the fire had burned him. Jynx was watching, mesmerized, as she walked towards Jace. Jace flinched, moving away from Jynx for a moment before returning neutral.

"You're acting like I was going to smack you," Jynx exclaimed, worried as she quickly took the sword away from Jace.

"Well, yeah, especially considering you just took my sword!" Jace yelled before moving his arm, gesturing to take the blade back from her. Jynx moved away quickly, pointing the sharp edge towards him, jokingly indicating that she was going to stab him. Jace stepped back, also clearly jokingly. Then, the blood-made sword deformed once again.

It shaped a shield, then a spear, and a handgun, even a mace, and finally into a book. All in the span of a few moments. The blood book then exploded into mini dots of floating blood. Like little insects, so small, all you see is a dot.

The ethereal dots floated around the dimly lit hall before igniting into mesmerizing pink flares. They looked like pink fireflies, floating around frivolously and gracefully. They flew in circle patterns before they all just disappeared and died of color disgracefully.

"Yeahhh, that's pretty much all I can do," Dark exclaimed, a nonchalant grin forming as his hand healed swiftly. He gestured towards Infinity next, who had a nervous look on his face.

"Umm, I don't have any signature powers, just the natural lighting and healing," Infinity blurted, his gaze fixated on the floor nervously. Masquerade patted his shoulder, offering reassurance. A wave of sympathy coursed through Jynx, sending a shiver down her spine. Hyper, once again, was bouncing his feet and jumping around uncontrollably.

"ME NEXT!" Hyper shouted enthusiastically, electricity crackling from his fingertips like miniature fireworks. Jynx had a feeling the lightning was unintentional.

"Yes, please, you next," Jace said while smiling at him. Hyper stopped energetically moving for a moment while he stood still.

"I'll start with my abnormal speed," Hyper said as he disappeared for a moment and came back with leftovers from the breakfast menu. Eating the serving quickly, he whispered something unrecognizable. Then, the eggs on his plate started moving slightly. The leftover scrambled eggs had started collecting into a little ball before forming a little egg-man.

The eggs had formed into a little man. The egg-man jumped on Hyper's shoulder and squeaked something no one could translate. Hyper looked at it and whispered something. The only thing Jynx could make out was, "...for the others can understand too."

"Hello! My name is Egg-man, and I can produce infinite eggs!" The little man exclaimed with charisma. Hyper smiled at the little man while still unable to sit still. Jace, once again, had an amazed face. Even Jynx thought it was neat.

"What!? Infinite eggs, isn't that, like impossible?" Jace yelled. His voice was out of spite and extremely loud. He was clearly over-excited.

"No, not to me.." Egg-man said as he split into another lump of scrambled eggs. He remained the same size, thus creating eggs from nothing. Hyper's brothers were also amazed and confused at the same time.

"You were just... hiding a power like that from us?" Dark exclaimed while looking at Egg-man weirdly.

"Yeah, I didn't know how else to explain it to anyone, pretty much. I can do magical things by just kind of saying it. I can 'incant' them, different from 'enchanting'"" Hyper explained, "Although the power to incant objects comes with the power to enchant them, so I can make a sword produce fire by telling it to do so, it's enchanting, but I don't need to know the certain spell to do so. So I can do complex spells without having to learn the complex spell." Hyper went further into the explanation.

"You just explained it perfectly. What the fuck do you mean you didn't know how to explain it," Masquerade pointed out.

"Language, man, we're in a public area," Jace said while Dark frowned at him. Masquerade looked down the hallway and looked down the other way obnoxiously.

"I don't see anybody, so I can say whatever the hell I want," Masquerade replied sassily. "Okay, fine, chill out, Hyper. What else can you do?" Jace asked while paying half attention to Masquerade, who looked as if he was about to blow up the world for whatever reason.

"That's pretty much it—just speaking to things and unexplainable magic," Hyper said, his fingers fidgeting with Egg-man absentmindedly.

"You should also mention that you have more raw lightning power than any of us," Dark suggested. Hyper looked confused.

"Oh yeah, we should probably go talk to our trip advisors by now," Jace suggested quickly. Jynx looked at him weirdly.

"Well, yeah, but don't you want to see Lazer's powers?" Jynx asked. She was staring him down like he was in trouble for some reason. She was still clearly mad at him but didn't want to lose Jace.

"Oh yeah, right, Lazer, you next," Jace commanded like he was a military general, pointing at him firmly.

"No need to yell at me," Lazer said while picking at calluses on his hand. He stared at Jace with full confidence. "Well, damn, what do you want me to do?"

"Show me what you can do?" Jace said sarcastically, in a rude tone.

"In a fight? I'd rock your shit, I hope you know," Lazer said in a serious but joking tone at the same time.

"No, not in a fight. Are you dumb?" Jace said while maintaining eye contact. In return, Lazer held up his hand like he was trying to give Jace a high five. Jace stared at his hand wearily since Lazer was across the hall from him, nowhere near him. Then, intruding from Lazer's hand, a laser shot across the hall, hitting Jace directly in the forehead. With enough force to make Jace fall backwards. Jace quickly fell backward and hit the floor with a loud thud.

"What the hell, what was that for!?" Jace screamed at Lazer from the floor while he was squirming to get up.

"HEY, LANGUAGE, WE'RE IN A PUBLIC AREA MAN!" Masquerade intruded with an overly loud voice on purpose. Jynx giggled while everyone else started laughing as well. Even Jace chuckled softly, a hint of amusement playing on his lips.

"Well you told me to show you what I can do…" Lazer said while he walked over to Jace, holding his hand out, gesturing for him to grab it. Jace grabbed his hand as Lazer pulled him up. Lazer stared into Jace's eyes as he got up, and a bright light burst out of Lazer's eyes, blinding Jace.

"Flashlight eyessss!" Lazer yelled while chuckling heavily. Jace chuckled, shielding his eyes with his hands against the unexpected burst of light.

"Just so you know, I don't have any signature powers; all I can do is use lightning," Infinity blurted. Jynx looked at him while feeling guilty.

"It's okay. You don't need special powers to be cool," Jynx comforted Infinity as he stared at her weirdly.

"No one said that to me before, thank you. They usually make fun of how useless I am," Infinity replied, his gaze shifting from Jynx to Masquerade with a mix of gratitude and defiance.

"What? You want an apology? Well, too bad, come talk to me when you have a signature," Masquerade said while laughing.

"Shut up, my name's Infinity. That means I'm going to be infinitely stronger than you," Infinity replied with a playful smirk, injecting humor into the conversation.

"Ooooh, he got you good," Hyper and Dark started laughing. "That sounds about right. Uncle Mardo might have named him that because of that."

"Or, maybe he can see the future since there are infinite possibilities," Dark hypothesized.

"Let's go talk to the advisors, so you guys are guaranteed to go on the trip," Jace said, brushing imaginary dust off his pants with a smirk.

"Yeah, let's go. I'm pretty excited to go on this trip." Hyper said. "After all, it'll probably be the only time we get to explore outside of the country."

"I'll lead the way then," Jynx emphasized. She walked down the hallway, knowing the classroom was across the school. Before arriving, she turned to her followers.

"Alright, chill out a bit when you're in here. You don't want to make a bad first impression if you're going on the trip, because first impressions matter." Jynx said before knocking on the door upon entering.

"Mr Zander! I have some new associates for our art club!" Jynx said to the well-dressed teacher sitting in a roller chair. Masquerade looked disappointed but relieved at the same time. He observed the classroom closely. As Zander teaches anatomy, the classroom is filled with models and representations of the human body, and other corny science teacher posters and stuff.

"Oh wonderful, there's a meeting tonight at six. Bring them along, and we'll discuss our next projects with them," Zander said while observing Masquerade closely.

"I know you said there would be no more people tag along on the trip, but I really think they'd be a great addition to the team because Lazer has lighting capabilities and would make it easier and cooler to take pictures for the school..." Jynx babbled to the science teacher before being interrupted.

"Oh, Jynx, I'd love to bring any extras, especially if they're superpowered, but you'll have to ask Glicher for permission," Zander replied formally. "Plus, how many do you even plan on bringing?"

"These five right here," She said, presenting Masquerade and his siblings. And, of course, Hyper had his finger shoved in his nose, Lazer was fidgeting with a world globe, Masquerade was about to rip Infinity's head off, and Dark was sitting down formally.

"These five would be a GREAT addition to the group. I'll talk to Glicher later, and hopefully, she'll approve of your request," Zander said while observing Lazer. "Show me which one has the 'lighting capabilities.'"

"LAZER! Show Zander your lasers, NOW!" Jace yelled at Lazer for no apparent reason. Lazer quickly took his hands off the round globe and stared into Jace's eyes.

"Huh, oh sorry, ummm," Lazer stammered before throwing his hand into the air. "Any color recommendations?" He said, moving his fingers in a squeezing motion.

"Yes, purple and red, please," Zander asked with certainty. Observing Lazer, Zander looked very interested in him.

"Okay, your wishes are my commands!" Lazer said, like he was some sort of genie. Masquerade, Hyper, Dark, and Infinity all stood in a single file line, watching Lazer with awe. Lazer pointed his hand at the wall, streaming a purple light laser at it. With the other, a red light appeared on the wall next to it. He moved them around like they were watching a light show.

"Impressive. Can you do anything else with them?" Zander asked while writing something down in his little notepad.

"Yeah, I can make them smaller..." He said as the lasers on the wall shrunk into concentrated dots. "... and I can make them bigger," he said as the lasers grew like they were big spotlights in a play. Then, 8 more lasers of the same size hit the wall, each with a different array of colors. They all randomly moved and, when hitting each other, had made another color. "I can make different shapes, too!" Lazer exclaimed as the lasers turned into a cinematic masterpiece. The wall showed a story of a wolf that had eaten a deer.

"Very, very impressive. I will talk to Glicher shortly. Your suggestions will immediately be taken into account," Zander said as he walked towards the classroom door. "Now, now, everyone out, I have someone to persuade," He said while gesturing everyone out.

"But, you didn't see the rest of our powers," Hyper said like he was whining, with the Eggman on his shoulder still.

"I don't need to. I have what I need," Zander said as he closed the door, shoving everyone out of the classroom. Jynx walked out last; excited Zander was actually taking her request into consideration. She looked at Lazer with a gleam of happiness in her eyes.

"LAZER YOU MIGHT'VE GOTTEN YOU ALL INTO THE TRIP!" Jynx yelled with a voice full of joy.

"Psssh, he didn't witness the best of my powers. I could've given him a real shock..." Masquerade bragged, shooting Lazer a sidelong glance.

"You're just jealoussss," Lazer replied quickly, returning the weird gaze. Masquerade stared back, not saying a word in return. Jynx glanced down the hallway, a quick check of the time reminding her of the impending need to conduct a proper tour.

"Okay, guys, I'll do the tour quickly; after school, meet up here to see the final answer from Zander," Jynx said as she walked halfway down the hallway. Masquerade cast a nervous glance at his schedule, brows furrowed in concentration.

Chapter 5
Masquerade

Masquerade walked into his first class with Infinity. Everyone had their eyes on him like he was some sort of model, which he didn't like. First on his schedule was biology, which he already had a bad reputation with. The teacher was even surprised to see him there.

"Masquerade, Infinity, stand up, please," the biology teacher said in a plain yet promising voice. Masquerade and Infinity stood up accordingly. "Introduce yourselves." Masquerade stared at him like he was an actual idiot, giving him a dull gaze. Because of this, Masquerade released his restraint on the 'charm', entering the teacher's thoughts. Of course, the teacher was thinking about how the girl named Ryan was wearing a revealing skirt. Masquerade gritted his teeth so hard he swore they broke.

"Of course sir," Masquerade turned around quickly. "Hi, everyone. My name is Masquerade, and he's Infinity," he said, pointing at Infinity. Masquerade's eyes took a quick glance across the room.

"Infinity can answer for himself," the teacher said, even though Masquerade had turned his back to him, ignoring him disrespectfully. Masquerade slowly returned a stare back to the excuse of a teacher.

"He doesn't like social interaction," Masquerade said in a cold tone. The teacher's gaze quickly went away. For some obvious reason, he didn't like staring into Masquerade's mesmerizing eyes. Masquerade smiled in response. "Something wrong? Sir?" Masquerade said in a normal yet deceiving tone.

"Please just stop doing that, whatever you're doing," He said to Masquerade, so concerningly it sounded as if he were frustrated.

"Doing what sir? Just so you know, it's respectful to maintain eye contact in a conversation, especially when you're just meeting the person. Wouldn't you know that, Mr. Briggs?" Masquerade pointed out.

"I didn't introduce myself," Briggs said while still staring downward, embarrassing himself, even though he could care less about a bunch of high school students.

"Hey! He's got a good point, you know," A student piped up from the back of the classroom. Masquerade turned around, staring into his eyes immediately.

"Who? Me or him?" Masquerade asked conductively. The student looked at him weirdly once they made eye contact, something that occurs a lot for him lately.

Oh, I get why Briggs doesn't want to look at him. He's, he's, hot? The student thought to himself. Masquerade almost laughed out loud. His name was Tamer, and he was an angel, in disguise. His parents were angels, that was for sure. Masquerade definitely knew this guy wasn't homosexual, his reaction was just an effect of his charm.

"Answer the question, please?" Masquerade said sarcastically. Infinity was amazed at how he did it.

"Oh, uh, both of you, I guess," Tamer stammered and stuttered. Masquerade dug into his memories a bit, he found his background interesting. The fact that Heaven wasn't the afterlife, but rather a place, far more beautiful than Earth, however. He was born in the bloodline of God himself, carrying divine blood in him. He wasn't just some ordinary high school student. He had a crush on a girl named Angel, that he rivaled her love with some other kid in his grade named Stray. Angel was pretty, though, like an angel surprisingly.

"Fair enough, I'll stop causing a commotion, sorry Tamer. . ." Masquerade said as he sat down back in his seat. It took a moment for the class to audibly gasp, wondering how exactly he was able to find out his name.

"He also never introduced himself. . ." Briggs said as if he was smart. "What's with you?"

"I just did my research before I came, didn't want to seem disrespectful to my peers, you know?" Masquerade replied, holding back a huge grin. Tamer looked weirded out, and Briggs had a convinced look on his face, still salty about the earlier interaction.

"Okay class, sorry for the mini interruption. Let us begin." Briggs continued. "Take your notes out. Let us begin with that!" Masquerade looked at Infinity, as they sat next to each other.

You know, this school stuff is fun as hell. Masquerade invaded Infinity's brain, projecting his thoughts into him. He even jumped a little.

What the hell? Infinity thought to himself, smart enough not to say anything out loud. He quickly looked at Masquerade.

Yes, that was me. I can read minds; don't worry, I won't invade your thoughts though. I just thought it would be fun to spice things up a bit.

Oh my god, that's so cool. What am I thinking about right now? He said as an image of pineapples appeared in his brain, indicating he was hungry.

Pineapples, which is weird because I can see it so clearly. Also, I should mention that not only can I read minds, but I can file through memories.

How do I know you're not looking through mine?

You'll feel it in the back of your mind, like a sharp itching scratching sensation. You'll definitely know when it happens. Masquerade lied to him, of course.

Oh, sounds great, so we can just communicate through our brains? That's so cool. He said as a donkey's ass appeared in his brain, trolling with Masquerade.

That's not even funny. A donkey's ass? Really? If I wanted to see that, I would go find Lazer, idiot. Infinity giggled quietly, but loud enough to attract attention.

"Something funny, Infinity?" Briggs turned around quickly from the board, staring at him strictly.

"Yeah, your fat sweaty forehead." Masquerade blurted as he almost choked out a giggle. The class started erupting in laughter. "And your receding hairline…" He continued, and the class started laughing again. The teacher stammered in place, trying to come up with something to say.

"I would send you to the principal's office, but I wouldn't advise since it's your first day," Masquerade said, reading Briggs' thoughts out loud. He changed the phrase a bit so he didn't seem suspicious.

"Whahow the hell did you-" They both said and stuttered at the same time. The class seemed invested. Masquerade locked eye contact with the bio teacher.

"You're just very predictable. Don't think I'm supernatural or anything. I'm just a teenager, you know," Masquerade exclaimed. Briggs stared at him weirdly, forgetting about the charm. He fell into Masquerade's clutches. It took a while for him to realize Jace was staring directly into Masquerade's soul. He stared back, freaking him out a bit but was relieved and excited he was friends with such a manipulative force.

As Briggs cleared his throat to speak, the bell rang, dismissing the class. The class left in shock, Masquerade left, staring down the teacher intensely as he marched down the room. Infinity took a while before leaving the classroom, following.

"What the hell was that?" Jace's voice intruded from behind Masquerade, who was trying to remember where Jynx had shown him where the weight room was. In contrast, his next class was weight training. Masquerade looked at Jace, promptly deactivating the charm, still bearing the burden of doing so manually.

"Just having some fun, and do you mind showing me where the weight room is?" Masquerade avoided the question completely.

"Oh, you have weight training next, too?" Jace said excitedly. "That's exciting, especially since you can probably knock some sense into Tamer for me!" Jace emphasized. "He's a bully to me, mainly because I'm close to Jynx, and my family doesn't have the best history around here. . ."

Masquerade remained gazing at him before responding, "Oh yeah? I think I could do that for you." A sinister grin played on Masquerade's face, revealing an unsettling amusement.

"I think the others will be here too. . ." Infinity said. "Since we agreed to take this class together,"

"No shit Infinity I was there too," Masquerade said as Jace took the lead to show them where the next class was located. Masquerade made his way down the hall, where there were two locker rooms. One for the men and the other for the women. They all promptly walked into the men's with his backpack in hand. In the room, where groups of teenage boys were frolicking. Hyper, Dark, and Lazer stood awkwardly. Gathered by themselves, Masquerade, Infinity, and Jace joined them. Tamer already had his eyes on the large group.

Masquerade observed in silence, his piercing gaze fixated on the scene. He quickly changed into gym clothes, shorts, and a muscle shirt. The room reeked of body odor, a pungent scent that assaulted Masquerade's senses, fuming in his already oily nose, and to add on to the scenery, were dirty clothes scattered across the floor. He waited for Jace to lead him towards the actual class. Jace hesitated before walking out of the room, clearly indicating for them to follow.

Following Jace's lead, the group ascended the stairs. At the top was a set of doors. Once opened, it revealed a room filled with normal gym equipment. Hyper eagerly grabbed the free weights, swiftly loading the bar with 45-pound plates in almost an instant

"Take it easy, rookie. You might want to gauge the weight first," Jace advised with a hint of humor. The instructor was dozing off on his phone, waiting for the bell to ring. Masquerade chuckled, knowing exactly what was going to happen next.

The bench sat ready to use, and the bar was at the right level. Hyper sat down and got ready to move the weight as the rest of the group gathered around the weight cage. Jace got himself behind the bar, getting ready to spot Hyper if he were to fail.

Hyper readied his arms and hands, fixating them on the rough rusted metal bar. He took a deep breath and quickly took the bar off the hooks. Then, with no sign of discomfort or struggle, he repped it ten times in under four seconds. He put the bar back on the hook slowly.

"Put another forty-five on," he instructed. He said as Jace had the funniest look on his face. Masquerade was smiling too hard. Everyone else had surreal uncertain looks on their shocked expressions.

"I think you forgot to struggle," Infinity said, sounding like some nerd. Jace was still wordless and was staring at Hyper weirdly. Once again, Hyper over-prepared just to rep 225 pounds like it's nothing. Jace was still even more surprised than before. Masquerade watched as the door opened, and the rest of the class started filing in. A group of almost twenty boys stepped in. Tamer came in first, and Masquerade really couldn't see why Jace hated him so much.

"Would you look at who it is. . ." Tamer said while eyeing him down, his eyes directly fixing on the bright haired boy, Masquerade. He observed quietly before speaking up.

"Why are you so jealous all the time? Get over it, would you? Jynx doesn't like you anymore and doesn't want anything to do with you." Jace said harshly. Masquerade jumped up at the sound of Jynx's name. Oddly enough, Tamer wasn't even talking to Jace, he just decided to pipe in.

"Shush up. Jynx is the least of my problems right now." Tamer said, which clearly it wasn't. Masquerade entered his brain again, reading his memories. Tamer used to be Jynx's best friend, then lover, then back to friends, and then enemies. Masquerade was sympathetic and surprised, even a little jealous.

Jynx was nice and would be the perfect girlfriend, and that's exactly what she was to Tamer. Masquerade cut down his heart and realized exactly what he was feeling, a sliver of jealousy hidden deep on his emotions. Straightening up, Masquerade shifted his gaze toward Jace. Regret washed over Masquerade as he reconsidered his initial judgment of Tamer. He stood there thinking to himself, was Jace jealous of Tamer?

"Well, she wants nothing to do with you either, so it's best if you stop picking on me before she gets involved. . ." Jace explained to him, adding more to the already unnecessary drama. Masquerade observed closely as the tension between Jace and Tamer unfolded rather quickly.

Jynx and Tamer left off on good terms, Jace made this conflict up by himself, he made it all up himself to get Tamer away from Jynx on purpose.

A hint of jealousy lingered, sparking Masquerade's curiosity about the true nature of Jace's feelings. Did Jace have a crush on Jynx? Masquerade recognized Jace's overprotectiveness towards Jynx, yet the exact reason remained elusive within Jace's memories.

"Oh, and by the way, I didn't come here to talk about any of this nonsense you're always bringing up, I came to talk to the new boys..." Tamer said while staring at Masquerade. Hyper looked excited, Infinity was zoned out, Dark was looking at Masquerade, expecting him to tell Tamer's entire life story, and Lazer was completely lost. Tamer's cold, golden eyes hinted at an otherworldly aura, suggesting an angelic presence. He had gleaming white streaked straight hair, highlighting a defined face and a nice sharp jawline, he was definitely handsome in male standards. He wore a black pullover and some gray sweats. Tamer waited for a response from anyone.

"I'm Masquerade. These are my siblings." He announced while pointing at his four subordinates. Tamer smiled, amazed at the chance of quintuplets. Masquerade couldn't help but wonder why everyone remained so fascinated by them, but then he remembered the chances of quintuplets to even occur. What makes it worse is the fact that his parents had multiple batches of them, adding more to the table of possibilities.

Masquerade didn't know if his dad was really the Greek god Zeus or if they named him that for whatever religious reason. He was definitely sure his father had god-like abilities, but the question was if he really was the real deal. It was easy to tell from his chubby and retired appearance, if he was actually a god. Now, he regrets telling the soul keeper that Zeus was his father, which was also weird how Anubis knew his name after mentioning he was the son of the god.

Tamer's sarcastic tone cut through the air. 'Can I get proper names, or are guessing games your whole thing?"

"Oh, I guess you're going to have to guess. . ." Lazer said while shooting light from his fingers. Tamer was staring at him weirdly, observing his otherworldly demeanor.

"My name's Lazer because I'm cool," Lazer said, trying not to sound stupid. Dark was chuckling, almost as if he was trying to hide something. Promptly delving into his mind, Masquerade sensed Dark's readiness and quickly responded.

Nature and I thought it would be funny to drug Lazer up on his first day of school, so she grew a Cannabis plant and made him eat some, and I put my blood on the leaf so I could heat it up later. Which I just did, and now he's high and doesn't know why.

Honestly, I wish you guys would prank me like that. He said to Dark, who was still chuckling. For context, Nature, as her name suggests, can use nature to her power. She can grow any plant she likes as long as she knows what it is, however. She used this power to her advantage and studied almost every species and type of plant available in the textbooks they had limited to in their old house. She can create poisons and substances in her body as well, which secretes from her skin, oddly enough. She can also use many powers of animals and use their instincts to her advantage, which gave her the weird quirk to make their noises from time to time. Meaning that sometimes she barks and meows at people. Masquerade could go on and on about his siblings, their accomplishments, and their powers.

"Hi, Lazer. . ." Tamer said in a confused, concerned tone. Lazer responded in an unusual manner, as if experiencing a high for the first time. First off, he took a while to respond since marijuana is known for such abilities. Second off, he responded in an accent, which isn't something notably associated with weed, but it passed off as so.

"Yes, of course! It's cool because I'm the son of Zeus himself," Lazer bellowed in a commanding voice, his vocals collapsing just as deeply. Dark and Infinity gasped, as Hyper was being distracted with other things. Masquerade had no clue as to why they were so surprised, as it was the unbridled truth. Following Lazer's reveal, thunder had rung the halls of the school, clearly offending Zeus for a reason that was hidden behind old mythological law.

Dark said something that Masquerade didn't even know, "Lower your voice, Lazer. You know it is forbidden to say anything related to Zeus in any manner." He whispered.

"Wait, what?! Since when could we not talk about our own dad in vain? He sucks anyways, so of course I'm going to talk shit." Masquerade presented with certainty. Thunder boomed down the hallways once again, which surprised him since Zeus's name was nowhere mentioned in that sentence. He theorized that the event occurred because he insulted his name.

"He has definitely said it before, and it's just common sense. No one should know *we* are the sons of *Zeus.*" Dark emphasized the words 'we' and 'Zeus.'" Again, following the tone, thunder once again violently vibrated the school.

"We're the sons of a god?!" Masquerade was still shocked that he couldn't speak of Zeus or his mother, Hera. "Can we use this to blacklist him?" Masquerade asked lowly.

"What are you talking about? Sometimes I feel you're actually stupid! We had already broken the first rule our father entrusted us with. They discussed this before we even attended the school!" Infinity said while looking at Dark weirdly. "And now, some random weirdo knows of our descent," Infinity continued, looking at Tamer. Hyper budged in like he knew what was going on.

"What was all the thunder about, and why are you glorifying dad like he's not an idiot that eats potato chips all day?" Hyper insulted while picking at his nails. Thunder did not follow up this time.

"Some random? I am the nephew of Michael himself, the Lord and Creator of Heaven itself." Tamer blurted. Surprisingly, thunder did not roll. Masquerade snorted.

"Why is his name Michael? That sounds stupid for the lord and savior 'Michael'." Masquerade blurted, disrespecting the Lord of Heaven.

"Do not speak so lowly of Michael. He can go by Michael if he wants to. For now, we call him Michael." Tamer explained, Masquerade contracted.

"You called yourself 'nephew' of Michael. I thought Michael had no brothers," Dark asked while scratching his head.

"To put it safely and normally, there is a heritage to the ruler of Heaven. As of now, he is Michael, whose reign is declining, and he has to find a new predecessor to the throne. This person may be anyone the previous ruler wants; it can stay in the family if chosen, but the first "God" had chosen someone other than Jesus, so the family could not stay in reign. Thus making me the nephew of Michael, because he actually had brothers."

Tamer explained well. "Although I shouldn't get into details, Hell is the same way. Satan has to pass the torch down to the next ruler. They are more complicated, however, because Hell is split between many rulers. Hades, Pluto, Susanoo, The Shinigami, Satan, Lucifer, Hel, Izanami, and Malekith." Tamer explained further. "You know, your father should teach you more!"

Hyper was shocked, "Wait, so where do we go when we die?" He waved his head around, moving his hair out of his eyes. "There's Heaven, Hell, and Masquerade talked about some jackal named Anubis?"

"Oh, you go to Anubis. He decides whether or not you go to Hell or his realm. Otherwise, Heaven is only for those born there and heroes who became strong enough to be praised. Also, any kind of god that would be able to reach Heaven."

"This is so confusing, I hope to-" Hyper said before being interrupted by an entire flash of yellow lightning crashing down from the roof. Zeus stood in front of Lazer, and Tamer's eyes widened in shock. Masquerade couldn't tell if it was in fear, shock, or both.

"You five dare disrespect your father and disobey the only rule placed on you?" Zeus bellowed in the ancient way of speaking, with a heavier accent than a russian. He was more muscular in appearance than usual, his beard was also more shiny. His eyes glowered with a bright shade of stormy blue, and a lightning-shaped scar was placed carefully through his eye. He looked like the Zeus described in the ancient tales, wearing a loose white robe, with muscles in places muscles shouldn't even be, that even Dark was shocked by his appearance.

"I will take you five to Olympus for such an act of treason," Zeus's voice felt like thunder itself, making Masquerade feel as if he shouldn't even be allowed to be near such a presence. Tamer looked impressed; Masquerade didn't know who would be stronger, Michael or Zeus.

"Very funny boy, of course, me, the ruler of Olympus, would be stronger than a joke which goes by 'Michael'" Zeus laughed. Tamer looked insulted, although he really couldn't say anything in the name of Zeus, who's whitening presence stood right before him.

"I thought being brought to Olympus would be an honor, not a punishment," Hyper squeaked.

"Not for the reasons I intend to bring you for." His voice rumbled.

"You say ruler of Olympus, but you haven't been there in ages-" Dark got interrupted as Zeus teleported everyone but Tamer and Jace away. In an instant, and flashes of a storm of lightning, they all appeared in the holy air of Olympus itself. Heavy white light filled the scenery immediately, and the pollen of flowers could be seen in the clear, void of pollution air,

"Asgard would be better-" Masquerade blurted.

"Shut your trap boy."

"Yes father."

The flowers bloomed, making their petals and stamens huge. Being in the presence of many gods, Masquerade would have guessed they should be that way. Zeus led them towards a waterfall, a waterfall of fairly huge glory and size, it glistened in the sun.

Clear blue water that filled and followed the river was huge enough to host sharks, fish, and other ocean creatures. Zeus stomped on the water, and as he did, clouds foamed up from the water, creating a path straight to the waterfall. Around the river were multiple fields of different colored flowers, almost like they were going on endlessly, giving off an harmonizing aroma.

Behind the entrance they had arrived from were multiple elemental-made bridges, there were twelve of them. These bridges connected each to different islands, representing the twelve great Olympian gods. Masquerade didn't even want to meet them all, instead he wanted to go back to school and talk to Jynx. He didn't like the fact there were outside influences, he wanted a considerably normal life. Zeus softened his gaze, almost like he heard Masquerade, which he forgot that he probably did, since he can mind read.

As the waterfall approached, Zeus waved his hand in front of it. The waterfall split itself, revealing a 'hidden' room behind the clear blue aqua. As Masquerade's eyes got used to the light change, he saw the beauty of the room. In a semi-circle shape, the room consisted of twelve gigantic thrones, each with different colors and accessories. It was easy to tell that each throne was associated with each and every god of Olympus there was. The room had a decorated interior. However, you could still see the remains of cave walls, right under and beneath the authority of the large chairs. Torches lay in between each throne, and different colors of fire burned furiously. Dark's eyes lit up in amazement to the god-full scenery.

"The Flames of Olympus," He said, pointing at one of the colored torches. "It is said if one of those flames dies out, then the god associated with said flame has died." Dark explained.

"Very well, son, you are correct." Something inside Masquerade made his blood boil. He called Dark 'son', but he called Masquerade 'boy'? Where's the respect? Masquerade observed his father, and saw his ear twitch in reaction.

"The flames connect and make The Eternal Flame," Dark's eyes scattered the room, looking for such beauty. Zeus started flying, levitating majestically to the biggest throne in the room, with the torch that had a golden flame of absolute power. Then, from the throne, he snapped. The middle of the temple started to rumble, which had a huge circle engraved in the middle. A huge wine glass-shaped bowl extruded from the surface, everyone watching in silence and astonishment.

In the bowl lay The Eternal Flame, a mixture of each god's power. The fire was rainbow-colored, keen to the jumbled up colors of each culture it represented. The flame was said to be used to hold back even Odin in an ancient war between the two religions. Zeus was even surprised at the look of it, the beauty of it still able to emphasize its authority upon even the greatest of gods. The silence was loud between the group of relatives.

"Enough loitering, around the age you are now, I brought your other siblings here to Olympus to treat them and teach them of my past. However, disobeying my orders has concluded that you are not ready for that yet, and I will have to teach a few lessons first." Zeus reached out his hand, a lightning bolt quickly obeying to his command and teleporting to his hand.

"For the starting of your punishment, I will send you with Artemis, Goddess of the Hunt. Together, you shall gather resources and food for the annual Olympian Festival," Zeus snapped, and the throne with the silver torch lit up. The throne had engravings marked on it, showing multiple stories and pictures of the legend of the one that is 'Artemis'. Those engravings then started glowing a silver hue, shining brightly, bright enough to make a normal being go completely void of vision. The fire from the torch emitted a thick fray of smoke that started forming a figure. A figure of a gorgeous body that only a model would have. From the figure appeared a shockingly beautiful young woman. The woman had long, thick green, brownish hair that was put in a ponytail. She wore a tiara that symbolized the moon, which was a huge part of her power. Her eyes were piercing, hoisting crescent-shaped pupils.

She had war scars through one of her eyes, showing that she was a rather tough warrior. Her attire consisted of a tight green robe that had white fur on the shoulders, neck, and the bottom by the waist. A belt revealed many different arrows that had many uses to them. On her back, you could see a bow intruding, that was large and colorful.

"Yes Lord Zeus?" Her soft, mediocre voice vibrated good vibes. Lazer looked as if he would pass out any moment now.

"Take these children, and punish them, use them to your advantage in hunting, and certainly train them for when the monsters back on World Infinite start noticing them." Zeus demanded. Artemis simply nodded as she slowly slid off her throne. Walking towards Masquerade and his siblings, they attempted to act normal. Masquerade's eyes slipped downwards, his eyes scanned her leggings, and Artemis wore nicely fitted boots that were also furry, like her robe.

"Heyy-" Hyper tried sounding cool before Artemis simply shut him up by growing a plant root to cover his mouth.

"Now, now, what kind of thing could kids like you possibly do to piss Zeus off?" Artemis said, with her beautiful eyes piercing Masquerade.

"We said his name?" Masquerade replied.

"It has got to be worse than that."

"We said that he was our father. . ." Lazer blurted.

"Now that will certainly do it." She said, Masquerade just now noticed her accent. "It's very dangerous to reveal you're the offspring of any god. If it gets out to the wrong people, you and your father will be in grave trouble. Hades is still looking for revenge, and so is Michael. The list goes on: Odin, Satan, Anubis, and definitely Misa." She nodded disapprovingly. "They'll come after you."

"Misa?! But he's a primordial god. How could he possibly have problems with Zeus if he's that powerful," Dark blurted.

"Only they know, child. Do not speak of Misa's name so lightly," Artemis said as she reached for her belt. From her belt, she pulled a bell and raised it up above her head. Everyone looked in surprise as she called the bell. The bell made a sacred sound, and from the depths of nothingness, six spirit deer had summoned from thin air. The deer had antlers more complex than any deer Masquerade had ever seen, even though Masquerade hadn't ever seen many. The antlers glinted with a light white color, indicating that they were definitely spirit induced.

Artemis climbed atop the deer quickly, gesturing everyone else to do so as well. The deer had soft fur, which was also silver-colored. The hooves were different, glowing light blue instead, and wherever they stepped, they left a white hoof mark in the ground. Artemis stretched her arms out, grabbing her deer's antler lightly, and whispering chants to its ear.

"For the first lesson, I will teach you how to ride a spirit deer. My personal favorite species, however, wait until you claim this as your favorite because you will meet many spirit animals during your time with me," Artemis said jokingly. Everyone followed as instructed, climbing atop the spirit deer that she summoned with her bell.

"Good so far, now push lightly and imagine going forward. The deer will respond to your mind and intentions." Masquerade's deer walked smoothly, and so did Dark's. Their respective deers walked in front of each other and lightly touched antlers together. Dark smiled with Masquerade and Artemis. He looked over to Infinity and Lazer, whose deer were also touching antlers. Then everyone stared at Hyper, whose deer was jumping wildly through the air. Like a bull ride you'd find at a carnival, the deer kicked Hyper off his back, making him fly in retaliation, hitting the wall with a loud thud.

Everyone laughed, including Zeus, who was watching menacingly from his superior throne. Hyper got back up and quickly got back on his spirit buck. After a long moment, Hyper got used to it and finally rode it like a normal person, or god, for that matter.

"Now to the forest, hunting for this feast will not be easy." Artemis said.

"Why can't Dionysus, the God of Wine, just summon food like before?" Dark asked, his knowledge of mythology further impressing the two Olympians that lay in front of him.

"He could, but his food isn't summoned from spirit animals. It's summoned from mortal animals, which isn't as refilling and good. So harvesting spirit crops and animals tastes tons better, for us at least" She explained with her soft voice. Masquerade forgot to notice that the deer was walking and galloping in mid-air.

"Is this your true divine form?" Dark asked yet another question.

"Yes sir, why do you ask," Artemis responded.

"The true forms of gods should disintegrate normal beings," Dark stated.

"Yes, but you aren't a normal being Dark."

"The same rule applies to demi-gods, though..."

"Your mother is god-like too. You're not no demi-god. You're full-blood! Like the rest of us." Artemis explained. Dark examined his hands, as if realizing a change in his fifteen years of existence. The great forest of Olympus approached, the trees glistening with white sparkles, the wood consisted of a straight gold color, and the leaves were another silver white. The grass was still green, but it glowed majestically. The rivers were clear blue, but they were still pretty.

Animals exploded with life all around the forest: rabbits, more deer, boars, bears, wolves, and even in the distance, full bulls and cows shadowed their beastly presence. Masquerade could even swear he saw a large dragonfly overhead. The forest's flowers were similar but smaller than before. Masquerade glanced around for any first victims that were ready to be eaten. The deer descended on Artemis's command, slowly walking towards the ground, and all the other deer even listened to her commands.

"Starting off, you do not need the deer to hunt," She said with precision, the deer disappearing from thin air into multiple sparks of white ashes. Her bow happened to start glistening in the sunlight, the string glowing a bright gold, with the wood being a clean bronze color.

"You want us to hunt with our hands?" Hyper disrespected the animal god, who glared at him just as disrespectfully.

"Do not be so impatient, Hyper. I was just getting there," Artemis said in a polite tone. Artemis wavered her hand in the air. Nothing happened at first, but after a moment, similar bows to hers were summoned in their hands. They were lighter, smaller, and less cool than

Artemis's own sacred bow, but they still looked extremely similar. Artemis smiled at Hyper, who was already holding the bow the wrong way.

"First off, we will need around thirteen exact deer. We will give extra rations to the mortals, so we know we didn't over-hunt."

Hyper tried drawing his bow, but he had no clue what he was doing. Neither did Masquerade, but that's beside the point. Dark and Infinity were naturals, already showcasing their skill greatly. Lazer appeared to have the hang of it, but really looked like an idiot, in Masquerade's eyes at least. Masquerade lightly stroked his bow slowly, observing its details, scraping his finger on the sharpened fiber. The string was made of all colors, changing from time to time. The wood still had a copper bronze color, the same as Lady Artemis'.

"Now, if you know how to use a bow, you can go right ahead and find your first kill," Artemis directed, looking at Dark instinctively, with her command, Dark and Infinity ran off into the distance. Artemis started with Hyper, grabbing his fingers to show him the correct way to hoist it. Lazer and Masquerade followed her direction shortly after. Lazer already had prior knowledge of wielding a bow, so it was not a challenge for him. He had a perfect aim straight off the bat that even Artemis was impressed with.

"My power, you see, forces me to aim with precision, so I already have the aiming practice needed." For demonstration, Lazer aimed at a low-hanging branch and quickly shot it down with a red-beaming laser, directed by the depth of the angular weapon.

"Very well, you are ready. Now go off with your other brothers. I will guide the hunt after finishing with these two," Artemis spoke with gleam. Masquerade sat down at a nearby rock while waiting for what could have been hours before Hyper got the hang of it. After he mastered such archery, he went to brag to Lazer, even though Lazer knew before him. Artemis walked slowly to Masquerade with something in her hand.

"I have a gift for you, not from my power but from another Olympian god," Artemis said with a sparkle of determination in her eyes. "Accept this offering in the name of Zeus," Masquerade glanced at the gift in hand, no clue how to respond.

Masquerade let out his hand and hesitated for a moment, "I accept this offering, uhgift," Masquerade said with low pride. Artemis looked at him like he was an idiot.

"Say, 'I accept this offering in the name of my father, Zeus.'" She offered.

"I accept this offering in the name of Zeus!" Masquerade bellowed. The charm in Artemis's hand glowed a bright gold color, bright enough to make someone blind, something that happened a lot here in Olympus. Artemis handed the charm to Masquerade, who glanced down at it. The item was a golden keychain of an owl. Initially disappointed, Masquerade then recognized the owl's significance, that of Lady Athena.

"Now I know this isn't my gift to be offering, but boy, there's something about you, and I feel that this gift should be yours. . ." Artemis bestowed down to Masquerade. ". . the gift comes from Athena, Goddess of Wisdom. It will allow you to learn any skill in a matter of minutes." Artemis looked at the bow. She grabbed the charm from him and clipped it down below on his belt.

Masquerade concentrated on the bow in hand, his mind becoming extremely blank. The charm started glowing gold again, flashing gold for thirty exact seconds. Masquerade graced the bow and now realized that he now knew how to use it. He drew the bowstring and quickly shot down an apple from a nearby tree, with exact precision. Artemis smiled, evoking a sense of pride in Masquerade.

"Now, I will begin the hunt," Artemis walked with Masquerade into the heart of the forest. "Your brothers have already succeeded in capturing three spirit deers by now. Ten remain. Go, boy, show me your skills" Artemis alarmed. With bow in hand, Masquerade dashed into the forest. He had to capture more deer than his siblings, he was determined to.

The one who captures the most deer will claim a prize, while others face punishment. Lady Artemis's voice echoed in his head. Now, Masquerade finally remembered he was in Olympus for punishment, not a treat.

Artemis had presented everything as a gift until now, then glancing overhead, Masquerade smartly considered: Artemis is the Goddess of Animals. Raging bulls filled the horizon hills, stampeding in this direction. A moment's hesitation, and Masquerade noticed the bulls' horns were made of steel, their tails transformed into snakes, and fire erupted from their mouths.

Chapter 6
Jynx

Jynx eagerly awaited the final bell before heading to Zander's room for confirmation. Excitement mingled with anxiety about the impending reveal. Notably, she hadn't seen Masquerade since the first period, leaving her to wonder if it was just new-kid problems.

Upon meeting Masquerade, her nightmare visions vanished, and though she didn't understand why, she appreciated it. The bell rang, and Jynx hastily left the classroom. Anxiously reaching Zander's classroom, she waited at the door, opening it slightly, hoping to see Masquerade, Lazer, or literally anyone else. Disappointment set in as she entered an empty classroom and walked toward Zander's desk.

Glicher and Zander sat, engrossed in their discussion, but halted when Jynx arrived. Surprisingly, both sported smiles, raising Jynx's hopes.

Jynx, we've considered your request, and we approve," Glicher announced joyfully, her usual nasty expression turned bright. Jynx then noticed Jace, who had been silently listening throughout. Suppressing her excitement, she cheered inwardly. "Speaking of which, where are these five?" Glicher asked, her tone notably rude again.

"I haven't seen any of them since the first period, Ms. Glicher," Jynx defended, growing increasingly concerned as she had instructed Masquerade to meet her there.

"I had weight training with them during the second period, where they, uhh, disappeared?" Jace said with uncertainty in his voice. Jynx observed that something had clearly happened, and he was being cautious about revealing it.

"You sound very uncertain of that, Jace sir. What really happened in the second period?" Glicher pushed for him to answer seriously. Zander watched attentively, not uttering a word, but also pushing for a truthful answer, by looking with eyes of disappointment. Jace held his tongue for a moment, likely attempting to fabricate a lie. Jynx intensified the pressure with her eyes as well, making everyone in the room hoping to hear the truth. Jace looked ready to burst. He opened his mouth slowly before the door burst open loudly.

Everyone turned their attention to the door. Tamer, one of Jynx's ex-boyfriends, stood in the wide door frame. Glicher looked amused, Jace looked ready to die, and Zander stood up in his chair, getting ready for some drama.

"Yes, Tamer?" Glicher said, her voice getting sassier by the second.

"I have something to propose against Jynx's request. . ." Tamer continued.

"Go on, I have places to be; make it quick." She snapped. Jace was staring at Jynx wearily, like he wanted to attack Tamer for whatever reason.

"We can not bring Masquerade and his siblings on this trip; it will be the downfall of the school, and it can be the death of us. . ." Tamer continued. Zander, Glicher, and Jynx looked at Tamer like he was actually insane.

"Have you taken your meds, Tamer sir?" Zander proceeded carefully.

"Yes, I certainly have." He frowned, Jynx knew he didn't have a prescribed medicine.

"Why would you propose such a statement?" Glicher asked.

"Bear with me here. I know it may sound like I'm crazy, but it is completely real," Tamer looked out of the window like he was waiting for something to happen.

"Stop tripping over your words, Tamer! Continue the story," Glicher persuaded.

"Masquerade and his relatives are the sons of the Greek God Zeus himself," Tamer declared as a loud thunder strike reverberated through the room. Zander scanned for the source of the noise, while Jynx, terrified, fell to her feet. Glicher still looked amused, completely ignoring the shock of the thunder just now. Jace looked more worried than usual.

"And why do I have any reason to believe that?" Glicher said, laughing. The thunder made it more believable, but Jynx still didn't believe in any gods. She stared at Tamer weirdly.

"You have to trust me with this. It will save lives, I'm telling you. . " Tamer said, fidgeting with his knuckles anxiously. Zander cracked his knuckles nervously as well, once he observed that Tamer was.

"Give some evidence, Tamer" Zander said, staring at him convincingly.

"Thank you, Mr. Zander." Tamer continued, "To start, I had a class with them during second-period weight training. Even Jace was there, correct?" He said, pointing in Jace's direction.

"Uhh, yeum, correct," Jace stammered, his proximal anxiety issues showing prominent.

"Great, so it started with Lazer. He quoted, by himself, that he was the son of Zeus." Tamer concluded. "Now, normally, I wouldn't believe things like that, but just like earlier, thunder had shaken the school." Already, Zander and Glicher looked convinced. "After moments of arguing about the cause, Zeus himself had spawned in a cloud of lightning. His voice, appearance, eyes, everything, it was so real." Tamer looked at Jace weirdly, awaiting his input.

"I can, uhh, approve of this. . ." Jace sputtered quickly, his saliva sputtering from mouth.

"Now, Tamer and Jace, two witnesses, are already convincing, and the surreal thunder strikes. I believe both of you. . ." Glicher started. "But however, if they are really the sons of Zeus, what makes them disqualified from coming on the trip? I don't see a problem with that?" She played on the defensive, making Tamer roll his eyes accordingly.

"How do you not see the son of a god being dangerous in any public place?! People who know or sense any young god will be preying on them the entire trip, especially since we're going across the world. . ." Tamer explained. "Young gods are often victims to power-seeking fiends."

"We'll see what these five have to say about the situation tomorrow, Tamer. Thanks for the information. You are all dismissed." Tamer, Jynx, and Jace exited the classroom. Jace wore a worried expression, while Tamer appeared determined.

"Jynx-" Jace began before she turned away.

"Sorry, Jace, I have to get home quickly. Just text me when you get home," Jynx replied. She didn't intend to be dismissive, but she sensed something was amiss at home. She could sense that something disrupted her household. Jace turned the other way, disappointed. Jynx noticed the difference in his personality lately, from cocky, to joyful, to depressing, and back to normal. Although she couldn't pinpoint his bipolarism today. She stepped outside in the cold air and quickly walked to her car, trying not to slip on the slick ice barrier over the concrete. It took a while, but after she started the car, she drove home in a flux. Pulling into the driveway, she could see Stitch in the living room window, clearly talking to a foreigner.

She opened the door and rushed inside quickly, ignoring the smell of fresh bacon and eggs. It was odd that Stitch was outside of his room this late, especially since he was in the living room, usually he'd be in the weight room. Rushing into the doorframe and glancing across the ever so anxiety inducing event, was the sight of a room that was filled with more than two people, which was the count of the other people in her household. Jynx's heart dropped as she saw the person sitting in the lounge chair, quickly she did a head count of the people.

One, Two, Three, Four, and Five. Mason sat down next to Stitch, and across from them sat an unfamiliar face, but sitting next to the unfamiliar were also two clear faces she despised, Jake, who often appeared in times of horror, and her own bastardly deadbeat father. Jynx felt as if she was about to collapse then and there, her life feeling like the plot of a poorly written mystery novel.

"Have a seat, ma'am," Jake's voice still chills down her spine, even now, quick flashbacks were replaying in Jynx's mind, her brain feeling the reverberating feeling of being thrown to the floor.

"Do not order my sister around you fucking traitor!" Stitch said, walking towards Jynx protectively.

"No need for strong language now-" Jake tried speaking before getting interrupted by the unfamiliar person. He had white glowing hair, chilling blue eyes, and burns on the left side of his face.

"Jake, shush for now, Jynx, why won't you join us? The name's Echo," The voice made Jynx's brain foggy, and it looked as if it did the same to Stitch and Mason. Jynx could almost describe it as an over-exaggerated brain freeze. Stitch then guided Jynx to sit next to her.

"Jynx-" Mark tried speaking up, it took her awhile for a response through her tear-filled eyes. Jynx was starting to panic, every single one of her enemies was in the same room as her, and all of them more than likely wanted to kill her. She looked up with her watery eyes. She couldn't tell if her father was sympathetic towards her or something else, more devious.

"WHY CAN'T YOU GUYS JUST LEAVE US ALONE!" Jynx screamed, alarming everyone in the room. Her voice faded through the excessive crying, but still loud enough for her to get her point across. "Just when I thought things were getting good, when I thought I met someone worthwhile, you guys show up and ruin it all!" Jynx whimpered.

"Woah, who says we're ruining things now. . ." Jake said, twirling his fingers in his brown hair. He stood up menacingly. Jynx tried remaining eye contact with him, but couldn't. Quickly, he was across the room, in front of Jynx. "Your fathers the only sinful one in this room, darling." He whispered slowly. "Watch your tone when regarding anyone else," Stitch was even too surprised to respond. He stood, terrified. Mason had no clue what was going on either, as he was asleep that horrid night. Jake retreated just as quickly as he approached, appearing back to the spot he sat in before.

Jake just had to remind Jynx who was on top. He just had to come back and traumatize her some more. Jynx still remembered the cuts she had on her body, engraved there for months and months. Mark looked at Jynx disgracefully, yet so honorably. Echo was sitting normally, awaiting a perfect time to talk.

"Jynx, we've come to talk and clear some misconceptions. . ." Echo's cold voice ran down her veins. "Your father here did not kill your mother out of cold blood-"

"Do not even START there. He was insane from the beginning! There is no reason in this world that would justify what he did." Jynx interrupted. "Not even a punishment either. . ."

"Oh, of course, Ms. Jynx-"

"Call me by my name, nothing fancy." She snapped.

"-Jynx, don't get me wrong, your father did unacceptable things, and he will atone for it, but there was a valid reason for his actions.' He continued, glaring at her so-called 'father'.

"No reason is good enough for cold-blooded murder. . ." Stitch budged in.

"Once again, this reason may change your mind," Echo continued. "Your mother was something far worse than you believe. She held a power that could destroy the family as we know it."

"Something? You refer to her as she's not even a human," Jynx's voice was coarse, still fighting through obvious voice cracks, caused by prolonged anxiety.

"She threatened the family with this power. She could control anyone at her will and make people do anything for her. . " Echo continued, ignoring Jynx.

"You're lying, she could never, and she WOULD never!" Stitch said with emphasis.

"Oh, but she could! Underestimating your own mother-child?" Echo snapped back effortlessly. "I'll just tell you the truth; that way, you can decide for yourselves." Jynx couldn't believe it, and she didn't want to. Echo's cold voice still discomforted her, further adding to her violent shaking. Jynx tried recalling anything about her family having powers. Surely, if her mother had powers, Jynx would too. Her father, Mark, also did not hold any power. Echo started the story, somehow displaying the exact moment in their brains with exact precision. Jynx feared his prowess, wondering if he was truly divine.

Flashback

Psyche stood at the broken door frame of the rundown restaurant. The night's rain wailed against the rusty metal ceiling, accompanied by the distant roar of thunder as she approached the building. As the co-owner of the business, she possessed the keys to the establishment. Lightning intermittently illuminated the windows, revealing the otherwise darkened dining area. She moved slowly and quietly toward the illuminated kitchen door, the only source of light besides the occasional flash of lightning.

Mark, the owner of this family-made restaurant, had been distant lately. Tonight, Psyche was determined to find out why. Her heels clicked silently along the checkered floor. She appeared in the doorway slowly, observing the room. The light remained on, but no presence was to be seen.

Then she remembered the breakroom, where Mark would happen to be that stormy night. She approached the room swiftly. Recalling previous shifts in the restaurant, the breakroom never had a door, but tonight, it had a loosely bolted plate of metal attached. She heard voices muffling in the room, recognizing Mark's vocals immediately.

Psyche swiftly employed her skills to easily unlock the door. In the dimly lit room, eight figures sat—Mark, Echo, a random fifteen-year-old she recognized as Jake, a handsome man armed with firearms, one of Echo's older friends (potentially Zeus), and two shadowy wolf figures. She stared worriedly. Mark had a scared look on his face, and Echo looked amused, which was usual for him.

"Oh look, who cared to join us!" Echo said sarcastically. Zeus stared at him revengefully. The were-wolves stood like soldiers and didn't seem to respond to the situation. These wolves stood on two legs and looked humanoid, which crept Psyche a little.

"I came looking for Mark, which seemed like I found him," She recoiled.

"Have a seat, ma'am," Jake said wistfully and looked her up and down disrespectfully, admiring her gracious body. Psyche disregarded it and walked closely, watching her step. Echo watched her every step, waiting for something to happen. Zeus watched carefully. The guy with the gun pointed it at Psyche vengefully.

"Step closer, ma'am, and I will not be held responsible for my actions," The guy's soft voice said, which did not match his tough-looking face. Psyche stopped in her tracks and quickly thought of a comeback. Zeus had a troubled look on his face, as if he was going to do something stupid, which now was genetically implanted into his son.

Psyche stepped closer, followed by a gunshot that reverberated like glass shattering in her ears. Thunder roared, and lightning flashed. Zeus swiftly stood before Psyche, holding the bullet fired from the pistol. Psyche now realized that Zeus was the reason that the storm outside was due to him and his stress buildup. Echo scowled at Zeus, marking the first of their vengeful backstory. Mark looked terrified at everything. And Jake, for some reason, was laughing.

"I told you Echo! He was going to betray you! You can never trust the Olympian gods!" Jake teased, cheering triumphantly. Echo maintained a foolish glare on his face, standing up from his chair. Psyche glared at the wolves, who were still standing in place. Mark also stood but tried inching away from the scene.

"Blast! Sit down, you've done enough. Zeus and I will settle these affairs elsewhere. Mark, for now, conclude what we've discussed. If you're still indecisive, hand the knife to Jake. . ." Echo ordered, clearly the mastermind behind this entire event of chaos. Mark's hands shook like he couldn't do what he was ordered to do, whatever that was. Psyche presumed that 'Blast' was the soldier with the guns. Zeus still stood in front of Psyche, protecting her

"II still need more time to decide, Echo," Mark said sadly.

"You always need more time! Dammit MARK!" Echo screamed while cracking his knuckles, he looked extremely frustrated. "Fine, whatever, this is so perfect! This is exactly what I wanted happening!" Echo had a hint of sarcasm and rage in his voice. He raised his hands and snapped, the wolves responded to his call, finally moving. Grabbing Zeus, the first wolf disappeared and teleported quickly with Zeus. The second wolf stood right behind Echo, waiting.

"Jake, brainwash her and take her home with Mark; this way, he can have more time to decide what to do." Echo said, staring at Psyche the entire time. "I hate this is the way you find out, Psyche dear, so I'll remove this from your memories. . ." Echo's voice sent a chill straight through her, usually his voice charm never affected her. Psyche had numerous questions, but she kept her mouth shut, aware that speaking out could lead to her demise. She kneeled on the floor respectfully. Mark had tears filling in his eyes as Echo disappeared with the remaining were-wolf. Jake walked to her slowly, putting his hand over her head. The memories washed away like water pouring on paint.

Jynx awoke in a haze, struggling to comprehend what she had just witnessed. Glancing aside, she noticed Stitch in the midst of a panic attack. Echo looked amused as Jake watched observantly. Jynx collected the dots as much as she could, she tried at the most. She looked up at Echo fiercely.

"You, you planned this, planned it all!" Jynx's hoarse voice screamed. The memory was hard to break down through a fog filled brain.

"What the hell are you talking about, child." Echo worriedly alarmed, his expression becoming overwhelmingly anxious.

"YOU KNOW WHAT I'M TALKING ABOUT!" Jynx screamed as she stood up bravely, now knowing what Echo was capable of. Echo looked extremely stressed. Jake looked amused and was even chuckling a little.

"I don't, now tell me," Echo's look explained that he had done something very wrong, his eyes piercing with ultimate coldness. He stared towards Jake, who was leaning on the wall across the room.

"You showed her the wrong memory, you fucking idiot!" Jake laughed and mocked Echo loudly, which for some reason he did very often. Echo's eyes widened, proving Jake right. Mark looked worried now, staring at Jynx.

"You know the truth then?" Echo observed. Jynx stared back with tears still falling down her glossy cheek. "Jake, hurry and get it done the way you did the first time, better than Mark could ever do," Echo continued, something sinister twirling throughout his thoughts. "Kill her." The cold sound collapsed from his breathtaking vocals.

Jake bolted across the room in a flash, straight towards Jynx. She didn't know what to do as she saw Jake running straight towards her. Stitch sidestepped in front of him, giving Jynx time to think.

"Out of the way, Stitch! You know it has to be done, the same way it was with your mother!" Jynx connected even more of the dots just then, knowing why she was victim number one. Echo had shattered his hopes of keeping the murder quiet, but the chance of him showing that memory truthfully still rang through the open air of possibilities.

"Jynx! Run, get out of here!!" Stitch screamed, fending off Jake bravely. As Jynx jumped straight through the living room window, she realized her family's dark past. Keys in hand, Jynx landed in the fluffy snow. She didn't know why, but she felt as if the snow was going to attack her, she was reluctant to escape the growing coldness. Getting in her car, she drove as quickly as she could, wondering why Echo, or literally anyone else, had tried chasing her, but at this point, she didn't care.

She recollected her thoughts and reminisced about the previous events. She realized Echo, Jake, and her father would be after her soon, at any favorable moment. She realized after this that all the females of her family did really hold a dark power, and the great moment of complete realization hit her, she could be next to inherit that same dark power. Her brain filed through memories, coming to the conclusion that Mark teamed up with Jake and Echo to plan the blood curdling idea to slaughter her mother. More info rose, noticing that Zeus was there to protect Psyche. Now, Jynx understood one thing and one thing only, and that was that her other members of her family would want to kill her before this power awakened.

Mark had been too scared to kill Psyche himself and made Jake do it for him, explaining why there had been a voice that Mark was hearing that violent night. Now the only thing she questioned was why Jake would make Mark turn himself in, as they were partners in crime.

Through the interactions she had seen, she concluded that the duo didn't even like each other. Jake sees Mark as one thing; a coward. Echo had planned this all, and Jynx had no clue who this man of authority even was. She looked in her car mirror, her eyes were glowing a bright pink. The first sign of power she had ever seen in her entire life until now.

Jynx couldn't trust Stitch or Mason, as they could've been in this entire scheme too. She wanted to go back and rescue Mason, but it was too risky to be considered a real thought. She made her last turn to her only trustable friend's house, Jace. She pulled into Jace's driveway and parked the car. She hesitated a moment, now realizing that Masquerade could really be the son of Zeus afterall. Now she just wished that he would return from wherever he was, and do it quickly. Jynx put her hands together in a praying motion, closing her eyelid, and facing downwards. She prayed to Zeus that someone could save her from her family's problems. Zeus probably wouldn't even hear such prayers, but she can only hope. Jynx opened her car door and walked inside Jace's house, finally feeling safe. The stress left her body immediately as a message filled her dark filled head.

You'll be safe, Lady Jynx. I will send a hero to protect you from your relatives' behavior. For now, you can only wait. Zeus had answered her prayers.

Chapter 7
Masquerade

Masquerade sensed someone in need of rescue, but it didn't matter at the moment. The raging bulls had drawn closer, leaving Masquerade indecisive about his next move. Artemis had mentioned the capture of three deer. Masquerade couldn't help but ask himself *How on earth are we supposed to fight mutant cows and hunt deer simultaneously?*

The only thing he could do at this point was to stop complaining and try. He put an arrow in his bow and shot overhead. The arrow actually hit one of the bulls, who at this point were already sixty meters away (or around 200 feet). The arrow didn't even faze the bull; it kept galloping. Masquerade tried counting them, but there were too many on the horizon. He estimated around fifty to seventy. They seemed practically invincible; an arrow did nothing to deter them and their hides.

Masquerade drew another arrow in his bow, this time generating an explosion from his feet. His body soared into the air, adrenaline rushing through him as he remained airborne. Utilizing the wind's current, he gained a clear view of the landscape. He flung his finger through the bow, flinging the arrow with his flashy fingers. The arrow flung with great force and speed, with the push of a little explosion. The arrow successfully penetrated the bull's hide. Masquerade readied more arrows, firing multiple times, with the same strategy as before. *One down. Only a million left.* He got ready to start firing again before a blast of fire interrupted his plans.

One of the bronze bulls had shot a fireball at Masquerade. He quickly tried maneuvering around it, but he still burned up his left arm pretty badly. The burn quickly healed a little, but the fire seemed to disable his healing capabilities. He guessed this was due to the fact these bulls were the creation of the gods, and came with god-defying abilities. Masquerade turned his focus back to the battle. While he wasn't paying attention, a few other of the bulls had fallen. His brothers were helping somewhere on the open battlefield.

Masquerade held his bow up again, this time trying something different. In his brain, he imagined an arrow made of lightning. He fumbled his fingers as the arrow came to reality. Pushing the lightning arrow with an explosion and a gust of wind, the arrow was able to successfully one-shot one of the bulls in a quick strafe of violent compressed air, making a thundering sound of wavering oxygen. Masquerade was happy with his power combo, feeling proud of himself. Once again, he shot another, taking down one more. He laughed at himself as another fireball was hurling towards him, unexpectedly.

He unsuccessfully dodged the ball, and the fire spread to his body. Unable to maintain balance, Masquerade plummeted to the ground. With a thrash, the bulls caught up to him. He looked up quickly as the cow was only seconds away from turning HIM into the ground beef. Masquerade tried getting to his feet, almost tripping over a rock. The bull looked like he smirked at him, mocking his minor mistake. He waited for the bull to charge, and then when it did, he jumped from the ground and grabbed the bull's steel horn from the front.

Fire snorted from the bull's nose, and Masquerade used this to quickly maneuver around and grab the second horn. His hands hurt from the sheer heat of the metal, but that didn't stop him. Quickly, Masquerade used all his strength to steer the bull directly into the ground. The bull tried fighting, but it worked in the end, his entire body crashing through the dirt.

 The dust collected in Masquerade's eyes, wiping it off with his arm. With the horns in hand, Masquerade steered the mutant cow backward and made him crash directly into another nearby bull. The bull moaned in pain, but he still wasn't done with the assault.

Masquerade snapped the horn off and backflipped off the bull, slapping him in the face in the process. He landed on a nearby tree branch, maintaining a quick squatting position on the tree, and snapped his fingers. Then, in the place where he had smacked the bull, a massive explosion erupted, successfully taking out both of the cows. The smoke cleared the height of the forest trees quickly. Masquerade looked overhead and saw what he fully expectedmore bulls.

He went airborne again and used the same trick as before, going as quickly as he could, he cleared seventeen bulls before he got tired, fuming with anticipation. His brothers had helped, and in no time, together, they had killed every bull. He wondered if Artemis was impressed with their skills. He glanced over the forest. He did not see a single one of his brothers, but he did notice a deer. He shot quickly, succeeding, and the deer fell.

Masquerade flew around looking for someone. After a while, he found Hyper frolicking with two deer, eventually killing both with a jab of a knife that he found on the floor. He landed next to him, startling him.

"Oh, Hi Masquerade! I've killed five already. I don't know how long we're going to be here," He said in a positive tone. Masquerade stared at him, before Artemis appeared before both of them, spiraling from a pile of leaves. The same occurred for the rest of his siblings, a whirlwind of leaves appearing before their eyes, acting as a portal to their forms. A pile of deer lay in the middle of the group.

"Thirteen deer! Well done guys. Now, I guess I'll hand you over to Lady Demeter for your next task," Artemis exclaimed. "Be careful, though. She isn't as nice as I was. Good luck to all of you!" Artemis said as she transformed into a crow. They all watched as she flew away, the deer disappearing just as fast as she did. Everyone stared at each other silently, clearly excited to talk but now knowing what to say. Hyper started, of course.

"That was so cool!" He started. "I didn't think the gods would be real."

"Me neither, but I'm worried something happened at home," Masquerade exclaimed, still having that gut feeling from earlier.

"That's not like you. By now, you'd be arguing with the most dangerous god there is," Dark said while smirking lightly. "Lighten up, I like that about you." Masquerade smiled in response.

"You want me to argue with a god?" Masquerade responded.

"I'm not saying you should, but it could be a possibility," Just after that, the goddess Demeter showed up before them. Same as Artemis, she radiated a nice presence, making Masquerade feel safe and warm. She wore a white dress that had icicles scattered around the perimeter. Her hair was nice and braided, its color was a bright and vibrant brown. Both her eyes were different colors, the same as Lazer's.

"Perfect. I know exactly what to do with you five," Demeter's voice sent chills down Masquerade's back, the same way Echo's did. She seemed exactly how Artemis described her, rude and not polite, something that deeply infuriated him. Masquerade searched her body, looking for what flame color she was associated with. Then, as usual, the five were teleported away with another god.

"Start here, harvest these crops and continue for the rest of the field." Demeter demanded. At first, it didn't seem as bad as a punishment, but then, when you looked up and saw over the horizon, it really was. As far as you could see, there were fields, fields of corn peaked at the back of the landscape. Other than that, it was all flat lands of potatoes, carrots, and other various field crops.

Now, Masquerade could explain in detail how he picked these crops and how he spent his time in this field of hell, but you probably wouldn't want to read about slave labor. The five got to work as soon as possible, using their supersonic speeds to finish as quickly as they could. There was no easy way to do this, even with the use of their powers, they couldn't speed up the process. This was forgetting about Hyper's ability to talk to inanimate objects.

In a haste of disappointment, Hyper quickly spoke to the soil itself, "Soil! Reject and eject these crops out of yourself, and slowly bring them upwards!" Masquerade thought he was in some fantasy wizard RPG, and he was dumbfounded when the crops quickly picked themselves. Layers and layers of corn, potatoes, carrots, beetroots, types of wheat, beans, beets, and other field crops had appeared in a lovely design, all organized respectively in high mountains. Masquerade wished he could see the look on Demeter's face when she saw their work.

They were all getting hungry by this time of the day, so they munched on raw vegetables, waiting for Demeter to rescue them. Before they remembered Hyper's powers, they spent around eight hours straight picking crops. Their god stamina really paid off, and Masquerade suddenly knew what it felt like to get paid minimum wage.

"You think we could use your blood fire to heat up some potatoes?" Masquerade had asked Dark, who was sprawled over the pile of carrots. The group decided to start moving the crops in big hills. Which looked cool at first, but after a while, it just got boring.

"We could, but I don't feel like getting up," Dark responded. Masquerade wouldn't be surprised if there was a carrot shoved up his ass at this point. His siblings were acting like zombies, and his ADHD wouldn't let him sit down, so he advised a plan. This plan would either piss Demeter off, or make her release them in an instant. He guessed the gods could just watch over them at any point in time, so he assumed Demeter was playing cards with some other god, which really pissed him off.

"Everyone! Stand up!" Masquerade yelled on top of the pile of potatoes. Hyper got up immediately, his energy shooting up back to normal. He already knew Masquerade had some fun planned. Dark groaned as Lazer and Infinity helped him up. "I have an idea, a great idea!" He continued, holding a potato in hand. By the looks of everyone else, they knew this idea was stupid, but the least they could do was to have some fun. "Pick a crop of your choosing and stand on top of the huge hills we already arranged!" He screamed like a camp director. "I already chose potatoes!"

Hyper stood on top of the carrot pile, and Dark chose the beetroots. Infinity claimed the sugar beets, and Lazer had chosen apples, which were an obvious smart choice for what they were about to commit. The apple trees were hard to find as the land was mainly fields.

"Now, on my mark, we will have the biggest and most dangerous food fight known to man kind!" Masquerade yelped, and his brothers suddenly raged with energy. "Begin!"

Masquerade didn't specify any rules, which made this an easy win for Hyper. But he had a plan, a master plan. Now, the very specific rule was you could only use the crops you claimed at the start. So Masquerade chose potatoes because they were easier to throw, and they hit like rocks.

Carrots started flying like homing missiles, and Masquerade dodged effortlessly. Hyper had targeted him first. Lazer was creating some weapons while Dark and Infinity fought each other. Masquerade grabbed a potato, staring at Hyper, they were both ready to fight. He threw the potato quickly and grabbed another one to launch. Hyper said something but he was too far away for Masquerade to understand.

Then, the carrots started flying out of the ground vertically, making an almost exact replica of a tsunami, except it was made of carrots. The wave made its way to Masquerade, who thought the wave was too short to reach him from where he was, he was wrong. The carrot wave reached its way to his level, and Masquerade panicked. He called the skies to his aid, using the wind's current, he pushed the wave back just enough to reveal that Hyper had created a carrot cannon. Masquerade was already incredibly jealous of his power.

In return, Masquerade harnessed the wind to conjure a swirling tornado of potatoes, even Hyper looked surprised and challenged. The tornado traveled around Masquerade, putting himself in the middle. Giving him the all inspiring nickname of 'The Eye of The Storm of Potatoes'. The vortex moved with his every move, picking up other seeds with him. He boosted himself with explosions from his hands and feet, the potatoes flying around him from the blast. He was airborne, his favorite place to fight.

Hyper looked up at him, the sun glaring in his eyes. He shot the cannon, sending a mush of orange vegetables, which was useless to Masquerade's defenses. The mashed ball had gotten stuck in the tornado, wrapping around and shooting directly back at him. He looked surprised, shooting another. The ball simply retracted back to the vortex, and he had two balls of carrot flying towards him.

Panic flashed in his eyes, and Masquerade couldn't help but smile. He wasn't done. He summoned more potatoes with the wind and made two huge boulders of raw potato. With this, he shot them with precise accuracy. All four of the vegetable boulders smashed directly into Hyper. Satisfied, Masquerade advanced towards him quickly. Gracefully, he landed beside him, shielded by a storm of potatoes.

"Join my side, Hyper; together, we will be unstoppable. . ." Masquerade urged. Hyper stood up, with mashed carrots and potatoes covering his entire body. He wiped his eyes and face off. Masquerade expected him to start screaming like a lunatic.

"That was fucking awesome! Of course, I want to team up. Imagine a storm of carrots and potatoes! I'm in!" Hyper reacted. Masquerade chuckled. They both focused on the other three, already having a formation as well. It was Hyper and Masquerade versus Lazer, Dark, and Infinity.

"Alright, it's a 3v2, so we're uneven, but Infinity has no special power, so we won't need to worry about him," Masquerade explained. Hyper stared incisively.

"Mhm mhm," was Hyper's only response.

"So, Dark's fire could probably be a problem. Flaming apples, beetroots, and sugarbeets would be a disaster. Lazer won't be able to enhance any of the crops, but his base lasers are dangerous enough,"

"Mhm, mhm." He repeated.

"We'll attack first," Masquerade decided. He ascended into the air again, the storm following him. He picked up some carrots while he was at it, making the storm have more volume. Masquerade prepared multiple boulders of potatoes and carrots. He made them slowly levitate under him.

"Make some more cannons! I'll make them float above me," He yelled down to Hyper, who had carrot and potato turrets made, these things could fire carrots bullets at lightning speed. Masquerade smiled at himself, realizing how stupid this event would be if it were ever put in his biography.

Since he was a god, his stories and life events would be written somewhere to be taught at school or something. He thought about how cool Hercules was, and then envisioned his own, and how his book would be about him fighting his brothers with a bunch of potatoes.

He focused back on the battle ahead. Dark and Lazer were arguing, and Infinity was staring at the monstrosity ahead of him. Then, an idea struck Masquerade. Swiftly, he manipulated the wind to draw the boulders closer to him. He simply touched it faintly, remembering what he did to the bulls. He shot the boulders full force at the three, and they were ultimately defenseless.

Masquerade chuckled as the boulders crashed into their faces. Just as they crashed, Masquerade snapped his fingers. The boulders exploded, leaving scars in the land and sending the crops flying all over the air in massive shockwaves. Masquerade continued to laugh, relishing in the chaos he had caused. Hyper watched as his turrets decimated their forces, which weren't much, but at least they tried. Masquerade released the tornado in an explosion of swift air, the potatoes and carrots dispersing across the landscape, creating a cool meteor effect, furthermore confirming Masquerade's victory.

"WE WIN!!" Hyper cheered obnoxiously towards the defeated trio. The looks on their faces were priceless. The turrets disintegrated at Hyper's command. They all started walking towards each other, Hyper still cheering excitedly.

"Good game." The three losers muttered shamelessly. Masquerade smudged potato skin off Dark's face, and he smiled.

"I gotta admit that was pretty fun," Dark mumbled, still cleaning mashed carrots from his pants.

"Yeah, I think we can all admit, anyways, Demeter is probably gonna be pissed when she sees this mess." Infinity exclaimed like an idiot.

"No shit stupid, of course, she's going to be mad," Masquerade hissed at him. Infinity replied with a smug smiling face.

"You're right, Demeter is going to be pissed," A lady's voice appeared behind all of them. Masquerade quickly turned around and lifted his hand upwards, throughout this read you can obviously tell this one obvious trait about Masquerade, and that was that he was incredibly stupid. His hand faced Demeter with one goal in mind. Instinctively, that was that he just blew up the Goddess of Agriculture and Seasons. Demeter had shock on her face as Masquerade's body flew the other way from the momentum of the explosion, smoke emitting from the initial blast.

He didn't mean to try and blow up a god, it was only his mere battle instinct. Now, he was in more trouble than he was before. Smoke smutted from his hands, and smoke was still left on Demeter's cold face. To make matters worse, Masquerade's stupid self couldn't stop himself from smiling.

Now, he faced two significant challenges. OneHe blew up a god out of cold blood, and the obvious secondHe smiled immediately after. Demeter took a while to speak again. Masquerade looked down at his hands, disappointed. He looked among his brothers, who were in just as much shock as Demeter. He felt so stupid and annoyed with himself. Demeter collected her thoughts.

"I will take you all to Zeus for messing up my fields and attacking a god of Olympus," She said strictly.

"But it was MY mistake. I don't see why they need to be punished for it," Masquerade snapped back, making things worse than they already were.

"Silence, boy. You attacked me, and your brothers trampled my crops," She replied. Masquerade couldn't help but ask himself how far her head was up her ass.

"Your stupid crops aren't trampled. They are only picked. Stop whining and maybe do something for yourself, you lazy excuse of a god," Masquerade blurted, and everyone gasped audibly.

"You DARE backtalk me. You have gone too far for being so young and naive. You know nothing about the culture of the gods, you ignorant prick," Demeter said. Masquerade only now realized that she could probably read minds, but that didn't matter.

"I know very well the culture of the gods. Growing up around Zeus himself, the only thing he knew was to make everyone do his bidding. You feel the same way, don't you? You dare argue in the name of Zeus and try insulting his own kid?" Masquerade fought back. He was now on his feet, smoke erupting from his hands. His heart pulsed angrily.

"SILENCE, your father gave me every right to punish you at my will. And I will not take disrespect from someone that has no experience in the ages of gods,"

"You keep talking about gods this and gods that! Why can't you argue with normal philosophy? The gods' logic is stupid and outlawed. I don't care what they think. It's just filled with lies and ideas that basically mean 'I can do whatever I want because I'm a god", which is not fair!" Masquerade's voice raised with every single sentence. His hands were filled with smoke, and it was rising to his nose.

"I've had enough arguing with a mere godling, enough!" Demeter mocked, and the smoke coming from Masquerade's hands was now steam. His hands were hot, boiling, and of all the decisions Masquerade has made in his life, this was by far the worst. Masquerade raised his arm and charged Demeter, with his hands ready to bring down the world with him.

Quickly, Demeter teleported everyone back into the throne room. Normally, this wouldn't bother Masquerade, but in the second they teleported, Demeter evaded Masquerade's hand. The explosion flew past her and hit someone else directly. Zeus and Poseidon sat in their thrones, their face shaken with absolute shock. There was a red flame present on the throne that clearly represented the God of War, Ares. And even Artemis was sitting on her throne.

Everyone watched as clear as day, that he blew up another god. Once the smoke of the explosion cleared, lay a well-built man with many war scars all over his face and body. He wore a military vest jacket. His face was defined, and his eyes filled with rage. His hair was black slicked back, with one red strand sticking out.

Masquerade wasn't dumb, he knew exactly who this was. Artemis, Demeter, Zeus, Poseidon, and his brothers watched as he successfully made enemies with the God of War himself. Ares had a stupid grin on his face, saying that he definitely wanted to make enemies with a fifteen-year-old child.

"You really have the nerve to strike me down, boy?" Ares's commanding voice compelled him. Masquerade only had one encounter with these gods, and he hated half of them.

"You set me up!" Masquerade pointed at Demeter, who was also in a fighting position. Zeus watched before stepping in and saying something.

"I should really just kill you already. You've been causing problems since you got here," Ares said. Masquerade's ears were hot. He wasn't going to let anyone push him around.

"Then do it yourself, coward. Demeter couldn't fight her own enemies, so I really hope you can do what she couldn't," Masquerade exclaimed. The rest of the gods had a look of shame on their faces. His father had a look of disgrace on his face.

"Show him, Ares; clearly, hard labor couldn't teach him the lesson I tried to teach, so it's clear it has to be a physical beating," Zeus ordered, and Ares had a big grin on his face. Dark and Lazer looked scared for Masquerade. Hyper looked hyped, as his brother was about to fight a god. Infinity waited to show emotion. Ares readied himself, closing his fists. Masquerade felt adrenaline fill his veins, he was really about to fight the God of War.

He thought about the biography again, adding to a food fight of potatoes was the fact he was squaring up to a god. Hercules couldn't even do that, from what he remembered at least. Masquerade waited for Ares to make the first move. Smoke already fumed the area, coming from his hands. Ares charged quickly, even quicker than Masquerade realized.

Masquerade went airborne and flipped to Ares's other side. Ares tried turning around quickly enough but instead met an explosion to the face. He grunted as Masquerade went under his feet this time. The smoke obscured Ares's vision completely.

Masquerade used this to trip Ares as he went underneath him. Keep in mind they made physical contact at that exact point. He tripped forward and met eye-to-eye with Masquerade. Ares smiled and raised his fist. He hit Masquerade point-blank in the nose, causing red flashes of lightning to erupt, distorting space itself, making his face bruised and expelled with blood. He recoiled and hit the stone floor with a thud. Ares went for another blow, but Masquerade caught his punch.

"That was a rookie move! Come on, boy, be better than that!" Ares called. The second punch came quickly. Masquerade miraculously dodged under it, grabbing Ares's arm. He used the momentum to flip him over, and used all his strength to do so. Ares was in his hands now. He used an explosion to throw him straight into the floor, making him crash directly on his back. It happened so fast that the stone under them cracked, and Ares had actually started bleeding.

"I'll show you, Ares!" Masquerade yelled as Ares got back to his feet. Everyone was watching the fight attentively. He boosted himself in the air. Ares watched from the ground, smiling huge. Masquerade used both hands to release a massive explosion to boost him straight into Ares.

Ares tried dodging, but Masquerade got his attack ready. He landed the nastiest drop kick from the air in human history. Masquerade had hit him in the stomach. Ares coughed blood. He punched him in the face, backflipping away from Ares's next attack, remembering the attack he landed on Ares's face.

He snapped, and it was all over. An explosion landed point-blank on Ares's face, knocking him straight through the wall. Zeus looked impressed, and his siblings were cheering. Masquerade bit his tongue to stop himself from smiling. Demeter attempted to conceal the reality that Masquerade wasn't merely all talk. However, this moment of joy did not last for long.

"You dare disrespect the gods to this extent?" Ares's voice came from the wall. His silhouette appeared from the smoke.

"I don't know, how long will you only care for yourself?" Masquerade snapped back before he was in red-searing chains. He couldn't move. Ares walked up to him slowly. A widening grin on his face.

"Your impertinence has worn my patience thin."

"Great, so have-" Masquerade said before getting his jaw locked. His anger rose again, but that didn't really help him anymore. Another jab to his jaw, followed by a punch to the stomach. Ares beat him there while his arms were bound by chains. He beat him till he was satiated.

"Haven't you had your times of being an abusive father in your immoral life?" Masquerade snapped in pity. Ares had a pitiful look on his face.

"Enough!" Zeus sparked. His lightning bolt had called to his hand. "One last punishment for you five, and that is to deliver messages with Hermes." Zeus summoned Hermes, and he appeared quicker than anybody had expected.

"Yes, Lord-" Hermes burped. "-Lord Zeus?" He finished. Masquerade didn't know if he meant to be disrespectful or not, but it made him chuckle, and Hermes noticed. He had brown curly hair and wings attached to his sideburns. These wings were gold, the same was attached to his feet. He wore a tight white robe, which was stained severely with buffalo chicken sauce. His boots were abnormally huge and were bright brown.

"Take these disrespectful children and show them a day in the life of the messenger god. . ." He bestowed on poor Hermes.

"Yes sir," He responded, looking at his inmates. Masquerade was bruised but smiled faintly. Dark waved awkwardly, and Hyper jumped up and down. Masquerade couldn't help but ask himself how much time had really passed.

"It has been twelve hours, which converts to two days in World Infinite, or as you call it, Earth." Zeus read his mind, and suddenly Masquerade's body was free of the chains, and Ares still had a smug look on his face. It has been two whole days since he last spoke to Jynx,

Masquerade was getting worried. The trip was in ten days since he left. Which meant he had eight days to get back home. Or in Olympus time, he had two days, forty-eight hours to complete his punishment. If he didn't, then he wouldn't make the trip on time.

He glanced back at Hermes, who twirled around in a dance, oblivious to Zeus's disapproving scowl. His siblings looked ready for another day of torture.

"Alright, kiddos, first things first, I'm here to, uhhurt you and make your life worse!" He stuttered. Dark put his hand on his forehead. Zeus sighed loudly, and Ares was laughing. Demeter was gone, probably sorting the mess Masquerade made. Artemis was still watching quietly.

"Until later boy, don't forget my beating. If you disrespect me or any other gods again, we'll be back at square one," Ares said as his body disintegrated into a body of blood-red smoke.

"Ignore him; he's the Olympians' resident hothead," Hermes reassured, a twinkle in his eye as he absentmindedly picked his nose. "Also, you might want to put some protection on or whatever you do normally. Because we're going to Tartarus for our first stop," Hermes contradicted. "It's very hot down there, and we'll be delivering to Hades himself!" He held up a basket full of letters and envelopes. There were even a few packages in there.

"Is Hades selfish and self-centered like the rest of the gods?" Masquerade sputtered while Zeus gave him a dirty look.

"Of course! What else did you think," Hermes said. "We might make a stop in the mortal world, too. Get us some snacks for the trip, y'know?" Masquerade and his siblings exchanged smiles; Hermes had swiftly become Masquerade's favorite god.

"Do not treat them, Hermes! This entire trip here was supposed to be a punishment!" Zeus thundered.

"Well, if you weren't gone for almost three years, maybe I'd listen," Hermes rolled his eyes, and Masquerade was amazed.

"My family business is none of your concern!" Zeus responded.

Hermes fell silent, and in an instant, the six of them were teleported out of the throne room, another thing he's been getting used to. Hermes and his siblings were in a Burger King parking lot. On the outskirts of the Burger King was an overwhelming river of great importance that Masquerade had no interest in. He'd never been to any restaurant before, until now. They entered the burger joint with a determined stride, driven by a singular goal: to sate their hunger. As they looked around, there was something about this place—it had a museum exhibit. In the hallway near the bathrooms stood a podium in a glass casing that had an unidentified object lying in it.

Masquerade scrutinized the object: a vial filled with pink blood. He read the description of the bizarre item. 'Ions ago, a clan of gods known as Kokoro existed, which were extremely powerful. Only in this establishment were we able to find a sizable amount of this blood.' Masquerade had many questions, but then Hermes snapped and all of a sudden, they were in a large castle-type room with their burgers and drinks. He wanted to go back and learn more, but Hermes insisted otherwise.

The room was massive. It had a black stone for the interior. In the front of the room lay a massive entrance that was bound with huge chains and metal locks. It had what looked like one of those magic spell locks on it that you find in video games.

Hermes devoured his food, while Masquerade hadn't even touched his own yet. Hermes walked to the massive door, and in a quick motion, he undid the magic spell, removed the chains, and opened the door with no struggle at all.

"I think you forgot to struggle-" Hyper said, laughing to himself. Inside the door was all darkness, although it seemed. Out of the darkness, suddenly poked a huge snout, followed by red glowing eyes. Dark gasped loudly. Masquerade observed before saying anything. The snout quickly emerged, turning into a head.

A black-furred dog had emerged. It had lava for saliva. Masquerade was so focused on one of the heads he didn't even notice a second one pop out as well. The third followed shortly after. Masquerade tried making eye contact with all three heads at the same time, which seemed to piss the dog off for an odd reason.

"Cerberus! Sit down!" Hermes called. The dog growled viciously before lying down with a loud thud. "I said sit!" Hermes yelled again. Cerberus listened and stood back up, sitting down correctly. Hermes gestured his hands towards the huge dog. "Hop on, guys! Nothing like Burger King on Hell's largest hound!" Masquerade could not believe he was getting a ride on Cerberus himself.

Masquerade and his siblings listened intently, swiftly mounting the colossal dog's back. Hermes stood on the middle head. "Take us to Hades' throne room, please, Cerberus puppy?" Hermes talked to the dog in a baby voice, which Masquerade thought was a bad idea. Cerberus emitted a canine whine, its three heads moving in a dance of anticipation. They all found it hard to stay on. The dog wrestled and jumped, making it hard to keep balance. Then, the dog turned around to face the darkness, which looked extremely dangerous to Masquerade.

The dog sprinted towards the door of the everlasting void and jumped. Masquerade didn't know why the dog had jumped until he realized they were 3,000 feet in the air. And there was an ocean of blue, yes blue, lava underneath them.

Chapter 8
Jynx

Jynx hadn't done much in the past two days. She slept in Jace's spare room. And lived off whatever Jace could cook himself. Jace's parents were out on a business trip, so everything lined up perfectly for her. The interactions between them weren't great, with Jynx in a bad mood the entire time, she snapped at him every time he came to comfort her. She felt bad sometimes, but the creeping thought of betrayal from him was always lingering in the back of her ever so important cerebrum. She lost her phone purposefully for two reasons, oneStitch and Mason would not stop blowing up her messages, which caught Jynx off guard because Mason never texted her.

And twosocial media wasn't improving her mood at all. Her Instagram feed was about how Nature, Masquerade's sister, had aced a botany test because she was able to grow the world's rarest flower. No matter where she looked, she was reminded about Masquerade and his family, which only made her feel worse. Masquerade and his quintuplets had been missing for two and a half days now. She could only wait to go on that stupid trip, eight more days before she felt safe.

Due to paranoia, Jynx skipped school, fearing discovery by Jake or anyone else. Now, Jynx wanted to do some research to find out who Echo was and, most definitely, Zeus in her mother's memories. Although online sources were hard to find, the Echo didn't have any real identity. Jynx couldn't help but wonder: Was Zeus really Masquerade's dad? Earlier, Zeus had answered her prayer. Jynx couldn't help but wonder who her savior was going to be.

She waddled out of her bed, tripping over her bed sheets and blankets. The extra room was small and had a mini TV that Jynx never used. Her bed was on the floor, and the mattress was smelly and old. She covered the only window with heavy blinds. Jynx had heavy eye bags, a result of her excessive crying.

Jynx slowly approached the door, hesitating to touch the knob. Standing there, her head in a daze, she opened the door. She was the only one awake, sharing the house with only Jace. She made her way downstairs and into the kitchen. She couldn't tell if it was day or night.

The kitchen window was wide open, revealing that it was the middle of the night. Jace sat on the dining table, eating cereal. Jace's house was modern, with a table positioned in the middle of the kitchen, like an island. Jace looked up at her weirdly.

"It looks like you haven't slept in days. Are you okay, Jynx?" he asked, and Jynx flinched at the question.

"Yeah, I just needed some space," she croaked. Jynx realized she hadn't seen Jace since she moved in two days ago. She also hasn't eaten anything in forty-eight hours. She'd slept through most of it. Her stomach grumbled, and Jace looked concerned.

"Do you want to talk about it yet?" Jace said, his voice still in a concerned tone.

"Yes I do, over a fine course meal," Jynx said, sitting down on the other side of the table. Gracefully, she looked at the fridge while Jace prepared instant ramen noodles. Jynx wasn't fond of them, but she didn't argue as she would eat literally anything at that moment. As the noodles were brought to a boil, Jynx explained the entire situation to Jace, who had a terrified look on his face the entire time.

"So you do believe that Zeus is real now?" Jace asked. Jynx recalled when he and Tamer had apparently seen Zeus in their second-period class.

"Yes, of course. He appeared in my mother's visions when Echo messed up and showed us the wrong memory," Jynx explained. Jace had a weird look on his face.

"Echo messed up that bad? But how? He's one of the strongest gods out there!" Jace said, and Jynx felt fear shave away at her body. "Then there's the possibility he messed up on purpose, because anger can bring out an awakened god's power. . ." He said, rising the calamity of the situation.

"What?! Echo's a god?!" Jynx's voice shuddered. "If he's a god, can't he just kill me himself?"

"Yes, Echo is the son of Sura. The way you described him, he has to be Sura's son." Jace said. "Sura is Misa's brother; they are both primordial gods. Which means they're very dangerous, and so are their kids," The way Jace described it gave her goosebumps. Jynx shivered. "Normally, I'm not into mythology, but since I saw Zeus, I figured I better study it,"

"So, how long do you reckon I have to live?" Jynx used all her mental strength not to have a mental breakdown right now. Tears started filling her eyes again.

"He's messing with you, Jynx. He could kill you any second now, and II just don't know how long you have," Jace said, with an extremely saddened look on his face. "I bet he;s waiting for the power to finally brew up inside you, so he can see what exactly it can do."

By this time, tears rolled down Jynx's face and cheeks. She couldn't stop it. "Jace, I'm scared. . ." She sputtered, finding it hard to talk. Her breathing stopped, and her heart skipped a few beats. She was losing control of her own body. Falling from her chair, Jace quickly grabbed her.

"JynxNot now, we need to come up with a plan. It'll be hard fighting a god, but we have to try. I will not stand and let you die," Jace comforted her. "You know, you gotta be pretty dangpowerful if a god wants you dead." He tried comforting.

"They don't know if I'll awaken my mother's feared powers, but if I do, I bet we can use it as a weapon against Echo." Jynx hiccuped. She sniffled in between sentences.

"Of course, we just have to wait. It might come soon, who knows?" Jace replied, still nurturing Jynx, who calmed down. Her body still jerked.

"It might be dangerous for me, we don't know, I didn't bond with my mom much before she died. And she definitely didn't tell me anything about a hidden power," Jynx explained.

"Wait, how come Echo wants to kill you? Why is Echo even involved with this whole mess anyway? Why would a god involve himself in human affairs?" Jace asked, confusing Jynx even more.

"I don't know Jace. Maybe he got bored."

"Well, this adds to the possibility of your power. It could threaten the lives and flow of the gods as we know it. No wonder they're so scared," Jace whispered. The oven beeped out of nowhere and scared both Jynx and Jace. He served Jynx, and they ate in silence for a while. It didn't take much to make Jynx happy, but she knew eating ramen at three in the morning didn't help much.

"Get your jacket on. We're going outside," Jace said while standing up.

"What are you crazy?? It's three in the damn morning! And it's snowing!" Jynx argued.

"Trust me, it'll take away all this stress." He argued back. Eventually, Jynx gave in and geared up. Hat, jacket, gloves, scarf, and an extra pair of pants. Jace's size was a size too extra, but it made her warmer and feel safer. Jace turned on the back porch light, and the two walked outside. Jace's backyard was huge, with apple trees in the background, it was winter though, so there were no apples anyway. Jace looked at the stars from the patio.

"Remind me why we're out here again?" Jynx asked, staring at the stars as well. She was still anxious, her hands were still shaking, not from the cold but from anxiety instead. Jace ignored her and walked towards the end of the porch, walking off into the lapse of darkness.

He stepped into the snow and bent over slowly. Jynx looked at him, making a face. He made a snowball, and before Jynx could react, he threw it at her. The snowball hit her shoulder, and Jace giggled.

"Seriously! This is what you made me come out for?" Jynx said in a harsh tone and rubbed the snow off her shoulder lightly.

"Come on, Jynx, just throw one back!" He said playfully while preparing another. Jynx still scowled at him before she stepped forward, smiling at him. She ran to the other side of the porch and prepared her own snowball. Jace smiled lightly and tried covering it. She threw it lightly. Jace stepped away from it and winced.

"That's it? You have to do better than that, you know?" Jace mocked. Jynx formed another snowball, and Jace decided to throw his first, before she did. Jynx ducked under the attack and she threw hers accordingly. The snowball hit Jace in the stomach. He looked offended, making another one quickly. Jynx ran in the other direction and picked up more snow. She ran towards the trees, and Jace still followed. The snow glittered across the yard, the silver moonlight bathing the yard.

Jace kept pressing Jynx with snowballs as she tried to escape. They threw snowballs back and forth as the moon illuminated them. In the moonlight, Jynx's hot pink hair glowed, contrasting with Jace's messy brown hair turning white from the snow. This event showed more of her unforeseen power, promising something interesting.

Their laughter lightened each other's moods as they effortlessly threw snowballs. Jace tried wiping his clothes off, but Jynx threw more snow before he had the chance to. One snowball fight wiped out Jynx's entire mind and problems. Hiding behind trees, bushes, and rocks, the two played for a while. It took them a while to realize how much time had passed. Jynx's hands were getting cold.

"Hey Jace, I'm ready to go inside! My hands are freezing. . ." Jynx yelled from behind a tree trunk. Jace dropped his snowball and took forever to respond.

"Wait! I have something to show you first." He screamed from the darkness. Jynx walked up to Jace slowly, hoping it wasn't some trick. Jace held up his hands. Jynx had just noticed he didn't have gloves on. Jace grabbed her hands and cupped them in between his. Jynx stared at him for a moment, their eyes locking. Jace's eyes seemed to glow a brighter blue than usual. "Watch!" He exclaimed loudly, as he noticed her eyes drifting.

Jace's hands warmed up quickly, and steam arose from them. Jynx's hands were toasty in no time. She was surprised. The two remained in eye contact.

"Woah, you have powers!? Why didn't you tell me?" Jynx felt a little betrayed, but she couldn't stay mad at him, as he's helped a lot lately.

"It's not that big of a deal, it's only, fire-" He said, as he raised his hand higher. From his hand, a blast of blue fire erupted. "I can regulate it from any part of my body." He raised his arms as steam smoked off his jacket. Jynx took the hint, plus she was shivering anyway. She locked into his jacket and wrapped her arms around him, allowing for a very warm and promising hug. Jace's body was warm and comfy.

The snowball fight only distracted her from the drama. Tears rolled from her eyes again. She couldn't help it. Jace was there to comfort her, however they didn't say anything. Jace knew she just needed to cry. Jynx didn't know how long they stood there, but it was probably for the best of them. Then, as the moment was about to die out of its grace, Jynx's eyes glinted with absolute pink, and her hair started beaming with the same color. Soon enough, the pink color enlightened the snow around them, overshading the light of the moon. In contrast, Jace's hair started glowing blue from his affinity of blue flames. The mental image played in her mind, imaging the colors of blue and pink mixing, making an absolute parallel between the signature colors of male and female. Jace was the peanut butter to her jelly.

For a moment, the hug felt surreal, like there wasn't that constant other pressure that Jynx always felt when hugging Jace. Usually, she'd feel another presence on top of her whenever the two made contact, this time there was nothing. He even breathed more normally, with a collapse of passion. She noticed she only felt this for two reasonsher power changed something from within him, or it was his power that changed his overall presence. She wondered what her power could even be, now that it's lightened up almost three times so far. At least she knew it had something to do with the color of pink, which made her happy.

"I finally feel free, like there isn't that stupid force tugging on me, all the damn time. . ." He said, before Jynx locked away from the hug, ready to head inside.

"What do you mean?" She looked up at him, before noticing his eyes change from blue, back to brown, and eventually black. He snorted, coughed, and looked terrified for a quick second.

"Nothing! Holy, I just overheated myself in that jacket. My bad!" He reassured. "Let's go inside." Jace gestured the two inside the house and finished their noodles.

"You're going to school tomorrow..." Jace said demandingly. "We don't need you failing any classes either now." He said as he washed the few dishes they used.

"I'll go the day after tomorrow. I still don't feel well," Jynx couldn't help but wonder if Jace was the savior Zeus was talking about. After all, anyone could be an angel in disguise. Or a devil, for that matter. In Jynx's mind, still the only thing that occurred was Jake and how he was probably hunting her at this very moment.

Chapter 9
Masquerade

Masquerade detested the flavor of lava, and Cerberus wasn't making it any more enjoyable. The dog was fireproof, but that did not mean his passengers were. The three-headed demon dog was running across an ocean of blue lava. Naturally, the creature could swim. Masquerade found that peculiar. The azure lava was quite stunning, he had to admit. However, it didn't make him appreciate the scorching heat.

Hermes was accustomed to it, while Dark observed it as if it were some ancient weapon. Masquerade was consciously restraining himself, avoiding accidentally pushing Dark into the lake. Infinity wore an uneasy expression throughout.

"Hey, Hermes! Mind if I take the lead?" Masquerade called out from the back of the hellhound. Hermes turned back instinctively.

"What? Do you want to lead this behemoth? He might throw you off, but sure!" Hermes said, almost sounding like he didn't care if Masquerade fell into an ocean of lava. Hermes snapped, and the two teleported places. Masquerade was standing on the middle head of the huge hound. He held two chains that connected to the muzzle attached to the head. The first thing Masquerade did was hoist the chains upwards with all his strength, this prompted the monster to charge forward at full speed.

Almost knocking Masquerade off, the chains were the only things keeping him in place. Cerberus took that personally and jerked his head upwards. This forced Masquerade into the air. He held on for his dear life as Cerberus showed no signs of mercy, or slowing down.

"Dammit! You dumb dog! Put me down now!" Masquerade screamed as sparks of lava found their way into his open mouth. It hurt, but Masquerade didn't pay attention to it much. Cerberus smirked at Masquerade with disrespect, staring back in a menacing manner. Masquerade wasn't going to let that slide. Cerberus accelerated through hidden sparks of azure glow.

Masquerade scaled the chains as they flailed through the air. Hermes was watching. Climbing the chains as if they were ladders, Masquerade and the hound accelerated even further. This almost knocked him off the chain, but his overwhelming growing strength saved him. Once Masquerade reached the end of the chain, he climbed atop the dog's snout. Cerberus responded by exhaling through his nose. The air was strong enough to blow Masquerade off, but before he flew off, he grabbed the chain again. However, this didn't save him, and he fell straight into the lava on his butt.

Now, Masquerade definitely expected to die just now, but the lava was shallow, which surprised the Hell out of him (no pun intended). The entire left side was burning up as he was being dragged by the huge dog. Masquerade anchored his feet, ignoring the pain of the searing lava. He tugged on the chain with all his strength. At first, this did nothing, but then it caused the dog to slow down. For scale, Masquerade was the size of this dog's toenail. Masquerade was practically water skiing, except the boat was a hellhound, and the string was a huge searing chain, and the water was lava, blue lava.

Masquerade tugged even more, summoning strength out of nowhere. This made Cerberus stop completely and turn in the direction, making him steer across the lava like he was doing a donut in an open parking lot. The dog swerved to this side as Masquerade steered it. In response, Cerberus tugged the chain upwards, propelling Masquerade swiftly skyward. The dog then tugged downwards, launching Masquerade toward the lava with a resounding impact.

That still didn't kill him for some reason, his god-like durability carrying him through the harsh conditions of this battle. Masquerade was pissed now, he was not about to be thrown around by a mutt.

"You stupid pooch! You'll regret treating me like a chew toy!" Masquerade yelled defiantly. Cerberus looked at him faithfully, probably wondering how he was still alive. The dog laughed at Masquerade, they exchanged vengeful glares.

Masquerade tugged on the chain downwards. Cerberus was thrown off his guard, and the dog tumbled heads first into the lava. Masquerade smiled at this feat, as he was actually able to outstrength it. Cerberus tried getting up, but Masquerade tugged even more, this time however, instead of pulling the dog, the chain snapped off. The force made him fall backward and sit down in the lava on his ass. Cerberus took this opportunity to stand back on his feet. The dog then roared, and the wind that exerted made Masquerade fly into the air.

He was still holding onto the chain, which followed him into the air. Masquerade started flying slowly and whipped the chain at the hound, like you see in those movies where cowboys catch animals. Cerberus tried catching the chain in his mouth, but this caused more injury to the canine, making a red slash incur inside its pink gums. The middle head's eyes started glowing a fiery red color, and he opened his mouth, which also had the same color intruding from it.

Fire blasted from its mouth, and Masquerade found himself caught in the middle of it. He fell back into the lava, still not giving up, the fierce flames covering his entire body. Steam fused, his skin reattached, and his muscles nourished, quickly healing fast enough to attack once more. The head on the left charged something as well, this time its eyes were light blue, and so was its mouth. Masquerade tried whipping the chain again but failed miserably, dropping it in the lava, and scratching his already burnt wrist. A wintry cold blast extruded from the dog and hit Masquerade directly, once more.

Now, Masquerade was burnt and frostbit. He put himself in this and would get himself out of it. The third and last head charged yet another attack. This time, it was purple. Masquerade had a crazy idea. He took the chain and jumped directly in front of the head.

"Masquerade! What the hell are you doing?!" Infinity screamed at him from the back of the dog, he was surprised he was still even holding on.

"I got myself into this, and I'll get myself out of it! DO NOT HELP ME!" He screamed as the purple attack erupted from the hound. The plan went according to plan. Masquerade was pissed that he hadn't won a single fight he got himself into since he's been in Olympus. He was going to win this time. To Masquerade's aid, the attack was lightning. He lifted his hand upwards, and all the lightning absorbed into him, aiding his strength, speed, and energy. This was due to his already natural affinity for lightning, given to him at birth.

Lightning pulsed through his veins and poured out of his eyes, power coursing through him. There was so much lightning that it was pouring out of his body. He flew towards the middle head quickly, with a flash of lightning, smoke, wind, and an explosion. Cerberus recoiled and tried dodging. Masquerade uppercutted the dog, and in one swift attack, the fight was over. The dog went flying upwards and thunder struck so loudly it could probably be heard through the entirety of Hell.

Hermes had saved his siblings from falling into the lava, as they were floating on a golden raft. To his surprise, Dark and the others were actually cheering. Cerberus hit the lava with a loud thud, but it still wasn't louder than the thunderbolt.

"That was badass!" Hyper said, jumping up and down and swinging all over the place. Lazer was hyped as well, as he shot celebration lasers everywhere. Hermes was even impressed.

"Great feat, boy, the first since Hercules! But now we have no way to Hades!" Masquerade was surprised at how he said negative things in a positive tone. He looked disappointed.

"Wrong again, Hermes." A sinister voice appeared out of nowhere. Hermes looked up and directly at Hades himself. His presence made Masquerade shiver and everyone else did too.

"When was I ever wrong? What do you mean 'again'?" Hermes asked while staring at Hades weirdly.

"You talk too much. No wonder they nominated you for the messenger." Hades exclaimed and laughed with his sinister tone.

"You didn't even answer my question!"

"Silence, excuse of a god!" Hades bellowed, and Hermes shut up quickly. He looked at Masquerade. He shivered. He didn't know what to do. "You," Hades pointed at him with his black painted fingernails. Masquerade shuddered again, looking at him fearfully.

"Yes? What do you want?" Masquerade said with a tone of disrespect. Dark looked at him, warning him not to say anything stupid.

"You knocked up my dog pretty bad. I might have to punish you, but I already have something in mind for all of you!" Hades exclaimed with joy, which Masquerade thought would be impossible since his voice was so unbelievably deep. Everyone else looked scared except Hermes, who was picking at a scab on his arm.

"Which is?" Masquerade questioned.

"A spot in my arena, my tournament. I'll have you fight any heroes that got stuck in my lovely Tartarus." Hades explained. "If you win, you get to escape! If you don't, you'll die and spend eternity with me!" He threatened. Masquerade sweated, well, he already was since it's a zillion degrees down where he was.

"What! What kind of deal is that!? NO! I DECLINE!" Masquerade raised his voice. He looked at Hades with impulsivity.

"You're way too loud and impulsive, little one. I think you'll be the best fighter there!" Hades said, his voice still uncomfortably happy.

"I hope you know we're the sons of Zeus! You won't get away with this!" Lazer yelled at him. Masquerade was surprised, as Lazer hadn't back-talked to a god until now, especially since it was Hades, the menacing of them all, maybe except Demeter because she was ugly as the potatoes she grew, according to Masquerade.

"You think I'm stupid, Lazer? No, I am not. I know who my brother's offspring are." His voice boomed. Lazer shivered. They all stood in the middle of a huge lava lake, with nothing else to be seen for miles.

"I'll get you guys situated!" Hades expressed. Then, the group was teleported in the middle of a huge arena. Like, the arena was really huge, bigger than anything Masquerade had ever seen. The stadium around it was filled with seats that were occupied. Occupied by millions upon millions of people, maybe demons. Masquerade didn't have stage fright, but even he was horrified.

"Spirits of the Dead! Listen up!" Hades exclaimed, and the crowd listened accordingly. "I bring new contenders!" He said, wavering his hand towards the five. "The games will continue today! VERY SOON!" Hades yelped in excitement. Then he snapped, and the five were teleported away once again, again, something they were getting really used to. They were in a room filled with equipment, and Dark looked extremely worried.

"Infinity, you should gear up well. I doubt he'll put us in duo fights, meaning you'll fight alone. With no signature power, you'll die against your enemy." Dark explained to Infinity so casually, as if he didn't care if he actually did manage to die. He gave him a shield, Infinity also looking gravely frightened.

"How long is he giving us to prepare?" Hyper said while grabbing a sword.

"I don't know, but it's Hades, it more than likely won't be very long. . ." Dark said while still fitting the shield on Infinity's arm.

Lazer didn't grab anything, and neither did Masquerade. Dark used his blood, so he grabbed a few knives. Then, just when Masquerade got comfortable, they were all teleported once again, but this time, one sibling was missing—Infinity. And on the end of the arena, he stood with a sword and shield in hand. On the other side of the stadium lay three siblings, or at least they looked related.

"The Furies, otherwise known as The Kindly Ones," Dark mumbled as he cracked his knuckles. If it came to it, Masquerade would jump into the arena.

Infinity was scared out of his mind; he had no clue how to fight, and he had no special powers, and he was fighting three sisters who looked like they would shred him. Infinity raised his sword miserably. The Furies laughed at him from across the arena. Infinity covered himself with his shield. He had no clue what he was doing, and now he was going to die. He tried his best, but he wasn't going to die without a fight.

He charged the three like an idiot, catching them off guard. The Furies got into formation. They all had wings. One flew to the left and the other to the right, as the last stood in the middle. The left Fury flew in to attack. He raised his shield and blocked. He felt proud until the right Fury attacked at the same time. She scratched Infinity's arm and kicked his head into the ground. His shield was taken from him almost instantly.

Infinity swung his sword quickly, but the Fury dodged and hissed at him in return. He tried getting to his feet, but the first Fury attacked him head-on. Using her massive claws, it scratched his face directly. Their wounds burned his skin. He tried dodging their attack but failed. They were already beating him down horribly.

Infinity's vision blurred. He felt like he was going to die already, barely thirty seconds into the fight. Infinity fell to his knees, his body gave up on him, it wasn't even healing itself anymore. The crowd wasn't cheering anymore. Infinity felt as if he had failed his entire family. The son of Zeus couldn't even beat a few bats, and now he couldn't even get up. He looked over to his siblings, who were disappointed instead of worried.

He knew if he didn't win, he would die. Infinity got to his feet once more. The Furies looked surprised, their plan didn't come to fruition. Infinity stared at them with fierceness. He felt he at least needed to try. Standing up, he felt stronger out of nowhere. A voice rang throughout his head.

Do not feel so down, Infinity. I will show you a path. Zeus's voice played in his head. Take my offering, and you will see your true power. Infinity accepted. His spirit rose.

"INFINITY, DO NOT DIE TO A BUNCH OF RAT-LOOKING DEMONS! STAND UP AND SHOW THEM WHY YOU'RE BETTER!" Masquerade screamed from the stands. Infinity smiled. The Furies tried attacking again, but Infinity dodged everyone effortlessly with exact precision. As one swiped by, he shocked her with a quick jab of lightning. It didn't affect her much, but it was something, something he couldn't achieve before.

Then, throughout his heart, arteries, capillaries, and veins, he felt a new pulse deep within him. His body felt as if it would split, his blood vibrating deeply. Then it actually did, making an exact clone of himself. He glanced at his siblings, who had shocked expressions. Then it happened again, and a third clone appeared. And again, making four. Infinity and his clones looked at the Furies, who were still hissing viciously. The clones jumped in at the same time, overwhelming the three at once.

It was now five versus three. That five quickly turned into ten, which then turned into twenty. The clones kept duplicating, filling the arena and overwhelming the Furies. The crowd in the stands started cheering wildly as his clones beat the Furies to a pulp.

"Infinity, the Son of Zeus wins!" A speaker from the stands had announced loudly as the crowd cheered even louder. They started throwing items, like food and even golden tokens into the field, all for Infinity to collect. He finally felt proud of himself for once. Infinity was teleported back to the stands, replacing Hyper. The other three looked amazed to see him.

"Bro! That was sick. How'd you pull that off?" Masquerade said, spilling his concession stand drink. Infinity looked at his hands and diverted his attention back to the arena. His clones were cleared, and Hyper stood in his position. Infinity winced.

"I don't know, but we should probably focus on this fight-" He said lightly, pointing in Hyper's direction. Hyper didn't look scared; however, he looked ready. Masquerade focused on the other side of the arena. On the other side was a large bull, dubbed The Minotaur.

Hyper didn't need weapons to show the Minotaur who was going to win. The bull tried charging him desperately, but Hyper played it safe. When it charged, Hyper moved out of the way, jumping on its back quickly. The Minotaur tried reaching for him but failed. Hyper grabbed onto his horns and threw the thing straight into the ground.

The bull roared, knocking Hyper into the air with one swift head movement. Once Hyper was in the air, it used its massive legs to launch itself into the air. Hyper had no time to react, and the Minotaur grabbed Hyper's entire head with one palm. He smashed his entire body into the ground. Dust arose into the battlefield.

"Bind him!" Hyper screamed at the dust in the air, and it responded accordingly. The dust had turned into chains and bound the bull down, branching out to create strong whips. Hyper generated lightning throughout his body quickly, walking to the chained Minotaur and taunting the poor thing. He swung his fist so hard it almost dislocated itself. The punch landed directly across the Minotaur's jaw. All the lightning in his body dispersed in that one attack, sending shockwaves throughout the thing's afferent and efferent nerves. The bull flung across the stadium faster than the lightning it was just shocked with.

The bull got back up and charged once again. Hyper coated himself in lightning quickly. He got himself into a racing position, putting one knee on the floor, and his hand in the same position. The bull still charged and was getting closer. Hyper charged back and in a flash, the two collided, but Hyper was ten times faster. And in the end, Hyper was fast enough to phase straight through the bull. The Minotaur fell to the floor in exhaustment. Hyper stood right next to his body, with its heart in his hands. The crowd roared in excitement, and he crushed the bull's heart with his lightning coated hands, making the crowd cheer even louder.

Dark was surprised Hyper had gotten rid of his enemy so fast. He didn't know what to expect from his own. He was pretty confident he could win, however. On the other side of the arena stood a normal-looking person, he'd say at least. He had purple curly hair, with eyes that emitted spirals that made Dark sleepy just looking at them. He knew who this was already; Hypnos the Greek incarnate of sleep. Dark couldn't help but feel sluggish and trip over his own feet, as he attempted running towards the god, he couldn't make it even a few feet without falling to the ground. The crowd was disappointed, and Dark lay, couldn't even open his eyes. His mind fell into a deep sleep.

Once he opened his eyes, he was in a completely different area than before. His brain was foggy, and he saw miles and miles of trees. The forest contained many whispers of a promising silent night that haunted him from the void of shadows. A thick layer of fog covered the ground, making the trees appear towering over him. Dark walked forward, trying to see if he could get anywhere.

What's your motive, Dark? Your goal? The reason you keep going? A voice intruded his brain, its noise echoing in his mind. He tried thinking about the question, there was no real reason to keep trying. This was his first adventure, but he suspected it definitely wouldn't be his last. Dark thought about every god there was, still even now, he knew what he wanted in the end.

"I want to be recognized by the god known as Misa. In the books I've read, he seems to be the most powerful god there is. I would like to meet him and his brother. I'll push myself as a god to be able to be compared to the two." Dark said, thinking about his distant future, he had also wanted to meet Mardo.

Oh Dear? Misa!? He's a tough one, and very, very. . . how do I put this. . . mean! The voice responded.

"You've met him? How?" Dark questions. "Who are you?"

Oh me? I'm the person you're fighting Dark. Hypnos! Dark felt bad. He would have to kill Hypnos to be able to succeed in life. If he didn't win this fight, he would die himself. Dark didn't know what to do.

No need to worry. I won't hurt you. I just want to make sure that your motives are right, which, yours are not youngling. You shouldn't want to be compared to a liar like those two. Misa is the worst of them all. He manipulates his children into doing his dirty work. I've never met Sura, but I bet he's just as bad. If anything, you might want to fight against them if you can. They've been controlling the gods for far too long. Someone needs to put an end to them, and I believe in you. I truly believe you can bring a stop to their reign of terror.

Dark didn't understand what Hypnos meant at all. "You want me to fight two primordial gods?! How am I supposed to defeat them?! It's near impossible." Dark said.

You may believe that at first, but there is a way. Your father was able to stand up to Echo. Who was the son of Sura, so I don't doubt you'll be able to beat one of them with help.

"That's my dad, thoughHow will I be able to stand up?" Dark asked.

Gods get stronger with age, but the offspring of a god will always be stronger than its parents. Which means you and your siblings will all be stronger than Zeus, one of them may already have surpassed him. . .

Dark was surprised. *I'll return to you now. Everyone in the stadium will see that you have defeated me, although that's not what happened. I hope I can inspire you in this quest to defeat Misa and Sura. Bring an end to their torture.*

Dark was in the stadium again. The crowd cheered loudly through the violent reigns of dark memories. He looked down at his feet to see Hypnos's dead and bloody body.

I'm not dead, Dark. Hades's helpers are immortal, so no need to worry. His siblings were also cheering with excitement. He was then teleported to his spot. This time, Masquerade was gone. Dark smiled, he had no need to worry this time. Masquerade would win his fight with no problem, and all his brothers thought so too, kicking their feet back on the stand, shoving their mouths of popcorn. Thinking back to Hypnos and his dialogue, Dark felt that even Masquerade would help him with his quest, he imagined himself and Masquerade versus Misa and Sura. He truly loved him, no matter how many times he got into fights with the gods. Dark watched the arena. Masquerade's opponent stood tall and muscular. The entire crowd was roaring in absolute relativity, and he knew why. He squinted at the enemy, only for Dark to realize this was Hercules.

Masquerade was stupid, he knew that by now. He wasn't stupid enough to know he was fighting Hercules, however. He had to get super lucky here, or else he would die and fail. Hercules stood there, chest high and a wild smirk on his face as the crowd cheered him on. Masquerade felt his hands start smoking up. Then, his energy level rose high, and adrenaline carried him through this battle. The sound of explosions echoed through the stadium, making the crowd silent.

He was already high into the air, which wiped Hercules' smile straight off his stupid face. Masquerade used more explosions to boost himself towards Hercules. Once he was right next to him, Masquerade cupped his hands together. He looked like he was about to shoot a laser from his hand, but instead, a massive explosion covered the floor. The blast radius was so large it almost hit the crowd, the debris flailing into the hellscape.

He landed on the floor, thinking he won. Out of the rising smoke, Hercules' huge body moved faster than Masquerade could imagine. His pure hands were bigger than his entire head. Then, he couldn't react, and Hercules grabbed him by the head, gripping with all his strength, bringing a small crack to his mandible. He smashed his entire body into the floor. Then, before Masquerade could recover, he was grabbed by his feet.

"Nice try. I appreciate new warriors, but your path ends here. I'm truly sorry." Hercules then whipped his entire body to the entire side of the arena. He smashed straight through the wall. The force of it broke every single bone in his limp, fierce body. Masquerade was going to die, and his heart pounded with rage. The crowd cheered for this man for too long, and he wanted to be the one to make him fall. Masquerade blacked out as he heard his siblings screaming for him to get back up.

He wasn't finished. He refused to die at the hands of some loser in hell. Masquerade opened his eyes, he saw Anubis, once more.

"I believe I've seen you before?" Anubis said, his voice was lightening, alleviating the feel of the room. He observed Masquerade. "Oh right, you! Masquerade! How's it been, buddy?" He asked. "You were lucky last time, I reckon, but it seems to me that you died due to Hercules. Very reminiscent of dying to such a hero!" Anubis talked small.

"I don't want to be here. I won't give up. I refuse to die!" He screamed at Anubis. His bones and body were healed perfectly, something that occurred twice since he's been dead.

"I'm truly sorry, young one, but no one wants to die-" He was interrupted.

"No, you got it all wrong. I REFUSE! I'm not asking you to save me. I'm going back and winning. I'm telling you, IT'S NOT OVER UNTIL I WIN!" Anubis had a shocked expression as Masquerade's body turned into particles, yellow energy dissipating into flashes of anger and power. His heart's ventricles contracted, pushing his blood through the arteries of his body. He then blacked out again.

The crowd was still cheering, unknowing of what was upcoming. His siblings now seemed to be crying in despair, and Masquerade couldn't help but smile. Hercules was posing. Hades was on his throne, cheering the man baby on. Hermes stood next to him, also cheering for Hercules, he couldn't help but think of how much of a fake the gods were, which ramped his rage through the roof. Masquerade stood up, revenge boiling in his fists. Hercules turned around like some battle sense activated within him, even more anger rose in his body.

"Hey, look who it is? Came back for round two or what?" Hercules bellowed from across the arena.

"Consider it round one," Masquerade said as he moved towards Hercules, unaware of a speed boost hidden inside him. In seconds, he was across the arena, in Hercules' face. His entire body ached like needles piercing every single pore in his skin, and he didn't know why. There was no smile on Hercules anymore, this time, it was on Masquerade's. "Got anything cocky to say before I kick your ass?"

"I accept your challenge," Hercules said, his humbleness soaring through the air like a plane landing. Masquerade nudged his shoulder lightly, a spark of explosive lightning occurred upon impact. He didn't know how to explain it, but all the energy stored in his body was released in that one interaction. His body no longer ached, and an explosion occurred, sending Hercules straight across the field in one swift movement of air. His eyes darkened, staring down at Masquerade as his body ragdolled against bare concrete. He raised his foot, and Masquerade was across the arena again, it was hard for him to adjust to this new speed.

He kicked Hercules once more, more explosions erupting in his face. Masquerade could now understand his new power; he could make explosions produced from any part of his body now. This time he made an explosion from his elbow, boosting his punch force, where he then used an explosion in his fists as well, double attack power. He landed a quick, clean hit on Hercules' face, knocking a few teeth out with one quick jab, the wind then followed, producing a nasty double impact. Hercules tried countering, but Masquerade was too fast, already approaching his back side.

He was stepping around every part of the floor of the arena around Hercules. All at the same time, punching him in several different directions. It reminded him of a dance, one that you would see at a masquerade, and at this point in time, Hercules couldn't even see him blitzing around. Masquerade quickly made a lightning sword and cut into his hamstring, making him fall to his feet with a large gush of intruding blood. He then stood in front of him and stared into his soul.

"Normally, I'd feel bad for doing this to a man, but I would call this a treat, considering you're one of my brothers. You've been too disrespectful, so I'm not sparing you," Masquerade said. He got his feet ready and looked like he was going to kick a soccer ball, Hercules harboring a terrified look on his face. Masquerade released his foot, kicking Hercules straight into the crouch, the crowd cheering.

Then Masquerade snapped. First, an explosion blew up his crotch some more, but then, in every place Masquerade stepped, touched, and looked at in the fight, had erupted into erupting large explosions. In quick seconds, Hercules' body was scattered across the arena in ligaments and mangled parts of limbs and tendons. The arena was going crazy, with Hades having a displeased look on him. Hermes stood up quickly.

"We better get going, Hades. Zeus might want his children back. . ." Hermes stuttered. Hades looked ready to kill Masquerade.

"Right after you killed my best champion? No, these five aren't going anywhere!" Hades' deep voice alarmed. Hermes winced, unable to do much, before Masquerade jumped directly into the air, facing his fierce fangs of destruction towards the strongest god in the scene, which was no other than Hades. His brothers, astonished, jumped over the railing and ran into the open battlefield, knowing exactly what was about to be revealed. Hermes' expression changed immediately, teleporting in advance. Then, the two gods' eyes matched, locked and pulsed with energy. Hades, the god of the underworld, and Masquerade, the god of destruction, were flying towards each other with their powers charged at a standstill.

However, Masquerade was one step faster than the darkened abandoned god, which proved his quick and successful one handed victory, that was only caused by a mere underestimation caused on Hades's part. In one quick judgment of Masquerade's wrist, and a flicker of energy in his eyes, an explosion was released that was able to replicate that of a vacuum bomb, filled with explosive tons. In a quick second, the realization of destruction was seen to the crowd, as the entire arena was flattened, killing the 'innocent' demons that happened to be in the blast radius, in almost an instant.

Then he was teleported away, once more, Hermes met him eye-to-eye, their expressions gazed with disappointment. "Now I see why Zeus went through so much trouble to punish you guys. You just seem to attract danger." Hermes said while picking at a scab on his arm. "Don't feel bad, however, as the offspring of such a powerful god, it's only natural that demons track you," he continued. "They want to kill you before you grow strong into a powerful god such as Zeus," Hermes explained.

Masquerade saw the familiar entrance to Olympus again, realizing nothing has changed since they've been gone the first time. Hermes pointed towards the throne room, and he quickly left again, indicating that they're on their own for this one. Dark had a grim look on his face.

"Hey, Masquerade, before we go home, I have something to tell you," He said. Masquerade stopped, Dark then explained all about the experience with Hypnos and how Misa was an enemy they had to take out.

"I don't know Dark, Misa is very powerful. I don't think we could take him out." Masquerade stared at him concisely, ignoring his already rise in power.

"Yeah, but Hypnos mentioned the kids of gods being stronger than their parents in the future, so maybe we have a chance when we're grown?" Dark suggested. the stones in the river didn't appear like last time, making an already disruption in the overall scenery. Masquerade stepped into the water and winced, the others following and copying his expression.

"Isn't Mardo Misa's son?" Hyper asked, "So, does that make us related to them?"

"It's just a saying, and he's not actually our uncle. He's just very close friends with our parents." Dark explained, which scared even Masquerade. *Why would they be considered friends if Misa is such a bad influence?* He concluded that possible, they were friends by force, meaning they HAD to comply with whatever he said. This made him feel more aware of the impact that Misa had upon the world. Masquerade invaded Dark's thoughts by accident, who was already thinking about the probabilities of them even meeting the god of shadows.

Negative thoughts crept into their brains as they got closer to the waterfall, almost like there was some dark presence that swept the area. Two voices murmured from behind the waterfall, discussing something incredibly important. One of the voices that could be recognized was their father, and the other was unknown, so far. The second voice was dark and brutal, giving off an eerie vibe. A voice that sounded horrible and charming at the same time, giving the bittering feeling of grief right after doing something that was good. The voice was so convincing it could tell Masquerade to kill someone, and it'd actually convince him to do so.

As they approached the waterfall, the presence binded them down almost like pressured air. Masquerade stepped into the water, dipping his feet in the cold freezing temperatures of the Greek river. The room was unbelievably dark at first, producing the same negative vibe as before, still he felt as the presence grew hands itself, and choked their throats so they couldn't breathe. A collapsed lung covered the feeling of his alveoles not being able to expand. He tried adjusting his eyes, but the dark mist remained in a thick covering sensation that crept into his open dilated pupils. The voices were louder, but they couldn't make out anything. He tried looking towards his siblings, they haven't even crossed the water yet, something that Masquerade didn't blame them.

He raised his arm, the wind current following gracefully. With one sweeping swing, he tried moving the dark mist out of the way, but nothing happened. The voices stopped, the room darkened even more, and he could barely see three steps in front of him in alarming moments. In response to the wind, the mist died down quickly, sweeping away like dust traveling across the soil. The room revealed itself faster than he expected.

He saw Zeus on his throne. And a tall skinny, but still muscular man, who had a tan tone, and his eyes glowed purple, brighter than the sun. His hair was mainly black, with many shades and streaks of gray. His smile was devious, yet so pretty at the same time. He wore all black, which looked oddly like a clown's attire, and on top of that, he had a black polka-dot party hat as an accessory. Around his eyes, it almost seemed like heavy mascara and eyeliner that was heavily smeared, making him appear like a woman that had been crying for too long.

The tip of his nose was also dipped in black, and to top it all off, he had black lipstick that smeared too far off to the side of his cheeks, making his mouth look bigger than it was. Masquerade found it oddly attractive. Two long slices also consisted of makeup that represented deep scars that intruded over his eyes. These were clown-shaped across vertically on the eyes. The two stared at each other awkwardly in silence for a long moment, his siblings broke the silence as they ripped through the water. The look and expression in Dark's eyes made the clown smile wide, making Dark almost choked on his own saliva. He stared the man up and down, nodding his head, and observing his features. No one said a word, painting the canvas of silence.

"Well well well, look who it is, interrupting *my* private meeting!" The man snarled before Dark could even open his mouth. "How much of that did you hear? Do I have to kill you?" The man approached Masquerade, walking like he was hungover. In quick succession his eyes felt drowsy, making him feel sleepy, making him almost fall over in deep response.

"I thought you had put a spell up? Even if they tried eavesdropping, they would hear nothing but mumbling-" Zeus countered, only to be rudely interrupted.

"Yeah yeah yeah, I'm only toying with them, Mr. King of Olympus. . ." He stopped right in front of Masquerade, their noses almost touching as he bent over, showing his unfair advantage in height. "You know actually that this private meeting was all about you!" He said, jabbing his pointer finger into Masquerade's chest violently, his black fingernails slightly poking through a thin layer of dried skin. "Oh my gods. Is my presence bothering you? I completely forgot to watch my manners!" The dark presence lowered immediately, and his smile widened once more, his taunting personality engraving the part of the brain that holds memories. Then all of a sudden, Masquerade could actually breathe normally now.

He held out his hand to Masquerade, reluctantly shaking it. "I'm sorry, I just realized I haven't introduced myself yet," He said, looking at Infinity, clearly disgusted for a reason that couldn't be marked. "The name's Mardo. You might know me as the man who named you all. You know me! I tend to be very famous for the ability to see the future!"

Masquerade and Dark gasped audibly, and Hyper actually looked scared for the first time on this adventure of chaos. The group immediately looked as if they all had millions of questions to ask him. Mardo looked annoyed already, as he was probably reading their minds. Zeus was rolling his eyes, losing his short tempered patience, just as quickly as a flash of quick lightning.

"Get it over with, Mardo, tell me what you foresee. . ." Zeus said. He was holding back, not to raise his voice, which made Masquerade wonder if he was scared of Mardo. Mardo turned towards Zeus slowly.

"What I have to deliver is not a fortune, instead a threat," Mardo continued. Zeus shuddered on his throne, Dark was cracking his knuckles. "A threat from Misa!" Zeus' and everyone else's expression widened in shock to the absolutely sparkling intensity of the reveal. Everyone in the room was getting anxious, and it showed, because Mardo's smile grew larger with every dark thought. "Misa wishes for a sacrifice. . " Mardo said, his voice lowering.

Hyper moved along the other four and walked behind Masquerade quietly, showing obvious signs of horror. Mardo didn't notice, showing huge red flags of danger. It was surprising that Mardo had Zeus anxious. Hyper lightly touched Masquerade's hand. He turned around and made eye contact with him, his eyes told him he was scared. Their minds intertwined like a wife wrapping around a coil. *Masquerade. Do something! We're all scared.* Hyper's brain expressed.

He glanced over to Dark, who had the same troubled expression on his face. Masquerade focused back on Mardo, and then fixed his posture and looked Mardo in the eye.

"Misa has requested a sacrifice. He wants this sacrifice to be ritualic, showing promise to the normal way they used to be donein a temple. The Temple of Misa. In Antarctica." Mardo said. Zeus discarded this. "He requests this sacrifice to be one of your sons."

Zeus stared at Mardo for a moment, fear immediately rose in Masquerade and his siblings. "I have too many sons to count! Are there any specifications to this request?" Zeus negotiated. Even fear peaked within him.

"Oh, of course, he only wants the pure children of power. Sooo, the younglings that were born with 100 percent god-blood." Zeus tried shaking off the fearful expression on his face. Mardo couldn't help but smile sinisterly, a huge trait of his mysterious demeanor. This only left eight options for a humane sacrifice. Masquerade, Lazer, Dark, Hyper, Infinity, Tazer, Bow, or Gray. Hyper was shivering while holding Masquerade's hand reluctantly. The dark feeling crept through the cracks of stone, clenching their throats once more.

"ME! I'll go," Masquerade piped up. Zeus automatically had an expression that said 'No'. "I don't want anyone else to go. I'll even fight to be the one that gets sacrificed."

"Woah! Misa would be honored in you boy! That's settled! Sacrifice ready. Misa has given you ten days to complete the ritual." Mardo's dark voice vibrated, Masquerade was getting tired of these huge deadlines.

"NO! We are not done with this meeting, Mardo. What if I decline such immoral requests?" Zeus asked.

"Then it means war on Olympus. It's as simple as that, so I wouldn't go and piss off Lord Misa." Mardo said. Zeus took a while before responding, showing very clear signs of stress. He had no clue what to say next, but Masquerade was ready to respond for him.

"Then so be it!" Masquerade grabbed his shirt roughly. Hyper's hand tensed. Dark looked at him, giving that same look he gave every other time on this adventure. He gripped it and tore his shirt off recklessly. "I WOULD sacrifice myself, but I changed my mind. I won't give my sacred blood to some idiot who thinks he runs everything!" Masquerade yelled at Mardo, who was on the other side of the throne room. "This is just the beginning. This is the end of Misa's reign! And I'll be the one to stop him." He bellowed to Mardo, who showed signs of immediate interest.

"This is going to be exciting!!" Mardo yelled back in excitement. "If you wish to fight, then I'll deliver!" Mardo said, his muscles tensed, and he faced Masquerade quickly. "Sad to see someone willing to change the world die so soon!" Even after confronting the god, fear boiled in Masquerade's stomach again.

He stared at Mardo before attacking, "Would you dare kill a son of Zeus?" Mardo stared at him like a dumb dog.

"That rule does not apply to me, or anyone outside Olympus, I'll have you know. You can't hide behind words your entire life." Mardo said, charging at Masquerade with a coat of black whispering over him. Even he knew he couldn't beat him alone, so Masquerade went airborne, giving Hyper a shock of lightning, charging his power into him. From above, he blasted Mardo with an undodgeable blast. Then Zeus snapped. He was in chains, and so were his siblings. Mardo stood perfectly still, being completely unaffected, the explosion hadn't even damaged him.

"Enough! Mardo, you may leave. I will have a sacrifice ready in ten days." Zeus said, Mardo giving a look of confusion. Then his face shifted to a satisfied look, and he disappeared into black mist, tangling away from the fray. Masquerade was disappointed, not even attempting to try breaking free. Zeus stared at the five angrily. "I will not argue." He started. "You have a quest to fulfill first. On said quest, you can decide who will be sacrificed." Masquerade felt fear rise once again.

"What! You can't be serious about this! Who would sacrifice their own kids because of a puny threat?" Masquerade argued. "I will not let any of my siblings die in that loser's hands!"

"Misa is not some puny threat! He is extremely powerful. Not even the hands of Olympus together would be able to successfully kill him." Zeus continued. Masquerade let him finish. "You have ten days to decide. And in those ten days, *you* will save a young woman named Jynx. . ." Zeus pointed at Masquerade. Every one of his siblings gasped. *Jynx is in danger?* "I see you have met her already. . ." He continued. ". . . the enemy at hand is also hard to beat, but I entrust you five to be able to save her and her family."

The chains loosened, and they were all freed. As Zeus was going to free them of punishment, a familiar foe from about ten minutes ago made an ultimate appearance. A black scar bathed the entire right side of his face, and charred bits of dry skin peeled from his arms. Hades erupted into his throne from gray and red streaks of baring smoke, his keen frown being a prominent feature of his unforeseen blackened side of his face.

"Just when I thought things were getting better!" Masquerade trifled, his fingers dancing across each other nervously, his brain nurturing upon the trouble he was about to get into. In the heat of the moment, Zeus sighed, ready to hear about what his sons have done this time.

"This boy has committed a crime of terrorism!" He cried out loud, everyone in the room came to a deep sigh, looking towards Masquerade disapprovingly. His finger was pointed at Masquerade, who was looking at his own fingernail, making sure they weren't as ugly as Hades'. Zeus sighed.

"What exactly was this act of terrorism? Did he knock over your lemonade stand by chance?" He snorted wearily, his expression set in stone with sheer disappointment. Hades frowned.

"No! He bombed my coliseum, and killed hundreds of innocent demons!" His hoarse daring voice continued to yap. Zeus had a shocked face this time around, his burrow furrowing, and his mouth quivering with shaking anger.

"Masquerade. . ." His voice spoke with careful directed anticipation, which represented resentful anger. He snapped his fingers, blasts of lightning covering his forearm. His brothers backed away, inching towards the edge of the entrance, all while Masquerade still stood in the middle of the twelve towering thrones. Upon reaction to Zeus' command, came all the torch lighting to a blazing indescribable color. Shadows of smoke turned into quick figures of human gods, who didn't look pleased to be forcefully summoned. "You have committed multiple acts of treason, assault, and now even terrorism upon an entire different realm!" His voice boomed, even louder than lightning this time around. All the gods gasped in return to hearing his unlawful actions. "Normally I would dismiss such an act since you're still a learning god, but now you have pushed the limits too far!" He continued viciously. "You will be banished to the deepest depths of Hell to rot for the rest of eternity, all because you couldn't maintain yourself like a normal god!" His brothers shook their heads in fear, disappointment, and absolute shock.

Zeus, Hades, Poseidon, Artemis, Athena, Ares, Dioynsus, Hermes, Demeter, Aphrodite, Apollo, and Hesphaestus sat in their thrones of authority. His fingers looked ready to snap, ready to banish his own son to the underworld. All the gods nodded, approving of such distaste in punishment, still all of them awaiting the cold agreement to grace from Masquerade's lips. "Then. . ." His voice rumbled with anger, smoke arising from the extended glory of his palms. Zeus noticed the build up of energy inside his son right away. A quick and yellow burst of color rising deep within Masquerade's chest.

". . .bring it." He said softly, before every inch of his skin turned bright yellow, eventually erupting a large explosion that ate the entire room in under a second. The rest of his siblings escaped through the waterfall, running for their lives. The rock from the cave opened immediately, scattering through the air like a volcano throwing ash after a large eruption. Lazer looked at the scene, absolutely derived from reality, struck with shock that Masquerade just nuked the Olympians. The only thing that remained undestroyed was the thrones, and the capsule underneath their feet.

The smoke cleared rather quickly, showing the explosive destruction that is known as Masquerade, who was standing bleakly in the clearing wavering black smoke. In seconds, each olympic god blitzed forwards, ready to achieve victory against him, except Zeus remained the only one who didn't rush forwards. With immediate thrusts of the wind, Masquerade soared over the bodies, attacking a group of them with a quick cluster burst of explosions. Zeus' lightning bolt traveled to his hand, and Posideon's trident came to view as well, their elements ready to clash against Masquerade's destructive standpoint. Just as quickly as lightning can flash, Masquerade blitzed in front of Zeus' face. Their eyes made contact, before his muscular hand crushed forwards, grabbing upon the weapon of lightning.

Everyone came to a stop, watching as son and father wrestled for access to the bolt of light. At first, Zeus seemed superior in strength, until an explosion blimped across his face, and in mere seconds, Masquerade yanked the bolt out his grip. He then weaved his hands across the open canvas, grudgingly slashing the metal bolt into his fathers chest. The other eleven gods in contrast, watched the showdown between the relatives, before joining the fray. Winds encased their bodies, making them levitate into the air quickly, where they then readied to attack.

"Let's go lightning bolt for lightning bolt!" Masquerade exclaimed while reaching his fists for the sky, the weapon in his hand generating an unholy amount of electricity. Zeus readied, his own lightning power coming to the surface of his epidermis. The power of lightning charging into the shape of a bolt, with many jagged lines that could take down any normal person. Then, the two watching in anticipation, released their bolts, which then collapsed and collided in great energy. An explosion of plasma occurred shortly after, which fell in Masquerade's favor. He took the opportunity to blitz into the smoke, and take the bolt away once more. Now that Zeus was stunned, he ran towards his brothers, who still stood running across the river.

"We're jumping over the edge of the mountain!" Masquerade screamed, in regards to Olympus Mountain. His siblings did not fight back in retaliation. Zeus got back to his defense, and he was quickly stopped by a flash of lightning that Masquerade absorbed. He landed on the floor, a few feet away from Hyper, where he was met with the two war gods, Ares and Athena, who stood in unison. Athena was strategic, and Ares was blunt force, both of their vows together enhancing their hatred to take down Masquerade. Quickly, all three of them held their hands out, ready to fight at any moment.

Masquerade moved first, blitzing his fast fingers to make mini explosions, which then erupted into fireworks. Their hands moved fast, Ares attacked his left plank and Athena his right. He was able to keep up in hand-to-hand combat despite being inexperienced and young. Jab to the stomach, jab to the chest, jab to the chin, and a nasty right hook to Athena's jaw, she went flying to the ground quickly, ready to use her trump card. Ares was more proficient with his technique, but ultimately failed to dodge a lightning bolt that came crashing down from the skies at his call.

Ares tanked it, landing a heavy blow to his arm, sending Masquerade into the ground. He responded by flipping in the air and doing a handstand, where he then pushed his arms upwards, flipping once again, this time to stand on his feet several meters away. He glanced to his left where he was met with Aphrodite, her blond striking hair catching him off guard.

"Won't you stop this for a treat with me?" She spoke with a seducing tone, Lazer looked at her willingly, and then glanced at Masquerade.

"Hell no." He said, slapping her across the face with fists enchanted with lightning. He pushed her away from her, and bolted for the edge or the water, which fell down to a void of whiteness. He hypothesized that jumping down would lead them directly to Earth. Masquerade held the bolt, looked at the approaching gods, and back to the bolt. Their jump to suicide only lay a few feet from them. "Jump!" He screamed, pushing Hyper and Infinity off the edge. He charged the bolt with the most explosive power he could, and chucked it towards the group. He raised his hands, throwing the middle finger up as he fell backwards down the void of absolute death. The last thing he saw was each and every Olympian god get blasted with the largest explosions he's created thus far, large enough to destroy an entire city block in diameter.

He turned his body, and perceived the deep blue sea from miles away. To be precise, twenty miles above sea level, with the danger approaching quick, fast, and deadly.

Chapter 10
Jynx

The trip squad got to school and was getting the bus ready for takeoff. They took forever loading luggage and other essentials. There was still no sign of Masquerade at all, but they still had time, however. She thanks god that Zander hasn't arrived yet. He was usually late, which Jynx had actually appreciated this time. The bus remained turned on, parked in the school garage with the rest of her classmates, who were cold, waiting for the heater to turn on.

Tamer, Stray, Jace, Jynx, Russel, and Jacob were the original members of the trip, along with Masquerade and his four siblings. Jynx stared out of the bus window. Russel and Stray were late as well. From the outside was the flashing light of the top of the bus, which annoyed her deeply. Jace sat behind her on the bus, warming the seat with his power. Her mind glanced towards the terrors of the previous nights, her mind glossing over her stalkers, wondering if any of them were going to attempt murdering her from within the safety of the school trip.

"Hey, Jynx, when are these quintuplets going to be here? You surely hyped them up a lot," Jacob teased her. Jace tried speaking up for her, but Jynx stared at him, telling him not to.

The bus door slammed open, "We're here!" A voice boomed from the front of the bus. Jynx looked up immediately, excited. Zander walked in with huge suitcases slowly after. Jynx wondered why he said, 'We're', but then Stray walked in. Jynx had only seen him a couple of times, with no clear look. He had a handsome, sharp jawline. His hair was split, dyed red and black, and parted in the middle. His eyes were bright red that gleamed with power. His clothes were defined and matched well.

Following Stray was Russel. He had brown, rigid hair that wasn't combed at all. He had dark, glistening skin with bright golden eyes. Jynx was disappointed it wasn't Masquerade. Jacob's face lightened, and he approached Stray with excitement. Glicher and Zander were both on the bus. The luggage was placed, and now everyone was ready to leave.

"I am sorry to say that our new subordinates will not be joining us on the school's first trip out of the country. . ." Zander exclaimed. "We will not wait any longer, and we will be leaving-" He was interrupted by the sound of a large explosion. Jynx stared out the window and saw the sparks of a bomb, smoke filled the area as well. From the smoke, five silhouettes approached the bus. Each was holding their own luggage.

Zander smiled as he opened the door to let them enter. Jace stood up in his seat respectfully. Tamer had a worried look on his face. Everyone else looked excited to see the five. Masquerade entered first, his eyes still mesmerizing to watch. His hair was ruffled and fluffy but still well done, sort of. He had many new scars all over his face and hands. He wore casual attire, but he still looked good in it.

Jynx blushed slightly as he walked by, when he stopped at her seat, staring down at her giddily. His brothers marched in next, who were also in shape and ready. Masquerade set his luggage down and took his seat, right next to Jynx. This was only the third time they had met, she realized. She smiled lightly at him and awkwardly waved at him, she felt stupid since they were in the same seat. He opened his mouth to talk before he was interrupted.

"How long will the bus ride be?" Hyper had asked, getting comfortable in his seat. He had four separate blankets and a body pillow, everyone stared at him weirdly, but he disregarded the stares. Zander even hesitated before answering.

"Our first stop will be at a hotel in the next four countries over. They're pretty small, though, so around seventeen hours. Of course, with bathroom breaks and a few stops to eat. Masquerade fiddled with his fingers, and in seconds the bus started moving.

"So, where have you been the past ten days?!" She said in a harsh tone, making extreme eye contact. He stared at her weirdly, like he was holding back something to say, Masquerade opened his mouth slowly.

"Uhm, I don't know how to say it without it seeming like a lie." He admitted. He put his hands on his pants like he was amazed they were there. "It's amazing these jeans aren't ripped."

She scrutinized him. "That's the worst way to start a conversation when you've been gone for a week and a half." He giggled quietly, and his eyes even dilated a little while looking at her. He put his hand to his mouth before speaking, revealing hands that were scarred severely.

"I'm telling the truth!" He exclaimed. "I've been running errands for a few uhhh, jealous family members..." He said, rubbing his forearm gently, which also revealed many scars. He undid his sleeve, pulling it upwards

"That's how you're going to put it?" Jynx said. "You're the worst liar I know!" She giggled. "What are you going to say next? Your family are gods in disguise?" She guessed, getting straight to the point.

Masquerade stared at her seriously. She almost gagged. "What if I told you that you were correct?" He said. Jynx still believed he had something to tell her.

"Yeah, I wasn't guessing completely in the dark. . . Jace said as he saw Zeus in the weight room. So tell me, how much does he lift?" She joked.

"Oh, he'll pick up a weight when pigs fly. Trust me, he's a lazy sack of potatoes." It seriously concerned Jynx that he wasn't joking, or maybe he was, and it was hard to tell. He was still very fidgety. He had much to talk about, so she waited for him to slowly come out of his comfort zone. "Yeah, he punished me for talking about him, which I'm still mad about. Then he made me hunt with Artemis, where she tried killing me with a stampede of mutant cows." He expressed his voice full of joy.

"It's comforting and frightening that the gods are real." Jynx said.

"I would agree on the frightening part if they weren't so self-centered. . ." Masquerade exclaimed.

"Go on with your little adventure," She told him. He smiled gently. His hot pink hair seemed to light up the bus, and his smile made her day.

"Then we got to harvest crops with Demeter. We had a pretty big food fight! It was fun. Then she set me up and made me fight Ares. I totally won, by the way."

"You won a fight against the god of war?" She said, surprised. "I don't believe you,"

"Meh, it was more of a draw, then Hermes took us to Hell. And I won the most intense game of Tug-o-War with Hades' pet dog." He continued. "Then Hades put us in a tournament, and I killed Hercules. . ." He quickly added.

"All of that in ten days?" Jynx asked. Her brain was filled with questions, she didn't feel like any of it was real.

"More like two days, time flows differently in Olympus. And in the underworld. I'm pretty exhausted from fighting so much." Masquerade untensed and relaxed his body on the seat.

"I'll let you rest. Goodnight," She said. And in seconds he fell into a deep sleep just like that. He breathed quietly. Jynx couldn't help asking herself how he managed to look attractive when he was simply sleeping. She rested her head on her seat, watching the trees quickly pass by.

After a while, she looked up to examine the rest of the bus. She had no clue how much time had passed. Everyone else was sleeping as well, except Zander, who was driving with a troubled expression. A town had approached from the front view.

"Everyone up! Our first stop of the trip!!" Zander exclaimed loudly. Masquerade jumped awake immediately. Jynx was surprised he was able to wake so quickly. Everyone else groaned silently as the bus came to a stop. She waited for Masquerade to get up first before leaving. The group entered the restaurant slowly; they were still all tired.

They were all situated at their tables. In total, there were thirteen people, so they split into two tables, one of six and the second of seven. Zander managed Jynx's table as Glicher took the other half. Masquerade and his four siblings sat with Jynx and Zander. The others sat with Glicher at another table.

"We have something to discuss over our lunch," Zander exclaimed. Everyone at the table looked concerned, they clearly weren't used to being talked to by a teacher. Masquerade looked at his menu nervously. "Jace and Tamer both said they saw you five with a god, during the second period ten days ago." Zander exclaimed. Jynx sat excitedly.

"Well, I'll have you know, Mr Zander, sir, that Tamer and Jace saw wrong. I don't even know what a god is!" Lazer said stupidly.

"Lazer, please be quiet and let us discuss this." Dark chimed in with an exhausted look on his face. They stared at each other for moments, exchanging glances of discomfort.

Zander chuckled a bit and started talking again, "So, is this really true or not?" Zander refocused.

Masquerade hesitated. "Yes, it's true," He flinched at nothing like he was expecting something big to happen. Everyone shuffled through their menus. "How does this affect the trip?

"It doesn't, really. We'd just like to know such information. Just in case anything gets out or if it gets brought to legal action." Zander explained. They ordered as the waiter came.

"Legal action? For what-!?" Masquerade was then interrupted by Hyper loudly.

"Where are we headed to next?" Hyper asked, excessively drinking his soda.

"The hotel has a pretty big waterpark, so it'll be fun." Zander said. "However, the boys have to share one room, and Jynx gets an entire room for herself." Masquerade gasped audibly.

"What!? That's not fair! Nine people in the same room!?" Masquerade raised his voice, attracting attention from other tables with his loud voice.

"Yes, I know it's absurd, but that's all the hotel allowed, four rooms. One for the boys, one for the girls, and two for the supervisors." He explained. The waiter came by and served food.

"I can change that. . ." Masquerade grinned.

"I suggest that you don't," Zander advised. "No need to worry. We had to save the budget for later activities on the trip. After all, you all have to fundraise when we return home." His words went straight through the ears of everyone else. After finishing their meal, everyone boarded the bus. The journey continued, and soon the group approached a sprawling city. The beautiful skyline unfolded as the bus smoothly navigated the highway.

As they pulled into town, Zander was looking at his phone. Glicher drove this time around. He displayed a map on his phone and held it up. "The city is huge, I know, but this is only our first stop." He approached, "We'll stay here for three days, and we have many activities to do. It's going to be overwhelming. You won't get much time to rest, there's much time to cover!" Zander said. You would either be very excited about that news or very exhausted, never in between, everyone seemed excited, however.

They pulled into the hotel parking lot. Jynx looked the suite up and down. It was the most

fancy thing she had been to. The hotel shimmered white, with warm beams of lights illuminating it. It was nighttime by the time they had arrived. Masquerade didn't look too surprised, and she stared at him harshly.

He gave the same look back, "Why are you staring at me like that!?" She giggled and kicked his foot.

"Nothing, it just baffles me that you aren't amazed by the hotel!" She raised her voice.

Masquerade responded by putting his foot back on top of hers, "I've seen better. Olympus is really, really fancy, you know." He stood up as the bus came to a stop.

"I don't doubt it, but you know it's going to take more convincing than that to make me believe you!" Zander gestured for them to grab their luggage. Everyone waited as Jacob took forever to find his suitcase.

"Wait! It's on the bottom, I think!" He screamed as everyone told him to hurry up.

"Then why'd you go first, you idiot!" Masquerade bullied him. He pushed him out of the way and grabbed his own. He turned back and made eye contact with Jynx.

"You want to grab mine too?" She said in a puppy pleading voice. Masquerade frowned and grabbed her case wistfully. Jacob stared at him weirdly, cracking his neck, still struggling to find his luggage. Everyone grabbed their luggage and left the bus accordingly.

They checked in, went up a pair of fancy elevators, and went into their rooms. Jynx stared at the three beds she had to herself. She wondered how the boys were handling themselves, who had the room next to her. She unpacked and set the room to her needs, fixating her sheets and tables. She wondered if the supervisors had anything fun planned for the night at all, or if she should just fall asleep on the majestic beds. As she was getting settled on her bed, a knock sounded at her door. When she opened it, Masquerade stood shirtless.

"Hey! We're going down to the pool, and I thought it'd be rude not to include you." Jynx blushed like an idiot as Masquerade caught her eyes, looking at his stomach. He was really built. Jynx wondered if he worked out. He smiled, which gave Jynx butterflies.

"Uhyeah, just let mechchange!" She spat out, "Oh god, sorry, just caught something in my throat." She slammed the door on him, Jynx's brain only thought she was a complete idiot. Quickly, she rummaged through her clothes and put on her bathing suit. She looked in the mirror to make sure she looked good, fixing her brownish pink hair quickly and left the room. Masquerade was still waiting.

"Are the others down there already?" She asked him. Masquerade walked to the next room down and knocked on the door.

"No, they're fighting over the bathroom right now," he opened the door and walked in for a split second. When he came out, he had Lazer and Dark.

"Hyper says he doesn't know how to swim." Lazer said with full confidence, clapping his fists together. Everyone else started laughing, Jynx even chuckled. Hyper came out of the room on Tamer's back.

"He may be right! But I'm making this guy teach me!" Hyper said, pulling both his ears forward, it appeared as if Tamer was a horse. Masquerade chuckled.

"The name is Tamer!"

"Okay, Tamer! You can swim, right?"

"Yes, I'm not an idiot like you!" Hyper responded by slapping him across the face.

"Woah! Me too!" Jacob came next out of the room while Stray gave him a piggyback ride, he had a clear expression that said, 'Please get this idiot off of me.' Jynx rolled her eyes. Jace and Russel walked out on their own feet, Infinity coming last, holding everyone's room keys. He closed the door, nudged Hyper, and they all started walking to the pool area. Getting in the elevator was awkward however.

"Before we get in, we must pick partners for a chicken fight." Hyper announced. Jacob smiled.

"I agree!" Jacob raised his hand, taking Stray's hand with it, both of them raising their arms in response; Stray still looked miserable. Lazer smiled and ran up to Jace, and jumped on his back.

"I choose Jace. He's a walking heater," he said. Jynx smiled at Jace while he had an annoyed look on his face. Masquerade looked at Dark and pushed him into the elevator. Everyone followed. The elevator was crowded, and it took forever to get down, since they were on the twentieth floor.

Once the doors opened, the group approached the pool door. Upon entering they notice a huge water park. There was a massive wave pool that caught the boy's attention immediately, and of course, Jynx was forced to follow them.

Infinity and Russel, Jacob and Stray, Hyper and Tamer, Lazer and Jace, which left Masquerade, Dark, and Jynx. Masquerade hesitated before choosing.

"Sorry, I don't like the water much. I'll sit out." He said, winking at Masquerade, which left Jynx and Masquerade. Everyone was already in the pool, ready to rip each other apart.

"Let me get on your back!" He said, approaching Jynx. She gasped like he just insulted her.

"What! NO! It's supposed to be the other way around, are you crazy!?" She bellowed at him. He held his hands up menacingly.

"Why not!? I'm gonna blow everyone up!" He screamed, and the other groups stared at the two weirdly while they argued.

"I'm not that strong!" She argued back, and Masquerade looked insulted.

"I don't weigh much!" He pursed his lips, "I'm not fat!" He laughed and bit his tongue. Jynx couldn't tell if he did that on purpose or by accident.

"I am not carrying you!" Jynx yelled back.

"Fine! Whatever shuts you up. . . " He said sarcastically.

"What!"

"Nothing, nothing," He smiled, his tongue still being held down by his clenched teeth. Jynx climbed on his back as they got into the water. Masquerade grabbed her thighs, tightening his grip on her inner thigh. She couldn't help but feel her stomach start swirling, his hands being incredibly hot, like temperature-wise.

The groups started fighting. At first, it was normal until lasers started flying everywhere. Masquerade advanced the two towards Lazer, who was on top of Jace. Lazer smiled down at Masquerade. A laser was hurling towards Jynx, but Masquerade dodged it for her.

"This is why I should be on top!" He said, and Jynx ignored that his dialogue could be taken entirely out of context, which made her stomach swirl even more. "Stay on track, Jynx!"

Lazer tried pushing her off. Masquerade took his hand off her thigh, and the next thing she heard was ringing. She opened her eyes to Lazer on the other side of the pool. Jace had his hands up. Masquerade readjusted his hands back on her thighs.

"Get ready because we're attacking Jacob!" He said, walking in his direction. Jacob turned around, who just took Hyper and Tamer out of the fight. It was easy for them to take Jacob out, mainly because Stray was distracted. Right as they were going to fight Infinity, the waves in the pool turned on. It didn't last long for Masquerade to throw Jynx off of himself and dive underwater.

"Hey! What was that for!" She yelled when she resurfaced, realizing no one was there. Masquerade was still underwater, then she felt a hand pull her leg. The hand tugged and dragged her under. The waves distracted the others. Jynx opened her eyes underwater, ignoring the searing pain that the chlorine caused. She was eye to eye with Masquerade. His pretty hair floated elegantly in the currents. Jynx stared into his eyes for a moment. He stared back, and for a split moment, they stood there in the blue of the aqua. She could have sworn she saw him look at her lips.

Then Jace swam in their direction, they all surfaced, and Jace looked distraught. Masquerade looked at him weirdly, asking him what had happened, but Jace just nodded.

"I'm kind of hungry. Let's go to the snack bar and see what they got." Jynx suggested. The two agreed, and they all left the pool. Masquerade was shivering, and Jace smiled.

"I can help you with that," Jace said as he raised his hand toward him. Masquerade flinched for a moment, staring fiercely at him for a moment. Masquerade gave in, and Jace used his heat powers to dry him off. Satisfied, Masquerade tried racing the two to the bar, Jynx could still tell he was very obviously clearly anxious about something.

"You know Zeus approves of you," He said while trying not to cut in front of her.

"Me!?" Jace piped up excitedly, "What did he say about me!? Does he really like me?" He started smiling.

"No, not you, sorry,"

"Oh. . ."

Jynx fiddled with her fingers, "Me?" Masquerade nodded effectively. He moved to her other side, looking at Jace disappointed.

"Yes, he sent me here to protect you from something, you know! The entire reason I'm on this trip is because of him. . ." Jynx's heart sank deeply. She now realized that Zeus had sent Masquerade to be her protector, which meant that he had to be the one to fight her family, and Echo. Her eyes darkened, and she looked him in his eyes, worried deeply, her anxiety making her shiver slightly.

"I don't need saving, though." She lied, she didn't want him to die trying to protect her.

"That's not what he said! He mentioned the enemy's strength, but I'll be ready to fight anyone who tries to harm you," he asserted. Jynx couldn't help but feel flustered. Jace stared at him, concerned.

Jynx hesitated, deciding whether to tell him, her brain scrolling through memories. She looked at Jace for an answer, who nodded approvingly. Jynx took a deep breath, ready to reveal. "Uhm, the enemy is my dad, Mark," she started. "He killed my mother—wait, no, Jake did," Jynx explained the situation, with Jace adding extra details where needed.

Masquerade clenched his fists as they looked at the snacks, like they were his next victim. "How can anybody be that cruel?! Not even the gods are that obtuse!" he sputtered. "And that's saying something!" Smoke was rising from his hands. The clerk raised his eyebrow, and Masquerade snapped at him.

"Chill out. I know it's bad, but really, my mother could have been a really bad person tooWe don't know the full story," She explained. Masquerade still looked like he would blow up the next stranger who looked at him the wrong way.

"We'll find out then!" He bellowed. "Who's first on the list?!" He asked, "Jake or Mark? Or Echo!?" He held three fingers up in response.

"You think you can take on Echo? He's the son of Sura!" Jace argued.

"YES! And his fathers up there, too! Both of them need a lesson, all of them need to die!" His screaming further concerned the clerk, who was fully invested in their conversation.

"What's wrong with Sura?" Jace asked, and Jynx was invested in what Masquerade really knew. The three left the food bar with many snacks, and the clerk looked disappointed when they left.

"Dark had an encounter with a god, and he explained how Misa and Sura were manipulative forces and they needed to be stopped. And then, when I returned home, Mardo was in a meeting with Zeus. He said that my father was to hand over one of his children to sacrifice, and I volunteered to and threatened to kill Misa," The information harmed them, it was a whole lot to take in.

"What!? You volunteered to be killed?!" Jynx yelled, her fear rising even more. "How stupid are you!?" Jynx tried not to sound obsessive, Jace looked confused.

"You both really are the root of danger, huh?" He said, his tone lowering. A smirk appeared on his face. "Together, you'd attract even more, maybe even each other!" He teased her.

Jynx blushed and faced away from Masquerade. "Shut up, Jace! This is serious!" She pushed him straight into the wall as hard as she could. Masquerade laughed. Jace stood up straight.

"No need to resort to violence! We should come up with a plan, let's go to your room and see what we can come up with." He said to Jynx, ignoring Masquerade, who was blowing smoke into the vents of the hotel hallway. They all agreed and went to her room. Jace sat on the first bed nervously. Masquerade dived straight onto the second bed and lay there for a few seconds, showing the contrast between their personalities. Jynx realized that the one he sat down on was her bed, the one she picked. She sat at the foot of the bed, trying not to startle him.

"We should settle this over a dominos pizza," Masquerade's muffled voice came from the bed. Jace laughed and grabbed his phone.

"On it!" He dialed the number, "What kind are we getting?"

"Pepperoni." His voice mumbled. Jynx grabbed a pillow and threw it at his back.

"Get up and talk normally. . ." She demanded. Masquerade stood up and stared at her with the pillow in his hand, crawling over and smacking her with the pillow directly. Jynx pushed him off the bed and asked Jace to hurry up. Masquerade got back up and tackled her back onto the bed. She screamed, and then pinned her down on the bed. The two stared at each other for a long moment, before he grabbed a pillow and shoved it on her face, forcefully making her quiet.

"Shush, women, the guys ordering pizza!" Jynx kicked Masquerade off her.

"Maybe you shouldn't start fights you can't win!" She argued back, and Masquerade shut up just as fast.

"You started it-" He mumbled slowly. Jynx threw the pillow at him. Jace put his phone down and clapped weirdly.

"Pizza's on its way. Since we're in a luxury hotel, it'll be a few minutes," He stared as Masquerade stopped himself from blowing Jynx's head off with a pillow. "So about this plan?"

"I say we find their lair and blow everything up!" Masquerade said, dropping the pillow on the floor. Jynx and Jace both stared at him like he had brain issues. "Oh, come on! I don't see you coming up with anything!"

"Well, I don't know how we'll surprise a god," Jynx said, waiting for the pizza.

"I've done it before. It's possible." He had a look of nostalgia plastered over his expression. Jace looked like he didn't believe him, then someone knocked on the door. "Pizza's here!" Masquerade ran for the door, opened it, gave the guy a bill, and told him to have a good day. He opened the box and stared, swiftly taking the first slice. "I bought it. I get first bite."

"No one tried getting the first bite." Jynx said, rolling her eyes. Masquerade glared at her, shoving the pizza down his throat like he hasn't eaten anything in days.

"We'll settle the plan with a pillow fight!" Masquerade grabbed a pillow, Jynx instinctively grabbed a pillow as well, Jace followed and did the same. Masquerade jumped on the bed and hit Jace in the abdomen, dodging under Jynx and hitting her in the head. Then Jace hit him overhead, he grunted and counterattacked.

Jynx got up and hit Jace in the head. Masquerade picked the poor guy up and slammed him into the bed, then he turned around and looked at Jynx. Her eyes trembled with fear, waiting to get plummeted by a soft fluff of fabric. He rushed towards her, but Jace hit him again. He turned and smacked him with the pillow, the impact sounded like it hurt, even if it were just a pillow.

Jynx laughed, and then the two both threw their pillows at her head, making her fall directly into the bed. They high-fived and sat down satisfied.

"So much for planning!" She said harshly, eating a slice of pizza.

"I don't make plans. We find them, attack them, and kill them." He said, "Easy as that!" Masquerade said as he swallowed his third slice, no thoughts behind his pretty pink eyes. His eyes widened all of a sudden, his brain suddenly remembering something. "WAIT! I know who Echo is! I know him! He kidnapped my brother!" He bellowed, his tone becoming angrier. "Now I'm definitely kicking his ass! How many lives does he think he can ruin?!"

Jynx was too shocked to respond, her brain overstimulating. "I'm done. We'll talk about this tomorrow. I'm going to bed. Now get out, both of you." She demanded, and Masquerade smiled. He tried arguing with her, trying to stay, but she physically kicked him out afterward. Jynx covered up and dozed off, knowing tomorrow would be better.

Chapter 11
Masquerade

He woke up, his mind still shrouded in a disorienting fog. A commotion erupted as everyone jostled for the first turn in the shower. They were taking too long to get ready, so the teachers decided to let them shower in Jynx's and Zander's rooms. After a while, the group was ready to leave. The teachers hadn't told them where they were going yet.

"Eat breakfast in the hotel, and we'll go from there." Zander said with a sleepy voice. The rest of the group listened accordingly, he was so tired Masquerade slapped himself awake. He only had nine days until he would have to sacrifice himself to Misa, nine days to save Jynx, nine days to unlock the secrets behind his father, a time frame that continued to creep up on him. He had no clue how he'd pull off defeating Misa, the only thing he could do was try, and wait for the time to come..

Following a lackluster breakfast, everyone filed onto the bus. Masquerade ended up next to Hyper, who chattered incessantly throughout the journey. Zander stopped the bus in a foreign parking lot.

"For today's first activity, we will explore the God's Museum!" He said enthusiastically. Everyone seemed anxious to begin, but Masquerade already had his fair share of the gods. Leaving the bus, Zander held a map, Glicher followed quietly, her sassiness was rather toned down lately, as if Masquerade's return made her feel better. "Additionally, you gotta jot down notes on whatever catches your fancy! It's all part of the grading gig, naturally." They all groaned in response, their notebook nowhere to be seen. As they neared, the bright golden letters of "God's Museum" came into view, a very lackluster name for a tourist attraction.

Masquerade thought it sounded dumb. As they walked in, the museum was certainly magnificent, the floor was made of white quartz, which sparkled in the sunlight. Huge golden pillars were designed and used for support, replicating Greek architecture. In the lobby, a huge diamond chandelier hung over the check-in desk. The clerk smiled lightly as the group walked in. The museum had many exhibits, being shown in the board hung over the clerks head. The teachers had told them to explore freely as they wished, except she put them in groups first.

Masquerade was paired with Infinity and Dark. Lazer, Hyper and Tamer were next. Jynx, Jace, and Jacob were paired. Russel and Stray were duos. Insisting, Masquerade steered the group straight to Misa's exhibit, and no one raised a fuss.

"We can dig up all sorts of background info for our impending showdown with him." Dark suggested as they walked down the exhibition hall. Masquerade looked at the cases, noticing many paintings pinned to the wall, showing what the god looked like. In the casings were items that were once owned by Misa, a lot showing descriptions of the item.

However, none of the text was important to them, as it didn't describe Misa at all. He could tell Dark was frustrated. Just as they were about to leave, one of the items shined orange, which wasn't Misa's signature color at all. Infinity approached it and slightly made contact with the glowing gem. They all watched as the light emitted into a human being. In a mailman's outfit stood Hermes, who had so much mail it was sticking out from his bag. Masquerade had just now noticed there weren't any humans around, which was a huge coincidence, considering there was a Greek God in their presence.

"Hello again, younglings!" Hermes announced, his hair sticking straight up. "Zeus is mad at me," he frowned. The two made fierce eye contact, and he was able to notice a large burn in his forearms, still there from the blast let out the last time they confronted each other.

"What, why?! What happened?" Masquerade asked the traveler, god.

"Nevermind Zeus, I have a message for you! From your father!" He said enthusiastically. He rummaged in his pouch, after a while, he pulled a letter from it. The paper then disintegrated into golden ashes. "It says, 'Hermes, return my children from the Underworld. This instant or there will be consequences. Signed Zeus." Hermes' face said it all.

"You're a bit late to deliver that," Dark said. "I give you one out of five stars. Really poor performance, Hermes." Masquerade chuckled.

"I see that now! However, that's not all the reason I came here. Another message must be delivered to another hero, but he's dead." Hermes overshared. "So I'll give you the quest!" Masquerade didn't like the sound of this. "A rip in the underworld has opened, and demons started crawling out into the open world. You are to find and seal this rip, send the demons back to Hell, and try not to get yourselves caught by Hades! Or Satan! Or both!" Hermes said.

"How the hell are we supposed to do that!?" Masquerade said, looking at him like he was a mad man. Hermes responded by giving him a majestical-looking goat horn and a purple sphere made of an unknowing material.

"The sphere will open a portal to Hell, and the horn will seal the rip!" Hermes said as his body dissipated. They all looked at each other.

"For my sake, I already decided that the gods would ruin our trip." Infinity said.

"It's not supposed to be fun! We're supposed to save Jynx."

"I got everything under control!" Masquerade bellowed. Dark and Infinity snorted. "We should find Hyper and Lazer first, then we go from there." He whispered.

"How are we supposed to find the rip?" Dark asked sarcastically, and Masquerade was ready to go to Olympus and rip Hermes' head off.

"I don't know, look for demons?" Infinity said sarcastically.

"Well, what do demons look like!?" Dark argued back.

"They can look like anything. You'll tell by their presence." Masquerade explained, and Dark didn't argue back. The three searched the museum frantically, trying not to attract attention. In all places they could be, they found Lazer, Hyper, and Tamer at a concession stand. The three looked surprised to see them.

"Yo! We have a problem!" Masquerade announced, and the three looked exhausted already, even without hearing what he had to say. Masquerade smiled and explained what happened.

"Oh, I see, that's why I felt off lately," Tamer said as they walked down a flight of stairs, everyone staring at him weirdly.

"You can sense the demons already?" Dark asked, and Tamer winced, like that was a question he should already know the answer to.

"Yes, the demons have a connection to me, as they were originally angels too." He explained, and Tamer's eyes glistened gold more than usual. Masquerade pushed him in front of the group.

"Lead the way, angel boy!" He screamed, Tamer looked annoyed, but he still listened and led the group outside of the museum, walking into the clear streets of what seemed to be Berlin Germany. They hadn't had permission to leave, but Hermes gave them permission, so it didn't matter if the teachers had said so or not. Tamer led them into an underground subway, which worried him a bit, scared if Tamer was trying to sell them drugs or something weird.

At first glance, all you could see were normal humans walking around, but once you squinted, you could see their fiery signature eyes, some had invisible limbs, and many others were disguised as animals, which Masquerade found weird. He found a lot of things weird, especially Lazer right now, who was picking his nose oddly, his pinky finger shoved up there digging for gold.

Once the army of demons sensed the group, they all stopped and bared their at them, ready to pounce with absolute power. Masquerade now realized the subway was completely abandoned, and overrun with hundreds of entities. Masquerade handed the horn to Tamer reluctantly.

"Find the rip! I'll distract the demons!" He yelled, exploding towards the army to face them. The demons roared in advance, and many of them started flying towards him with their black charred wings of volcanic rock. Masquerade responded by blowing up everything that he saw, a lot of the demons falling one by one. None of them truly died, however, with a lot of them resurrecting to fill the shoes of the last that got pulverized. Tamer was still standing still with the horn in hand, doing absolutely nothing with it. His other siblings either joined the battle or searched for the rip.

The demons were overwhelming because they truly couldn't die without a demon-slaying blade. So after Masquerade 'killed' them, they just came back for more. Infinity's clones were helping a lot, but it didn't take long for the demons to understand what they were doing. Dark's fire was useless, so he used his blood weapons instead.

Masquerade stood still, watching over the overrun subway. He watched as everyone frantically tried to find the rip, everyone being overwhelmed by demonic forces.

"BLOW INTO THE HORN!!" Masquerade screamed, and the army of demons looked in his direction, Tamer looked terrified, like he knew what the horn could do. Despite that however, he didn't hesitate, huffing into the horn, the demon's expressions changing immediately. Automatically, the rip revealed itself. The clear disruption of the air revealed itself, quickly vibrating into colors of purple, blue, and black. It was revealed to be three long scratches, as if some creature that looked like a wolf was responsible. The demons howled in fury, their shapes contorting into more menacing forms.

Infinity made more clones to fight the up-rage, but they didn't last forever. Hyper tried controlling them with his speaking powers, but nothing occurred. Lazer's lasers weren't doing anything effective, and Tamer only had super strength, and Masquerade's explosions were ineffective. Dark's blood was the only weapon that seemed to damage them, so eventually, they would be exhausted and overrun.

Launching into the air, Masquerade seized the horn. Instead of blowing outwards, he blew inwards, using his control over wind to make a current in the air. The rip showed the other side of hell. It wasn't blue this time, instead it was a scorching red. After he inhaled, the rip seemed to seal a little, getting ultimately smaller by the second. Just when he thought he did something, a wolf's claw stabbed him through the gut, intruding through a disruption in the canvas of the open air. The thing was almost as long as Masquerade himself.

Everyone had shocked looks on their faces, seeing a large claw through his abdomen, you know, he would too. This didn't stop Masquerade, who inhaled in the horn again, the rip sealed ever so slightly, he used all the force in his lungs, then sealing it completely, and the wolf's claws disappeared. Next, he took the portal ball and threw it in the middle of the demons, now that the rip was sealed A huge purple sphere appeared in the middle, sucking the demons into it like a black hole. It was a one-use weapon, with it being destroyed upon use.

Just when Masquerade thought he saved everyone, another rip tore through the fabric of reality itself. Quickly, the wolf's claws returned and stabbed straight through Tamer's back. The two closest to Tamer were Hyper and Infinity, who tried helping him when the claw tried retracting back into the portal. They failed, and the wolf took them right along with Tamer, sucking them through the depths of Hell. Dark, Lazer, and Masquerade had locked shock as their main expression, as the rip sealed itself.

Hyper, Infinity, and Tamer were stuck in the depths of hell by themselves. Tears filled Dark's and Lazer's eyes, their hearts unable to beat fast, as well as their brains filling with bad thoughts of underlying death. Masquerade couldn't hold back his anger, something he was known for.

"GODDAMMIT! THIS IS ALL HERMES' FAULT!!" Masquerade screamed. "I'm going to kill that stupid dog, and then Hermes is next! He probably knew this would happen!"

"Woah woah now, chill out a bit! Getting angry isn't getting us anywhere." Dark advised, and Lazer nodded, the two remained sobbing.

"WHAT AM I SUPPOSED TO DO? My siblings are going to die because of me!" He screamed at Dark. Masquerade's eyes watered, blurring his vision.

Dark stumbled over his words before finally responding, "Ease up on the yelling! We need to find a way to Hell and rescue them." Dark suggested, wiping his tears, trying to bring longevity to the group, who were having trouble cooperating.

"We still have to save Jynx! And we have to figure out how to stop Misa and Sura. We have to stop Echo! And I have to sacrifice myself in the next nine days!" Masquerade blurted through tears. "Tell me how I'm supposed to do any of that in nine days! TELL ME DARK!" Dark couldn't answer, his voice stuttering a few mumbled noises, but nothing audible came out.

"The gods won't help us. . ." Lazer spotted the obvious.

"Figured that out just now, huh?!" Masquerade and Dark exclaimed simultaneously. Masquerade rubbed his eyes.

"First things first, we pray that Hyper, Lazer, and Tamer make it through Hell until we figure out our way down there," Masquerade outlined. "We'll have to figure out how to beat that wolf thing."

"Garm's his name, he's a real menace, and he can hop between realms at will," Dark explained as they exited the underground subway. Lazer remained silent.

"We'll deal with getting to Hell later. Starting off, we'll have to save Jynx. The only way to do that is to kill some guy named Jake, her father Mark, and Echo." Masquerade expressed.

"That's by far the hardest task on our list." Dark pointed out.

"Yeah, I know! Then we'll find a way to save our family, and automatically, we have to find out how to navigate Hell and kill Garm." Masquerade explained.

"Still not an easy task. . ."

"And last, I'll sacrifice myself and try putting an end to Misa then and there!" Masquerade explained. His voice was trembling, and his voice hoarse from going over the same threats over and over the past few days.

"How are you supposed to end Misa? You'll be dead once you sacrifice yourself!" Dark said as they approached the museum again.

"I guess it's time to reveal my secret. . ." Masquerade tensed, following Lazer and Dark's eyes. "These series of missions will be entirely possible because I'm immortal." They both gasped with excitement.

"WHAT! HOW!?" They both screamed at the same time. "How is that possible?!"

"I don't know, but I'm sure it'll catch Misa by surprise. I'll for sure at least injure him." Masquerade guessed.

"Huh, I guess that's how you survived Hercules, then?" Dark hypothesized. Masquerade opened his mouth to speak before he was interrupted by screams of a crowd. They all sighed and started running in the direction of the screams, ready to face the danger. As they arrived at the scene, they observed crowds of people running down the corridors, away from a large threat

Jynx was standing in the middle of the crowd, with Jace trying to protect and shield her. Jacob was screaming like an idiot, pointing at the monster in threat. There was a monster trying to kill her, a werewolf. The wolf seemed familiar to Masquerade, but he couldn't tell where it was from. Jynx seemed to know the wolf, however, and it seemed to know her, their eye contact proving sentiment. The second Jynx and Masquerade made eye contact, her mood seemed to improve immediately.

Masquerade tensed his hands, getting ready to blow everything up, once again. The werewolf stared at him in return, also readying to attack. Masquerade found out where he was going to release his anger. He exploded towards the wolf in haste, sliding under the wolf's feet. He popped on the other side and punched the animal in the stomach, then he charged an explosion and blew the wolf through the wall. Jynx cheered, and Jace was heating his hands with fire.

"SCORE! ONE POINT FOR OUR SAVIOR MASQUERADE!!!" Jacob screamed with joy, Masquerade smiled. The wolf got back to his feet, taunting them. Then, a stream of millions of lasers penetrated through the wolf's skin, successfully severing the arm off completely. Masquerade looked at Lazer impressively. He went airborne and gestured for Dark to fight underneath him.

He pointed at Lazer to stay where he was, commanding him to be the long-distance fighter. Masquerade flew towards the wolf, and Dark ran towards him. Lasers flew past their heads and hit the werewolf. Masquerade bopped him in the head a few times and flew around him, hitting him with occasional explosions, like he was an annoying fly. Pink flames seared over his lower body already, and there were many slices in his stomach.

The wolf let out a roar and a voice condescended. "These lunatics won't save you from your demise, Jynx!" A familiar chilling voice sounded from it, making their ears ring with icy tone. Large black scythes appeared out of the wolf's body, slicing Dark and Masquerade directly. A familiar force of power then blew them both towards the walls. The wolf howled, and all its injuries healed in an instant. The hound snapped, and sword cuts shaved down Lazer's, Dark's, and Masquerade's bodies, creating even more scars to his already fucked-up body.

Dark smiled, releasing blood that turned into arrows and projectiles. Masquerade stood up, giving Dark the blood from his injuries, and Lazer did the same. Arrows, lasers, and strikes of lightning volleyed toward the wolf quickly. Masquerade charged him again, and Dark followed.

A lightning laser hit the wolf in the chest. At first, nothing happened, but then a lightning strike from the sky shot through the roof, bounding the wolf down, rendering it unable to move its muscles. Dark quickly made a blood-fire sword and cut the legs off, making it fall to its furry knees. Masquerade took this opportunity to make a lightning sword and behead the creature, in haste, the head popped off effectively, blood splurging across the shattered glass.

Masquerade kicked the body over and warned everyone to close their eyes. He picked up the head and exploded the thing into a billion pieces. Their entire body and injuries were healed by this moment.

"You can open your eyes now. . ." He warned, everyone looking in amazement. Dark was able to clean the blood up pretty easily with his prowess. He stored it in a jar of already collected juices, which would have been weird if it weren't due to his power, he did this just in case he got into another fight. Jynx looked scared again, Masquerade approaching her subtly.

"Who was that, and how did he know your name?" Masquerade asked, and Dark walked up to his side. Jynx nodded reluctantly.

"That was one of Echo's wolf servants I'd seen in my mother's memories." She explained as she scratched her forearm. "He had two of them, meaning we only got rid of one." Then it hit Masquerade, he knew these wolves, and he already had fought one of them before, when he tried to rescue Bow, he felt so stupid and worthless. He seemed like his memory was the main cause for his low lacking IQ.

"I could've used that thing for answers!" Masquerade sweated. "That thing kidnapped my brother!" He announced. "Once we find him, we can rescue Bow! And then we'll rescue Hyper and Infinity!" Jynx looked confused.

"Wait, what! What happened to Hyper and Infinity?" Jynx questioned. Dark looked anxious. They explained everything that happened in the last hour. Jacob actually looked worried for the first time. Jace looked ready to leave and shut the world out, something he'd never actually consider doing. "You have a lot of rescuing to do." She tried adding humor to the wound, which was something only Hyper was good at.

The group searched for the teachers and attempted to explain the situation. Initially skeptical, Glicher didn't buy it, but Zander seemed more receptive. Three of their classmates were missing, and it was all Masquerade's fault, everything all seemed to be his fault. Bow was gone. Hyper was gone, and Infinity was gone. If he didn't get his shit together soon, Jynx and Jace would be too. The teachers advised they all go back to their rooms for the rest of the day and get some rest, they were already considering postponing the trip, and going home as soon as possible.

Everything was stressful the entire rest of the day, no one tried to cheer anyone up. They sat on their phones depressingly, waiting for some good news to arise. No one left the room, and no one argued. The teachers warned them of a concert later tonight with a quick lousy text, advising them by saying they were forced to go. Masquerade locked himself in the bathroom. He needed to find things out.

He looked in the mirror at himself. His eyes were bagged, and he looked stiff, and he quickly grabbed his hair and scrunched it violently. He noticed quick wisps of smoke erupting from his wrists, his brain subconsciously did this, something he realized he did unknowingly ever since he obtained the ability to produce explosions. His eyes plowed with pulses of pink that abruptly switched to a probe of purple lightning. Staring into the mirror, he lost himself. He lost his brain, wandering off into nothingness, a feeling that he actually could get around with. He then realized he was daydreaming, daydreaming of a girl, a girl with bright pink eyes, just like his own. His smile went unnoticed to himself, and so did his dilation in pupils.

Daydreaming is defined by the act of dreaming while awake, in other words, lost in thought. When you daydream, it affects two parts of the brain, the hippocampus and the visual cortex, these two parts communicate with each other, making the phenomena occur. However, the same parts are used when considering actual sleep, which made this next set of events happen for Masquerade. Upon dozing off, he closed his eyes for an extended period of time, the blackness of his eyelid was immediately shrouded with a spark of purple coloring. He awakened, forcing his eyes to open, only to see the scenery of an entire other world.

His body lay in a dark river that consisted of only black water, black water that had white speckles in it that looked like distant stars that engraved their centuries of history into the cries of the stream. He stood up, letting the mystical water trinkle its way down his body, he let the white grace of it make him glower with night-time glint. At the end of the river, consisted of a drop off that fell into the most vibrant waterfall he's ever seen. He followed the stream, edging off the side of the ledge, looking downwards. Purple jagged rocks made the water split like branches on a tree that grew for an eternity, except its leaves were replaced with magical bubbles that happened to be tinted black as well.

On the sides of said stream, were flowers that bloomed purple and white petals, the pollen was black speckles however. A field of these flowers revealed to follow the slithering river, revealing a pattern that you'd only see in a dream. Masquerade looked up, realizing this entire area was shrouded in darkness, because it was encased inside a huge cavern. The stalactites had a white tip, making the cave appear as if it had stars. He sat down in the translucent white blades of grass, letting their presence graze upon him.

His meditation was interrupted, when a familiar pair of eyes approached him from the darkness. "I found you." His voice said, Masquerade recognized the brooding tone, but couldn't pinpoint the man. "You dream a lot, you know that Masquerade? It's a symptom of the ADHD you have." His tan-ish body revealed itself, it was no other than Mardo. His arms were rolled back, revealing multiple shocking tattoos that were engraved deeply in his skin, they all represented something sinister, something Mardo could never share with anyone. His makeup glistened with the white light of the grass.

"Did you bring me here?" Asked Masquerade, who was still awed in the beauty of the realm. Mardo smiled, even though his makeup made it seem like he already was.

"Yes I did, like I said, I found you through your dreams." He plucked at a scar on his left ring finger, a scar that never seemed to heal away, despite his godly healing factor. "You've been dreaming of Jynx, haven't you? Not only that, but your thoughts are full of the dangers of the outside world. . ." He observed, walking across the blackened water, to sit next to Masquerade.

"How did you-" His voice shuddered. "Are you a mind reader?" He asked.

"No I can just tell by your dreams!" His finger snapped, and in between them, formed a pit of fire that glowered and raged with a hue of purple. "Haven't you guessed yet? I'm the god of dreams!" Masquerade was dumbfounded, once again. "This is the dream world, a world only I have access to." He stood up, grabbing Masquerade's hand slowly. In this realm, he felt his injuries level, and his emotions were floating. "Your subconscious can be your greatest enemy, but so can your conscience." He stood up, directing Masquerade to the water once more. Mardo raised his hand quietly, and a canoe came to formation in the ripples of the river. He boarded, getting ready to thrust the paddles, but he was surprised when they rowed themselves.

"What's the purpose of this?" He asked, his anger was unable to rise. Mardo smiled once more. Masquerade almost flipped out when the canoe started traveling towards the waterfall. He was left in amazement when the water underneath them; continued over the open air, allowing them to travel in the air without the ground's aid.

"Guidance. . . which is something a lot of heroes lack, someone to tell them what to do, and how they can do it." Mardo spoke, and now Masquerade was remembering their last encounter, which was resentful and filled with rage. He recalled them trying to kill each other. "Do you know how you're going to continue your quest?" His low voice made him want to fall asleep then and there.

"Kill everyone that gets in my way!" He yelled. Mardo frowned and shook his head in disapproval.

"No, that's not the way you should view. What if one of those gods in your way was your own friend, turned evil. Then what would you do?" He put him in a mental headlock.

"I guess you caught me there. . . What's with you anyways!? Stop acting so linear as if you weren't trying to kill me a few days ago!" He pressed.

"Regret is one of the most prominent feelings in a god's life, especially mine. However to answer your question, it's all just a mere act. Here, my thoughts and actions are hidden from everyone else, especially from my father, Misa. He's the reason I was acting the way I was that day, by using my power for his own good. But enough about me, what are you going to do to save Jynx?"

"Empathy? Trickery is my answer? Maybe I can persuade them to leave us alone, by carrying out a task?" He answered truthfully.

"That's far better than your first answer." The boat came to an abrupt stop, revealing that they now appeared in the presence of a huge celestial body, a large asteroid with life on it. A small planet, like the ones you'd see in a video game. Mardo jumped out, and Masquerade followed, quickly realizing there was no gravity. They jumped around the floating rocks, still continuing their conversation.

"I see myself deep inside you, a past that was only relevant eons ago. However, I want you to find out why, and realize why there's an ember of my past persona inside your soul. FInd out your true nature, Masquerade. If you can do that, then I bet you this entire realm, that you can start a revolution against my father, and win." His smile started fading. Then, unexpectedly, Mardo punched Masquerade with full force, forcing his brain to wake up.

He saw the mirror once more, and saw his eyes consisted of spirals of purple smoke. Masquerade walked out the door and decided he wanted to cheer the room up. Everyone was either sleeping or scrolling social media depressingly. Someone was knocking at the door, and everyone got up excitedly. Even though Tamer, Infinity, and Hyper were gone, they were still pretty excited to go to a concert.

Once they opened the door, the two supervisors and Jynx stood there waiting. It was dark by the time they had arrived at the concert, but it was still exciting. Mardo's speech still raced through his veins. The teachers had managed to get front-row seats, where the neon lights thrived the most. The concert masked everyone's emotions for a while, and the music was loud. Jynx seemed nervous, and Masquerade didn't know why. Jace also appeared to be extremely anxious. However, everyone else ignored their emotions and continued to have fun. He observed the and ahead of him, normal looking humans, although one of them had brown hair with black streaks and a killer smile.

Masquerade made an excuse to drag Jynx away, wanting to talk about her problems once more. He told everyone else they were going to get concessions. Once away from the loud music and crowds of people, Masquerade stopped the two. They were in a dark hallway next to the bathrooms.

"What's wrong? Don't you like concerts?!" He said teasingly, and Jynx still had that nervous look.

"No, it's not that, it's the one of people playing. That's Jake!" Jynx revealed, scratching her arm. Masquerade felt so dumb, as usual. He scratched his head for a long time.

"Well, what are we supposed to do?" He asked, his eyes gleaming red instead of pink. He thought for a long moment. "He knows we're here!? How can he track us?"

"I'm not sure, but I think it has something to do with Echo and his supernatural powers," she concluded. "It's not safe here; we need to stay in this city until tomorrow morning,"

Masquerade's eyes gleamed some more. "I've got an idea, but it's a bit reckless, however it might just save your life, so you better appreciate it," he said in a flirty voice. Jynx's eyes lowered, and she smiled, her eyes sputtering on and off with pinkness. She reached up on her toes, where her eyes finally started to flicker the right consistency. He felt compelled to stare into them, and in response, he grabbed her cheek softly, his hands smoothly caressing her pearlescent skin. He didn't know if it was an effect of her eyes or not, but he liked the jerk of command she conflicted. She smiled, as Masquerade's hand moved by itself to move her now pink glowing hair, to behind her ears. Then finally breaking the tension, he leaned in throughout invading thoughts and kissed her plump lips lightly. He blushed a little and didn't know what to say, but even more flustered was Jynx, who's cheeks glowered more pink than her beautiful eyes.

In response to this all, Jynx leaned in once more, kissing him back. The effect felt ever more compelling due to her demanded stare. "Now we're even." She whispered with such a giddy voice, that Masquerade tried delivering another peck, but she blocked. "Enough. . ." Her voice flicked, and with that, her features returned to normal, her green eyes returned, and the strands of hair glistening brown. So then, he left, gesturing for her to follow.

They returned to their seats with some popcorn; otherwise, it'd look suspicious if they didn't. Masquerade nodded at Jace, indicating he knew of the problem, and his anxiety dissipated. He noticed that Jake was eyeing their group almost the entire time, he was the one playing the guitar with some other concert friends. The two made eye contact viscously, which resulted in Jake smiling.

He needed a plan to ensure Jake wouldn't follow them out of the concert without causing a scene. Suddenly, Masquerade knew what to do. After all, he knew two things: every time he died, he seemed to unlock more of his abilities. One of these was to blow up items that he's already touched, and it's very common for concert fans to throw items on stage.

His only problem was that he only had one item to throwa crumbled Snickers bar in his back pocket. He took it out disappointed and stared at Dark, who smiled and fumbled in his pockets. The sound of loose change came from them, one thing he never thought he would do was throw money at the worst guitar player in the world. Jynx and Jace looked more anxious than usual, which Masquerade hated because he was the one saving their butts once again. First, Masquerade grabbed the Snickers bar.

He looked at it in his hand for a long moment. Then he hurled it on stage directly towards Jake. His long brown hair looked yellow in the neon strobes, but his stupid smirk was wiped off his face in seconds. Masquerade then grabbed all the change in one hand. Four pennies, three nickels, and two quarters, racking up ten explosions at hand. He scattered the change across the band floor. No one noticed at first, and then Jake looked a little suspicious, as if he knew what Masquerade was capable of.

Masquerade smiled and held his fingers high in the air, his thumb laying on his middle finger, ready to snap, and as he released, time seemed to stop. The music slowed, and everyone else around him stopped as well, the slow motion killed the moment of anticipation caused by the eventual sweet release of a drumming explosion. The only other person who could move was Jake.

"So you're the savior, huh?" Jake's voice bellowed down to Masquerade. His senses were deteriorating. "You don't look very heroic, and your attitude could do a makeover!" He teased. "If Zeus really thinks you're the one who's going to stop me, then he's got a lot of highschool classes to retake!" Masquerade's anger boiled, and he didn't even seem to question how Jake knew anything about Zeus.

Time returned to normal, and suddenly, the entire stage was ablaze, smoke billowing. The last few explosions went off quickly, and broken instruments flew out of the rubble. People were screaming, guards were running, and alarms were sounding. Masquerade stared at the stage floor. Six innocent people were dead, Jake was gone, and bodies were scattered. He was a cold-blooded murderer of six normal people making a living. His memory then retaliated, remembering when he killed a stadium of innocent demons earlier against Hades. Was he really the hero he claimed to be? His brain pulsed one more time, reminding him of what Mardo had said, 'I see myself deep inside you, a past that was only relevant eons ago.', was this what he meant?

This didn't put him above Misa at all! He hadn't thought about these guys being actual humans, his only violent thought was that they were working with Jake, but clearly it had been a scandal. He stood expressionless, unable to articulate the cause of his actions. Jynx and Jace dragged him out of the concert seats. One thing led to another, and he was on the bus, looking out the rainy window, stuck with his own thoughts once more. He was still shocked he had murdered someone; he couldn't bring himself to pay attention to anyone. The teachers were lecturing the students on something, but he wasn't paying attention, something Mardo said he did a lot.

Staring out the window, tears streamed down his face. It was nightfall by now, and the road was darkened due to rain. He didn't know if it was him, the gods, or the emotional standpoint everyone was at that made the weather extreme. If it weren't for the glowing stream of light coming from the car that seemed to stay on their trail for the past fifteen minutes, then he wouldn't have snapped back to reality. The car had been in the same place the entire time, which wouldn't have been odd if they hadn't taken such a complicated route back to the hotel. Masquerade rose in his seat, locking eyes on the car. Immediately, the thing took off and sped up towards the front of the bus, most likely in response to being caught. Masquerade felt goosebumps on his forearms, feeling the urge to act, but the teachers were already fed up with everything that had happened.

Then, the sunroof of the car opened. A familiar face jumped out from the roof and landed on top of the car. The car then swerved to block the path of the bus, disrupting the traffic. It drove right in front of them, making black etchings in the street. Jake turned around and faced the windshield of the bus, jumping straight through the glass. Glicher was driving, and Zander sat right behind her. Their fear rose immediately, and Jake smiled at Jynx, his eyes gleaming with the anticipated spree of murders that came with being born a female under her family. Everyone on the bus looked ready to give up.

Jake held his hand up, and a sword appeared out of thin air. A meter-long purple blade with a misty black handle. Rain drops scattered atop the bus roof and made the scene all the more intense. Everyone's bodies almost seemed paralyzed, because no one came to Glicher's defense when the blade was plunged straight through her gut. She tried to scream, but nothing came out, only a fountain of black blood. It was almost like the sound was muffled to Masquerade, like it was when time slowed.

Jake lifted her body with the sword and threw her straight out the windshield. He then pointed the sword at Zander and told him to take the wheel. He walked down the aisle of the bus, looking at the kids in the seats one by one. His blade rested by his thigh as he walked viciously, hanging with the intent to stab someone that tried defying him. But the second he raised his blade, Masquerade was in the air, ready to attack. His hearing returned as Jynx screamed something, Jace was being oddly quiet again. Masquerade dodged Jake's first strike. The second time, he wasn't so lucky.

His blade cut the side of his shoulder, and he retreated backward. The people on the bus started filing away from the two, shuffling seats. Masquerade wasn't going to be turned into a kabob today. Jake thrust his sword towards him, and he couldn't move all of a sudden, which was most likely Jake's power. Then, the blade was parried, and Dark came to his defense. Time slowed again. Lazer was shooting about to fire a laser, but it turned to ash.

Jake pierced Masquerade's stomach and threw him straight through the bus ceiling. Jake then climbed atop the bus and stomped on his back as they stood on the roof. Rain trickled down on them, making their bodies wet and shiny. Jake then stabbed the sword into Masquerade and pinned his hands together with the blade. He squatted down to his ear and giggled manically. Dark quickly tried coming to his defense, but Jake almost kicked him off the bus. He held on by a few lucky fingers.

Masquerade was praying to the gods that Lazer would keep himself hidden. Jake whispered in his ear. "Told you Masquerade. . ." His voice faltered. "You weren't strong enough to defend yourself. So now you have to watch Jynx die as well. So sad!"

Masquerade's veins pulsed, and anger rose, smoke steamed out of his hands and the sound of beating drums roared through the rain scattering winds. Jake watched observantly. He tried producing an explosion, but nothing came out, no matter how hard he tried to release. Dark observed them quietly, blood seeped into the bus via the hole they made. Everyone stayed quiet. Jake was laughing silently until he was hit by an unknown force. He staggered a little and released the blade from Masquerade's hands in quick succession. Lazer appeared out of thin air and helped Masquerade to his feet, his hands glowing with the power of light energy.

Jake scowled as his blade seemed to extend out longer. Swiftly, he let out his blade and almost cut the two with a singular strike. Dark took this moment to get to his feet and throw his blood at Jake, who dodged, almost like he knew that the blood was dangerous. Lazer shot his lasers, but he dodged every single one so elegantly. Masquerade tried blowing him up, but once again, he evaded perfectly.

The next thing he knew, the blade was stabbed through his chest once more. Jake held him up high in the air and mocked him. He was turned into a kebab, fair enough.

"I was going to spare you, but I changed my mind," He said as he flicked his blade towards the edge of the bus. Masquerade flew through the air, and the blade raged through his chest down to his crotch, slicing him down cleanly, his body couldn't heal. His body splattered on the wet pavement, and he was run over by ongoing traffic. A semi-truck finished the job for Jake, and Masquerade hoped that the two could hold out longer.

He saw everyone's faces of terror from the side view of the bus. Jynx, Jace, Jacob, Stray, all of them, their faces were distraught. Then he blacked out.

He saw Anubis once again. "Third time's the charm aye?" He said sarcastically with a smile on his face. Masquerade looked down miserably.

"I need help, Anubis. I'll never be able to protect Jynx if you don't." Masquerade explained. Anubis looked confused.

"I never try to believe in immortality when I see it, son. You are the first truly immortal god I have witnessed." Anubis stepped forward. Masquerade let him talk. "I'll help you, mainly because you're probably going to be back here over and over again." He giggled. "Meaning I'll be forced to comply with you!"

A black blade formed into Anubis' hands. He stared at it for a long while. "I have to explain something first." His expression changed, and his appearance became more clear. "So, as punishment for the both of us, Misa had sealed Mardo inside me. So, we share the same subconscious but have one body. So his power is trapped in my body, and he can't get out without either my or Misa's permission. He's quite annoying from time to time, but that's behind the point. We are good friends. However, we fought alongside in the war against the Egyptian pantheon, which is why there are none of them present to date. Misa, Sura, and their kids led a war against them, where Misa brainwashed me into fighting for him, and I was forced to kill my brethren Osiris, with the help of Mardo of course. Misa had started this war so he could have access to the afterlife and use the dead to raise an army, just in case the other pantheons tried fending for themselves. After Mardo tried saving me from him and his clutches, he made us both stay down here for eternity and greet the dead and decide where they go." It was only seconds for Masquerade to connect the dots, Mardo was just as bad as he was, killing innocents, talking badly about others, having a potty mouth, and praising the wrong people, but he changed with punishment, and that's why he has deep regrets. That's why he wanted Masquerade to be careful of his actions, because he wasn't careful himself, and now he paid the price. Mardo wants Masquerade to be the god that he himself could never be.

Anubis held the blade towards Masquerade, gleaming with white streaks, although the entire thing was made entirely of shadow. It reminded him of the scenery from the dream world that Mardo took him to. "This was the blade that killed Osiris, and it holds both mine and Mardo's power in it. Osiris' soul keeps the blade alive." Anubis gave the blade to him. "Now return to the overworld and show Jake who you were meant to be!" His eyes seemed to water.

"I know of your end goal, young Masquerade, and I'll say that you have mine and Mardo's blessings. We both hope you are able to stop Misa once and for all." Masquerade faded back into nothingness. He blacked out again.

Masquerade jolted awake on the side of the road. The bus didn't make it far, meaning that it had only been a few quick seconds. Traffic also hasn't stopped yet. Masquerade flew upwards and blasted towards the bus. The sword was in his hands, all its power glowering with ultimatum. Jake seemed to be walking away from Lazer, who was injured on the floor. Dark's pink flames glittered in the rain, and Jake stepped away from them. Masquerade landed on the bus and yelled Jake's name.

He held his sword upwards and towards Jake. He didn't hesitate and swung his blade. Masquerade parried it and thrust towards his stomach. He remembered his gift from Athena, and watched it glow gold, giving him the knowledge and art of swordplay. Jake dodged and counterattacked. Sparks flew in the air as the two fought. Their blades clashed repeatedly. Masquerade used his explosive prowess and out-strengthened Jake. His blade flew towards the ground, leaving him weaponless. Then Masquerade landed the first attack on him.

His blood oozed onto the metal flooring. Quickly, he evaded around and grabbed his sword again, almost cutting Masquerade. Immediately, Dark came around and slashed at him with a flame blade. Jake parried him over and over until Masquerade joined in. He tried defending against both of them, but it didn't end well for him. Dark slashed his shoulder, and Masquerade thrusted his stomach.

Jake coughed blood, and the two almost fell off the bus from an unknown force. Then Lazer came into the fight. The three waited to attack him, the rain droplets making a melody that Masquerade could follow.

"Well done, but I was just testing you. Now I'll get rid of all three of you," He threatened. His eyes changed from blue to purple, his blade extended again, and he charged Masquerade first, who didn't even care to notice how he was still even alive. Lazer created a sword made of a light material. He was faster than before and ten times more aggressive. His combos became deadlier, and his slashes did more damage.

They tried out-maneuvering him, but he quickly succeeded in multiple attacks. He seemed to stop when it came to attacking Dark. He used blunt force, like the end of his blade, when attacking him. He was avoiding drawing blood from him. The three couldn't land any successful attacks, so Masquerade kicked him instead. He released an explosion and blew him off the bus. He then used his sword as a projectile, and another explosion came.

The sword was now struck in Jake's chest. Dark released his blood, and even though Jake avoided a lot of it, pink flames still devoured his body. Masquerade's blade was back in his hands, and he didn't know why. Jake's body hit the pavement with a loud thud, and he rolled aggressively. He wasn't dead, but it bought them some time to recover quickly. Masquerade jumped down into the bus, followed by his siblings. Everyone's faces lit up at the sight of them.

Zander still didn't slow down one bit, focusing on driving. Masquerade told him to find them a completely different destination. Zander agreed and decided they would talk about this unfortunate series of events later. Masquerade was exhausted and sat down next to Jynx. Who had her eyes buried in her hands. He put his hand around her shoulders and tugged her in for a tight hug. She leaned into him and sobbed quietly into his chest. Masquerade remained quiet, and so did the rest of the bus. There was a hole in their roof, and they had no clue where they were going next.

Chapter 12
Infinity

The side of Hell they landed in this time wasn't the same as their first arrival, the lava was a normal fiery orange and red instead of wisping blue, and the demons were ten times more aggressive. They've been attacked almost ten times by the time they've been trapped down there. Tamer kept saying an army of angels would descend into Hell and save them from every bit of danger there ever was, but Infinity doubted it every time Tamer mentioned it, mainly because nothing ever happened, considering they've been burning for almost twenty-four hours.

The trio walked down a dark cave, their feet already being sore from excessive hiking. Infinity hated the smell of Hell, which consisted of overcooked steak with a hint of heavy smoke. It was boiling in the wild of Hell. During his trip down here, he learned that Hell consists of actual cities, where the heat isn't as bad. It mostly consisted of dark and red volcanic rock, but often, you could see vegetation, which was odd. Tamer suggested they move towards the capital of Hell.

Infinity was confused, thinking Hades' palace was the capital. Apparently, there are many rulers, and every ruler holds a capital, so there is no true capital because the rulers are at constant war, something that reminded him of his own hometown back at his home planet. Tamer said they've landed in Satan's domain of Hell. Infinity didn't know who was worse, Hades or Satan, but he had a feeling he'd find out very soon.

After a while of navigating a huge cave system, they appeared in the front view of a massive medieval-looking city. When he says massive, he really means massive. The city line spread so far across the pool of lava that he couldn't even see the end of the city. Tamer seemed to smile, which was weird because why would he be happy to see Satan?

"This is it. . ." Tamer said as they struggled out of the tight cave. The city sat on a huge block of black stone, supporting the entire foundation from the raging ocean of lava. The block was placed in the lava and seemed to absorb the heat well, containing the thermal energy for conservation. At the bottom of the block ran a line of huge boat docks, and on said docks sat huge pirate-designed boats that were designed to withstand high temperatures. These boats seemed to be made of blackish-purplish wood material, which looked flammable from afar.

Now, the only thing they needed to do was cross the lava without dying. At first, Infinity suggested making clones they could walk on, but Hyper had a different plan in mind. He spoke to the nether rock in the wall, and it quickly formed into a raft that was able to float. From there they went on to the docks and entered the city. The best way Infinity could describe Hell was by calling it a huge cave, meaning flying straight upwards, you'd hit a roof of stalactites. Although the ceiling of Hell was so high up, you can't even see it from ground level.

Upon reaching the docks, they entered a dark hallway carved into the side of the massive block. Inside was a large ancient elevator that was at most three meters huge. There was a lever that, when pulled, brought the elevator upwards.

Once they reached the top, it revealed the interior of the city. It brought them to a main road, and although there weren't any cars, they had carriages pulled by hellish-looking horses. Many 'people' stopped in their tracks to view the odd-looking trio, who definitely didn't appear to be one of them. Although demons looked very similar to humans, they had huge horns intruding from their heads. They also had spanning bat wings that were often held back in the outfits they wore, but it was still hard for them to hide the massive wings that held a huge part of their genetic makeup.

Their eyes were almost always different shades of red, orange and yellow, with the occasional pure black or pure white eyes. Their hair had a range of colors that could be anything. Lastly, they had long black or red tails that had a point at the end. Tails, wings, and horns could be genetic, and all have different varieties, shapes, and colors, meaning one demon could have one horn, or two, or three, and so on.

The demons stared at them weirdly, but no one stopped to say anything, judging them silently. Infinity stared at Tamer weirdly. "How exactly are we supposed to reach Satan? Isn't he like, you know, royal? And protected by bodyguards and other important stuff?" Infinity asked. Tamer smiled.

"Great question, but you see, I'm an angel. Any time angels are seen in Hell, they are automatically brought to the nearest ruler, who are then sent to prison and tortured. And since I'm related to Dave, they can't kill me, so we'll have a free ride to Heaven." Tamer explained correctly.

"Great plan I guess, but how do we know that he won't kill you? Or even me and Hyper?"

"Because I'll bribe him and make sure we'll get out of here safe, and he'll listen to me because if he tries killing me, then Dave will declare war on Satan, and they don't want another war after they just lost to Hades." Infinity felt relieved. "Now we just wait. . ." His angelic presence roared through the ranks of the demons.

They walked into a nearby store, which was filled with weird-looking candies that looked as if they'd blow up upon eating. Spending their afternoon shopping at a demonic candy shop wasn't exactly what they had in mind, even if it was afternoon time right now, which was hard to tell under the wraps of rock. Automatically, the cashier of the tiny shop looked suspicious. He eyed the group the entire time they were in there. Honestly, you could take one good look at Tamer and automatically decide that he's an angel.

Especially since he has a huge glowing gold halo, the cashier demon rang the security alarm. Tamer smiled and waited. Soon, the demon police broke through the door with heavy weaponry and bullets at hand. The three let the police take them in, and the next thing you know, they're right in front of Satan. Infinity had no clue what Tamer's plan was, but he followed reluctantly, because he himself had no plan.

"Another angel, huh?" Satan's voice boomed. Now, Infinity wasn't attracted to Satan, but he couldn't deny the overwhelming presence. He sported black slicked-back hair and massive horns protruding from his head, with eyes filled with hate. Tamer watched intently. "Kill all three of them!" He announced, and his bodyguards swooped in immediately. Tamer was surprised, and Infinity was disappointed. Infinity jumped towards one of the guards, ready to attack. The demon gestured his head forward, and Infinity almost ran into his horns.

He dodged under him and tried punching him, but it wasn't effective, as his skin was as tough as an iron chestplate. He had heavy iron armor on, Infinity forming a lightning sword and sliced the armor like butter. The demon's blood spluttered lava instead of blood, making a scenery of shining orange light. He sliced through his waist, and the demon fell to the floor, the shining light of the sword glinting off its blackened body. Satan's expression changed almost immediately.

Guards stormed the room, leaving their measly group of three against a roaring army of twenty. Infinity looted the soldier's body and took his sword. He charged the group and attacked the first person he made contact with. Hyper was attacking as well, and Tamer stared mindlessly before he did anything. Hyper mumbled something, and the ground itself came rising into spikes. With Infinity-made clones to match the army in number count.

Even with the clones, which were weaker than Infinity and had the durability of a tree, they were overwhelmed quickly. Tamer had also tried fighting, but it didn't go well for him. Infinity had to think of something, his mind racing, and sweat was bouncing off his back more than usual. One of the guards raised his blade, ready to slice Infinity's face off.

Infinity flinched, his eyes closing tightly, but the attack didn't come. Upon opening his eyes, he saw that the demon was frozen in place, unable to move. His mind felt fresh, refreshing with rates only capable of a computer with an overly high CPU. He didn't know how or why, but when he raised his hand, the demon flew straight upwards, his head hitting the ceiling of the throne room with a loud thud, crashing directly through the wreckage. He aimed his hand at the nearest demon and flicked his wrist, its limbs responding according to his mind. He flew straight through the rest of them, throwing them around like a mother cleaning up leftover toys on the floor. His clones dissipated, and Infinity held control of all the demons, even Satan.

Everyone stood frozen, unable to move, Infinity smiled and walked towards Satan with a devious smile that was more menacing than the demon lord right ahead of him, although Satan quickly broke through the defense. He stared down at the three, showing signs of a clearly impressed-looking expression. Then he huffed, and a wave of fire came spitting out.

Infinity didn't know how he knew, but he guessed the fire would've vaporized him to dust. He held his hands up and prepared to die, attempting to push the flames away. Then everything went black, he didn't know if he died suddenly, but then the next thing he knew he was flying through the air. Tamer and Hyper were next to him, and below them was a pool of red lava, glowing a color that represented blood.

Infinity screamed and held out his hands once again, this time, a portal opening. The space was outlined in a purple color, making the shape of an oval Inside the purple portal was another pool of lava, but it was blue. All three fell through it forcefully, feeling the intense change in heat difference. He released more power, and the portal stacked upon itself, making multiple layers of portal covered lines. They fell through a series of colors all ranging from blue lava, purple lava, green lava, orange lava, and even black lava. The portal seemed endless, but eventually, it closed, and the trio found themselves on a snowy mountain with cascading frozen peaks. It didn't look anything like hell, and the heat from hell quickly faded and turned into a freezing cold. The mountain range was high, this time he couldn't tell where they were. He quickly looked at Tamer, who was shivering excessively.

"Now what?" Infinity asked, and Tamer shook his head disapprovingly.

"I have no clue. . ." He said, and Infinity could only guess they were back on Earth, hopefully in The Himalayas.

Chapter 13
Masquerade

Thirteen was a number that Masquerade always despised. He always had, and he was reminded of his hatred even more when he boarded the plane. He sat a row away from Jynx because there was no row thirteen, and the omission angered him, sparking curiosity about why it was skipped. He knew that Jake was alive, but he hoped to Hell that he didn't want to duel on every type of transportation there was, because last time they fought on a rental bus, while it was pouring.

The class was in a really good mood lately, which was surprising because one of their teachers had just died. Their adventure was eventually plastered through every article in the newspaper, and broadcasted carefully through the news. They had to provide extensive explanations to the authorities just to be able to board the plane. The only one who wasn't in a good mood was Zander, who was grieving the close death of his coworker. No one bothered him, though. Masquerade sat next to Jacob, who had a great sense of humor.

Moreover, Jynx had to reveal her secret to everyone, the class had to know due to safety measures, and that way, Zander knew what really was going on, so not everything was blamed on Masquerade, and his expressive desire to destroy every place they had been. His sword could conveniently absorb into his body, cleverly avoiding detection by security. He wondered how the mechanics of it worked, quickly thinking about Anubis and his backstory. Masquerade's mind wandered, thinking if the gods back then ever had to drive cars, and if they had showdowns in their Lamborghini's or if they just gaveled at each other with lame old horses.

Zander tried cheering himself up by telling everyone that they were going to a zoo when they landed, everyone was excited except him. Jacob was messing with his phone and insisted Masquerade give him his number. He gave in, and the two played 'Imessage games' for a good portion of the flight.

Upon Masquerade getting up to use the restroom, Jace inexplicably followed him, who had been eyeing them throughout the plane ride. They both went into the restroom together, which was odd, to even Masquerade. He let him fluctuate.

"I have to talk to you about Jake. . ." He trailed off, his voice faltering. Masquerade flinched at the mention of him, remembering the encounter he just had with the force of mystery. "I kind of know his history and where he comes from." He continued, revealing secrets that should've been revealed a long time ago. "I hid this even from Jynx. I didn't want her to know, O feel she'd be paranoid out of her mind if she ever found out,"

Masquerade didn't like where this was going, "It might be better that way. . ." He replied.

"Jake was a childhood friend of my older brother. He often hung out with the both of us, however he betrayed me, and I hated him for that. I'm too weak to get my revenge, so I was hoping you'll be able to achieve that for me."

Masquerade nodded, assuring, 'He will meet his end by my hands. I promise." Masquerade smiled and patted Jace's shoulder. "Just play the memories in your head, and I'll be able to experience them pretty well." Jace looked a little anxious, but he eventually agreed. He usually loved this part, shuffling people's memories and all, but this memory hurt even him. Masquerade gazed into Jace's eyes, and still noticed that wall of fog from the dance a while back, and how he wasn't able to read his thoughts clearly. Then the flashback happened, its clear contents filtering through the retinas of the two teenage boys.

Young Jace raced through vast fields of tall grass. He, Cosbi, and Jake often went hunting for frogs. Jace was around ten years old at the time, his brother being slightly older. They were preparing to fish with each other. He lost where Jake went, but he knew they'd eventually find each other. He kept searching for frogs, doing what he was expected of. Jace was often blown away by Jake's manifesting abilities, he was able to do supernatural things, like speak as other voices, which often got him free candy from the supermarket. His appearance didn't seem to change, however.

He was running mindlessly through the grass, and the next thing he knew, he had run into Cosbi, who had multiple frogs in an enclosed bucket. His brother smiled at Jace and patted his head, with a grin that could enlighten the dark world.

"Found you!" He giggled and lifted his hands in the air. Jake appeared behind him. "We better get back home. It's getting late." He suggested while looking towards the horizon. Jake nodded reluctantly and gestured him forwards, taking them hours to leave the huge field, but eventually they managed to get out.

"We'll fish early tomorrow morning, and don't worry, I'll be staying the night to wake you guys, since you both aren't the best at getting up early." He mocked and continued walking. Jace glanced down at his belt, noticing a knife with a striking purple glint, he didn't know why Jake always kept that knife with him. It really creeped him out sometimes, but he ignored it as they approached his house.

Jake was a constant presence, and Cosbi provided unwavering support. He went to every football game Cosbi had, and always defended them in any situation. He was just the best kind of friend anyone could ask for, one that came once in a lift time. Once they reached the house, they ate dinner and quickly went to bed excited.

He was anxious for tomorrow. They often went fishing together, but this year, they had full schedules of sports and other events. Jake slept in Cosbi's room, and Jace had his own. He fed his dog and quickly tried to sleep. It took a while, but the excited young kid eventually put himself to sleep.

In the morning, he was jerked awake by Jake, who held a frog to his face, and Jace jumped out of bed immediately. The sun hasn't even risen yet, but the three of them got ready quickly. It was perfect conditions, the weather was amazing, and they had collected enough worms and frogs for bait. Jake smiled as they walked out of the door. He had a nice grin that was often deceiving, with brown eyes and his gleaming brown hair.

Cosbi drove the ranger, driving them and making it to their favorite spot. The ledge had a perfect view of the poorly lit river, with the sun just barely now rising on the horizon. Fishing poles were ready, chairs and drinks were set, and bait was ready to use. It would have been the perfect day. The three threw their hooks in with baits and readied themselves for a labor filled hours.

They caught many fish and shared many laughs. Then Jake told Jace to find some more bait. They had run out of frogs but still had many worms. Jace didn't hesitate and quickly started searching for them. He figured he'd capture only three and return as quickly as he could. He found one stuck in the cracks of the ground. He quickly grabbed its hind legs and started searching again.

He found another frog hidden in a patch of long grass, and in the same area, he found many frogs. He took all of them, around four. So, in total, he had six. As he returned with the frogs in hand, he walked back to camp. He found it weird that he didn't hear Jake and Cosbi talking about some stupid video game. As he approached, he heard Jake's heavy breathing instead of murmurs of joy, and a searing stabbing sound was evident. Jace sprinted up the rocky hill. Once he was able to see Jake clearly, he gasped.

Jake stood hunched over Cosbi, his body was limp and spread across the floor. Blood pooled along the equipment, falling into the river water. Jace covered his mouth, stopping himself from screaming. Jake smiled hysterically.

"He didn't deserve this, Jace!" He screamed as his blood-covered hand reached for his face, the blood smearing on his cheeks and lips. The blood dripped down horrifically. Jace tried thinking of any moment where Jake could've actually been this insane. In every memory he had, Jake was always happy, with slight hints of bipolar disorder, but nothing that wasn't too evident. He always had a smile on his face, this time however, it was covered with the red gleaming blood of his first brother. He was always cheering them up when he needed to, but now, he stood on his brother's body, responsible for his death.

Jace started to tear up immediately. His tears swelled and blocked his vision. Jake stared at him like he was confused, piping down and staring at Jace.

"I'll spare you, although I originally planned for you to die as well. But now, since you'll live, you can't tell anyone that I killed your brother, or else I'll find you, and mark my words. You, will, die." He spoke in gaps between his words. Jace nodded and stood in fear. Jake pointed at him for whatever reason. "Now scram home before I change my mind. GO!" He screamed.

Jace flinched and trembled, stumbling out of the way, limping his way home. He couldn't hold his tears, both of his parents were at work, and he plumped down on his bed. Anyone could piece together the puzzle, mainly because Cosbi died once Jake disappeared. He just wished he got to say goodbye to his brother.

The flashback fainted away like a ghost, and Masquerade remembered that Dark had mentioned the name 'Cozbi' before, which meant a big liar and deceitful. Dark was always spitting random facts like that, something he was grateful for. Masquerade pulled away from the memory in haste, his mind filling with hatred and depressing thoughts. Jace held his own forearm uncomfortably. Masquerade unexpectedly through his body against Jace's. Forcing him into a hug. It was awkward, but the two sorted it out normally, especially since they were in a plane bathroom. Jace's eyes watered, and he cracked his knuckles.

"How can someone be that evil?" Masquerade's blood seemed to boil again, smoke rising from his hands. "He's going to die the next time I see him!" Jace seemed to lighten up after he said that. They both left the bathroom awkwardly, as there was a nice woman waiting in line, batting them a worried eye. Masquerade returned to his seat quietly.

He sat next to the window, staring out of it decisively. The deep blue sky was beautiful, no clouds were to be seen. It would've been a beautiful day to do anything fun. The land below was hard to see from the height of the plane. Masquerade looked directly at the plane wing. His mind filled with shadow. Suddenly, a flash of yellow lightning filled his vision.

The wing was struck. Automatically, it exploded and fell off the plane. Masquerade was never more confused than ever before in his life. Just when he thought it was over, another flash came from above, and thunder struck even louder. More lightning had destroyed the top of the plane, making a large hole in the ceiling.

Everyone started panicking as gas masks dropped from the ceiling. The power shut off in the plane, and the lights went blank, strobing delicately. The entire plane was dark, and the only light source came from the windows, and the large gaping hole in the material above. People screamed, babies cried, and Zander clearly had enough. He grabbed Dark's and Lazer's hands and rushed them towards the pilot's room. The pilots gave them an unexpected glare.

"We need to get outside and on the wing. Trust us, we can fix it." The head pilot sneered and nodded reluctantly.

"It's clear daylight, and we just got struck by lightning, so why not trust three teenage boys to save our plane." He said sarcastically, and he opened the pilot door. Wind soared through the door and interrupted them. Masquerade climbed out first, followed by the other two. The pilots looked at each other and decided that they were absolutely crazy. On top of the plane, the wind almost knocked them off. The wing was badly torn off, wavering the movement of the plane. Crouching down, they examined the issue.

"How the hell are we supposed to fix this!?" Dark screamed, his knuckles looked really sore, and he was cracking them again. Lazer looked the same way, and Masquerade couldn't help but think how dangerous he was, something a lot of people had said would be the case.

"Easy! I got a pretty cool solution to this." He put his hands on the plane and smudged them together. "We put our lightning powers together and make a new wing made from straight lightning!" He yelled in excitement, his arms zipping in electrical energy immediately.

"You better pray to whatever god that you didn't offend that this actually works!" Dark yelled at him. Masquerade smiled as the three put their hands down, gripping the side of the plane. The first lightning wing that formed had a deformed look, and it made the plane more unbalanced than it was without one the wing. They tried one more time, and the wing looked worse than the last time, the lightning scattering into a jumbled up shape.

Lazer sighed in frustration and attempted to create it on his own, but his efforts ended in failure. Dark's hands emitted steam, and red smoke trailed from them, his prowess continuing to grow in power even more. In a quick moment of despair, they saw Dark's hands observingly shift shapes, the powers in his palms turning large polka dots. It seemingly absorbed the metal under him, taking the particles of the matter directly into his dermis. The tiny patch of the plane's material underneath his hands disappeared out of thin air. It was obvious to tell; his hands had just destroyed matter itself. Dark barely held on by a scrap of the plane, his knees placed down on a thin wire of metal that revered with the wind. Passengers stared up at them from the gaping hole in the plane's surface.

Masquerade waved sympathetically at Jynx; she responded with a thumbs down. He smiled back, while Dark focused intently on something. They all gestured back to the destroyed wing. The next thing they knew, the wing completely formed itself, the same exact way it was before. It spiraled to life from the ripped seam. Dark's hands steamed even more, his concentration proving keen, and his fingers seemed to have deep wounds all over them. He stood up, amazed, staring at Masquerade.

"What the hell was that!?" Lazer questioned him.

"I don't know! But it hurts like hell, and my hands are burning with pain right now." The wing functioned normally, bringing the plane to ultimate balance. Masquerade had no clue what just happened. "It seems to me that I can destroy matter and store it for later uses or reshape it into something else completely." His body trembled a bit, looking down at the distorted metal that he destroyed moments prior. The power to reshape matter came with overwhelming drawbacks, which showed prominently when he fell to his knees once more.

Lazer pointed towards the hole in the plane, shocked expressions fluttering like sparks of lightning. All three of them turned at the same time., hearing loud screams coming from the plane. From the hole, a werewolf on two feet came crawling out. His fur was entirely black, which vibrantly contrasted against the wisping rays of the yellow sun. This was the one Masquerade fought long ago when saving Bow, his angered look was ready to fight. Masquerade readied his hands, and so did Dark.

"We're sparing this one boys!" Masquerade went hysterical, laughing and jumped high in the air. He let out a little laugh that seemed to scare the people on the plane, who were watching closely. This time he felt like the villain in this situation, his arms flailing with destruction. The werewolf snapped his claws, he didn't know if it could even snap. The same move occurred as before, deep cuts invaded their skin, but this time the blood automatically turned, shaped, and formed into arrows, shooting and piercing into the wolf's hide.

Masquerade felt a twinge of jealousy towards Dark, whose power was glistening in difference compared to his own. The plane's material disappeared and started turning into lunges of vines made of silver metal. They started wrapping around the enemy and bound him to the floor. Masquerade jumped and threw an explosion that threw him straight off the plane.

Masquerade flew towards the enemy, tackling him in midair. They spiraled around the plane, engaging in a brief aerial skirmish. They orbited it as Masquerade continuously punched him over and over, thinking of it as water current in a river, except in the air.

Then he grabbed the wolf by the chest and threw him straight upwards in the air. Dark crossed his arms and watched. Lazer shot lasers, but they missed the target., ultimately making shines of light in the clear blue sky. Masquerade used his explosions to gain momentum in a circular motion, making his entire body spiral at millions of miles an hour, the vision around him was blurred but the smoke from his hands created a vortex. Then he released wind from his hands and evenmore explosions. Soon enough, an entire tornado twirled around him, except the tornado was made entirely of explosions and smoke.

One push upwards, and he burst towards the flying mutt. His hand ached, holding it out like a superhero. His entire hand grabbed the wolf by the snout, and he released the energy that built up, causing an explosion bigger than he imagined. It almost hit the plane but missed safely. Landing back on the plane, Masquerade couldn't help but feel impressed by his own performance. Instead of a massive explosion, he transformed it into a picturesque firework display. This awed the passengers, and even the pilots. Dark mumbled. "So much for sparing him." He rolled his eyes. Masquerade smiled.

"I read his mind, and the wolf's basically brain-dead. He's being controlled by Echo, so pretty much it was a spy the entire time." He explained, and Lazer gasped in shock, his eyes vibrating in terror. "I should also mention how Jake seemed to know that your blood was dangerous, so that spy has been around longer than we think."

Dark grabbed his chin, saying 'I guess, but now I can store matter inside me, so we can surprise attack him with something next time." The three sat down in their seats as if nothing happened. Of course, the passengers didn't let that slide. They asked too many questions and it annoyed Masquerade, although it made the plane ride ten times more interesting this time, as Masquerade was lighting sparklers for toddlers the entire time. The hole in the roof also made everything more fun, everyone cheering through the hole. There was a chunky asian boy sitting in the corner of the plane, his family was cheering them on, however the boy was rather quiet, holding a bald baby. Then, some guy asked how lightning struck the plane in broad daylight, which made Masquerade think.

Dark lowered his gaze and stared at Masquerade, "Because some loudmouth idiot doesn't know how to keep his mouth shut every once in a while!" He said, Masquerade having no clue what he was talking about. "He insulted almost every god there was in Olympus, and now they try to sabotage everything he does. Zeus probably struck us down in pure hatred!"

Masquerade chuckled and smacked his thigh. "What! Do you really think I would do that!? I'm on a mission, here to save a lovely girl!" He mocked Dark, and Jynx blushed.

"That doesn't mean he won't punish you. Sure, he knew we'd survive this encounter, but that doesn't ensure he won't make it hard for us to reach our goal." He had a point, and he realized the Greek's were most likely hunting them down. Masquerade spaced out for the last moments of the plane ride. Zander once again was able to convince the pilots not to let the group get caught in legal action, wondering if he had some sort of power to persuade.

They un-boarded the plane and made their way to rent a bus. Everyone was anxious still, and Zander was incredibly anxious. Masquerade hoped the zoo would cheer everyone up. They rolled up to the zoo, and everyone got out depressingly. Jynx stood up reluctantly and raised her voice high.

"I know we lost many people on this death trip! But that doesn't mean we should always be in a bad mood! We need to have fun and mourn the others later. I know it may be hard and traumatizing, but we need to push!" She cheered, and everyone cheered with her, even Zander. Masquerade really had to thank her for that. They all walked into the zoo in a happy mood. Masquerade was smart enough to infer that they might attack them here, so he warned everyone else. This didn't seem to lower anyone's mood. However, they agreed to be ready to fight.

Entering the zoo gates, they embarked on their tour. Immediately, it became apparent that something was amiss in the zoo, there was no one there at all. The animals were still in place and making a commotion, but there were no people roaming around. Masquerade now realized that the clerk who had checked them in was peculiar too, his eyes matched Mardo's, a shade of deep purple. He stared at his group members, reminding them of Jynx's speech.

"We need to be prepared for a fight," Masquerade declared to the rest of the group members without superpowers. Echo has taken this as an opportunity to ambush us with a full-out attack. If Echo does decide to fight, I'll be the one to take him on. Dark, you'll fight Jake. Lazer will have to take on Mark, if he can fight. Otherwise, the rest of you will be back-up because he may not have any other forces."

They all stared towards the zoo gates, and Zander raised his fist. His voice was hoarse, but he nodded, "We'll fight for the both of you!" Everyone cheered as they walked into the more than likely booby-trapped animal zoo

Chapter 14
Jynx

The group had already split up. Jake revealed himself and followed Masquerade, Lazer, and Dark elsewhere, claiming Echo didn't need assistance. As far as anyone knew, there weren't any other monsters to deal with. Jynx dashed through the zoo, searching for a way to help. Jace, Stray, and Russel trailed behind her. Zander and Jacob stayed behind, engaging in casual conversation. However, they couldn't locate where Jake had taken the three. Jynx hoped it was only Jake present. Jace warned of potential others.

"Masquerade had already killed the werewolves, and Jake said Echo wasn't here, and he was fighting those three anyway, so that would leave my dad and Blast." Jynx said, and the group members winced.

"Who's Blast?! You never told me anything about him." Jace exclaimed. Jynx frowned and explained the memory again in detail. Blast was another of Echo's servants. He wielded a gun. Jace shivered at the thought.

The group stood arguing at the monkey exhibit, oblivious to the lurking monster ready to pounce from the cages. The monster pounced directly at Jynx, and Jace instinctively shot a geyser of blue fire upwards. The monster was a werewolf, the exact one that was just defeated on the plane. Its body was engulfed in the flames, but it still ran directly through it. Jace's fire didn't seem to bother it at all.

Jynx stepped backward and avoided the wolf, but it swooped its massive claws through the group. It missed Jynx, but it sliced everyone else. Stray, Russel, and Jace all went flying backward with deep cuts in their bellies, leaving Jynx left defenseless. She turned around and tried running, but the wolf caught up in two steps.

Jynx would have accepted her death there, but more intense flames burst in her direction. The heightened heat bothered the wolf, making it howl and redirect its attention towards Jace. Jynx looked and saw his hand was burning black, almost like his own fire was hurting him. Stray stood crouching on the floor, holding his stomach, trying to stop his blood from pouring. He coughed blood and fell over suddenly.

Fire blazed through the air once again. The wolf evaded, however, and almost made his way to Jace. His claw was one inch away from poking his entire face off. Then Russel intervened.

Jynx knew Russel had no powers at all, so she was confused as to why he would try attacking a monster head-on. His body looked vulnerable to an open attack. Russel closed and clenched his fist with all the might he had, landing a punch on the wolf's cheek. At first, it seemed like a normal force, but then a shockwave of air followed. It was delayed, but then the wolf went flying straight through the animal's metal fencing. The fence was bent and shattered as the human-wolf flew through the monkey exhibit, breaking every tree it came into contact with. Dust rose into the air when the wolf finally crashed and landed on the ground. It made a crater on impact. Jace stared at Russel in amazement. Stray was still on the ground, he witnessed the main impact of the wolf's fury. Jynx hurried over to him and tried helping him.

"That was amazing! Why didn't you tell us you were a bodybuilder in disguise!" Jace joked. Russel smiled, opening his mouth for what seemed like the first time on this trip.

"Since we're all revealing our secrets lately, I guess I must reveal mine too-" His nervous voice sputtered and stuttered. 'I'm Tamer's cousin, in other words, I'm the son of God.' Jynx and Jace gasped, and Stray continued coughing. His blood seemed to heat up, plopping steaming drops of liquid into the dusted floor. The ground sizzled in response. The next thing they heard were gunshots, blaring and disorientating the surface of air, everything happened so fast that Jynx couldn't process it correctly. Russel had a bullet through his stomach, and he hit the floor hard, however it seemed he wasn't dead yet. Stray coughed up more blood. Jace had his hands in the air, and a ringing noise annoyed Jynx deeply. She looked in the opposite direction, where the bullet came from.

Standing in the midst was Blast. His pistol was steaming as he aimed directly at Jynx. He had black hair that was ruffled and frizzed up. He wore snaggy red-framed sunglasses. His pistol gleamed with red flames around it. He reloaded his gun quickly and continued aiming at Jynx. He raised his voice.

"Jake gave me permission to kill you. He's pretty busy with the other two. They're pretty strong." He announced. Jace's eyes widened.

"Two!? There were three of them!" Jace said as he knelt down, scared to get shot. Jynx's body trembled, wondering if it was Masquerade, who appeared to have superhuman durability. No one was here to save her this time.

Blast's expression changed as well, "Oh yeah, the third one is fighting Mark, who's not much of a fighter, but he tries." He raised his gun again. Jynx's father was really trying to fight the son of a god, she wondered how well that was going for him. Blast reached his gun upwards and shot it. Red smoke filled the air.

It was a danger signal, and almost immediately, the werewolf came to his defense. Then, the second one came from the shadows, the second one that was supposed to be defeated back at the museum a while ago. They should've both been dead. Jace moved his arms down and tried shooting fire out, but Blast pointed the barrel at his face.

"Don't do anything stupid. I will not hesitate to kill you!" His finger toyed with the trigger. Jace stopped. Then, the gun swayed in Jynx's direction. His eyes tightened, and he smiled sinisterly. Jynx heard the sound of gunshots. Her life flashed before her eyes, time seeming to slow, then memories flooded through her brain. The memories of Jace and Masquerade, all the happy ones, tears came next through the heat filled air.

Then the bullet seemed to melt out of thin air. Jynx gazed. The atmosphere was warming up, you could see the heat and, of course, feel it. Jynx stared behind her and hoped to see Jace had a hidden fire powerup, but instead, Stray was standing, almost completely healed. His eyes were entirely black instead of the normal red it usually was.

His hair was normal, but a massive streak of it turned fire-red. His eyes pulsed directly at Blast, who winced, his confidence seeming to disintegrate. More shots were fired, but as they passed by Stray, they melted into blobs of metal. The werewolves both attacked at the same time, attempting to overwhelm him with quick successive attacks. Stray dodged effortlessly and jumped upwards. His hands were smoking with flames.

He held them out, and blasts of black fire burst forward. The wolf's fur disintegrated off like it was tall grass, quickly spreading to the werewolf next to him. Stray smiled a not-so-reassuring smile. His eyes pulsed, an actual ring traveling out of them, that appeared as a circle of absolute fire. This ring appeared on his skin, around his eyes, having the look of a tattoo. The wolf, who landed in his exact line of sight, erupted into flurries of ash and disintegrated in the response of Stray's immense eye contact. He landed on the ground and glared towards the second wolf.

In the same occurrence, the wolf disintegrated into a flurry of black ash, it seemed like the poor soul tried latching on for life, but eventually, it just disappeared. Blast charged towards Stray, unloaded his magazine. Stray charged back in return, with black flames curling into his hands The black flames licked Blast's legs, and they burned him to the bone, revealing layers of connective tissue that stretched and squirmed due to intense heat.

Blast screamed for his life and tried running away, but Stray showed no mercy. He grabbed Blast by the shoulders, making him maintain direct eye contact. From the eyes, Blast's body crumbled and turned to complete ash. In the end pf the fray, lay three piles of dark gunpowder, resembling the appetite of a monster with a stomach that represented a bottomless pit.

Jynx was torn between fear and relief. Three of their problems had disintegrated into thin air. Stray nodded, and his eyes returned to normal, the ring of black remained, but his eyes were now red like usual. Russel stood up, his wound completely healed. Jynx was astonished, now emphasizing on the dark fact of supernaturality. Everyone on this trip had been supernatural except for Jacob, who more than likely had secrets of his own. This made Jynx wonder of the set rules that were detained in the flaps of existence she lived in, were the keeping of secrets something so important that it engraved into the natural thoughts of the newer generations? She knew the course of adaptation, and how animals evolved to stay alive, in which her brain rang with the thought of her previous ancestors adapting to keep secrets from a higher entity in existence. But this thought raced through her brain, and disappeared as quickly as it appeared.

Her eyes were glowing pink again, and her classmates near her noticed the ethereal unnatural appeal to her look. Jynx tried holding back the pulses of power she felt deep within her cerebral cortex, but it was such a scarce feeling to her that she wanted to contain the vibrations. She wanted to define the unnatural pains as a migraine, but she knew this pain was ultimately different, excessively more vibrant and deceitful. Then her optic nerve contracted, making her vision darken for a moment of haste. The lobes of the cerebrum relaxed, alleviating her to another plane of existence, instead the sensation was only a figurative flunk of her thoughts, sending her to illusions.

The onslaught of memories she wanted to forget came back in a quick and successful chomp, sending impulses through the gray and white matter of her brain. Her vision returned, and now she stood in the basement of her old household, the structure of it completely engraved in her hippocampus, the branch of her consciousness that stored memories. She was never allowed in the basement of her house, something her parents both forbid deeply. Now, she stood freely, in a dim light room with only one source of light; that being a hanging lightbulb that was attached by a loose string. The LED bulb only lit a large pool table and a portion of the stone ground, the rest of the room being pitch dark.

Jynx noticed the pink glow of her hair once more, seeing the light glisten the reflective glares of the pool balls on the green fabriced table. Then, she saw the faint pink once more, this time in the mere darkness, extruding from a dark corridor near the front end of the wall. Eyes and hair that ultimately glowed pink just like her. She thought this was going to be an evil version of what she could be, but instead, emerging from the light, was her mother, Psyche.

"You really do look like me, sweetie!" Her charming voice said, growing closer to Jynx. She tried touching her cheek, but Jynx backed away from her fingers. Her mother frowned, realizing the anticipation of her return in this memory of hectic present, she concluded that her daughter didn't know the real truth despite her deserving such. "Oh my baby. . ." She whispered lightly, trying not to alarm her offspring. ". . .let me tell you the story, and the contours of *our* power." Her voice became smooth, void of any signs of aggression. Jynx fell into a pit of comfort, her muscles tensing back to normal.

Psyche's hair had purple and black strands imbued with the glistening pink, but Jynx couldn't pinpoint the origin of the split colors. "Why do they all fear us? Is there something wrong with me?" Jynx's voice shuddered, faltered, and shook, her anxiety ranking up to tiers that she thought was impossible. She put her hands to her face, attempting to scratch her own eyeballs out.Psyche frowned empathetically, her emotions playing a huge part in the restoration of her daughter's safety.

"Controlling people is a very tempting power to try and suppress. Our bloodline is known for negative thoughts being able to influence the way our abilities manifest, and if it's always brewing from the cause of a negative environment, then the power will awaken with a relatively dark downside. For me it was tempting to not kill people with my power. I'm not sure what the full capability was, because I wasn't able to manifest it completely. . ." She paused, looking into the darkness of the room. Jynx's mind wandered, wondering what exact phenomena she was experiencing.

"Are you still alive? I thought they killed you before you could awaken your power?" Psyche winced, as if her words physically hurt her. She patted her daughter on the shoulder quickly. "Or did you implant this memory inside me the same way Jake was able to do?" Her mind wreaked havoc of incomplete trust for anything that could be double-glanced upon.

"I can't tell you that just yet, but know this my love, your power is valuable. Do not let it awaken with negative emotions, awaken with the intentions of doing good, and you will shine, shine brighter than any star, and god, and any entity. I believe in you, my only sweet daughter." She ended, her voice fading, her image faltering, and the ground turning black.

Chapter 15
Masquerade

Dark was gone, leaving Masquerade and Lazer left to fight Jake. Masquerade was frustrated that he couldn't beat Jake; they had been fighting for a while. His blade emerged from his skin, a gift from Anubis. Lazer advanced, shooting lasers everywhere, the only power he's had since he was seven.

Jake dodged, parried, and showed the two he was severely superior to them. He was thrown around embarrassingly. Masquerade even attempted to blow everything up, but it didn't work. He also tried fighting strategically, but with no success. Lazer was getting tired, and Masquerade was too fatigued to think clearly, lunging towards him. Jake held his sword up and thrust forwards. In response, Masquerade rolled under and used his sword to slice around Jake's arm. He glanced over his shoulder and poked Jake in the back, catching him by surprise. The sword pierced Jake's skin, the blade doing more damage than an average sword. Jake turned around hastily and swung his sword harder than usual, trying to finish him off. He held his guard, trying to block every attack thrown at him. Masquerade tried maneuvering around him, but Jake caught on quickly. He then went airborne and tried swordplay in the air. Their swords clashed, and Masquerade had the edge in strength from above. He smiled deviously as he pushed the sword downwards and sliced Jake's cheek.

Jake lowered his guard, and then was met with a laser to his face. He staggered backwards, Masquerade kicking him so hard he flew backward, and his blade left his hands. Jake struggled to his feet, defenseless. Lazer ran towards him, followed by Masquerade. Jake held his hands out, like he was going to attempt to use a new power. They both winced and dodged in different directions. Masquerade realized that the move he pulled was the same movement Jace did before charging his flames.

Then, a similar blue fire blasted through the air, grazing their legs violently, leaving Masquerade distraught. He hypothesized that Jake might've had the power to copy or even steal others abilities. He then threw his own blade, slicing through Jake's arm like butter melting. It landed, the blade spinning itself into the ground, making a swinging motion. Masquerade then grabbed Jake's blade from the floor, holding it out to his forehead. Jake sat on the floor, defeated.

"Any last words?" Masquerade mocked him with Jake's own blade. Jake smirked, his smile revealing that of a million lies. Both of them felt a feeling of precognition, the emotion of knowing something big was about to happen.

"Yes I do, I think I got the best last words anyone's ever heard!" Masquerade hesitated for too long, and failed to slice his head off. When he finally threw the blade up, his body turned to pure smoke, his body disappearing. Then Jake's voice was heard from behind. "The question is, are you ready for my spiel?" Jake was completely healed, then his sword burst out of Masquerade's hands and returned to him, with a magical force that called for glory. Except that glory was hidden behind a wall that consisted of thorns that represented joy, but those thorns were ready to be picked and snapped off, both of the rivals stood in realization of that exact representation.

Masquerade ran over and picked up his own blade, but in an instant, Jake was on top of him, his quick speed clearly showing he was the compensation that was regarded as the force of glory, and Masquerade was the wall of poisonous joy filled thorns, the one thing stopping the glory from traveling further.

He realized that Jake was glory because glory came quickly, and didn't last long, but Masquerade representing joy was perfect, as it lasted for eternity, just like he would due to his immortality. The representation of glory, Jake, held Masquerade down and pinned his hands to the floor, stabbing his stinging blade through them, trapping him to the floor. His blood boiled, hating the fact that Jake thought he was so much higher than him, which made perfect since in their battle of symbolism, glory was usually seen as a higher form of enlightenment versus that of pure unbridled joy. Lazer attempted fighting him one-on-one, but he failed miserably, Jake threw him to the side with one swipe of his enlarged sword.

Then Dark approached out of nowhere. He held a body in his hands, throwing it towards Jake. The man was alive, but he was tied together with strings made of his blood. Jake frowned instead of smiling for a change.

"Oh great, all three of you are here!" Jake used his sword to cut in between the blood, and the man was free of his bindings. "Mark, you might want some popcorn for this! It's going to get real emotional." Jake smiled, waving his hand with power, his glory shining through his chest, overshadowing Masquerade's joy, which was quickly declining to fear and despair. Popcorn appeared in Mark's hands, the extra butter compensating his dead wife who always asked for extra. Blood arrows then soared through the air, but Jake dodged every single one and stared at Dark, who tried reforming the ground into a weapon, but nothing came. His blood flames weren't blazing from his arms either. "I deactivated your powers, so don't even try." He smiled, his glory shining brighter than ever before.

Masquerade tried creating explosions, but nothing happened, locking Jake's claim in point. His muscles struggled and contracted under the sharpness of the blade. Dark stared at him, signaling him to shut up and listen for once. Jake raised his voice and started laughing hysterically, his body moved autonomously, making obnoxious and devious movements, another reference to be connected with that and the feeling of glory. He laughed the entire time, opening his mouth, he said, 'I really can't believe all of you can be so stupid!' His voice gleamed with glory, his body dancing around with clear signs of deceitfulness, and of course he made sure to mock them the entire time while doing so. He danced with himself as his mouth spat out nonsensical words.

"Like come on, really?! Even Mark could look through his bipolar actions and see he's been a fake this entire time!" He knocked on Mark's hollow skull, who was eating the popcorn given to him. Jake's laughter turned to tears of glory and excitement. "I tricked that stupid brat from the beginning, for her entire life! I know her secrets, your secrets, I know them all! I know *your* secrets!" He pointed at Masquerade, who could barely keep himself from saying something, which directly attacked his egoistic persona. "I know everything, and soon, the destruction of yours and her family will be because you couldn't shut your damn mouth!" He stared at Masquerade, he knew this entire disaster was about Jynx, but he still didn't know what he was trying to hint at, at first he thought it was about the murder scandal where him and Mark switched roles.

"Your powers, your family, your stupid little stories, and your personalities! You're more impulsive than even I ever was!" He pointed at Masquerade once more. "And you! You're straight-up dumb!" His voice turned to Lazer, Masquerade realized that this secret was far deeper. He was still dancing like a lunatic, the glory coursing its way through the nerves, veins, and branches of his internal anatomy. " I give you credit for being the smartest of the bunch!" He pointed towards Dark, his body doing a quick arch, and Masquerade was starting to get mad again.

"Maybe if you opened your eyes a bit, you'd see what I'm talking about!" He clapped his hands to an unknown rhythm, his feet tapping into a song that only existed in Jake's mind. Dark was getting annoyed at this point, wanting him to get the point across already. "Day by day, how else do you think I know your abilities and your fighting styles? How else do you think I knew where you were every moment of this trip!?" He screamed some more, his voice was far from exhaustion. He smiled again. "Come on, really? Piece it together! Even Dark told you, Cozbi? That name couldn't really be that important to notice, except for the fact that it literally means 'liar' in biblical texts!" He shouted one last time, Masquerade recalled the time Jake murdered Jace's older brother. He realized that the moment he was talking about was only a moment that was shared between himself and Jace, how could Jake know about their relationship?

"Oh fine, I'll just tell you! I made it all up!" At first, Masquerade didn't know what he was talking about. "Cozbi? He's fake! I never murdered anyone by that name nor never knew anyone." Masquerade was piecing it all together, remembering the layer of fog in Jace's brain. Even now, Masquerade glanced inside the vengeful eyes of Jake, whose brain was covered in the same thick wall of glorified mist.

However, Dark still had no clue what he was hinting at, when all of a sudden, Jake's voice changed into someone they were all familiar with, someone that Masquerade could trust. "Does this sound familiar to you at all?" Jace's voice came from Jake's mouth, imitating his vocal cords down to the core

Dark and Lazer looked around, trying to find Jace, but little did they know that Jace was standing right in front of them, dancing like an idiot, who had a little too much knowledge on swordplay. "Still don't get it? Do I have to tell you!?" His smile widened wider than ever before. He laughed some more. "I AM JACE!" His voice faltered, turning back to his normal voice tone.

Jake's body then faded into smoke like a ghost, and once it reformed, Jace's form stood in front of them. Jace smiled and waved politely at the three, exactly imitating his kindness, but despite the mimicry of all of Jace's features, the one and only part that Jake's glory couldn't copy was his pure delicate joy . Masquerade's brain was filled with nothing but pure rage, and Jake continued his dance. "This is going to be so fun!" Jake screamed again, Masquerade opened his mouth even though he knew he should probably keep it shut.

"PROVE IT!" His voice shook with rage, his hands were still stabbed through the ground with a sword. Not-Jace smiled, and his body returned back to the features of Jake. "Hmmm Tamer, Hyper, and Infinity! They are trapped in Hell due to the hellhound known as Garm!" Dark gasped, which was something only the group would know.

"I can read minds! Jace's mind was completely free of treason! You're lying!" Masquerade bellowed again, although his suspicions were proven wrong as he remembered, clear as day, the fog wall protecting his friend's brain.

"Oh, it's pretty easy to hide thoughts and change perspective, especially with Echo by my side helping me out!" Jake yelled back. "It was pretty easy tricking all of you, and yours truly, enjoyed every single little moment of it." He snarled, Dark was terrified, and Lazer was spaced out.

"And even now, Jynx remains in the most dangerous position she's ever been in, right next to the enemy!" He smiled and crouched down. "You, the knight in shining armor, the one Zeus had sent to protect her, has failed. Your irrelevant and stupid choices have brought her to the death that she thought she was safe from!" He mocked. "AND IT'S ALL BECAUSE YOU CAN'T KEEP YOUR STUPID MOUTH SHUT AND THINK WITH YOUR BRAIN FOR ONCE!" Then, throughout the chaos, his brain flashed back to the moment of the dream world, Mardo's remains still hushing his negative thoughts that conspired at the back of his mind. Surely enough, he imagined Mardo's advice to change, shattering beneath the crumbling satisfaction of an earthquake, letting the rage filled thoughts course through the remains of his joy filled veins. His arteries clogged, with the rage breaking through said clogs, which represented the joy still left within him. The clogs traveled to the wastes of his kidneys, to be determined as filtrate, that would eventually leave his body in a rush of waste-filled liquid. This representation showed that he was no better than Jake, as the rage that filled his circulatory system was the phenomenon that was only described by the word 'glory'. Masquerade yearned for the new substance inside his veins, he yearned for the 'glory', ignoring Mardo's efforts to show him 'joy'. He practically joined the wrong side of the war, flipped the wrong side of the coin, and sat on the wrong side of the branch. He was no hero, only a person that did bad, even if it was for the greater good, it made him no better than the mischief ahead of him right now.

An explosion rushed from his hands and feet, disrupting the ground around him, making rumbles in the earth. Jake's sword snapped in half, and the next moment, he found himself on top of Jake, his body shook. Masquerade realized the power that came with choosing the path of 'glory', it was far greater than 'joy', but only later would he realize the downfall of his decision.

"Take. It. Back!" Masquerade released, and the explosion burst him into the floor. Jake shook it off, and his blade returned to his hand unharmed. He tried to attack, but Masquerade evaded and dodged everything perfectly, his guidance to 'glory' showing itself prominent. Jake's eyes straightened, trying to focus and rely on counter-attacking. Masquerade intercepted and parried every attack Jake had, finally able to overwhelm him.

Jake stared at his forwards, a familiar gaze was upon his eyes, a red flame flickering from the sockets of his skull. Ares. Then Jake's blade locked and swung, hitting Masquerade directly in the jaw, slicing his mouth. Jake then jabbed and pierced his stomach, making a piercing hole in his abdomen. Masquerade cursed the war god, knowing what happened. Dark had explained it before, the gods were punishing him, all because he insulted them. First Zeus, now Ares. Ares made him lose this fight on purpose, the battlefield was his domain. Jake kicked Masquerade to the ground.

"Hopeless and useless!" He pointed the blade at Masquerade's neck. "The roles are reversed! Any last words, kiddo?" Masquerade smiled and opened his mouth wide, he did what he was best at and started talking obnoxiously loud.

"DO IT! KILL ME! YOU FUCKING COWARD!!!" Masquerade's voice shook. He held his hand out and produced the biggest explosion he's ever done before, one that could destroy an entire skyscraper. Jake blasted towards the zoo gate and broke through them, bending the metal upon impact. Masquerade stood up, and Anubis' blade came to his hand. "Fight me. . .'' Lightning sparkled throughout his body, reaching his sword. The blackened sword rejected his power however, and Masquerade understood why, because it wasn't accustomed to withstand the power of glory, instead it was required to only be held by a warrior with a sensation of joy. THe blade dissipated from his hands, and then eventually his view.

"We've come to the rescue!" Jynx, Russel, Stray, and Jace—or Jake—showed up on the scene. Masquerade turned his attention to them, and automatically, Lazer, Dark, and Masquerade rushed towards Jace. Dark reached him first and pinned him to the ground. Jynx's joyful expression quickly faded, her eyes flashing a color of pink and then red, and then back to normal. Jake was back on his feet, charging the group with horrible intentions, they still had no hope to win.

"We have to run! We can't win against him! Take Jace hostage, and let's go! I'll explain later," Masquerade screamed. However, Stray stopped him and smiled, his eyes darkening with a deathly chant.

"No, we'll fight him, you and me together." His cold voice said, and his smile widened. Masquerade didn't know why, but he joined him reluctantly, charging towards Jake, and Stray's eyes pulsed with blackness. Automatically, Jake winced as if his power and energy were draining. Black flames blasted towards him, the foe rolling under them and slashing at Stray first. Stray grabbed his blade and burnt it with black flames, the metal melting over.

Masquerade raised his hands and readied to attack Jake's lower stomach. Jake used his blade to redirect the flames onto Masquerade's hands, burning them reluctantly and he winced backward. The two made direct eye contact, and he kicked Stray the other way. Then, he tripped Masquerade and prepared to trap him again. This time, he swiped his hand, producing a large cortex of wind and parried it, flashes of lightning shocking his chest.

Jake was caught off guard, and then the black flames engulfed his entire lower body. He stumbled backward and screamed in agonizing pain.

"Damn you! You burned my favorite sweats!" He glowered at Stray. "You'll pay for that!" He charged towards Stray and swiped his blade everywhere, he was reckless but ten times stronger. He sliced Stray once, then twice, and the hits started racking up. Masquerade charged in and kicked Jake in the back of the head.

Jake turned as fast as he could, but when he did, more black flames started spitting. Stray punched him twice, and Masquerade exploded his entire head into the stone. Jake staggered some more and cursed. The flames were eating at his skin. He got more burned every second, by blackened flames of death, and destructive blasts of glory. Masquerade pounded his fist into his arm, charging an explosion. It cut deep, and he kept pushing with wind gusts.

Stray kept pushing him with flames. Then, an air force sent the two flying in the same direction. Jake laughed as sword cuts ensnared their bodies, a move that only the werewolves could do. Stray glanced toward Mark, and Jynx seemed to wince as he did so. Masquerade didn't know why, but time seemed to slow once more.

Mark looked back in sheer fear, his body pulsed, and it was like they all could feel the fear inside the poor guy. Stray's eyes pierced through the guy's soul. Masquerade could see Mark's brain clearly, his eyes were flashing before his eyes. Mark's memories flooded forward and left an imprint in Masquerade's thoughts, he was reminded of the fake fate he was given by Jake, and how his family was stripped from him. Then, his entire body started turning to ash. Black ash swirled in the wind, Mark's body was turned into nothing but black shards.

Jake seemed to ring with fear also. His eyes remained looking into Stray's. The same effect didn't follow, and Stray seemed frustrated with his control over the power. Masquerade looked Jake up and down.

He raised his voice, "Until next time, Jake, just know that next time won't go so lucky for you, and you'll be dead." The threat sounded better in Masquerade's brain. The group fled the scene, picking up Zander and Jacob at the entrance. Jace was tied up with blood ropes, and Zander looked confused as they escorted his body. Masquerade gave him a hateful glance, something that came natural now that his veins were corrupted with glory. Jake had actually let them escape for some reason, a reason that he knew, which had to do with one specific person. They rented into the hotel that was originally planned, the group stood awkwardly in the elevator awkwardly, everyone coming to a silence.

"So, is anyone going to explain why we need to tie up Jace?" Zander asked and tried freeing him from the restraints. Jynx looked extremely anxious, which was normal, but she was never this stressed. The elevator opened, and Masquerade grabbed Jace by the shirt.

"We'll be right back, and I'll explain everything later. I promise." Masquerade announced, and everyone nodded and left for their rooms. Masquerade shoved Jace into the hotel janitor's closet, and he winced with fear and pain. The glory and the former joy stood at a standstill, that would reverberate memories to the reader.

"Immortality isn't as bad as they all say." Masquerade smirked at his sworn enemy, who lay sprawled on the floor. Masquerade pushed him down aggressively, Jace's eyes lowering, staring back fiercely.

"Come on, there's no need for this!" Jace pleaded awkwardly, stumbling over his often mixed up words. His anxious demeanor often slurred up his language skills. Jace had sweat covering his lower back, highlighting his shiny tan body. Masquerade already had him pinned to the floor, he knew that the janitor's closet wasn't the best place to do this.

"Oh my god, stop talking so loud. If someone so much as walks by this locked door, my foot will be up your ass." Masquerade mocked, ironically his own vocals staying rather loud. He started to laugh hysterically in grief, glory filled anger. Jace shook at the thought of his previous dialogue, and looked utterly terrified.

"I will hurt you, so please do worry. You don't even know the beginning of what you have done. You make me seem like a bad person, after all we both know what love can do to a person. How much longer can you put up with this act, Jace? After all, you are the one who tricked all of us and used me to get closer to her." He sighed between sentences. "That's why we aren't friends anymore. Crazy how you can ruin a great friendship, right Jace?" Masquerade said. "You're probably wondering how I'm still alive, huh?" Masquerade stared into Jace's soul, muttering.

"You're immortal. There's no way you can be alive after that! You're a liar, and I should've known!" His voice croaked with force, although he had no energy to scream.

"You think I believe you? Oh no, I know you, Jace; I know who you really are. You're just a psycho." Masquerade snapped back in a rather sassy tone, his words limited, trying to get him to break character.

"You think that, but the truth will show itself soon." Jace attempted to get comfortable under his terrifying grip.

"You're very funny; you can't gaslight or manipulate me this time. Not anymore!" Masquerade teased in a baby voice. "I absolutely hate your guts." Masquerade continued to bash him with heavy clenched fists. His voice and throat hurt from trying to hold back tears and trying to keep up this act. Jace stared at him. No sight of tears, no signs of emotion, no sign of guilt. His mind was completely empty, void of any signs of remorse.

Masquerade fought the urge to unleash his anger and beat him. He still loved Jace partially; he couldn't hurt him. Masquerade locked his eyes back on Jace. He put his emotions in check and bottled it up like normal. Jace's thoughts were filled with trying to protect Jynx from her damned cursed family, but that was Masquerade's job, not his.

Wiping away his tears, he stared Jace in the eyes. "What really happened then?"

Jace swallowed. His body was still covered in sweat, "Jake lied to you!" He bellowed. "There's no way you can actually believe that liar! We have to stop him together; you already know Jynx wouldn't want this. . ."

His eyes lowered, and he tried making sense of it all. "How can something like that be a lie!" He screamed. "You can't hide behind that stupid mask forever!" Masquerade grabbed Jace by the head, his face seeming to melt. Tears rolled down both Jace's and Masquerade's faces, a last resort to show emotional distress.

"It didn't have to be like this Masquerade." Jace's voice changed, his face changed, and even his clothes formed differently. Jake's body stood there in all its might, in all its ironic glory. Masquerade was terrified already. His sword lay by his side, and he looked ready to fight him in this tight place. "I don't know how exactly you intend to get out of this situation without being accused by everyone else. No one will believe you!" Jake's body formed back into Jace's. The sword was gone, and blue fire started swirling around his legs.

Masquerade took his chances, ignoring everything he just said. He tackled Jace straight through the wall, breaking the wall, forcing the two into the air, straight down the side of the building. The afternoon air smelled great. It was sad it would be the last time Jace and Masquerade could share it together.

"If you really want to kill me, Masquerade, then you'll have to kill Jace first!" He screamed as he fell to the ground. "And not even that will be an easy task."

Masquerade didn't know if killing Jace meant he killed Jake, but he was forced to take his chances. He charged toward Jace, who covered himself in blue flames. Masquerade forcefully threw his body straight into the flames anyway. He grabbed Jace's arm and threw him to the ground as they fell, catapulting him into the dirt. Jace tried catching his breath, but Masquerade didn't let him.

His flames didn't hurt, other than touching a hot baking pan. Masquerade realized that Jace didn't know how to fight, it was almost as if this wasn't Jake at all. He couldn't dodge anything, or perceive his attacks like his counterpart could. Masquerade was essentially fighting a punching bag, Jace taking every hit. He had good durability, allowing him to tank his blows, but he lacked everywhere else. Jace got to a point where he was about to pass out, his flames extinguishing.

"Is this really Jake? Come on now, if I'm going to kill you, at least make it harder!" He screamed, Jace's hands started burning black, his flames becoming more vibrant in contrast.

"If you want to kill me, then do it already! Stop toying with me, you murderer!" He screamed, this is when he noticed that they were practically in the middle of a public area. He now realized what Jake was doing, pretending to be Jace to make him look like a bad person. In contrast to his past decision, he realized Jace was a representation of joy, just like Masquerade used to be, and Jake was the flame of glory that sometimes overshadowed Jace's joy. However, this one time, was when 'joy' was able to completely reign more powerful than 'glory'. He charged again, this time, his flames hotter, but with a heavy downside; his skin burnt upon using them. Jace dodged an attack and returned with a wall of flames. Masquerade striked it.

By this time, fire was spraying from every direction of his body, burning his own body to fight on par with Masquerade. His hair was fireproof, but his skin was completely black. His eyes were also surprisingly intact. His body was destroying itself, just to be able to stand a chance against him. He charged again, his fire-engulfed fists reaching out. They were barely able to make a fist through the blazing pain it caused him to move. The heat seared Masquerade's skin off.

He jumped back. There was only one way to do this, and he utilized the wind to achieve this. Wind traveled around Masquerade, carrying him upwards. He then grabbed Jace, his body ignoring the searing heat. The two went spiraling into the air, exchanging blows, fire blasting everywhere. Jace seemed mute and continued to spam flames in the blue skies.

The duo continued until they couldn't see the ground. His fire was at the highest temperature it could be at, so hot the fire could almost kill Masquerade.

"It's sad you have to go this way." Masquerade flew towards him, Jace was able to fly with the force of the flames underneath his feet. He tried avoiding his attacks.

Then, Jace released all the energy he had left. The fire burned everywhere in Masquerade's body, almost killing him. He reached Jace and touched him lightly. All it took was one touch. He released his last explosion, making Jace's body reduced itself to complete ash. He was completely gone, the last flicks of his dead fire licking off Masquerade. The heat of his infused power was enough to make him drop dead, giving his entire top layer of skin third degree burns. He passed out and started flying towards the ground at alarming speeds. His last thoughts, hoped to be able to say goodbye to Jace at least once.

He opened his tired eyes. In front of him stood Anubis again, who looked proud yet so disappointed at the same time. Masquerade walked closer to him than usual, being used to his presence. However, he seemed to be discomforted by Masquerade. "Did you get anyone by the name of Jace?" He asked slowly, his eyes swelled, tears even trickled downwards. He sniffled.

"You chose the wrong path. . ." He whispered, his fingers fumbling with an orb beneath him. ". . .you may have noticed the blade no longer responding to you. Mardo is very disappointed." He said, regarding the corrupted blood within him, which had started clotting up once more, but only in small quadrants, due to his soul's natural impulsivity, wanting the body to route back to its original ways. Masquerade frowned in disbelief.

"I'm sorry. . ." He said, rethinking his choices. "Let me speak to Jace one last time, please. I promise to change my blood!" He responded, and Anubis nodded, slightly annoyed and distrusted.

"Jake's power is truly one of a kind." He ignored his yearns for help. "I'll tell you now that he was right, Jace was really completely made up, only a remnant of your memories. He never had a real heart, besides whatever artificial fake that Jake felt, he more than likely gave him a fake one, one that was coded to pump glory. The way I see his power is evident, pretty much, Jace was a complete clone of Jake. The two could appear in the same scene, without any real problems, because Jake trapped the soul of an innocent into the dead body, making it a lifeless doll meant for the sole purpose to cause deceitful lies. Really think of it as a clone. Don't feel so down, young one. You did what was right, you killed a portion of Jake's power, at least. Also, I guess I should mention that you released Jace's trapped soul, inside that second body lay a soul. If you want to feel the empathy you caused, you can imagine this, that the trapped soul was able to experience every moment it had with you, but it wasn't able to control the body."

". . .he was a friend that could never actually interact with you, no matter how much he wanted to." He flickered his hand in the air. "I can show you to that freed soul if you wish." Anubis suggested. Masquerade rubbed his eyes and nodded, crying in response to the absolute carnage. His adventures had a toll on his body, and they were finally catching up on him. Anubis snapped, and the scenery changed.

He stood at a familiar house, revealing the home of a young Jace. Masquerade observed the area, noticing the dark background. He walked to the steps and found Jace sitting on the porch. The sky had a tone of demonic delicacy, containing swirls of red and brown. It looked like the world and sky was rotting around them, and in his eyes, with him. The constant pressure of glory in his veins started to damage his pumping heart.

Jace stared at Masquerade, who ran up to him and fell into his arms. They both started crying, all the stress and anxiety that had built up was finally released, and they were both able to feel 'joy' warm their very body and soul. This was the real Jace, the Jace that actually felt emotion, the Jace that enjoyed being Masquerade's friend, and the Jace that wanted to protect Jynx. This time, his soul was pure and perfect, radiating a deep warmth that made him feel special. In seconds, their powers were being contrasted against each other. His pink eyes glistened the same brightness as Jace's blue. Their difference in colors also explained their difference in spirituality, Masquerade's glory matched Jace's joy, in terms of the ways that they changed. Jace went from a bastard that hated anyone that went near Jynx, to a kind soul that can warm the essence of anyone, and that was all possible because 'joy' could actually change. Joy came in all kinds of happy colors, it could be from obtaining a new dog, or saving a friend that definitely needed saving, which was Jace's case.

For the contrast, Masquerade's glory represented his personality exactly. He went from an aggressive brat that yelled at people who angered him, to someone that still does the same exact act, only for a different reason, or in his defiant case, a person. This was prominent because 'glory' never changes, it's always obtained through one mental decision, which is grief earned victory. The feeling of glory never changed either, only the ways to obtain the victory did. Now that they remained in a soul-snatching hug, their fates and spirits intertwined.

The intertwining of their souls only meant one thing, they exchanged their spirits. Jace's helpless soul absorbed the glory stuck deep within Masquerade's capillaries, exchanging all the unchangeable with the changeable, being the joy of his own soul. In quick succession, Masquerade realized why this had to be done. Jace, who can't change now, since his soul is at rest, didn't need the changeability of the 'joy' because now he would remain the same. A lost boy, with no real cause, and no real control over his body, this time because he didn't have one to host now. In the afterlife, the souls were able to roam freely, and all this swapping also represented the different ways to obtain 'glory', which happened to be two times with Jace's circumstances. OneJake being in control of his body, and twohis soul not having a body to host in the first place.

To finish the query, Masquerade needed the 'joy' because he still needed to be the one to change. He needed to change for Jynx, for Mardo, for Anubis, he needed to be a better person if he wanted to save everyone. Not some selfish brat that acted on primal instinct and rage.

Masquerade let him go, and Jace stayed quiet.

"I guess this is going to be our last goodbye." Masquerade sniffled. "I promise to tell Jynx that you said you love her. I'll make sure you get the revenge you always wanted." Jace tried looking happy, cracking his knuckles. Masquerade grabbed them. "You have no need to crack them anymore. You're free."

Then Jace started bawling to the point where he would have thrown up. Masquerade slightly touched him. His body quivered.

"I ffeefeel so bad-" He stuttered so badly to the point of exhaustion. He couldn't even talk right.

"Take a breath buddy. I'll tell Jynx your exact words, and I won't forget to add the stutter, I guess." They both cracked an anxious laugh.

"I couldn't stop Jake; he was too evil. He trapped my wretched soul, I was forced to watch it all unfold from the beginning." He was still crying and sniffling in between sentences.

"You were great—a great friend while it lasted. I was able to see your soul shine deep inside that monster. Just remember Jynx would still be proud of you." Jace smiled as he held Masquerade's hand in the red void. "I just want you to know that. . ." He paused, remembering their transfer of glory and joy. ". . .I can love you. . ." Masquerade stuttered a little. ". . .it's hard for me to emphasize that, but you protected Jynx long before I came around, so I respect you for that." He smiled at him. "I think I'm finally able to emphasize my feelings more due to your 'joy'." He finalized. Jace's body started glowing a faint gold that got brighter by the passing second.

"I'll be leaving soon—" Jace exclaimed with a stuttered voice.

"Don't, I want you to say. I still have a lot to say, I just wish you could stay alive with me and Jynx. Graduate high school and college together, get drunk, attend parties, have fun, and get into trouble. I just wish we had more time." Jace smiled as more tears started rolling down his dissipating golden face.

"We all wish we had more time. But for now, Masquerade, don't forget me, ever. And please, get together with Jynx for me. Kiss her, comfort her, make her feel loved, it's all she deserves, and that's all I ask from you. This is my final goodbye. Masquerade, don't tell Jynx that I love her, instead tell her that *you* love her. . ." He opened his eyes for a long moment. "Take this offering." He gave Masquerade a small golden ball of energy." Use it when you feel it is right, and trust me, you'll know when it's the right time." His voice faded, his body faded, and his presence faded, and just like his 'glory', Jace was gone. He still wished there was more time between the two.

Masquerade then returned to Anubis. He stood there disgracefully. He stared at Masquerade honestly. "You should return home now." Anubis snapped, and Masquerade jolted awake again. His classmates gathered around him, everyone was worried. His eyes were still sleepy from the transfer. He sat upright and stared at Jynx first, maintaining heavy conflicting eye contact.

"Jace is dead." He said slowly, sniffling. Jynx stared back angrily, her expression said everything. Jace's body was right next to him, burnt to a crisp. Everyone backed away from the two, who had a streaming connection of hate building up like pins rolling over due to a heavu thrown bowling ball.

"THANKS TO YOU!" She screamed hatefully. Her tears were swelling in her eyes, making them bloodshot red. "You're a cold-blooded murderer! No better than Jake! Who do you think you are? YOU'RE NO HERO, YOU MADE EVERYTHING WORSE!" Her voice beamed with anger. "You killed my only friend. The one who was by my side my entire life, he helped me against my cursed family. He made me feel better, and the only thing you could manage was to disappear and give us all false hope!" Masquerade felt his soul shatter. He tried reaching out to Jynx. She dodged and stood up. He couldn't even open his mouth.

"I can never trust anybody, I see that now! This is goodbye, I don't ever want to see you, ever again. I never loved you! I never even considered it!" Masquerade wished she only said that through blind rage. Deep down, he really felt like he murdered an innocent soul. Jynx stormed off towards the hotel again. She murmured something to Zander and pointed at Masquerade. The world turned upside down, and the next few hours flew by in his room by himself. Dark and Lazer let him be. He'd been crying the entire time, having no clue in the world what to do. Jace was dead, and no one knew the truth. Everyone thought he killed him, soon enough he'd be running from the national police force.

Jynx wanted nothing to do with him. Zander was forcing Masquerade to leave the group. He was just collecting his thoughts before deciding where he would go. He hoped somehow Jace's soul would make things right between him and Jynx.

Chapter 16
Jynx

Jynx really couldn't trust anyone. Her best friend was dead—all because of someone she thought she could trust. The person she once loved was a cold-blooded murderer. She stared out her window, missing Stitch. She missed Mason and his quiet, soft voice, but most of all, she missed Jace. Her brain kept flashing back to the memory she had of her mother, reminding her not to awaken during a time of despair. She ignored her brain's call for help, and slammed her phone at the ground, walking towards the bathroom door. She kept the light off, and watched the mirror, which was being illuminated by a singular hefting candle. Her face showing through the yellow warm light, her eyes started illuminating once more. The pinkish color zipped along the irises of her eye. Then in a different contrast to the first color, came glowing a violet hot pink, matching Masquerade's eye color.

Her hair then enlightened, the color washing across the strands like bioluminesce washing over a breach shore. She maintained heavy eye contact with herself, feeling her brian impulse with quick and short thrusts. Then, upon focusing her eyes, appeared a large crack through the middle of the mirror, shattering it indirectly. Her image disorientated, adding to the scenery. Then the light flickered on, the shower current ripped off, and the door slammed dramatically. Her brain again reminded her, not to awaken under stressful circumstances. This brought heavy and quick tears to her ducts, making her breakdown on the bathroom tiled floor.

After hours of torture, she turned around and decided to get ready for the group's next event. They were really trying to keep it together, but Jace, Infinity, Glicher, Hyper, Tamer, and now Masquerade were gone from the trip. They decided that they might cancel the entire thing and go home, obtaining several extended sessions of therapy.

That left Russel, Stray, Jynx, Dark, Lazer, and Jacob. They lost about half of their group all in the span of a few days. Jynx shuddered at the thought that she might be next. Her eye color shimmered once more, reminding her of Masquerade's latest actions. The fact that she loved him made her flustered and frustrated at the same time, the fact that she kissed that man. She scrunched her hair in her hands and sighed loudly.

She then picked up her brush and tried to mask her feelings. She was usually good at it, but too much has happened lately, then someone started knocking on the door. She put her brush down and answered it.

Zander stood in the way. 'Pack up, Jynx. We're returning home on an hour's notice. I should've done this a while back. Sorry for the inconvenience, and I'm truly sorry. I thought Masquerade was a good influence." His voice was hoarse.

"No need to be hard on yourself. It was my fault this trip turned out to be so depressing." He nodded and left for the next room. But when she turned to the side, she saw Dark in her room. He was sitting on the bed, flinging his feet and cracking his knuckles. He smiled slightly and opened his mouth. Jynx sighed, hoping to hear good news for once.

"I'd like to talk about Jace. I know it may be tough, but I know the truth." He spoke, and Jynx flinched. He was sympathetic, but she really didn't care.

"The truth? What truth is there to believe? All I know is that your brother is a murderer!" Dark's face winced, and he stared back.

"You're wrong, Jake is the murderer. . ." Jynx's heart sank, and she paced around the room. She thought about what she would say next. She wasn't about to argue with a soon-to-be god. She held back her emotions.

"I know that. Jake has been my tormentor for some time now." She convulsed, her brain pounding with anxiety, and the constant voice beating against her cerebrum, it said 'Don't awaken', in dark deep whispers.

"I'm aware, Masquerade told me everything, he knows the truth also. He isn't that bad, but I get where you're coming from. He's extremely impulsive and has a loud mouth. And that behavior can get him killed and others into a lot of trouble." The voices pounded and started whispering even louder, her brain barely able to contain the corruption. Then, her eyes started glowing pink again, much brighter than before. "He only does it to protect those he loves. He's only like that because deep down, he really loves you. He'd die for you, for me, and for his family. It's not saying much, considering he's immortal, but it's still the sacrifice that matters."

Jynx felt her heart drop again, "He's immortal!? Why wouldn't he think that's something important he should share?!" The whispers turned into yells for help, now saying 'Help us from the power! It's disorienting!', her eyes were only getting increasingly more powerful.

"He's only trying to protect you. It's better he likes to keep his immortality a secret. After all, he could just brag about it twenty-four-seven. And by the way, are you okay?" He asked and explained.

She nodded, the pink starting to escape the encasing of her eyes, stretching across her face. Then her veins started to glisten with pinkened embers of blood. The voices were screaming "Okay! I hear you!" She yelled, startling Dark. "Sorry, just tell me the truth, please. I want to know what excuse he has for murdering my best friend." She said through gritted teeth.

"I'll just say that Jace needed to die for your safety, let's leave it at that. You'll be too shattered to hear what really went down. . ." Her eyes of pink filled with anger, quickly setting her hair to fumes of the pink dye, which ensnared Dark's expression. He trailed off as he inched towards the door, her veins and arteries now fully pulsing with energy. 'Kill Him!', 'Stop him!', 'Ask for the real answer!', they all said in harmony.

"NO!!!" She screamed back, tears covering her eyes. Dark tried coming to her defense, but Jynx thrashed at him, yelling for him to stay away. In response to her thoughts, Dark was flung across the room with great force, crashing through the window of the balcony. Then she felt it, a valve in her brain turning and opening, the voices finally escaping from the clutches of her nervous system. She imagined Dark, who was hurt only slightly, to grab one of the shards of glass and hold it to his neck. His eyes turned pink as well, following the command that sequentially played in her mind.

She tried stopping him, but her thoughts decided it would be a bad idea. Dark put his head down, and Jynx finally came to a sense of conclusion. She awakened, and she did so despite her attempts to not do so in an evil environment. "STOP, DON'T LISTEN!" She screamed, falling to her knees, and safely deactivating her power. Dark fell to the floor as well, the glass cutting his hand only slightly. "Why's Echo after me and not anyone else, is this why?" She asked, her voice letting out gasps calling for help.

"Masquerade's tracking Echo down as we speak. Read the letter I left on your bed. It's from him. He advised us not to help him. He says he got it all under control, but I don't trust him. Lazer and I will be ready to fight if it comes down to it. I won't stand by and let him "die". He's saved me one too many times." He announced as he opened the door. "I'm just saying you should consider it, and just know Jace didn't die in cold blood." Jynx cried, again. "I won't mention your power to anyone else, I promise."

With that, he closed the door and left. Jynx shuddered and grabbed her blanket, seeking comfort from anyone. The letter fell off the bed. She stared at it for a long moment before bending over to pick it up. The letter was scattered with badly written handwriting. She observed the layout before reading it.

Signed Masquerade,

I'm truly sorry for whatever actions I might have done or look like what I've done. This final trip has been a disaster, and most of it was my fault.

I have left the group as advised by many. Hopefully, you all return home, but no need to worry left me, I'll be safe. I'm sorry Glicher, I'm sorry Jace, and I'm sorry for Tamer, Hyper, and really for Infinity. I hope they are still with us, but something tells me they weren't so lucky. The god Misa is who I pray to for all your safety. I have left to find Echo and hope to kill him.

Good luck to you all. I hope I return home. Be sure not to get attacked by Zeus. :).

My sacrifice for the art club is to atone for Jace. Good luck.

Jynx shed a tear at the thought that Hyper could've died. She finished packing and looked over the letter a couple more times, looking for a hidden message. It looked too spaced out for a letter. She wasn't an English major, but she knew it was odd to space it like that.

She took a deep breath and dragged her luggage for the bus. Once she got down there, she confronted Dark about the letter.

"I think he left a secret message in this letter…" She handed it to him. Dark glanced over it and winced.

"I didn't look at it very much because he told me in person." He seemed to be hurt a little all of a sudden. He called Lazer over. "The first words in every line form the sentence 'I'm final I left for Misa For My Sacrifice'. Normally, I wouldn't care for this." He put his hands on his head. "It's a long story."

Jynx sighed. She didn't know who to trust at this point, and now she wished she could have at least one moment of relief, a moment of relief that could draw her power back inside her, because at the moment, her brain vigorously sent impulses of danger down every nerve in her nervous system.

Chapter 17
Masquerade

The decision to leave the group was hard for Masquerade, his mind was racing with what to do first. The first on his agenda was to find and track Echo; he wanted to get rid of the most powerful enemy on his list. The first thing to do to achieve that plan would be to talk to Anubis, who might give him some insight on where to find Echo. He hadn't even left the city yet, but he walked far enough away from the hotel. He had no clue where he was in the world and how exactly he was going to get home.

Masquerade stood on top of a towering skyscraper. He glanced downwards at the night streets that were illuminated by lamp posts and raging traffic. His first hope was that suicide could take him back to the afterlife, and so he stood, on the top of a roof, ready to jump. Then he dove off the side of the building, the winds soaring against his body. It took a lot of self-control to be able to do so, with the ground approaching every lasting moment. His body splat on the sidewalk, however he felt no pain, and his body was completely undamaged.

He stood up, unphased, looking down at his unscarred hands. Cars had stopped traffic to check if he was alright, Masquerade simply modded and started walking down the street as if nothing happened. He was confused about what just happened. His energy remained the same, indicating that nothing had happened. No scars indicated that he had just fallen five hundred feet.

He wanted to try one more tactic. He then pulled his dark sword out of his body, which was now able to be used by him due to him cleansing himself of 'glory'. The blade quivered in his hands, and quickly, he plunged the sword into his gut. He expected it to break, but the sword pierced through effectively.

No pain came; however, the blade seemed to phase right through him. He tried cutting himself all over, but the sword would pass right through his skin. He dropped the sword, frustrated. He thought about how he would do this for a quick moment, and he started sprinting back into the depths of the city. He waved down the first person he saw.

"Hello, sir, can you do me a huge favor!?" He exclaimed to the poor guy. The guy looked at him weirdly. His eyes were golden, and he had a messy blond overlay with black undersides and sideburns. His blond hair shimmered in the moonlight, highlighting his tuxedo and fancy car. He glared at Masquerade.

"Sure, why not, kiddo!" He said enthusiastically. He walked up to Masquerade slowly.

"Thanks! But you have to promise me not to back down, no matter how disturbing it may sound. Okay?" Masquerade winced and held his hand out to shake.

The man shook his hand, "Agreed." Masquerade couldn't help but smile, but didn't know why he did so. He felt connected to this man on a spiritual level, the same way he felt with Jace, except this time the person was a complete stranger.

"So basicallyI want you touhh, how do I phrase this. I want you to kill me?" He said awkwardly. The man looked surprised at first. "Please don't worry! I'm immortal, but I don't think I can kill myself." He explained, his mind fogging with embarrassment.

"I see! My name's Alastair, and normally I don't go around saying stuff like this, but I'm the same way!" He announced, and Masquerade smiled.

"What!? You're immortal, too? You can't kill yourself either?" Masquerade asked, and Alastair nodded and smiled, who walked forward and patted his shoulder.

"Yes, I'll kill you. Hand me the sword." His expression narrowed. He nodded approvingly, Masquerade held out his sword and handed it to Alastair, who admired it for a while, the colors gleaming a vibrant purple. He quickly held the sword in a fighting stance. Masquerade stood ready to die. Then, the sword plunged into his stomach. The soothing pain felt releasing to him, it sounded insane, but he was glad he could feel the blood oozing from his chest. Alastair smiled and slashed the blade once more, making lines of blood scatter against the stove pavement.

Masquerade fell to the floor, his blood pooling onto the cement. He heard the clang of metal hitting the floor as he blacked out. Then, finally, he saw Anubis waiting in the same room as last time. The room had golden flashing chandeliers hanging from the stone brick ceiling, and many emeralds and other forms of gems were scattered around. Anubis had an abundant smile on his face.

"You're back again, Masquerade!" He said, his voice lowering. He stared at the blade, which was glowing heavily purple. Masquerade held it up and admired the glow.

"Why is it doing that?" He asked while slightly touching it.

"It's because it's in our presence." He explained, his eyes were glowing gold suddenly. Masquerade lowered his eyebrow.

"Our!?"

"Yes, me and Mardo. I thought I told you Mardo is sealed inside me?" His voice raised, and instantly, Masquerade felt another presence, the same presence he's felt two times before. Once at Olympus, and twice in his dreams. A hand appeared out of Anubis' stomach, its translucence quickly becoming solid. Then, an entire body came flying out, and two gods lay in his presence. Mardo's clown makeup was purple this time around instead of smearing black, which highlighted his key facial features. Mardo smiled at Masquerade, who held out his hand. The blade flew out of his hands and towards Mardo, who admired the sword for a long moment. "This blade killed multiple powerful people. I hope you know how important this thing really is." Mardo explained, and Anubis nodded acceptingly. "It was the sword that killed Osiris, and it wounded even Misa." Mardo's fingers seemed to make the blade more powerful, the metal growing in power in response to its owner's touch, but then it unexpectedly shot back towards Masquerade. "It holds a bond between me, you, and Anubis, breaking it would shatter that bond. That's why you weren't able to wield it with 'glory', because it would ultimately shatter the connection we all have through this spiritual item." Finally, was he able to understand the connection between the people in the room. That main thing that made them so easily able to have great chemistry was because at one point, they were all filled with 'glory'.

The blade felt more potent, and Mardo was grinning in return, but then Anubis interrupted. "What brings you here? It seems you died willingly, which isn't like you." Masquerade walked up to the two.

"I need to find Echo, Jake, and Garm." He spoke demandingly. Anubis' expression widened.

"Two of those people would be almost impossible for you to kill. Are you sure you want to do that?" Masquerade frowned, wondering if Anubis even believed in him. "I know. I just need to retrieve my brothers from Hell first. So if you could bring me to them, that'd be great."

Mardo smiled and butted in, "Well, hurry up while you're down there, because I want to see Echo get what he deserves!" He said chillingly, Anubis agreeing.

"What? You're not on Echo's side?" Masquerade sputtered, and Mardo laughed.

"Of course not! Why would I follow Sura or his son's ideals? All he does is manipulate the gods to do whatever he feels like doing. And my father is no better. Once I get unsealed from Anubis, he's the first person I'm killing." Masquerade smirked, realizing that their family bond was shattered, making an ultimate parallel between the two gods.

"Well then, we'll get along well." Masquerade recalled when Mardo tried fighting him back on Olympus, the first time they had conflict.

"No need to worry about that scramble in Olympus. I already told you back in the dream world, I was only acting for Misa. He doesn't like it when I disobey him." Mardo sighed, "He only lets me out of the spiritual world when he needs me. He always keeps me cooped inside Anubis's conscience; it's really hard to explain."

Masquerade ignored it, "Okay I get it, now take me to Hell!" Mardo snapped, leaving him time to be alone with Anubis, something he wrathfully despised. Even though he's been teleported a trillion times before, he still hasn't gotten used to the feeling of being instantly rushed forward. The next thing he knew, it was freezing cold. The last time he checked, Hell was a boiling wasteland of lava, but now there were ranges of mountains ahead of him. He looked ahead and saw three figures ready to fight a gigantic wolf.

He ran towards the group, and the air was filled with snow, obscuring his vision. The giant hound had glowing blue eyes and was ready to attack, its delicacy ready to slash its claws of fury to kill a group of underlying gods. Then it jumped into the air, its claws pointing towards the three. Masquerade went airborne and flew towards it, punching it with an explosion, making it fall backward violently. Soon enough, the sounds of howling interrupted the cold winter air. Hyper's voice cheered loudly in the background. Masquerade smiled and glanced back at the three.

Tamer was beat up, but happy to see him. Infinity and Hyper both looked like they worked overtime against the hellscape. The wolf charged a blast of ice; Masquerade dodged with great speed. He landed next to Hyper.

"What's the plan?" Infinity asked, his voice still sounding the same as the last time he talked to him..

Masquerade grinned, "I'm going to assert dominance over this dog!" They all laughed in response, standing still and doing what they did best, and watched. He rubbed his hands together, ignoring the freezing weather. Masquerade had now just noticed that a normal human would immediately freeze in these conditions. His skin wasn't damaged at all, but he ignored the peeling of his dry dermis. The dog growled in response.

This one had no chain, but Masquerade still evaded around his neck. Hyper was running around its legs. "Make me a chain!" He screamed down at Hyper. Then after a set of whispers, a glow of purple lightning, the next thing he knew, an ice chain erupted out of the mountain and wrapped around the dog's neck. He stood on the neck of the hound, tugging the chain upwards. It wrestled back, but Masquerade proved stronger. He didn't know where the strength came from, but he was hurling the huge hound towards the wall of the mountain. It crashed, and the mountain started coming down on them, starting an avalanche. Huge rocks and snow started to fall down. Masquerade summoned his blade and swiped it across the air. At first, nothing happened, but then gusts of wind slashed the avalanche right back into the air, creating meteors of homing rocks that poured like heavy rain.

The wolf got back to its feet and barked. The bark was loud enough to blow the four straight into the nearest wall. It then charged towards them, this is when he looked into its baring eyes. He realized the poor thing had no brain, it had no thoughts, with no real sensation of good and bad. He realized he might have been fighting the ultimate representation of 'glory'. Masquerade grabbed his wrist with his palm out and held it out to the giant, releasing a burst of power, and an explosion blasted it back into the ground. Masquerade flew upwards again to try getting to its neck.

Quickly, it got to its feet and pounced behind him. Its paw smashed him into the ground. The claw was stabbed into his stomach, and it kept smashing Masquerade into the ground, stabbing him over and over, with the dog hacking him into the ground. Masquerade clenched his fists into its furry paw. He gripped and redirected his strength again, swinging with all his might, and the dog flew into the mountain wall once again. Adrenaline pulsed through his veins, adrenaline caused by the deep depths of 'joy'.

The dog roared at him; however, this time, the air didn't push Masquerade back. He instead locked in, and roared back to the canine with no soul, and stomped on the floor as hard as he could, asserting importance and dominance over it. A crack fissured into the ground, and rumbles of energy started shaking the entire area. He didn't know if it was an explosion, but the mountain was falling into pieces, and the vibration of an earthquake whaled the stones in the floor. The ranges in the background seemed to split in half deep in the horizon, and Masquerade looked backward. He saw the entire ground split itself open, revealing a crack that was growing larger than the Grand Canyon itself.

Hyper, Infinity, and Tamer should've been eaten by it, but they were completely safe, completely put aside by Masquerade's prowess of air, floating slightly in the snowfields of the frozen hell. They were on a piece of land that didn't get swallowed by the earth that was also levitating. The hound was falling into the hole, trying to scratch its way to the surface. The crack extended beyond Masquerade's line of sight. He now noticed the earthquakes in the region. The mountain ahead of him was split in half entirely and was crumbling apart.

"Goddammit, why didn't Mardo name you Earthshaker? You're the god of destruction!" Infinity screamed, the earthquakes screaming in contrast in the background. Masquerade now realized he was also standing on a pike of land, barely levitating. Masquerade flew towards the group. Tamer was completely terrified, and in the depths below was an endless river of lava that cascaded the souls of escaping unworthy demons. The dog was trying not to fall down to its death, to join the rest of the demons.

"I don't know how I did that, but we got to get the hell out of here!" The ground around them was breaking and collapsing as they spoke. He grabbed his blade.

"How!?" Hyper looked worried, and Masquerade was now realizing how much he missed him. He reached in for a hug and turned around quickly, also letting Infinity reach in, which left out Tan=mer, who stood awkwardly. His voice lowered.

"I'll show you, just watch." Masquerade turned to face the struggling hound, its huge body struggling to stay on the ground that remained from the huge rumbling. He leaped off the edge and aimed for the dog's back, jumping and grasping it, finally climbing to its huge ears. It tried wrestling back, but Masquerade pulled his ears back like a lasso. He held the ear to his mouth. "I'll spare you, puppy. Take me and my friends to Earth!" At first, he didn't expect the dog to do anything, but then it started panting, in response to it almost falling down to its final demise.

It didn't actually talk back, but it howled in understanding. The dog's muscles untensed, and it calmed down entirely, its fur becoming fluffier. Masquerade jumped off its head and landed on the ground next to his paws, grasping on its fur again and lifted the hound to rescue. It was threatening and intimidating, but it let its tongue out and panted like an actual puppy. Masquerade stared and happily looked at Hyper.

"So, how will this work?" Hyper said as he jumped towards him with bouncing excitement. Masquerade petted the huge dog and shrugged, questioning the sanity of the situation.

"I don't know, we'll see!" He said, climbing aside the dog. Masquerade climbed atop its head and stood for a long moment. "Hop on!" Infinity and Hyper didn't hesitate, but Tamer did. It took a lot of convincing, but eventually it worked, with him reluctantly joining. They all buried themselves in the long fur of the gray wolf. Masquerade tugged its ears again. "Go! To Alastair!" Everyone winced.

Garm whined at first, then his claws turned a bright light blue, spiraling with power of great importance. He howled upwards, like the moon was there, but saw the depth of a cave instead. Masquerade thought they'd travel through a portal, but then the wind was knocked straight out of him. He almost fell off the hound; it traveled at light speed, and everything around them distorted into multiple colors. He clung on for dear life until they stopped suddenly. Masquerade flew off the fur and crash-landed in a nearby dumpster. He got up and saw Garm scratching his neck, the hound being externally larger than the two-story house right next to him. Hyper, Tamer, and Infinity were scattered on the street in different positions.

It was nighttime, and he was on the same block where Alastair had killed him. To his surprise, Alastair was still there, walking over to the group.

"Wow, you weren't lying, you really are immortal!" He announced it to the world. Tamer gasped, and the others looked confused. Masquerade frowned.

"Long story! Yes, I found a way back to the town and rescued my siblings and friends. Thanks, Alastair. But I still need another favor." His voice faltered. Masquerade turned to the group. "Return to the group, text Dark to give you an address. I'll be there shortly. I just have some, uh, business to finish." Hyper winced, and his arms flew into the air. The huge dog was panting loudly. Infinity smiled and opened his mouth.

"What exactly are we going to do about this dog!" He shouted and started pacing around the road. Masquerade flinched.

"Let him be. I'm sure he'll know where to go." Infinity nodded like he was crazy and started walking down the road with the rest of the group. Tamer smiled and patted Masquerade on the shoulder. "It's essentially a big puppy, just maybe someone will adopt him!"

"Good luck, we're counting on you." His angelic voice beamed through his worries. He smiled back and turned towards Alastair, as everyone else cheered down the road, their worried expression finally turning light, representing the contrast between the nature of Earth versus the nature of Hell. A single hike up a mountain on Earth resulted in sore legs, and maybe a threat from a grizzly bear, but a hike in Hell? Yeah you'd be lucky to be alive still, which made Masquerade feel better in Hyper's growth lately. He knew his hyperactiveness could get out of hand, but his actions were able to silence themselves for once to save them from the depths of a never ending pit-hole of fire, he couldn't help but wonder if any of his siblings had to make the decision of 'glory' and 'joy'.

"I need you to kill me again." The three down the road turned around with shocked looks on their faces, Masquerade grinned, "Keep walking!" They turned away with a few snickers.

"Whatever you wish for, dude." Alastair held his hand out. Masquerade gave him the sword. He swung, and Masquerade died. He blacked out, and he saw Anubis again. It's crazy how fast the process could happen. Mardo was still standing in front of him, talking about how certain dishes of beans are cooked. They both gasped and turned to face him, Marod being more interested in the boy than Anubis. He paused and took a deep breath. "I need help defeating Echo." He blurted, and Mardo took a long step forward. He grinned deviously.

"I thought you'd never ask." He said sarcastically. "Not to pick sides or anythinggg, but if you insist on killing him, I have a few tips." His voice said in a way that said, 'Oh yeah,

I hate Echo with my guts.' Anubis sat down on an old rusty throne. He snapped, and the room disappeared out of thin air, everything around them turned into a void of pitch black darkness, and the ground below them ceased to exist, making them float in midair. "So?" They both stared at each other in the pitch black. Mardo lifted his fist, black tattooed were shown prominent.

Especially in his hands, where a tattoo formed into the shape of a ring finger that was there since his birth. "Let me show you something important. Hold out your hand for me please." Masquerade followed his directions. Mardo held his palm in his fist. At first, nothing happened for a few moments, but then Mardo clapped his hand with his other one. A purple shockwave occurred, lighting the black area with the aura. Pain seared in his veins and hand, making him fall to his knees in agony. Mardo smiled as a black mark etched into his skin, and at the same time, smoke, lasers, string, and light exploded out of his hand. The pain was impossible to bear. He struggled to open his mouth.

"How the hell is this helping me!" He recoiled backward and readied to attack Mardo, who smiled.

"Don't worry, you'll see when you get there. This mark allows you to use your own powers to a greater extent. So those flashy explosions of yours will be more powerful, but only when coming out of THAT hand." His finger pointed. Masquerade held his wrist.

"Why does it hurt so much then!" His hand still stung with pain. Mardo smiled.

"Glory hurts kiddo. Next time you think about saving someone, just remember your past self and how he reluctantly chose a path of self resolve, rather than a path of helping people. Now you're forced to live with that regret." He whispered reluctantly. "I'll get you a quick ride to Echo, and you can go from there." Mardo snapped. Masquerade tried arguing, but the next thing he knew, he was falling through the air. He thought he'd be used to it by now, but there's just something about being two thousand feet in the open air. Masquerade was trembling with fear, not because he was falling to his death again, but because he would have to face Echo soon, all by himself.

The wind stopped his fall, and his body landed safely on the ground, landing directly in front of a massive door. In front of said door stood a massive mansion. It was heavily decorated with quartz, gold, purple and black colors. The mansion doors were brown with huge golden rings as handles. He didn't know what to do. Does he knock? Does he kick open the door and destroy everything? Without hesitation, he grabbed the golden ring, and decided he'd be the better person for once. He pulled the elegant door open slowly. It creaked with noise and slowly retreated open.

Masquerade slipped inside the crack and surveyed the mansion. If Echo was here, wouldn't this place be more secure? The mansion was decorated with black marble flooring, and huge golden pillars supported the white marble ceiling. In the middle of the room and pillars was a huge purple crystal chandelier, under said chandelier was a circular etching on the floor, like a tattoo on the ground that was designed with some old symbols like the ancient Egyptians used, but he didn't jump to conclusions. It looked like some gateway to another realm. The round platform was completely purple.

Then it hit him, he had been here before, with Hyper. Long ago, on Halloween night. He walked into the middle of the room, admiring its beauty. The floor had purple carpets placed on it, which bound off in multiple directions into different rooms. He held his hand out quickly, and his sword came into view. The gleaming purple blade shined in his bruised fingers, illuminating his spirit, showing that the warrior inside him was ready to fight. The white streaks of the blade started animating itself more frequently, indicating deeply that it was filled with 'joy'. He switched hands and placed it in the hand that Mardo had tattooed earlier, he glanced at it, wondering how it even worked.

He glanced around and spotted a room with a kitchen. He walked towards it, but was stopped by a hateful voice he recognized well.

"Well, look who decided to take matters into his own hands. I have to give you the benefit of the doubt and praise you for trying so hard." Echo stood a few feet away from him. His eyes were still chillingly blue. "Now that you came for me, Jake will have no trouble taking out Jynx and your brothers." His voice lowered. "Really, you should've seen this coming." He smiled and glowered at him. "You really do lack common sense, just remember that you need brains to survive in this world, and pure power isn't going to get you anywhere."

Masquerade raised his blade and grinned slightly. "I envy your enthusiasm, but there's only one thing I need you for." The sound of thunder struck the room, and Masquerade was in the air in seconds. Echo was moments away from Masquerade's landing zone, barely managing to dodge, and the two were eye to eye. "Where's my brother?" His voice demanded. Echo's mind went blank for a long cold pause, with the 'joy' of Masquerade's sword piercing into his toxified veins.

"Which one?" He argued, and Masquerade felt anger controlling him again.

"You know which one!" He swung his blade, and Echo ducked under it. His actions were hard to follow, and he was faster than usual. Echo stepped and invaded his personal bubble, closing the distance between the two. Masquerade tried stabbing at him, but he just dodged wistfully. His fist maneuvered lightly, punching him in the shoulder, sending him flying in the other direction, coming to a quick standstill.

"I don't know what you're talking about." He teased. Masquerade got back to his feet and charged towards him again, his sword clanging against his muscular knee-cap. Echo teased him more, sticking his tongue out in disappointment. He dodged every attack effortlessly, still keeping his composure. Masquerade managed to outmaneuver him once, and the blade was moments away from slicing his neck, the attack was undodgeable and would have killed Echo right then and there, but instead right as the blade was going to hit, an ice sword manifested from thin air and parried his black blade, a flurry of yellow sparks floating in the breeze of the room. Masquerade flinched and tried to counterattack, but was still proven outclasssed in terms of strength, skill, and speed.

Echo flicked the blade in his hand with his wrist using great strength, to lunge his diving swords into his opponent's thigh, and then swiping upwards violently, cutting Masquerade's leg off. From the knee down, his leg was shaved clean off and blood was rising just as quick as a hose spurting water. He lost balance in his stance, flailing his arms upwards, losing control of the blade. Once the blade soared through the air, Echo slapped the blade across the room, making it slide across the floor and making a metal clinking sound. He fell to the floor and tried catching himself with his hands, failing, he landed face-first into the marble. Echo followed by delivering a gut kick, the shear strength sending him to the other side of the room, away from the sword.

He grunted and attempted to get to his feet, which was impossible, considering one of them was missing. Echo laughed and quickly stepped over to the blade that lay on the floor. Masquerade eventually had no options, and had no hope left.

"This battle is over already. You have no weapon and you're missing a limb! How do you expect to win? Soon, you and Jynx will both be dead." Echo picked up the blade. "Pathetic, Mardo tried helping you, it seems?" He said as he observed the dark sword. His face turned grim, observing the shining glint of metal. Then Masquerade remembered what Mardo said about the mystical blade, if it was destroyed it would break the connection between the three. He tried using the neurons in his brain, trying to articulate what that would mean. The blade connected Mardo and Anubis, meaning if he broke it, their seal would become weakened. He quickly pieced it together if he broke the sword, Mardo would be forced to use Masquerade's body as a host. Then his eyes pulsed with a quick flash of purple, letting his body travel with the speed of lightning. Echo was caught off guard, leaving Masqueraded a quick receiving second to retrieve the blade.

Unexpected to his opponent, he merely pinched the metal, and the entire sword snapped in half. The metal cracked like it was glass, the power of it swifting into the etching on his hand, that also happened to be a result from Mardo's power. The sword's old parts fell to the ground, completely shattered. Echo mocked him as he started walking towards him menacingly. Then, a flash of black lightning struck from the ceiling, cracking the debris into smoke, and encasing Masquerade's entire body. Echo had a look of confusion on his face that quickly turned to hatred, and even fear.

"What did you do!" His voice screamed with contrast, the presence of Mardo finally able to be sensed. Oh, I see what you did! Mardo's dark and deep voice spoke, Masquerade's brain fluctuating with its power. With Mardo's power, his leg healed back to normal, allowing him to stand normal once more. You're cunning for your age, that sweetness that was able to conspire within me as well. I told you, there's something about you, something that reminds me of myself, maybe a reincarnation of sorts. Now with Mardo and him sharing a consciousness, he finally noticed the spiritual reason behind him and Echo's rivalry, and this reason was much more than just the spirit, this time it was something hidden in their genetics.

If he didn't win against Echo now, everyone would die. He clenched his jaw and his fists. He raised his voice and opened his mouth. "I don't need that blade to defeat you! COWARD! Fight me with your hands!"

Echo's expression widened as he prepared to counterattack. Masquerade had no clue what he expected to do without a weapon, but he tried. He jumped into the air and charged his palm with glistening energy. The enemy glared back indecisively. Spikes and blocks of ice started to rise from the floor, then he let it all out, the power of an awakened god, splitting his heart into two beats. An explosion destroyed all the created ice, shattering it all over the place. Echo was caught in the center of it all, his face burnt off from the heat of the explosion. His body stood firmly, although it was clear the explosion hurt him.

Masquerade charged him again and swung his fist. Echo ducked under and counter-attacked his gut, another ice spike intruded from the ground, threatening to stab Masquerade. He lifted his foot quickly, and the two flew straight into the air from large gusts of wind, almost hitting the ceiling of the mansion. Echo hesitated for a moment, before lightning came, striking down through the mansion ceiling, completely destroying it and sending debris flying through the air. The bolt struck Echo directly, sending him flying into the ground again, electrifying his nerves. His body was damaged, but Echo showed no signs of pain.

Hidden amongst Masquerade's bloodline was the power of the heart, and behind Echo's was the power of the brain, making their obvious interactions be decided with that of fate, and the cunning trick of knowledge.

Masquerade flew down quickly, landing directly on top of Echo. He started spamming explosions and fireworks. Every time he swung at Echo, explosions blew up around and with him. His mind formed a genius plan to beat him, which was as he was fighting him, he would build up and charge an explosion throughout his entire body. Then, he would release it when he thought it was the best time to kill him. Echo kicked him off with a large gust of cold wind. Masquerade continued the assault of graceful sparks of energy. Echo had trouble dodging explosion after explosion. He tried counter-attacking with walls of ice, but they were immediately destroyed and shattered no matter the durability of the walls.

Whenever Echo tried escaping to recover, a vortex of wind currents kept him close. Revealing a current of rain and thunder strikes, was the deep realization of fighting in the middle of a storm. Even inside the mansion, it was pouring with crystals. Masquerade used all of his powers at the same time, bolts of lightning rained from the skies, explosions decimated the area, and gusts of wind kept Echo in check, and to top it all off, every time the two made eye contact, he would use it to predict Echo's next move.

It was almost like Echo stood no chance against the now fused gods, although Mardo hasn;t shown useful just yet. Soon, you'll show your true potential. He spoke, his dark voice turning his anger into motivation. Just sit back and watch, I'm going to knock his fucking teeth out. Mardo chuckled. Mini me, mini me! Masquerade was always two moves ahead of him, following with nasty combos of destruction. He was winning this fight, his power of the heart proving supremacy over the brain in raw absolute power. He then hit Echo with the nastiest jaw lock ever performed in history, cracking and unhinging his mandible, sending multiple teeth sprawling to the floor . His facial expression went from joking to serious, and Echo clenched his fists. He's locking the fuck in, you have to stay sharp!

"Enough!" Echo snapped, and Masquerade flew into the nearest wall by an unknown force. All his defenses were gone in quick seconds, the lightning and wind stopping with an unknowing technique. His power over the brain shows supremacy over the heart in intelligence. Echo held his hand out, and black metal rods flew out of them. All four of them stabbed Masquerade, draining his power and energy. Then, the rods started levitating and forced his limp body to Echo's position. They stood eye to eye, with Echo being taller however.

"It was fun fighting you, young god, but what do you want your last words to be?" He smirked as the black rods stung with more searing pain. The most classical line a villain can say, come up with something original! Mardo teased. Masquerade moved the hand with Mardo's matte black tattoo on it, holding the hand right up to Echo's white, pale face.

"Say hi to Anubis for me." He whispered. Echo's expression dropped. Black lightning came from his hand, and soon enough, an explosion flattened the area. The explosion he had charged up for the entire fight was released and destroyed the entire mansion. It was so massive it formed a mushroom cloud in the clear blue sky. Mardo continued laughing, Get ready! Take some of my energy! He spoke, and they both realized the light and power that emitted from the light of his tattoo. In the smoke still stood Echo's silhouette. Once it cleared, you could see he was still completely unharmed. Masquerade flinched and got back to his feet. The metal rods had disintegrated from the fierce blast.

"Was that all?" Echo said, while the power that Mardo was harnessing grew in volume. Masquerade underestimated his own speed, stepping towards him, but instead of traveling one step, he boosted straight through Echo's unseemingly unscathed body. The speed was so insane it left Echo's entire left arm sliced off from the shoulder and down. And for the first time, fear was rising in Echo's chest. Masquerade stomped, his foot thirty feet away from the last spot he was in. He stomped on the floor and smiled.

"No, that's not all." The ground cracked again, and massive earthquakes started rumbling across the entire deserted plains, this however, still wasn't the power that Mardo was holding. Get ready! I'm almost done. . . Why don't you respond! I'm *focusing, dammit!* He responded in advance. Echo stared at him fearfully, but still angrily. The ground was splitting at their feet, and Echo had nowhere to run. Echo stood on an unsteady and unsafe platform of the splitting floor, his legs almost slipping into the crack.

Then he felt a nostalgic feeling, the feeling of his eyes being split, except by a force within his own body. Masquerade then experienced the sensation of being under a beating pulse. Except instead of him, it was Echo. Mardo was laughing hysterically, he knew this moment was coming. His dad's famous 'God Pulse' had activated within himself, he could now read Echo's every thought now, and he felt more aware of the area around him as well. His eyes pulsed and gleamed with absolute power. His power allowed him to gaze at Echo, the flux of power then carried and raised his hand in the air. This is it. "Prepare yourself Echo!!" Masquerade's mouth forcefully opened, making him yell something he didn't say. Then his hand, which was marked with the tattoo, flicked down aggressively.

The air compressed with heat, and the ground started forming black cracks of smoke. The clouds split, and the largest lightning strike in the world came crashing down on Echo's body. The diameter of the strike was so massive it bathed his entire body in pure lightning. At least a radius of 3 meters struck the area. The strike was so powerful the thunder was delayed by half a minute, and the sound created a shockwave of pulsing air. There were black marks on the ground around the strike, and the heat from it was still bending the air around it. At first, he thought the lightning had killed Echo, but then the strike froze in place, the lightning stopped streaming its strums of noise, and started to turn from purple to light blue. From the bottom of the huge bolt, it started getting covered in ice. He thought his vision was playing tricks on him, but it was clear as day. The bolt was frozen in place, and the lightning was still streaming inside a casing of cold, bright ice. Echo stood in front of the mess, laughing. Masquerade's arm was completely shattered with the energy of summoning such a strike. His arm was paralyzed for a few moments.

The ground was still falling apart, however, and Echo stood still as if nothing could kill him. Masquerade opened his mouth slowly. "Wipe that fucking smile off your damn face! It's over, Echo! Stop fighting, I will win!" He screamed as his body ached everywhere in power, the drawbacks of using such destructive capability were coming back. Echo watched and lowered his brow.

"I appreciate your warning, but now I see why Mardo feared you so much. You are the strongest Greek God. The embodiment of Zeus, maybe even stronger than him. I didn't believe a teenager could surpass him so fast. This is the end for you! It surely is sad to see a god that wants change to die so quickly" Echo's body started steaming, and his injured body started healing. That was my line! That bastard, trying to take my flow. Masquerade didn't know what to do. Echo waved his hand in the air, and a black mist came from him and attacked Masquerade. He forgot about his increased speed and blitzed sideways, forty feet away. The mist dispersed quickly and rearranged itself to attack again.

Trails of ice tried following him, but he sped in the other direction. He was so fast you could see after images of his traveling body. Echo tried attacking him with multiple combos of ice and black mist, but Masquerade weaved through them all in quick succession. He could see every attack before it came out, thanks to Mardo's future sight. He knew where Echo was every second of the fight and exactly what he was going to do next.

Masquerade planted his feet into the ground, his paralyzed arm could now move only slightly. Echo still stood in front of the frozen bolt, staring as frost started covering his own body, giving him an awakened state of flow. Their hands matched each other, both in a position to throw hands, and box. More than that however was their differences, the brain, Echo, was in a flow state, locked in, focused and ready to fight. In contrast, the heart, Masquerade, was in a state of heightened senses, caused by the increased blood flow caused by his pumping heart. His hands were in a boxing position, indicating he was ready to fight. Masquerade responded by putting only one of his hands in a boxing pose, since he could barely move his other one.

Three. A dark, deep, and mysterious voice whispered in his head, which he recognized as Mardo. Two. The voice continued, as ice spikes started to intrude from the ground once again and sparks of lightning started to illuminate the area as well. Wind whispered, clouds rumbled, and the ground roared.

ONE! The voice boomed as Masquerade and Echo started sprinting towards each other. Blocks of ice shattered as explosions started decimating the area. Echo hit him with a quick jab to the jaw, which he responded by blocking. Echo quickly jabbed at his stomach, which he couldn't block. Masquerade groaned in pain as his useless arm proved nothing.

Echo started giving him the works, he wasn't able to keep up with Echo in hand to hand combat with only one working arm. Masquerade followed with a bash to the head that Echo was hit by, recoiling his body backwards for a moment. Then Echo made an ice sword and tried slicing his head, he responded by dodging under it, doing the splits under the blade. Sparks of lightning flew everywhere, illuminating their contrasts in supreme spirituality.

Masquerade resorted to fighting with his feet. He swiped his leg under Echo's and tripped him. As Echo fell, Masquerade quickly positioned his leg to kick Echo directly in the stomach. This sent him flying, ragdolling across the floor. He quickly got back to his feet and started charging after Echo once again.

"It seems your arm doesn't work!" He screamed. "I'LL WIN!" He was completely unhinged by this point, only trying to destroy him. Masquerade went to punch him in the face, but Echo blocked with BOTH of his hands. A moment of anticipation raced through their nerves and blood, pulsing rage blinded both their visions. Masquerade smiled deviously, the most sinister unhinged smile you could see on a person. The moment was so tense that Masquerade could feel every one of Echo's muscles tighten himself.

He raised his own 'paralyzed' arm, as sparks of lightning and explosions started emitting from it. He grabbed Echo's fists with his 'working' hand, keeping them in a standstill. Masquerade lodged his fist into Echo's stomach, as legions of destructive power unleashed into his stomach. The force blew him several feet away, forming a gaping hole opened inside of his abdomen. His ribs were shattered, and his blackened burnt guts were pouring out of his cavity. His spine broke, and kidneys were crashing out from the bowel of his wound.

Masquerade blitzed past him once more and cut off his left arm entirely with lightning again. He catapulted lobs of explosive energy in his direction.. All of them exploded on the right side of his face, causing more burns and scratches. Echo tried attacking, but Masquerade was too fast. He created a blade of lightning and sliced both of Echo's legs off, and he fell to the floor, his breath trying to catch up. Masquerade then grabbed Echo by the chest and held him up straight, staring directly into his cold eyes.

"Tell me where Jake is, and maybe I'll spare you." His voice demanded. Echo coughed up blood, his face covered in ash.

"Nice try-" He coughed again. "-but you can't kill me." The scratches on his face

"In that condition you might as well say I already won!" He said, still hoisting up Echo's upper half. Echo hesitated on the floor, then he stood up quickly. He hit Masquerade with an uppercut that sent him flying straight twenty feet away. He stumbled and tried getting back to his feet, but the hit seemed to drain his power by a ton. His power affects the thermoreceptors in your skin that connect to the brain, allowing for the feeling of being drained.

Mardo explained efficiently. Masquerade fell to his knees and tried to regain his balance, but his energy was completely drained. Echo however, went above and beyond, excruciating that the brain lasts longer than the heart in exhaustion, his body's voltage ramped up, and his power increased above his normal potential that allowed for his legs to be healed back to normal strength. He then stepped towards him deviously, with a stupid wide smile on his face. His face was bearing the weight of disgust and lost ambition, but that lost ambition was quickly turning to exponentially growing power. Then Echo held his hand out to him, providing an offering of some sorts. Out of options, Echo seemed to be getting anxiously desperate to win.

"Take my hand, and I can offer you immortality, a life, something to live for. And reign over an entire kingdom, the world will be yours as we know it. Together, you, Misa, Sura, all my brothers, Mardo, and everyone. We can take over the world, and kill anyone in our way. Your old family will cease to exist, don't try to hide it because I know that you dislike your father; trust me, a lot of people do." Masquerade made fierce eye contact with him, considering his propose for a moment. He could feel Mardo's presence screaming for him not to.

He grinned, and let his hand out, and grabbed it for a cold moment. What the hell are **you** **d**oing! Dumbass, after everything I've taught you this is how you betray me! Echo's body relaxed, seemingly prosperous to believe Masquerade. Then, like a flame of embers enlightening due to a growth in potential, Masquerade spoke, his heart beating with the pulse of two powers. "I don't need immortality. . ." He finally said, anticipation rose, as crackling power emitted, millions and millions of jolts of lightning plugged inside Echo's hand. The lightning quickly spread throughout his entire body. He started hyperventilating and was shocked with the absolute power of the electricity. The final phase of the fight began, Echo losing neuros, with Masquerade's cardiac tissue forming another lump of muscular beating cells. Long red scars highlighted where Echo's veins would be. Smoke arose from every part of his body, and Masquerade stood up once more. Another awakening? Mardo spoke after witnessing the fact that Masquerade was growing a second heart of power. His veins convulsed, and their blood carried a second impact amongst his shockwaves of potential.

He quickly learned the symbolism, that the brain was seemingly more powerful than the heart, but two hearts however, were clearly superior.

Echo's body jolted upwards with energy, and he fell to the floor, still shaking intensely. "Tell me where my brother Bow is and what Jake's next plan is." He said as Echo was only seconds away from death, his second pulse of power energetically pushing his limits over the line.

Chapter 18
Jace

Jace walked up to the portal, after seemingly transitioning from the realm of his memory filled household. He noticed his soul was being weighed on a scale made of spiritual metal. Anubis smiled with a touch of nostalgia. "Your soul is as pure as gold." He smiled at him, showing signs of great impression.

Jace gasped, expecting it to be less pure than he thought, considering he absorbed Masquerade's glory, which was supposed to make his soul corrupt. "So, the actions in that body were not my own doing?" He asked.

"Correct because you see, Jake trapped you inside your body against your own will; he forced you to do those bad things, so really, the bad things 'you' did, were bad things 'Jake' did." He explained. His gaze shifted down to his feet. "He took away your life at a young age, and soon it will be his time to pay." He smiled, his eyes holding a great significance that reminded him of an old friend. Then with a snap of his fingers, Anubis shifted the scene.

The room was filled with mist, and standing in the middle of it was Jake. Jace was only eight years old, his hands were dirty and filled with scars. Jake stood right above him, stepping on his chest. His voice was low and cautious.

"Great thing I found you again, you'll be great for what I need." He said, Jace covered his mouth with his hand to stop himself from screaming terror.

"Let me go! What-?" He stuttered. Jake smiled.

"You'll see." He said with a grin. Jake grabbed him and carried him into the next room over. He had no idea where this place was, but it felt out of the ordinary, absorbing his presence like a n egg emulsifying a cake batter. Jake tied him to a chair, which was something he did a lot for an underlying reason. On the floor was a satanic symbol etched into the floor. Jake said something in a foreign language, and the symbol started glowing red.

"The sacrifice has been made!" He screamed. "ACCEPT MY OFFERING!" Then, the room filled with dark energy, the pressuring power bringing his wrists together. The presence was immense and made Jace feel like all the pressure in the world was on his back, resulting in him barely able to bear the weight. In the middle of the symbol was a humanoid figure that appeared upon formation of Jake's call. At first, he couldn't make out what it was, but the smoke cleared, and a strikingly beautiful woman appeared. Her body was model-worthy, and she immediately blew Jace out of the water.

She wore purple lipstick, and her eyes spiraled into madness, however such a pretty kind. Her hair was tightly curled, carrying hues of purple and black. She wore a long purple dress and had white heels. She walked towards Jace with interest. She had great posture, and her gaze made Jace feel loved.

"This is the one?" She said, focusing back on Jake, then back to Jace. "I remember you other sacrifice earlier, which didn't go too well, so I'll complete the ritual for you." Her voice was outstanding, controlling the fates of their brains. She opened her clenched fist, in response to a lightning power of wisping purple mist. Jace's body went flying towards her, and he landed next to her elegant feet. The woman stared down at him with a wistful smile. "Close your eyes, little one. The procedure is usually painful for the receiving end." Jace didn't close his eyes but instead watched what she did, unable to take his eyes of her.

At first, she walked up to Jake, lightly touching his chest, like she was reaching out for something deep inside him. Her long purple fingernails extracted a light blue substance that had highlights of dark red, representing the blotches of evil on his soul. It was a faint light, almost like it was his soul or at least a part of it. She played with the soul for a while before walking towards Jace. She stretched the blue substance out and gracefully arched it around her fingers.

Then she plunged the soul inside Jace and was speaking a foreign language the entire time. Once the soul entered, Jace could feel a second presence at the back of his mind, almost like he was sharing his little boy's body with another consciousness. At first, he thought it was just a dream, but then he realized he couldn't move his body, his fingers not moving in response to his call. He hypothesized that it was just sleep paralysis, but then his body started moving for him. He could see everything that happened but had no outside control of his body.

The woman smiled and turned back to Jake. "The ritual is complete. Enjoy your trade." She smiled as her appearance turned into purple smoke, and just like that, she was gone, her wispy beauty leaving a striking scar in his eyes. The same scar extended, reaching the front part of his brain, and etched itself in stone. Then his body started moving towards Jake, and he couldn't do anything about it.

"Good! Very good." He smiled and giggled hysterically as Jake's arm was wiggling, it was clear that this was Jake testing out his new prowess. "This will be amazing! This will be fun, outstanding! Finally that bastard could work her power." He said as Jace could only watch. The body moved towards the door by itself. "Now I have to find Jynx." He said, and Jace suddenly knew the entire reasoning behind this. Then his vision glitched, convulsing in the memory collapsing and flashing with distortion. The next thing he knew, he stood before the presence of three gods. In the death room, he watched Mardo, Anubis, and Echo discussing something.

"You died!? That's hilarious!! I can't believe that twerp actually managed to pull it off!" Mardo screamed, "I picked the right one to wager on!" He cried tears of joy. Echo had a disappointed look on his face.

"I don't know why you're so excited. Once you die, you don't have a second chance." Echo started, and Jace was worried about what he meant. Mardo sneered.

"Oh, you're completely wrong Echo! I have a *shadow* now!" He screamed in joy and jumped in the air like a little toddler, something he did pretty often according to Anubis' expression, which turned serious upon Mardo's latest dialogue.

"Wait! You used Masquerade as a *shadow*? You monster! That was going to be the kid to get us out of this horrible mess!" He argued with Mardo, who smiled back in return. His black clown makeup glistened.

"Don't worry, he's immortal, remember?" He explained. "Do I have to explain *shadows* to you again?" Anubis rolled his eyes and gave him the thumbs up. "I can give a portion of our power to my *shadow*, and I become much weaker in return for the chance to gain an extra life. Meaning that once I die, I'm able to resurrect in the place of the shadow's soul, so the sacrifice will die in response to the transferring. Since Masquerade is immortal, he won't die, and he can be my eternal shadow forever, making us both immortal!" Mardo laughed at his cleverness.

"And since we share powers and minds with each other, we will both be unstoppable; Masquerade's abilities and his strength mixed with mine are unbelievably chemistry oriented" He smiled. "That's the only reason he beat you, because of me!" He boasted.

"You're a cheater and a traitor! Just wait till our fathers hear about this, you'll be as dead as Masquerade soon. I'm resurrecting now, and I'm going to kill him!" He announced.

"He's immortal, you can't! Tell my dad all you want, he's the first I'm going to kill. . ." Mardo insulted him. Echo grinned back as a result, who stuttered backward.

"I have my ways." He said as he started walking backward. As he turned, he walked right into Jace. His expression quickly changed. His cold voice raced across his spine. "Who are you?!"

Jace stuttered before speaking up, "I'm JJace." Echo snorted and pushed him out of the way, and upon making physical contact, was the realization of fear. Then he turned back and realized who he was.

"Wait, you're Jake's clone, aren't you?" Echo's entire demeanor shifted in a moment. Jace rolled his eyes in response. "Wait." Echo grabbed his arm. "He's marked by Aella!" Echo pushed Jace onto the floor, making Jace more confused than ever. Echo reached out his hand and grabbed Jace's arm, following by poking his finger with a flurry of spiking ice. Then pain came, searing pain that made him scream in horror. A black tattoo started forming on the palm of his hand, a marking of the god. He observed it as it began steaming fiercely with wintery power.

"He died already! You can't make a dead person your *shadow*!" Anubis screamed. Echo smiled, his brain contracting with transfers of electrons.

"Well, I guess you have no choice but to bring him back then, huh?" Echo teased. Anubis stared back weirdly, as if Echo was trying to challenge him.

"You know that's against the rules! I can't do that!" He argued back. "Misa will kill me."

"Then so be it. No one wanted you to take over, all you've done is hold this idiot's power back, other than that you're a nobody. He's already my *shadow*, you have to resurrect him, by my order!" He echoed.

"I don't take orders from you, only Misa or Sura." Anubis recalled. Mardo smiled and opened his makeup smeared mouth, showing fangs of power.

"Just let him, Masquerade's gonna kick his ass again anyways." Mardo snapped. Echo rolled his eyes, and then Anubis snapped his fingers. The two appeared back on Earth. Jace looked over to the person next to him, Echo nowhere to be seen. He was some random man, who didn't look important to the gods at all, besides the fact he had a tuxedo on. Then, the man disintegrated into a flurry of black and white ash.

From the ash, Echo formed again, and he was completely different than before. His hair had changed from white to black, his facial features remained the same, however. In his hair was a tint of hot pink and purple, that was noticeable at a glance. He looked related to Mardo, which Jace had just now realized was actually the case, as Mardo was technically Echo's cousin.

Chapter 19
Jynx

As they reached the plane station, some familiar guests stopped them. Tamer, Hyper, and Infinity gathered with the lost group. Jynx felt miserable, her brain still convulsing in huge splitting headaches, her awakening power still being held back by an unknown face.

"WE SURVIVED!" Hyper screamed, his hoarse voice still carrying a charming tone. Jynx was happy to see them, but deep down, she was disappointed Jace wasn't among the group. Zander scratched his head, attempting to make sense of it all.

"How? I knew you guys got trapped in hell, but how did you manage to survive?" Zander said as he greeted the three.

"Masquerade came out of this purple portal! He showed up, wrestled Garm, made an earthquake, destroyed half of hell, and gained immortality!" Hyper's joyful voice resonated. Jynx tried not to chuckle, but couldn't stop herself.

"Wait, what!? Masquerade saved you? Why would he do that? As far as we know, he killed Jace and was deemed a traitor." Zander spoke up. Tamer winced.

"Jace is dead? Why? What happened?" He gasped.

"Masquerade killed him!" Everyone screamed except Dark and Lazer. Hyper's eyes lowered, and his expression underwent a complete change, his mood seemingly disintegrating.

"Liars! Masquerade would never kill anyone unless they had bad intentions! JACE WAS THE TRAITOR!" He screamed, backing away from everyone, causing a commotion. Jynx had never seen him this angry before. "I can't believe you think he would kill someone with good intentions! You guys are fakes! No one could be friends with any of you!" His face was starting to turn red, and so were his ears. He turned to Jynx ragefully. "The fact that he even liked you disgusts me!" He pointed at her angrily, she felt a quick pang of guilt that was replaced with evil.

"Does anyone know the truth, or are you going to believe that the hero of this trip is a serial killer?" He screamed once more. Dark stood up, and he tried touching Hyper to comfort him. "Stay away from me!"

He flinched and backed off. "Listen, Hyper, Masquerade isn't a murderer. Jace was playing an act the entire time. No one knew except me, him, and Lazer." His voice faltered. "No one believes me though."

"It's hard to believe that entire lie when Jace was a normal human his entire life!" Jynx stormed. "There's no way he was Jake! That doesn't even make sense!" She screamed. "He would've killed me ages ago if that was the case! You're just going to tell me all those memories and moments were fake?!"

"Listen, the truth will show itself. You just have to be patient. It's hard to believe, I know-" A loud clash interrupted the group. Hyper rolled his eyes.

"I see you guys just love hiding in public places!" Jake's voice screamed from the bottom of the escalator they were gathered on. "No worry, I have no problem killing civilians to get my prize!" He jumped on top of the railing and started running towards them. Zander looked ready to give up on life, an expression that wasn't new at all. Stray jumped up to attack, but Jake opened his mouth first.

"FREEZE! ALL OF YOU! Don't move a single muscle!" He demanded. Everyone was paralyzed almost immediately, Jynx had almost forgotten about that ability. "I've toyed with you guys too much, and now you will all die!" His sword came out of nowhere and almost killed Jynx then and there, but she felt her mind open once more, a valve closing and opening, resulting in an opening of power.

Her hair beamed with a glint of power, her eyes following the same beaming pink. Her brain contracted, followed by the sensation of her nerves being nourished. Then, a clunk noise sounded, and his sword was parried and thrown straight out of his hands. Jake gasped audibly, Jynx's eyes piercing through his sword. His power ceased to exist against her, and she felt all her neurons spike with power, following her fist upwards.

His sword clanged and clung across the smooth paving of the airport. To everyone's rescue, Jynx punched the enemy, sending him flying with a shockwave of energy. Jake fell off the side of the escalator, screaming with excitement. Then, a soaring wind thrust him into the floor with a crashing explosion. Masquerade stood on top of the escalator, his eyes were fierce, and his hands sparkling with explosive energy. Jake stood back up and glanced in the direction of the sword, although Masquerade watched attentively.

"Tell them the truth Jake!" He screamed from atop the nonmoving stairs. Jynx winced, as she had no clue who to believe at this point. She then jumped off the escalator herself, charging in her tormentor's direction. Jake stuttered for a moment.

"What truth!? There is no truth to be told! Everyone knows what you did!" Jake bellowed back and started sprinting to his fallen blade. He picked up the sword and opened his mouth again, "Now! You tell them the truth and bestow your mistakes! Murderer!" Jake exclaimed. "Take your final plunge and kill yourself right now!" His voice powers activated. Everyone watched in anticipation as Masquerade stood still for a long second.

"No. Since you don't want to say it, I will." He leaped from the top of the railing and landed on the floor flawlessly, then Jynx attacked Jake. He dodged the initial blow, but was caught off guard when Jynx was able to outspeed him. Her body produced a burst of pink, disappeared, and reappeared right behind Jake. Her heavy fists enchanted with power reached the side of his ribcage, cracking the entire thing into pieces. He gasped at Jynx's new potential, and sped off, looking at Masquerade, who pointed his sparkling hands at Jake and announced very loudly, "He pretended to be Jace this entire time!" At first, Jake laughed, and Jynx knew it had to be a lie. "Right before Jace died, I got to talk to his dead soul. He would like everyone to know this!" He announced, and everyone stared in his direction.

He pulled a golden ball of energy from nowhere and held it in his hand for a long moment. He crushed it in his hand, and the golden essence exploded into an image of a flurry of gold flickers of flames. The flames put themselves together and formed a figure made purely of golden light. The figure was Jace and his soft face. Jake stood completely still and observed the scenery that stood before him.

Jace's golden figure opened his bright mouth. "This is my message to anyone who distrusts Masquerade and his decisions. I am a message from Jace's soul. Anubis allowed me to send a message to the real world. I'd just like to say that, yes, Jace was really a traitor, but no need to feel betrayed. I really do remember all the memories I've had with you guys, and I remember the fun. Just know that Masquerade isn't lying, and you should give him a second chance to prove himself." Then, the figure disappeared and faded into golden sparkles.

Jynx's heart was filled with sadness and betrayal. She stared at Masquerade's distraught face. She owed him an apology, even if she couldn't really trust the message fully. Jake stood there, laughing.

"Looks like the secret is out!" His words still charmed with power. "I used that young idiot Jace. He was nobody but a tool! A tool to spy on Jynx and the person that was eventually going to kill her, which seemed to fail." His eyes lowered, glancing across the field to look at Jynx. "It seems your power has finally manifested, messing with my link between us. Now I have to end it, before it gets any more dangerous! The only one who you can rely on now is Masquerade. Even now, he is no match for me." The others were all still paralyzed. Masquerade had a slim grin on his face like he was trying to hold back from saying something.

"Is that what Echo would say?" He mocked, and Masquerade charged towards him in a quick flash. His speed increased severely. Jake's face had terror plastered all over it, trying to read his quick agility. He tried stabbing at him, but Masquerade weaved under the blade. He punched it upwards, and the blade went flying into the air.

Jake sidestepped and dodged his next hit, but he held both his hands out and exploded everything in his path. Sparkles of yellow started lighting up the area, resulting in the sparkles summoning lightning strikes from the air, which then exploded into their own explosions. Jake went flying in the other direction. Masquerade blitzed past him in a swift arc, lifting his blade which then made Jake's arm sliced off and hit the floor in a splat. He turned around and shot a beam of lightning at Jake's chest. The lightning sparkled and made an explosion on impact.

Masquerade made a lightning blade and blitzed the man once again, traveling through him. Jake's other arm fell off, and he fell to the floor himself. Masquerade smirked and seized Jake's own blade.

He opened his mouth, "Look away, guys." He turned towards the group. Everyone shook their heads disapprovingly, and Masquerade smiled. "Or don't." Then he charged and sliced the blade straight through Jake's neck, decapitating him in quick succession. Blood spurt from the severed vessels and Masquerade flung the body over the railing. He walked towards the group with a sassy walk and stared directly at Jynx.

"Jake, Mark, and Echo are dead. I saved Infinity, Lazer, and Tamer and tamed Garm. That only leaves for me to deal with Misa. What else do you guys want?" He snickered. Jynx felt a little remorse, and her body moved without thinking. She hugged him, and Masquerade took a deep breath, reciprocating the hug. The public stopped in horror, and Jynx realized all this had happened in an airport. People were giving them all disgusted looks, and some were protesting and screaming hurtful names.

Masquerade turned around to face the crowd. He opened his mouth and started to speak. Infinity ran up to him and tugged on him. "Let me deal with this." Masquerade held his tongue and patted Infinity on his shoulder. Infinity stood still for a while before he opened his eyes again. He snapped both of his hands and with force, a portal opened. It was circle-shaped, and it bent reality around its frame. The portal swirled around and stayed open as Infinity directed it. "You don't need the plane, everyone in the portal!" He said excitedly. His fingers were jittering a lot, but he kept the shaft open.

Everyone had a reluctant smile on their faces, and they single-filed through the portal. Jynx went last, as everyone was amazed by the twisted magic. The portal took them straight into

Zander's old classroom. To Jynx, it was amazing the thing was still standing. Infinity held his hands out like he was some god, and even though he was, it was still weird. Everyone cheered, but something felt off to Jynx.

As she glanced at everyone in the group, she realized none of them were, per se, 'normal'. Masquerade, Dark, Lazer, Infinity, and Hyper were all offspring of a Greek god. Tamer and Rusell were both born under the bloodline of the Christian god. Stray had control over death powers, although his origin remains unknown. Jace was dead. Jacob was the only normal one in the group, and he looked completely terrified the entire time.

Masquerade stood heroically in the midst of the portal. His forearms pulsed with veins, and he stepped inside the classroom. Once he stepped in, the portal closed like a falling guillotine. Masquerade held his hands out and started clapping, cheering and improving the mood of everyone around, his fingers emitting colorful blasts of fireworks.

"Woah!! We win!" He announced and started frolicking around the room like a toddler. Even though it was childish, everyone joined in on the fun. They started doing their own cringe dances, and everyone forgot about their problems. Masquerade lit fireworks, Lazer made shadow puppets, and Dark made pink butterflies. Everyone enjoyed the moment as it happened, that no one even realized it was turning nighttime.

Tamer and Russel stood close to each other. Jynx wondered what was next for them. She walked up to them. "So what's in it for you guys after all of this?" She asked them, and they looked down disapprovingly.

"We're returning home soon. A message has traveled over to all regions of Heaven. It told us to return home immediately, something to do with Misa. Messages dealing with Misa never end well, so we're expecting something horrible." Tamer said while fidgeting with his hands. Jynx frowned and replied carefully.

"Well, it seems like your story isn't over, but mine is. I'm glad that I met you two, really." She replied, and Tamer had a glint of joy in his eye.

"I hope that Masquerade grows stronger on his quest. Someone needs to stop Misa. I really believe in him, but this is goodbye." He stood up and walked towards Masquerade. Russel followed. They both said their goodbyes and hopes for the future and although Jynx didn't have much relation to them, she even teared up a bit. Tamer stood as his body started radiating gold, and soon, so did Russel's.

The two exploded with golden energy, and their presence was soon gone, leaving a lovely feeling of joy in the classroom. Everyone stood in a sense of conclusion, and they all agreed to return home, especially Jacob. Masquerade and his siblings offered to walk Jynx home, which she agreed to. Stray walked himself home, and so did Jacob. Zander locked himself in his classroom. The night skies were filled with stars.

She was distracted the whole time as Hyper tried explaining the mechanical engineering behind an ATV. Masquerade held Jynx's hand as they walked down the sidewalk, something she was hesitant to agree to. Dark and Lazer were catching up with Infinity and his experiences. It left Masquerade and Jynx to talk by themselves. It felt odd that Jace wasn't with them. Finally, Jynx broke the silence.

"So what did Jace say to you?" She said awkwardly. The skies were crystal clear, with no clouds to be seen, representing their clearness in their souls purity. The moon was shining bright and big. Masquerade hesitated before answering.

"He told me to, uh, I guess I should start with-" He stuttered anxiously. Jynx tightened her grip on his hand. She took a deep breath, barely managing to maintain the headache that contained her brain, which meant her power was back to hiding in the depths. She wondered if it could ever fully awaken and stop caging itself behind her brain walls. Her mind was filled with thoughts of danger that were quickly washed over by thoughts of joy, something that came upon her hand touching Masquerade's.

"Spit it out. Look, I'm not mad at you anymore. I guess I'm still just trying to process what happened in the last week." She reassured him, her brain filtering through what was real and what was deceiving. The delicate light from the full moon came with a hidden mask of a different meaning. That meaning was something that came deep from within the two lovers, their bodies glowing with white reflected lights. Something about their heritage made an electrifying indifference in their current relationship. Masquerade untensed due to their tension.

"He told me to live life and that I shouldn't be scared of. . ." He trailed off, continuing the theme of 'joy' and 'glory', his mind racing with dark thoughts that should be reconsidered.

Jynx giggled. "You? Scared? That's funny!" She joked with him, and pushed him jokingly. Masquerade tumbled forward a bit and stood back at her side. "Sorry, please continue." She laughed, trying to ignore the thought in her dark brain, and accidentally ignoring the feeling of connection in her veins.

"He reassured me that I shouldn't be scared of *you*." He finished, and Jynx felt her heart sink a little, however, her brain convulsed as well, comparing the wrath of joy versus glory.

"What am I going to do to you!?" She said, "I know my power is approaching alarmingly, but maybe that'll help us defeat Misa!" Jynx thought about the future, once more hearing the sounds of darkened voices. Masquerade still looked more serious than usual, and then looked worried when he noticed a spark of pink in Jynx. He stopped her in the middle of the street, observing that no cars came their way. The moonlight glistened in his eyes.

"Not in that way, I guess what I'm trying to say is. . . I like you a lot." He stopped, finally releasing his emotions, opening a valve in his heart, in the same way that a valve opens in Jynx's brain when her power is released. "Jace wanted me to care for you and love you. He wished that we could have a perfect relationship and life together since he wouldn't be there to witness it." Masquerade reached his hand up on Jynx's shoulder. Jynx smiled despite the seriousness, her eyes were locked, unallowing her power of control to come out.

"Listen, it's okay. We've been through a lot together. I guess I want to say I feel the same way. There's something about the way you really cared for me despite the way you made it seem." Masquerade smiled finally, the serious tone fading away slowly. The moonlight made the event seem all the more romantic. He slowly nudged his hand on Jynx's cheek. He reached in and kissed her in the moonlight. This time, without the use of her power.

"A god falling in love with a mortal seems wrong." He smirked, his tone fading back into that seriousness. "But that doesn't matter to me. Jynx, would you like to be my girlfriend?" He asked with a sly smile on his face.

Jynx couldn't help but feel excited, yet flustered. "Of course!" She screamed and jumped into his arms like they were getting married. She finally truly felt happy and felt she could trust him. Masquerade held her in for what felt the warmest forever in a while. It took her a while to realize everyone else was staring at them both weirdly, all of them having a smirk on their faces.

"Go Masquerade! Relationship goals!" Hyper screamed. The dark midnight made their voices echo. He smiled in response and ignored them. They had arrived at her house. In the stricken moonlight, the house looked abandoned, and even now, she wondered if Stitch was really on her side. They all walked inside, and Masquerade offered to stay a few nights just to make sure she was safer. She agreed and thought it would be a great time to bond, since they were girlfriend and boyfriend after all. His siblings were also going to stay, and they set up their beds in the living room. They all stared at the blank, dark screen of the television.

"All of us, slumber party in the living room!" Masquerade smiled and picked up a pillow. Jynx stood a few feet away from him, but he still slapped her with the fluffy pillow. She grinned and thought of all the old moments with Jace, but now wasn't the time to grieve. She picked up another pillow and joined him in the feathery pillow war. Dark, Hyper, and everyone else were targeting each other. They jumped over the couches, dodged, flew, and had fun for the first time in a while.

After they got tired, the living room was filled with the scenery of a long-fought war. Falling pillow cases were all over the floor, and the soldiers were all fast asleep in the middle of the living room floor. Some scattered on the couches, and others slept awkwardly on the carpet or the hardwood floors. None of them even bothered to cover themselves up, and in the midst of the scenario, they were too exhausted to.

Jynx stood as the only soldier standing. She watched as everyone snored and jittered in their sleep. She smiled, and for once in her life, she felt safe. She laid down, grabbed her blanket and snuggled herself next to her new boyfriend. She stared at the dark ceiling and closed her eyes, finally feeling a sense of release from danger. She fell asleep with no anxiety or any dark moments in her brain, even the dark ability in the back of her mind was silent as day.

Chapter 20
Jace

Jace found himself torn between feelings of relief and frustration upon returning to life. He never wanted to die, but now that Echo had control over him, he wondered of the underlying possibility of having to harm his friends once more. He walked alongside Echo, who, oddly enough, appeared more human than usual. Echo's communication style and expressions allowed Jace to understand his motivations better. However, Jace hesitated to confront Echo about the perplexing choice of targeting an innocent girl and her mother. Under Echo's black hair, heavy eye bags were turning white.

"What do you want?" Echo snarled in response, making Jace flinch before they continued through the forest, who caught him staring hard.

"I was just wondering about your background, your family, and the reasons behind targeting Jynx and her mother," Jace said cautiously, trying to avoid disrespect.

A faint smile appeared on Echo's face. "I can't tell you, but I can share the power we fear emanating from her," he began, turning to face Jace. "The power held by Jynx and her mother poses a threat even to the mightiest gods," Echo continued.

"But what if they aren't entirely malevolent? Perhaps they might spare you and channel their power for good!" He suggested.

"We can't risk that, though. Sura believes anything wielding such power should be eradicated immediately," Echo continued, his gaze fixed oddly on the floor.

"Well, Sura's spouting nonsense!" Jace declared, and Echo refrained from defending Sura.

"As his son, I can concur with that. He won't disclose the truth about Psyche and her true identity. All he mentioned was that I had to eliminate the two females before their power escalated," Echo explained, a hint of hesitation in his voice. "I agreed because I don't know what Sura would do if I disobeyed him."

Jace felt a little relief. He thought about how he would respond. Echo wasn't all that bad, but everyone believed he was. "Do you truly believe Masquerade can do it?" He asked him.

Echo flinched at the question. "Do what?"

"You know, overthrow Misa and Sura. He intends to eliminate them and put an end to their continued torment of the gods," he explained.

"Does he genuinely plan on doing that?" He pondered. "I suppose I'll never discover it if I end up killing him." Echo frowned. "Trust me, I don't have a personal grudge, but if I fail, Sura might as well just kill me." Jace shrugged.

"You don't have a choice?"

"No, I can't allow Masquerade to shield Jynx any longer. She must be eliminated."

"Why can't you both join forces?! Mardo and Anubis have already switched sides. They aim to assist Masquerade in his quest! This could be the most significant revolution the gods have ever undertaken!" Jace exclaimed. Echo squinted at him, but he, too, seemed to harbor hope.

"I won't betray my father. Masquerade and Mardo stand no chance against Sura, even if they collaborate." Echo argued. "And Anubis is bound to the afterlife, so he can't fight physically." Jace felt like he was arguing a lost cause. "Misa has the biggest army in existence. We can't ever hope to win, even with all the gods working together." He said. "Let me show you Misa's forces and his entire empire, then maybe you'll understand. Together h and Sura, they dominate the gods. There is no hope left for anyone. Once they decide they want something, it's theirs." Echo sniffled and waved his hand over Jace's forehead.

He phased back into reality and saw an entire kingdom. Purple and gold lights illuminated the entire horizon of the ginormous cityscape. It was modern yet medieval at the same time. All the buildings were constructed of black stone, wood and metal. It was so detailed that it seemed that it was sketched from the hands of a true artist, and in the middle of it were armies and families of people, who were appearing to live in comfort, all wearing signature black armor or purple casual wear. The city was so huge you couldn't see the end of it.

Jace was amazed by the decoration and detail of the streets and the buildings. In the middle of the city stood a huge palace, and from there, you could see a throne of towering importance. On the throne was Misa himself. His skin was olive tan, and he wore a huge purple and black robe that reached all the way to the ground. A fluffed coat ring was wrapped around his neck, connecting the robe together. His eyes were rings of purple, red and black that held a resembling emotion of ultimate control. He had a black tattoo intruding from his left eye socket, and his hair was long, so long that it reached all the way down to his lower back, and it wasn't straightened.

He stared down to the bottom of the throne, where someone who looked similar to him stood. The man at the bottom had the same skin tone. His hair was striped gray and gold. It was long, but not long like a girl, but boyish long. It was messy and made him look shaggy but still well-managed. His eyes were sparkling gold, and he wore a tight compression outfit. The suit was entirely black, with lines of gold tracing around them. He wore a gold belt, and his hands radiated golden power. Jace knew this as Peace, one of Misa's sons.

They spoke with great power. "Looks like the sacrifice still hasn't been made yet." Peace said, his voice was calming. "Zeus has one more day to his deadline."

Misa had his hand on his chin. "Yes, I know this. He knows what the consequences are. If in the next twenty-four hours, I don't have a godly sacrifice, then we punish him." His voice said deeply. Peace seemed annoyed at him in a way.

"Why even do this anyway? There's no point in punishing them. They didn't even do anything!" Peace argued, and Misa's expression was mundane.

"For the fun of it! Sura's carrying out some mission on Earth Infinite, so I might as well make myself look busy in the meantime. You know it's been a while since some drama went down." Misa smiled, and Peace rolled his eyes. Then Misa raised his eyebrow. "Speak of the devil." He sighed and rolled his eyes, Jace almost thought the god was looking at him.

Then, a fluffy-haired young man came out of nowhere, walking up to Peace. His hair was dark gray and had streaks of hot pink and purple, looking genetically comparable to Misa. His outfit was entirely black. He was Sura, and behind him stood the man who ruined everyone, Jake. His arms were cut off, and he was bickering some stupid gibberish. His neck also looked scarred up badly and was attached by a few loose stitches. His loud mouth was directed towards Misa.

Normally, Jace would feel guilty because this mortal was screaming at the most powerful god there was, but something was off. Jake contained an aura that was quietly impeccable compared to everyone there, like he had a hidden background. Sura pointed his fingers at him and whispered something to Peace. They both chuckled, and Jake looked ready to cut their arms off next. Misa finally spoke up.

"So? What brings you here!?" He said to Sura and Jake, who both glanced at each other weirdly. Sura opened his mouth.

"Jake and Echo have both failed to kill Jynx. At first, I assumed Jynx had awakened her power already, but Jake says otherwise." Sura smiled and widely opened his mouth on purpose. "You may speak now, Loki!!" He giggled like some teenager, Jace was entirely confused.

"GIVE ME MY OLD SOUL BACK YOU OLD HAG!" Jake screamed at Misa, who was playing with his fingernails. "I AM LOKI, THE GOD OF MISCHIEF!" He announced. "I'll steal your identity, turn into you, and probably bang your wife too!" He mumbled. Sura laughed some more, furthermore attacking his intelligence.

"By whose orders?" Misa even grinned.

"BY MY ORDERS!" He screamed back, and even Peace had a sly smile plastered on his face. "I need to go back and show that Masquerade kid who's the real god." He said, and Jace gasped.

"Wait, you knew this entire time that Jake was a Norse god?!" Jace turned to Echo, who looked disappointed.

"Yes, why else would I use him to kill Psyche and Jynx?" Echo exclaimed, and Jace felt a little stupid, who thought of the possibility a little bit more.

"Wait, you mentioned earlier that I was 'marked' by Aella? What does that mean?" Jace said, his head spinning. Echo sighed and turned to face him. He grabbed Jace's hand, where the tattoo was etched.

"Aella is one of the primordial entities that were born when existence was created. Think of them as manifestations. They feed off fear and other outside emotions. So, really, they are a result of the gods, humans, etc. Aella is the entity of chaos or madness. Not to be mixed up with destruction but instead with mental problems, like spiraling into madness, depression, anxiety, or other mental disorders. She is a master of manipulation and you were marked by her, and to put it into simpler terms, it means you share a portion of her powers. It's weird, but Aella doesn't like her *marks*; she often tries to kill them time and time again. So you aren't safe, is what I'm explaining." Echo stuttered, and Jace frowned, knowing that he was dead before, meaning she wouldn't be able to kill him twice, hopefully.

"So I guess what I'm trying to say is, I'm trying to save you from her. I don't like the Entities at all. I want to destroy every single one of them, but that's hard to do. You have to kill them all at the same time, and they are crazy powerful, considering they have the powers of what they represent."

"FINALLY!" Screamed Jake, interrupting their conversation. His body was completely healed. Jace turned to face what had happened. "I'm done going by Jake. CALL ME LOKI AGAIN!" He started dancing around the throne room, and Misa put his palm on his forehead. Sura was still laughing oddly, and Peace rolled his eyes. Then Misa turned his attention to Sura.

"Why don't you go kill Jynx yourself?" He said, and Sura winced.

"Loki's got it under control, and Echo should be going back for round two soon as well, hopefully. As long as they are two versus one, whatever killed them the first time, they should be good." Sura said as he turned around, showing the obvious signs of laziness. "I'm going home now, so if you need me, don't." He smiled.

"Wait, so Mason and Stitch are still alive?" Misa bellowed. Sura rolled his eyes.

"Yes, Psyche's kids are still standing, except Jynx soon." He replied. "And Psyche is dead as well." Sura snorted.

"Bring me Mason. I know Stitch had his rebellions, so I don't want him here." Misa said as Sura started to roll his eyes once again. Jace wondered what was up with these powerful gods acting like young kids, and rolling their eyes obnoxiously.

"I don't want to though." He started whining, and Jace found it funny. "I feel like your own nephew doesn't even want to see you. Mason doesn't like you." He chuckled. Misa grunted.

"They don't know of their heritage. Do they?" Misa asked.

"I don't think so. Psyche probably didn't say a word. She thought she could live a happy life and run away from us, but obviously, she couldn't." He grinned.

Misa frowned. "When you put it like that, it makes it sound horrible!" He awed, and Sura laughed. Jace was interrupted by his thoughts, did they seriously think what they conspired was a good cause?

Jace turned to Echo in shock, "Jynx is a god?!" Jace screamed, and Echo sighed. The two were teleported out of the scene with a flash. They stood on a familiar street, and at the end of it stood Jynx's house. It was midday, and Echo started fidgeting with his fingers. His hair was split dyed white and black. A look of evilness prompted his endless frost that was conspiring in his eyes. Jace gulped, ready to acknowledge his plan.

"You're going to kill Jynx." His voice shattered through the air like his power forming and breaking crystallization icicles. Jace felt a shatter in his soul once more, his prediction had come true. He now conspired with the entities above, knowing that he was cursed due to their influence, something he could never get rid of. Ultimately he knew, his soul was damned to be controlled, and there was nothing he could do to stop it. His veins filled with a new power, not 'glory', not 'joy', but this time, lust. Jace stared into the eyes of Echo, awaiting his next command. "I'll distract Masquerade, and if you fail, backstab, and think of escaping, I'll kill you instantly by using my *shadow*." He snarled. "Just know, you're under my control now, and there's absolutely nothing you can do about it." Jace felt exhausted, knowing that this happened twice to him already, but time around, he finally had open control of his body, but he was about to use it to cause harm to the people he loved most.

Chapter 21
Masquerade

Baking muffins wasn't on today's agenda. Seeing a dozen muffin pans on the drying rack, Jynx decided it was time to bake. As she sprayed the pan, Masquerade fumbled around in the cabinets and fridge, looking for the right ingredients. With prior baking experience, he knew the basic ingredients. He fixed up some salt, sugar, baking powder, soda, and all the other stuff that was needed.

Once everything was gathered, he watched Jynx fix it all up. Quickly, she separated dry and wet ingredients into bowls. The air was heavy with the expected scent of pumpkins.

"Stir this while I prepare the oven." She quickly slid to the other side of the kitchen. Masquerade picked up the whisk and stared down at the mix. He strafed it in and started violently mixing as if the batter had insulted him. Jynx started giggling from the other side of the room. He smiled in response and dipped his finger into the sticky batter. Jynx came to his side and playfully jabbed his side. She stood happily and watched as he stirred.

Masquerade grabbed a finger scoop of batter and quickly smeared it on her cheek. She frowned jokingly and did the same. They playfully exchanged smudges and ended with a faceful of raw pumpkin spice batter. Masquerade's hair reeked of pumpkin spice, but it smelt good, so he didn't care. His clothes were stained orange. He watched on the countertop as Jynx poured the batter into the muffin pan.

Jynx placed the raw batter in the oven, turning to Masquerade. She plugged her nose. "You smell!" She said, lightly pushing him off the counter. Hyper entered the kitchen with an sword made of ice, and Jynx gave him an incredulous look.

"It smells like pumpkins!" He yelled, walking in cautiously. His sword was raised like he was going to slice them if they said anything out of the ordinary. Masquerade raised his hand.

"What the hell are you doing?" He said, and Hyper raised an eyebrow.

"I'm looking for Lazer. We were sword fighting with these ice swords I made, and then he ran away from me." Hyper complained. "And then I smelled pumpkin pie!" He lured towards the oven and pressed his face into the glass. Masquerade constantly forgot Hyper was actually his age instead of a dumb toddler.

Masquerade rolled his eyes. "There's six of us, so two muffins for everyone." Hyper stared at him weirdly.

"Where's the frosting?!" He exclaimed, sounding puzzled.

"They're muffins, you tard!" Masquerade yelled back. "Muffins don't have frosting! Cupcakes do!" Hyper looked disappointed, and he dropped his sword on the floor. He bent down to eye level with the oven.

"It would've been better with icing, but nooooo." He said sassily, turning his head from Masquerade. " I'll keep an eye on them until they're done," he said, sitting down. Masquerade was about to join him before someone knocked on the door. Jynx nodded and went to answer it. He followed, making sure it wasn't some planned attack that would end them all. She opened the door, and it was revealed to be Jace. Masquerade was shaken, who almost killed him then and there. His hands started shaking with smoke, piling into the noses of the three that stood in silence.

Then, his fists extended, and Masquerade noticed the same tattoo mark on his palm. He stopped him in his tracks. "Don't move," he demanded. "Show me your hand. How did you get that?" Masquerade questioned. Jace looked too exhausted to continue. "Prove to us you're not Jake!" Jace sighed and looked behind him awkwardly. Then, Jace and Masquerade attacked at the same time. Shards of blue fire and yellow explosions glinted down the entrance of Jynx's porch.

Masquerade grabbed both of his arms and swirled his entire body around, throwing Jace directly into the front yard that happened to be filled with trees. From the side, Echo appeared, causing Masquerade to go into a fight-or-flight response. The grass quickly turned white, pressing him to move out of the way. Blue ice and flames then erupted on both sides of his body, causing him to fly upwards with wind. In seconds, his brothers flailed out the door to his defense, seeing the bright explosions decimate the remains of the lawn. "What the fuck did you do!" He screamed at Echo, who had that same cold smile wiped over his face.

"Mardo tricked you!" Jace said, his tattoo glowing in power in response to his words. Masquerade turned to face him again, ignoring Echo, all three of them coming to a standstill. "That tattoo on your hand symbolizes that you are a *shadow*. I take it Mardo lied to you. It only means that he gets a second chance at life for the risk of the *shadows' life*. But since you're immortal, they cancel each other out, so it's a win-win situation for both of you. Mardo gets true immortality while you gain some of his power." He explained. Masquerade felt betrayed at first, but now he understands why he was able to destroy Echo and Jake in a fight so easily. For our sake, I never tricked anyone! It was all a part of the plan. BEAR WITH ME!

"Also, Misa and Sura want their sacrifice in the next twenty-four hours, or else they're going to punish the Greeks," he said. "So someone needs to step up and take the toll."

Masquerade raised his hand. "It's going to be me," he said, and Jace looked shocked. Masquerade felt weird; he had never expected that all of this was happening now. "It's fine. I'm immortal. My sacrifice means nothing." He guessed, realizing he was talking to the *real* Jace.

"Well, then he'd just want another sacrifice. There is no excuse."

Jynx revolted."What do I have to do with any of this?" She asked and started pacing around the yard nervously. Jace took a deep breath inwards.

"Sura said your mom was his sister, and he called Mason his nephew," he revealed, and everyone took a while to realize what that meant. "So basically, you're related to Misa and Sura. Psyche is the third triplet to complete their family tree." Jace looked extremely nervous. "Which means you're an extremely powerful god, Jynx," Masquerade didn't know what to feel, scared, happy, or excited. Jynx remained silent for a long time.

"Does this mean I'm forced to be a slave?" She said with full confidence. "Do I have to be the way Mardo and Echo are?! Puppets to Misa and Sura!? I'm forced to put my life at risk for their benefits?!" She said, and Echo winced, who then lifted his hand out, calling a blizzard of ultimate negativity. Then the fray started, Dark and Lazer both sped forwards, ready to attack Echo. Jace remained in a fighting position, attempting to stand up against Masquerade.

"Jake's back, Sura revived him. And I should also mention that he's also a god. You know Loki from Norse Mythology?" At this point, Masquerade was done with hearing all these reveals. The blizzard raged on, trying to fight the presence that came from the opposing force. Masquerade ran forwards, catching Echo off guard, and grabbed him aggressively.

"Enough! If you're here to harm Jynx, then so be it!" Masquerade realized the development that happened to Jace. He was still being controlled, but this time by a different god, and his body was still his. He could tell the hesitance in his actions, as he was barely able to stand up to her. Jynx readied her fists, her power failed to activate against him. The sadness endeavors sparked between them, showing an underlying tension that was built up between the now enemy and ally.

Then, they clashed, with Jace showing superiority. Dark joined the fray, and Infinity joined Masquerade. He focused back on the battle, grabbing a hold of Echo's hands, and throwing him into the air with a quick spark of strength. A quick spark of lightning traversed through the air, obliterating Echo once more. Then Infinity, with power enchanted fists, punched his face, sending him back into the floor.

Hyper and Lazer were reluctant to join, staring at Echo, who landed back onto the floor, with his hands reaching out, ready to freeze Masquerade to complete bits. Infinity stood next to his brother, his wispy care for his brother finally showing homage to the moment he was saved upon his grace of destruction. "It's been a while since we got to bond. . ." He said, despite Echo charging up a powerful attack.

"After this, I'm planning a real trip where we actually get to enjoy ourselves." He smiled. "For now, let's blow this mother-fucker to bits!" He screamed, his explosions becoming stronger.

"Enough with the talking. Soon enough Jace will kill her! There's nothing you can do to stop us!" His voice wavered with certainty, and Masquerade knew their connection was over. He showed superiority in power, his two beating hearts were stronger than his one brain, there was no need to stretch out their fight any longer. The burning embers of similarity and differences between their deep ancestral bloodline was gone, and Masquerade was about to prove their gap in spirituality. "The Kokoro are supposed to be dead." He whispered, and a shock filled his brain that wasn't caused by his own realization, but Mardo's instead.

"Shut the hell up you coward! I already killed all those recipients! Me and my deadbeat father made sure there wasn't a single drop left!" Mardo's voice forced it's way from his throat. Echo smiled.

"Looks like I struck a nerve!" He yelled back, and Masquerade's body ran forward on its own, landing a nasty nerve-racking, bone shattering, teeth clattering, face reddening, and meanest blow in history. Mardo's power seeped through his veins, noticing the second overlay of blood vessels that led to a growing heart. Rip him to fucking bits. Mardo said. Echo's body was instantly knocked out, hunching forwards, barely managing to stand up. His eyes rolled back, and his body fell to the ground.

"Looks like that second heart of yours still can't help you from a surprise attack." A familiar voice said from behind him, he now realized there was a sword plunged directly through his chest, highlighting the place of his first heart. Blood oozed like the 'glory' that was drained from his body. Masquerade turned around, grasping the blade, and noticed that the 'glory' had returned, finally trying to end the triumph between a waging war of 'glory' and 'joy'. Jake stood before his eyes, his sword gleaming with more power than ever.

"Ready for round four, loser?" Jake smiled, his eyes glistening a dark emerald green this time around.

"Call me Loki. I'm about to win three-to-one, your siblings don't stand a chance." He looked over the wasted field, noticing a few new foes. Thor, the god of thunder, Mason and

Stitch joined the war, and Echo was awake once more. He felt anxiety build up as he watched each and one of his siblings, and Jynx ready to risk their lives.

Then, he threw his fist up and charmed his entire arm with yellow energy. The blizzard that encased the yard grew stronger, but Masquerade unleashed his explosion. The entire thing landed on Jake, the size of an entire skyscraper erupted, blowing the storm of ice and snow away with one sweeping blast. The gunshot howled, resembling the start of the final battle.

Chapter 22
Jynx and Jace

Her former friend and everything stood before her, ready to end her ever-edging life. She wondered if Jace had control over his body this time, and if he was doing this out of the fear that he would die, again. Her power was beating against the valves in her brain, ready to be let out, but she reluctantly waited for the best time to unleash it.

"You've come so far Jynx! From being vulnerable and weak, to fighting for yourself!" Jynx now understood their parallel. Jace was there to show her what a person should be, and now that she knew she was a god, her brain would now use him as a reference to save people. She wanted to be a god of importance and have a meaning to the people. Her power was to control and Jace's entire backstory revolved around being controlled by the demons of the world that resided around them so powerfully. She however, wasn't going to let her power control people the way Jake and Echo did, she was going to control Jace, to free him of his chilling chains that bound his soul.

"I'm going to save you. . ." She said, being reminded of all the times she had to be saved. Her entire development revolved around this one moment, and it was to save her best friend. Her brain contracted, releasing her power of restoration, and with that fully manifested, she rushed forwards, ready to strike against a person she once trusted.

"Let's hope you succeed." He whimpered back through a wall of glory that imprisoned him, his words cascading a feeling of warmth to her. Pink flowed through her nerves, changing her eyes and hair in coloring contrast. She landed the first blow, knocking the wind to his stomach. His hand restrained, as if he were holding back to strike at her. Then it pushed forwards with a force that wasn't his, and rushed towards Jynx's face. Her speed ramped up, and she disappeared and reappeared directly in the back of him, striking him with a blow that damaged his spine greatly. Then, she used her power. Every time she struck, it forced his brain into a moment of vulnerability, that made him have slightly better control over his body, making the connection between him and Echo fade away. She glanced upon Echo in the battlefield, who stood, fighting Dark and Infinity. She focused back ahead, channeling her power to control, into Jace's mind.

"I'm sorry for everything I've done!" He cried, still holding a deep grief from when Jake was in control of his soul. Jynx hit him with another blow to the chest, further weakening the chain that held Echo's souls together. Jace regulated his temperature, so the flames wouldn't hurt her as bad. Then, the onslaught of heat began. Blue hues of reminiscing fire rushed forwards in a blaze, Jynx's legs getting flooded by the sheer heat. She dodged into the air, hitting Jace with another attack to the face, once again, the control bond losing its strength.

"I'll get you out of there Jace! Don't worry!" She yelled through tear filled eyes, watching her best friend fight so hard not to hurt her. Then she was struck by a fist of more flames, knocking her to the floor. Jace then roamed over here, ready to kill her in one swifting blow. She raised her legs, but he grabbed them, slamming them back down to the floor.

"I can't do it Echo!" He screamed in pain, his fists stopping the rush of fire. His tattoo started gleaming a color of light blue ice. Jynx smiled, wondering if her power had destroyed their link.

"JOIN ME!" She screamed, her voice commanding his own brain to stop the tattoo from doing anything suspicious. He hesitated, knowing what was about to happen next. The tattoo was going to kill him if he betrayed Echo, which he still was deciding what to act upon. His lust filled veins, stopped pulsing. He remembered his great deciding factor that made him so relatable to Masquerade, his glory that he took from him. He knew it could be good in certain situations, which compelled him to take the wrong path, for the right action. This is what made him the hero of his own story, a broken warrior taking the road of injustice, swearing that he would never do bad again, even if it wasn't his own choices. His soul was still damaged from the wrong use of 'glory', but he was going to reverse that, by doing it the right way. He would use the 'glory' from Masquerade, and use it for a good cause, which would finish the story between the two men. Jynx, astonished by the power that was emanating from Jace, released the full brunt of her own power. The controlling aspect quickly released its affinity into his blood, turning the clots of lust that formed due to Echo, into smooth tissue of 'glory'. This 'glory' enchanted his prowess, his future, his decision, and with all that now pushing his soul forwards, he made his final comeback.

His flames, carried by ambition, lit brighter and hotter than ever. Its brightness and tone of shine represented Masquerade, who helped him through a journey of 'joy' filled with grief, and its heat and color represented Jynx, who helped him release the color of 'glory' that can also be used for good. His moment came, highlighting his change in personality, which was the 'glory' in everything. His flames started turning his skin black. Jynx cried tears of both astonishment and grief, realizing what had to be done, something that was told to her long ago.

Jace's flames, then burnt his body to a crisp of bones, killing himself directly. She watched as his glory turned to dust, and that dust turned to memory that was left to be observed by the greater good. His flames, burnt every aspect of glory, joy, and lust with one swift heat wave. She knew it was for the greater good, ridding of the need to be defined by a human emotion, something that shouldn't even be glanced upon by the gods in the first place.

Jynx wept, her demise still evident from her sight, because she let her guard down in grief. She jumped in fear as someone grabbed her by the back of her neck, lifting her high into the air. "NO ONE MOVES A SINGLE MUSCLE! OR SHE DIES!" Her killer screamed, tears were starting to fill her own eyes. She realized this was someone she thought she could trust, this one line being evident so prosperously to her, yet it defined the truth that came with awful power in a world of hungry gods. The person about to end her life was no other than her brother, Stitch. Everyone in the battlefield came to a quick stop, glancing over to see a situation of despair.

"Stitch! Don't do it!" Masquerade screamed from the grip of Jake, who was pressuring to defeat him. "You can join us!" His eyes showed evidence of a soon to come breakdown of emotions.

"And for what? No matter which side I join, I'll die! Sura and Misa will kill me if I don't do what they say, and you guys will kill me if I listen to them!" He raised a knife to Jynx's neck, his arms holding her down, as she gripped his hands that were tightly enclosed around the blade. He stood behind her, holding her tightly. Tears streamed through the air, and sorrow gripped every emotion.

"JOIN US! We'll start the end of the reign of Misa! We can do it together." He screamed. Stitch winced. Masquerade saw him untense and figured he had finally resigned. His eyes lowered, and he looked like he was seeing the future for them, but then he swiftly dragged the blade across her unprotected neckline. The blood splattered across the green grass. Jynx fell to the floor in tears of angst. Stitch was crying, his actions favoring that to the villains, as they finally accomplished their goal. Everyone had stopped fighting as the blood dripped down some more. Masquerade boosted himself with the most aggressive explosion yet. He almost reached Stitch before he opened his mouth to speak once more. Stitch snapped, and Masquerade froze in place as he was airborne.

"I told you Masquerade. . . You only further proved my point: no matter what side I take in life, I still end up dying, so why don't I take the easy way out." He paused as he gestured the knife upwards. "My mother's dead, and there is not a single reason to stay here at this point. If there's an afterlife, I know I'll regret this." Then his own knife plunged into his own throat. He violently shuttered it and split it through his hyoid bone. Swiftly, he used the blade to break his neck bone, and he splat to the floor dead cold. Jynx, who still lay alive for a moment, finally died, the blackening memories of her loved ones quickly fading. She opened her eyes, seeing Jace in a golden room of enlightened immortal joy.

Chapter 23
Masquerade, Jynx, and Jace

Turning to Dark, he embraced him and collapsed into his arms. "I have one request from you. A really huge one." He said, still grasping onto him, as tears poured into his chest. "I want you to kill me, please." Masquerade exhaled loudly and continued crying. Dark smiled.

"Of course." He said, quivering from the aftermath of the fighting, that was still halted due to the shock of the moment.

"I entrust you to not let any more harm happen, I will be gone for a very short moment." Masquerade didn't know how he did it so quickly, but the next thing he knew, he was standing in that similar golden stone room. Anubis and Mardo weren't there, however. In the middle of the room stood Jynx, and wouldn't you know it, so was Jace. She hadn't noticed Masquerade yet, but she observed the room like she might've been there at one point. He approached her and lightly touched her shoulder. She quickly turned, scared out of her mind.

"MASQUERADE!" She screamed and hugged him. "I'm so glad I survived! Where are we? What is this place?" That one sentence shattered his heart, Jace was astonished of the beauty of the room, despite him seeing it once before.

"You're dead. This is the afterlife, my love. . . You'll see Anubis soon after this." He said in a depressed tone. Jynx looked confused.

"What? How? You're here though-" Then she pieced everything together. "Oh. Right, you're immortal." She frowned, and Masquerade only felt his heart shatter some more.

"I came to say my last goodbyes. I just wanted to say that I love you." He said, his voice trembling. Jynx smiled. She didn't have a single negative emotion stirring inside her. She tightened her embrace, her power was convulsing in her veins more fiercer than usual.

"I love you too." She emphasized. "I hope you can visit every once in a while, but I get it if you don't, saving the world is a really hard task." She took a step back and looked into his eyes. He tried holding a smile but couldn't. "Look at the switch in roles." She continued. "It seems I'm the brave one here!" Masquerade couldn't even chuckle. Her skin started glowing pink, and Masquerade saw the phenomena of her blood being pulled back to her body, which was a feeling he felt way back to the first time he died. "Don't let any of your siblings join me any time soon." She said and kissed him. It was the best kiss in the world, he swore he could feel them live a thousand lives and futures together in just that one kiss. He felt memories start flooding past his fog-filled brain. Even if they were fake and never happened, he cherished them.

Then, after their moment, they turned to Jace, who was waiting patiently. "I guess this is goodbye?" He glared at Masquerade. "Again!" He chuckled. "I already gave Masquerade the spiel, but I bet he wants to hear the altered version. Right?" Masquerade giggled, showing that he obviously did. "Now that we are all parting ways, this is going to be the best talk of my life, my career." He smiled. "I stole your glory, both of yours. Just so your souls can be pure, so when Anubis weighs them, they won't be heavy." Masquerade wanted to spend more time, but their time was running out, and Jace's words were starting to fade. He stuttered, rushing forwards, and grouping them all in for one final hug. Masquerade's eyes glistened pink, following Jynx's and then Jace's, who contrasted blue embers. Jace knew it represented their connection being stronger than his to either of them, but he still felt empathy for them. In that consisting hug, Jace absorbed all the leftover 'glory' inside their veins. It was a lot, and he felt his blood start to clog. Then his body started fading into a bunch of golden flurries. He had a large grin on his face before he completely faded. Masquerade was left in that room with Jynx, who's image had no sign of fading. She stared at him with her pink fluttering eyelashes, giving him a look of love. He walked up to her, his eyes gazing into her beautiness.

"Looks like your power of control isn't the cause of me wanting to kiss you." He said, Jynx feeling flustered by his words. She remembered the first time they kissed, which was a result of her powers manifesting. Jynx felt the deep sensation of her blood pumping backwards. The feeling felt as if her heart was absorbing her blood instead of pushing it, and she quickly realized that Masquerade was feeling the same phenomena she was. Everything around her started creating lines of blur around her peripheral vision, causing that look of distortion you get from traveling too fast. The lines blurred past them, and the next thing she knew, her eyes were open and fluttering with delicacy.

Jace wandered for a while before Anubis appeared, he felt like a failure. "You shouldn't blame yourself." Anubis said. "It wasn't your fault." He continued. "You can't expect to win a war against the most powerful gods. All that matters is that you tried. You have a great heart and some of the worst parents I've ever seen." He said. The scale of souls was ahead of him again, and Anubis pointed at it. Jace's soul traversed from his body, quickly retching its contents on the metal plate. The feather on the other side glistened with power. Jace watched his soul closely, seeing the blotches of 'glory' overrun the surface of the perimeter.

"Not going to talk? No final words at all?" He had a look of terror on his face, as Jace quickly realized that the blotches of 'glory' made his soul heavier than the feather. The portion he absorbed from Jynx was too much, and now it was going to make him pay. Jace shook his head in response to Anubis' question. He addressed the power-craving god, the intense eye contact making them both tremble. Tears made his eyes more red than usual.

"Listen to society. Immortality is as bad as they all say." Jace said as his final call for help, watching his soul fall deeper in weight in comparison to the scale. Anubis frowned, his snout immediately becoming large in size. Jace now realized why 'glory' was so important to the gods, and why that was because they consumed it. The gift of glory came with power, and eating said power gave you a sense of spirituality, but consuming too much would result in corruption, which was a thought you'd assume. But, Jace felt his body start fading from existence, and his vision started shrouding with darkness. He witnessed one last horror before being cast away into eternal darkness, and that was Anubis grabbing his soul. His teeth turned vicious, snout became wide, and his tongue slimier. He grabbed the soul with two of his claws, playing with the fluid in great response. His tongue sucked off the remaining blotches of glory, as if it were an appetizer. Then, the soul plunged into the razor blades of his soul-consuming teeth, shredding the soul into billions of worthless pieces. Then it began its tract to the darkness of his stomach, quickly reducing it to nothing.

Jace knew the final moment of despairAnubis was the most corrupted God of them all.

Chapter 24
Masquerade, Jynx, and Mardo

Masquerade awoke in a panic, thinking he lost Jynx, but was relieved when he saw her body starting to stand up, glowering with pink color and energy. He observed the battlefield, and saw that every single enemy was defeated, by his brothers, who all stood with their awakened powers, reaching 120 percent of their potential. He looked at Jace's body, and realized there was a flaming light of blue embers emitting from him. The entire front yard was nuked with a bomb that wasn't Masquerade's, instead Jace's. The flames proved useful, as Jake's, Thor's, Mason's, and Stitch's bodies all remained burnt to a crisp. Masquerade walked over to Jynx and grasped her hand. "Stop crying. . . Jace didn't sacrifice himself for you to feel down." He leaned her in for a hug. Their eyes glowed pink, and they locked into each other's eyes. Jynx felt her brain's valves open, but this time it was one last time. All the valves opened, accessing every single part of her brain. Her cerebellum, cerebrum, brainstem, and diencephalon were cherished with such grace.

Her nerves filled with such power, enlightening the main difference between her and her boyfriend. In the same way he and Echo were explained, they had opposite organ systems as their bloodlines main symbolism. However, their love far succeeded the concepts of such rivalry, and additionally the brain needs blood to nourish, and the heart needs the neurons to pulsate. Together their powers alleviate each other, further defining their relationship in stone. Then, behind the scenes, Jynx finally awakened. The valves of her brain connected to the valves in her soul, allowing her full access to a great coursing power.

Deep down she felt a deeper connection to Masquerade, and she knew exactly what the reasoning behind it was. There was a reason the females of her bloodline were feared, and it was much more than the power to control others, it was now revealed as the power of pure and clear immortality. Now, the one in a lifetime occurrence beamed its importance into the yielding event of sacrifice.

However, their title wasn't complete yet and there was one last common enemy to defeat. Echo, who now had the risk of dying due to his *shadow* dying personally, had fully retrieved his full power. After we lose our shadows there's the risk of death, but the ultimate trade off is the full extent of our prowess. Masquerade shuddered in complete response, his eyes looking into Echo's. Their eye contact made him freeze in place, unable to move at all. *Are you going* to help me? Masquerade conspired, but Mardo declined. You have your help, a fully awakened goddess. Echo winced, finally showing his final prowess. "Do your worst."

Jynx's brain was drawing power, her final awakened form being equal to that of the other immortal by her side. The power of restoration, finally manifesting itself to show resemblance of that to Masquerade, who showcased the power of destruction. They both rushed forwards in advance, their fists ready to defeat the final boss at hand. Several quick ethereal pink explosions erupted throughout the yard, staggering Echo, who's ice was having trouble forming. Masquerade closed in, attempting to get a hit in, but was left in shock when Echo touched him once, giving him immediate frostbite. Echo then kicked him in the chest, freezing one of his broken hearts, and almost killed him in an instant.

He was stopped by Jynx, who attacked his backside, and cracked a bone in his lumbar vertebrae. Her power of restoration glamoured with perfect defense and offense, and Echo was immediately hit with multiple attacks, bruises, and scars. He turned around, trying to reach Jynx, his touch would be able to kill her instantly, but failed to slightly grasp her. She realized what her power could do, and Mardo was laughing as he analyzed the situation. Her power allows her to restore anything! What she did was restore all the attacks that he's received, THROUGHOUT HIS ENTIRE LIFE! He screamed in ultimate excitement. Echo staggered almost in defeat. His touch almost graced upon her skin, freezing only the first layer of her epidermis. Masquerade still was left defenseless, unable to move due to the frostbite that traveled down his legs. Then right when Jynx was about to accept defeat, Dark came flying forwards, attacking Echo with a roundhouse kick from Heaven itself. Echo staggered, reaching his hand out, the air being frozen due to his wintery power. Protecting Dark, came flying Hyper, who punched him directly in the chest, lightning spurting through the frozen cold air. After Hyper, came Lazer, who was spamming large blasts of lasers, and then met Echo with an elbow to the jaw. Next was Infinity, who's fists were enchanting with great force. His speed increased, and he blitzed through Echo, sending a vibrating blow of casualty through the nerves of his opponent.

He threw up blood, his mouth spurting both mist and darkened black blood. Jynx wrapped around the four, running away from an incoming blow of icing wind. A large blizzard brewed deep within Echo's heart, ready to be released with great force. Then, the ice in Masquerade's body was released from a power that wasn't his, and he felt his soul being ripped from his body. He felt a feeling of his eyes stripping away from the contours of his body, and he experienced his consciousness fall back. He looked to the left of the void and saw Mardo, his eyes glowing with blackness. "Take the backseat and watch! It's my turn to give this loser a run for his fucking money. . ." Masquerade nodded, his body switching places with Mardo's, who then took control of Masquerade's consciousness and movements. He watched from an arena that was assumed to be his soul, and he sat down in the midst of the chaos.

Mardo's presence made his body shift. He had the appearance of Masquerade, but his hair turned bright hot pink to a jet void black, and his clown makeup and tattoos appeared all over his brightening face. Echo stood in astonishment, sensing Mardo's ultimate presence. "Bow down to me you fucking coward!" He screamed once, and blitzed forwards with great speed. Due to Mardo's consciousness not being in sync with Masquerade's hearts, one of them lagged behind the other, resulting in two streams of blood constantly being pushed through his body. Mardo raised his hands, and so did Echo, their powers ready to clash once more, resulting in flashbacks of their first battle, where Mardo embarrassed the god of winter. They rushed towards each other, Mardo reigning superior, as Echo's fists didn't freeze his skin.

Mardo elbowed him, then punched his teeth, jaw, cheek, forehead, nose, chest, and stomach, all in three seconds. Due to Mardo pushing Masquerade's hearts to a lag, it resulted in double impact, because the second heart was there as a backup strength. Mardo clasped his hands as Echo was hit an additional eight times on top of the first eight times he hit him. Echo coughed up blood and yelled in rage.

A blizzard of power released, but Mardo simply laughed, and raised his hands. He released an explosion then Masquerade ever could, except this time the color of it was pure midnight black. He used another explosion to boost himself, and then used the wind to trip him forwards, and followed the combo with a flash of black lightning. The delayed heart allowed for Echo to be impacted by another three hits, further damaging the god. Ever since Masquerade destroyed the sword it allowed the two to bond, and when their *shadows* combine it allows the host to use their powers. Mardo proved better in using Masquerade's arsenal better than he could. Echo stood, already almost defeated, but Mardo wasn't done.

"I can'tbelieve. . ." He coughed more blood. "You would betray your own bloodline, Mardo!" Mardo smiled, sticking out his tongue in disrespect. A piercing revealed, but more importantly was a blackened tattoo that wrote 'Shut the fuck up and die!' in etching importance. No one understood what the meaning meant, until Echo's entire throat exploded with destructive capability. Blood erupted from the gaps in his teeth, throwing his teeth and gums out in streaming pools of redness. The nerves in his mouth exploded as well. No one understood the power emanating from Mardo just yet, until he sped towards Echo once more. He grabbed him by the chest, threw him into the air, and spit into his face. Then, a tattoo formed on his left cheek. The black marking represented the shape of a train subway, and the railings glistened a dark purple. In response, with Echo still flying in the air, summoned an entire freight train through the air, and crashed directly into Echo's body.

Another tattoo formed, showing the symbol of a snake. A double impact occurred from the blow earlier, and all of Echo's bones cracked with pressure. The snake symbol then erupted into multiple golden scaled reptiles. The venom seeped into his arms, grabbing ahold of his entire arm. Mardo contracted his arm and ripped it off with full force. He swirled with the force of wind, and slapped Echo back in the face with his own arm. Quickly, he gave Masquerade control over his body once more, taking the backseat of the body. Everyone cheered reluctantly, although the enemy wasn't completely dead just yet. Jynx and Masquerade rushed forwards, both of their powers gleaming indifferently. She was slightly fasted, and reached him first, reaching her power covered fists into the cold air. Her rage was comparable to Masquerade's, and she smashed her fists directly into his skull, cracking it with her shear strength. Then, Masquerade finished the job, and made an explosion with the stomp of his foot, scattering every single piece of Echo's body throughout the air. The kill was satisfying, finally all Jynx's problems were dead, with underlying gruesome endings to their stories. Masquerade leaned in for a kiss, and the two finally realized their title of importance. The Immortal Lovers stood in 'glory' of the victory, experiencing the 'joy' of being next to each other, and finally void of any 'lust' that may come their way.

THE END

Epilogue

Masquerade stood at the peak of the cold mountain. The temple of Misa stood shining in the blizzards of Antarctica. The God of Everything awaited him. His father didn't approve of it, but Masquerade insisted it was him. His body wanted to give in, but he had to continue for his family's sake and their survival. He approached the run-down temple. Once he entered, he expected no visitors, but in the middle of the sacrificial dome stood a fairly tall man. He stared at Masquerade. His eyes glowed rings of purple and red with black outlines.

They pierced his soul. His presence troubled Masquerade. It almost pinned him to the floor. The gravity of it was immense. The man had pitch-black hair, with half of it being purple. His hair was long, reaching all the way to his lower back. He opened his mouth.

"Don't even open your mouth! You ruined my life! You took everything from me!" He screamed at him, his voice shaking. He tried holding back tears, but nothing held. The god stared back reluctantly. Masquerade held out his hands, and smoke was arising from his palms.

"Be quiet and stand where I am." His soft voice whispered. It chilled Masquerade. Depression, anger, grief, and anxiety stirred up inside him. His hands pulsed and ached worse than ever before. Misa looked at him. Masquerade sprinted towards the god.

"You know I wouldn't give up without a fight!" He couldn't smile like usual, but he still held his spirit. Masquerade held his hand out towards Misa. "I'll kill you!"

Misa stood and smiled viciously. Masquerade released his held-up emotions. The god's expression said it all. An explosion was released. The biggest Masquerade ever produced. Bigger than even what mankind had achieved. Two times bigger than the Tsar Bomba.

"I saved this for you."

Authors Note

In the entire 372 and so pages of this book on my google docs, I never expected to be able to set my story in words, but here I am. This is only the start of a huge story, and I think I did very well in using this as the starting point of many eventful stories to come. It was even more of a journey working with Amazon to get this thing actually published. Enough about the future of my series, and more about me, and a lot of my thoughts that I had going into this book.

As a kid, I had many thoughts about the characters in this book. Even my sister was able to help me with some of the namings of the characters. We would both play with our legos, or various amounts of stuffed animals and build a world from there. Of course back then, we had no clue how to create an actual plot. So looking back to that, and then seeing this novel completely finished really brought a fat tear to my eyes. I never expected to get this far with this, so I thank whoever happens to be reading this.

You made my day just by reading this piece of literature. Hopefully I feel the same about the sequel, and the book after that, and after that. Before I finish this up I just wanted to say to never give up on your dreams.